WINTER'S WRATH

THE HERALD'S SAGA: BOOK ONE

COURTNEY NIBLETT

Book Cover and Illustrations by Jeff Brown

ISBN: 9798396645509 (Paperback)
ISBN: 9798396651401 (Hardback)

To the twelve year old girl that sat on her bedroom floor with her first story idea and a big dream. We finally did it.

CONTENT WARNING

This book contains situations that include strong language, brief mentions of past child and domestic abuse, sexual assault and discussions of sexual assault, monsters, and graphic depictions of violence which includes torture and death.

This book is intended for mature readers and contains graphic sexual content. Reader discretion is advised.

CONTENTS

PROLOGUE

Spring

My power waned sharply. With every passing moment, the little that remained ebbed away as I shot through the sky like a bolt of lightning. My very bones ached from the strain as I urged it to carry me faster, hoping I had enough left to make it home.

The sun hung low in the sky, casting a golden glow on the thick clouds overhead. My stomach dropped as I glanced past the band of sparkling purple light beneath me and into the trees of the Great Forest far below. The snow-covered peaks of the Fire Mountains loomed in the distance. The band of light arched towards them, following the ribbon of road cutting across the land.

I breathed a sigh of relief. The appearance of that winding road meant I was almost home.

Suddenly, the purple band flickered beneath me, and I dropped several feet. Fear sliced through my chest, and I swore, shoving everything I had left into the light and silently pleading with it to hold on a few moments longer.

I made it to the base of the mountains when I felt something snap in the back of my mind. The light vanished with a final subtle twinkle and for one terrifying moment, I was suspended in midair.

Then, I plummeted.

Dark trees rushed up to greet me. The wind roaring in my ears dulled the sound of my curses as I scrambled and flailed, digging into the last few wisps of my power for salvation.

The power sputtered and coughed as I threw my hand out towards a large oak. It shuddered at my command. Branches creaked and groaned as they twisted around me into a ball and slowed my descent.

More branches cracked and snapped against the wooden shield as I crashed through the canopy. I squeezed my eyes shut, bracing myself as the shield slammed against the soil, rattling my skull with the impact.

I released my power with a groan, panting and wincing in anguish. The oak untangled its limbs and stood tall, dropping me face first into the dirt. The heavy scent of dried leaves and soil filled my nose. I rolled onto my back, clutching at a sharp pain in my chest.

I was about to sit up when a sudden creak split the silence.

I looked up and saw a large tree branch jolt towards me, clinging to the trunk by a few fraying splinters. I gasped and rolled as the branch snapped free and smacked into the ground with an earsplitting crunch, missing me by inches.

I blew out a breath and got unsteadily to my feet, dusting myself off with shaking hands. My skin, usually the color of a bright pink carnation, had paled significantly and was streaked with dirt and mud. My heart was pounding against my ribs, and an empty ache filled my abdomen.

I tried to turn, pausing to look down at my feet as something restricted my movement. The bottom of my bright green robes had become tangled in the fallen branch. I huffed and tried to tug them free, wincing as a tearing sound filled the air around me. Several large holes ripped open, and a number of the red silk roses stitched around the hem now littered the forest floor.

"Damn it," I hissed, releasing the stained fabric. "These were my favorite."

I sighed and started yanking the twigs out of my loose green curls, tossing them to the ground. I shook my hair out, freezing as I realized that something was missing. Something vital.

I reached up, gasping when I found nothing but empty air. Panic shot through me, and I spun in a circle, desperately scanning the shadowy underbrush until a golden glare caught my eye. I pressed a hand to my chest in utter relief, dropping to my knees.

Wedged in the soil, underneath the fallen branch was a circlet of lush, full roses cast in brilliant gold. Set in its center was a large emerald the size of my fist. The gem glinted dully as I wrenched the crown free and began brushing the dirt from it.

Normally the power stored within the stone's deep green facets would cause it to glow like the stars in the night sky. Since I'd just left the World's Tower, my power was still locked there, keeping the world in balance until the next herald arrived to begin their season. Summer would place her stone on the throne and her power would push mine out, freeing it from the bonds of the spire. But she was late. Again.

I set the crown carefully back on my head. Its weight was a small comfort as I scanned the surrounding forest for anything that seemed remotely familiar. The sun streaming through the thick canopy above cast the ground in watery light. The huge trees stretched high above me, blotting out most of the sky. Their trunks were packed so densely together, I couldn't see beyond a few feet into the shadowy woods.

"Where am I?" I said loudly, half-hoping someone would come stumbling through the underbrush to rescue me. The only response was the cry of a startled crow taking flight.

When no other reply came, I stepped forward to examine the moss on one of the tree trunks. I vaguely recalled something about moss growing on trees being an indication of some sort of direction, but I couldn't remember what it was to save my life.

"This isn't happening to me," I whispered, wringing my hands anxiously. "This cannot be happening right now." The other heralds should've met me at the temple that marked the halfway point. They should've escorted my sister there and then taken me home.

I waited for three days before finally giving up and trying to get home alone. A decision that I was severely starting to regret.

A desperate thought struck me. I looked up and reached into the vast depths of my well of power, wincing at the resulting ache. I fixed my eyes on the sliver of sky visible through the treetops and strained to manifest the band of purple light.

The Cosmic Bridge was the link between places, crafted of pure cosmic energy. If it appeared, even for a second, it would at least point me in the right direction.

I threw my will out with all my might. Nothing happened.

I reached a desperate mental hand into the recesses of the stone's power stores, silently pleading for something. Anything. But not even a spark of energy remained.

My shoulders slumped in despair as the gravity of my situation settled in my chest. I was powerless and lost in the Great Forest. No one had any idea where I was, and I had no way to contact Fall, Winter, or Summer for help.

I stepped into the shade of a tree and leaned against its sturdy trunk to try and catch my breath. The sun had dropped lower, casting ominous shadows across the forest floor.

Once the light was gone, the forest would be too dark to navigate. My situation was looking more and more grim by the second. I was considering my options when the leaves above my head shuddered. I looked up and spotted a pair of glowing green eyes.

"Who are you?" an angry voice hissed. "Why are you in my forest?"

A willowy figure with huge antlers jutting from the top of her angular head dropped before me. The entity's feminine figure was covered in moss and leaves from her neck down to her hoofed feet. She peered into the shadows at me, narrowing her eyes and baring her pointed teeth. Her razor-sharp claws were out, and a growl rose in her throat.

Dizzying relief flooded through me. I stumbled out into the light and recognition flashed across her face. She dropped to her knees and bowed her head, flattening her long pointed ears against her skull.

"Lord Spring!" she exclaimed. "I-I didn't realize it was you! Please, forgive me!"

I rushed to her and fell to my knees, pulling her into a tight hug. She gasped, startled by the sudden gesture.

"Calliope!" I breathed. She hesitated before patting me gingerly on the back. I pulled away, meeting her eyes with a sheepish grin. "Thank the Ethereal Two you found me! I am so utterly, hopelessly lost!"

"I can see that," she said, arching a thin eyebrow. She stood and brushed the detritus from her knees before offering a hand to help me up. "So... Why is the herald of spring lost in my woods? Shouldn't you have returned to the palace by now?"

"I should have," I agreed, passing a frustrated hand over my face. "No one came to replace me. I tried to make it home on my own, but I seriously overestimated how much power I had left." I dropped my hands to my sides with a heavy sigh. "My sister has been late for her last six cycles. But she's never been this late before. It's like she doesn't—"

I glanced at Calliope and winced. Her expression was drawn. Tension lined her shoulders as she avoided my eyes, crossing her arms protectively over her chest.

Guilt and shame twisted around my stomach. "Ah. I didn't mean to—"

Calliope's eyes shot furiously to me.

"Didn't mean to?" she repeated tightly. Her finger trailed across a silver oval hanging from a piece of twine tied around her neck. "So, you just forgot what your sister took from me?"

"I—" I swallowed. The pain in Calliope's face made it hard to breathe. "I'm so sorry."

"You're *sorry*?" Calliope snapped. Silver lined her glowing eyes. "She's the reason Brynn is dead and all you have to say is you're *sorry*?" I flinched and fell silent. She stared me down for a long tense moment before she let out a sharp breath and looked away. "Just go. Get out of my forest and don't ever come back." She pointed off to the left before she turned and launched herself into the canopy.

I watched her glide through the branches like a wraith, guilt squeezing around my chest like a vice. Tears blurred my vision. I wiped them away on the back of my hand and headed off in the direction Calliope had pointed.

My heart sank lower with each step I took. Summer was my twin sister and had caused me nothing but anguish and heartache for as long as I could remember. She'd learned from an early age exactly how to bend me to her will. And after years of being broken down with guilt and shame, I'd stopped fighting back. But despite all the pain she caused me, she was the only family I had left. Or at least that's what I tried to tell myself when she decided to be particularly spiteful.

I'd been trudging through the forest for Ethereal only knew how long when I finally stumbled past the tree line and onto the cobblestone-paved road. It curved upwards and disappeared behind the peak of the nearest mountain. I blew out an exhausted breath and kept moving, eager to finally make it home and put this whole mess behind me. The sun was a meager sliver of light peeking over the distant snowcaps when I finally reached the end with a huff of relief.

Nature's Palace stood proudly upon a high cliff, overlooking the lush valley below. Large windows glinted like diamonds set into the dark stone walls. Four towers, situated at the corners of the rectangular base, scraped the sky with their pointed peaks and a low stone wall formed the perimeter around the expansive grounds. I could see the trees in my orchard swaying gently in the evening breeze as I approached. I sighed, practically dragging my aching feet through the iron gate and into my favorite spot in the entire world.

My garden was a vibrant clash of color. Flowers, shrubs, and trees dotted the landscape. Roses of every shade edged the path that twisted its way to the large oak front doors. My relief faded as I spotted weeds peeking through the soil of my flowerbeds. I glanced around for any sign of my personal gardener. He was the only one I trusted to tend my flowers when I was away. I turned in a small circle, scanning the grounds, but I didn't see him anywhere.

"Kaelin?" I called.

No one answered.

My stomach fluttered uneasily as I suddenly realized there were no sounds other than my own breathing. The palace was as silent as a tomb.

I slipped through the doors and into the opulent grand hall. The walls and the high ceiling were gilded with gold and marble. Ahead of me stretched the huge staircase leading up to the second floor. There were no servants singing while they set the table in the banquet hall. There were no clinking plates or mirthful voices filling the air. There wasn't a soul in sight.

The quiet thud of the door closing behind me echoed like a rumble of thunder through the empty halls.

I held my breath, straining to hear even the faintest hint of life. I'd never seen the palace this empty. There were always servants and minor spirits bouncing about the halls. The air was almost always filled with music or the lingering smell of something delicious being cooked in the kitchens below. But there was nothing. It was as if the palace had been completely abandoned.

As I took another hesitant step, a strange gleam caught my attention. I lifted my gaze and sucked in a sharp breath. Thick black ice was creeping across the ceiling and down the walls. My eyes followed it across the hall to the altar room on the second floor.

I swallowed hard. Anxiety set my nerves on edge as I made my way slowly up the stairwell and crept towards the door. The ice was a bad sign. It meant Lady Winter was upset, and I had a feeling I already knew why.

My sister delighted in getting under the skin of our stoic, serious friend. And from the look of the creeping black ice slowly devouring the palace walls, she'd pushed her too far.

I reached the door to the altar room and twisted the knob, but it didn't budge. The door must have been frozen shut from the other side. Frowning, I braced myself and slammed my shoulder against it. The ancient wood creaked on its hinges as it popped open, sending me stumbling and sliding into the room.

The floor was covered by a solid sheet of ice. Ice and snow whipped around the room, stinging my face and neck as I squinted through the blizzard. I could barely make out a figure silhouetted by the moonlight streaming in from the large window behind her.

"Winter!" I screamed over the howling wind. "Winter, what are you doing?" She turned sharply and spotted me. The blizzard stilled, leaving only the faint chill of its icy presence in the air. My breath rose in a fine mist as I shivered and tried to move towards her. I managed a single step before I lost my footing and slipped, my crown toppling from my head. It clanged against the icy floor and rolled away before coming to a clattering halt at Winter's feet.

She bent slowly and lifted it. I watched, propped up awkwardly on my elbows, as she approached the large marble altar in the middle of the room. Four carved pedestals surrounded a statue of the Ethereal Two entwined in a lover's embrace. Three of them sported ornate crowns with large gems on their faces.

Winter carefully placed my crown on the only empty pedestal, rotating it so the stone was facing the statue. She then returned to staring out the window without so much as a word as I struggled once more to my feet. The sight of all four stones was unsettling. The last time I'd seen them together was six hundred years ago. My sister's stone should've been on its way to the World's Tower. And yet, there it sat. Something was horribly wrong.

My eyes slid back to Winter's rigid form. She was wearing her heavy robes of purple and dark blue. Her straight, snow-white hair tumbled down past her shoulders and her light purple skin sparkled like the world under an early morning frost. She was three inches shorter than me, with sharp angular features and deep blue eyes that were brimming with tears. They dripped down her cheeks, freezing into streaks as they went.

She fixed her icy gaze on me as I carefully slid closer. "Winter," I began hesitantly. "What happened? Where is everyone? No one came to the Crossroads Temple. Summer needs to..."

Winter balled her fists in barely withheld rage at the mention of my sister. Her face contorted in a blend of pain and fury. I quailed under the fierce intensity of her stare and sucked in a nervous breath. I'd never seen her so angry. Whatever my sister had done this time, she'd clearly pushed the usually reserved and calm Winter too far.

"Winter, what happened?"

Again, she didn't answer. She pursed her lips as I slipped closer, narrowly avoiding one of the growing stalactites of black ice inching towards us.

I met Winter's streaming eyes. "What's wrong?" I reached for her hand, grasping only air as she flinched away from my touch. My unease grew. The silent halls and overgrown weeds pressed on my mind, and I gulped again as a stifling fear clutched at my heart.

"Winter, where is everyone?" I whispered.

A fresh wave of tears spilled down her face.

"What did she do now?" I asked, terrified of the answer.

She met my eyes, glaring for a long moment before drawing in a shuddering breath.

"Did you know?" she whispered through a clenched jaw.

I raised my eyebrows in confusion. "I'm sorry?"

"Did you know?" Winter repeated a little louder.

I opened my mouth to respond, the breath freezing in my lungs as a horrible understanding raced through my mind. My stomach twisted and I looked away as a tirade of shame ripped into me. Whatever I'd been expecting, it wasn't this. This was so much worse.

Winter let out a soft, horrified gasp.

"Please. Tell me you didn't," she choked. I glanced back at her, unable to mask the guilt on my face.

Devastation wracked her beautiful features.

"Winter, I—" I trailed off. The pain in her expression cracked my heart in half.

She gasped, gritting her teeth and clenching her fists so hard, her knuckles turned white.

"You knew!" she accused, her shrill voice echoing in the silent room. "So, everyone knew! Everyone except me!" She heaved out a sob and wiped her tears on the back of her hand. "How could you do this to me? You of all people! I didn't want to believe it, but it's true! You betrayed me!"

"No," I stuttered hoarsely. "No, Winter, I'd never betray you. You're my best friend."

"Then why didn't you tell me?" Her despair morphed into simmering rage as she took a solid step towards me. "Because she's your sister, right? That's always your excuse."

"Winter, please. I didn't—" I scrambled to find the words to explain as she took another menacing step forward.

"Then why didn't you tell me? You just said I'm your best—" Winter took a shuddering breath and crossed her arms over her chest. I felt as though the heat of my shame would burn me alive. "All you've ever done is bend to her wishes. You've done everything in your power to excuse her actions. The humans worship the ground she walks on, and you... you let her take everything from me!"

I shrank back. A bone-deep chill settled in the air as I struggled to find the right words. "Winter, I..."

"Don't lie to me," she seethed. Flurries of snow and ice careened around us as she moved towards the altar. "Her servants have been whispering for weeks. Hissing behind my back. And that witch smirked at me every chance she got as she stalked around. I finally cornered a spirit in the garden, and she told me everything. How she'd seen Summer—" Winter's voice broke. "So, I confronted her. And do you know what she did? She laughed!"

The wind whipped into a frenzy as her grief overwhelmed her. A chair in the corner of the room was lifted by the swirling ice and smashed into the window, sending a cascade of broken glass into the valley beyond.

"She sneered at me!" Winter shouted. "She said, 'I always get what I want. Even if what I want is yours.' It broke me. Everyone who loved me... Or at least said they loved me. Fall. You. All of you let her steal my happiness." Winter stopped beside the altar and stared at me for a long moment before she shook her head.

"I wanted to believe in you," she whispered. "After everything she did to you. All the blood she tried to stain your hands with—"

I flinched hard. My heart raced and my hands began to tremble at the mention of my darkest shame. My deepest regret.

"You've tried so hard to hide it," she said. "But we all saw how it broke you. How it still breaks you. You don't smile anymore. You don't sing. You once filled the air with the sweetest music I've ever heard and now because of her, you haven't so much as hummed in two hundred years. Your grief leveled mountains and nearly changed the path of the moon. But she didn't care."

I blinked away the tears clouding my vision, unable to find the words to say to fix this. To make this better.

Winter locked eyes with me before gently lifting a circlet of silver icicles from its pillar. The large red garnet set on its face caught the guttering lamplight as she settled the crown on her brow. The light emitting from the stone brightened and her deep blue eyes began to glow.

"What are you doing?" I asked. Fear gripped my chest as Winter picked up a tiara of golden sunbeams and plucked the large, gleaming diamond from its front before throwing the crown aside. "Winter," I gasped, "Winter, stop!"

She kept her eyes on me as she moved to the next pillar and removed a sparkling purple amethyst from a silver crown of leaves. The crown slipped from her fingers and rolled away. She stopped beside my crown. The rage burning in her eyes shot straight through me as she removed my emerald and slipped it into her pocket with the others.

"Winter, don't." My firm tone was undercut by the waver in my voice.

I tried to step closer, but my feet suddenly refused to move. I looked down and found my green slippers encased in ice. Panic seared my mind as I tried to wrench my legs free. She flicked her wrist and the ice started to creep up my ankles. Burning cold touched my bare skin and made its way swiftly up to my knees.

"Winter!" I cried out. "Winter stop! Please, don't do this!"

She watched me struggle as the ice crawled up the hem of my robes.

"You brought this on yourself," she replied flatly. "You and the rest of this wretched world." She reached up and touched her crown. "I'm taking the tower."

"Winter, no!" The ice had reached my waist. "The world needs our balance! The humans—"

"The humans are just as guilty as you," Winter spat. "They worshiped the air she blew in their stupid faces. Committing horrible crimes because she commanded them to! Humans taught her that she could have anything!" Her deep blue eyes blazed with anger and determination as she continued, "I will find the *Book of the Cosmics* and take everything from them. Just like they let her take everything from me. Once I have the book, I will join the stones and destroy the Two. Then I will rebuild this world. I will create a paradise free from your wretched sister and her twisted human pets."

Blinding terror gripped my mind. In my panic, my power flared before it sputtered and died. The ice spread quickly up my chest and back, cresting over my shoulders and searing my skin as it went. I reached out, clawing the air in desperation as I stretched my hand out to her.

"Please, Kiora," I begged.

Pure wrath flashed across Winter's face.

"You don't get to call me that," she hissed. "Not ever again." She raised a hand. I managed to squeeze my eyes shut tight as the ice surged up and covered every inch of me.

I couldn't move. Everything started to go numb as I realized I had no way to break free and no way to save myself. I was going to die.

She said something, but the ice coating my head blocked my ears, and I couldn't understand her. Suddenly, I jolted forwards, sliding rapidly across the floor. My stomach lurched hard as she tossed me out the window and I plummeted. As I fell, the dregs of power lurking in the deepest parts of me surged through my blood and wrapped around my terrified heart. A soft, calm darkness enveloped my mind as I dropped through the sky. I felt a sense of peace. And then, I felt nothing at all.

CHAPTER ONE

LUMI

Twenty years later

"Lumi! It's time to get up!"

Mother's voice thundered up the stairs, startling me awake. I sat up with a disgruntled huff, rubbing the sleep from my bleary eyes and stretching my stiff muscles. My blanket slipped from my shoulders and the early morning chill sent a hard shiver rolling up my spine. I gasped and yanked the blanket back up over my head, pressing my nose into its warm folds.

"Lumi!" Mother called impatiently. "Let's go!"

I rolled my eyes and momentarily considered flopping back onto my bed. I had just turned to wistfully examine my pillow when my mother barked my name again and I cringed.

"All right, I'm up," I grumbled. The glaring sunshine made my eyes water as I glanced around my bedroom. The fireplace on the opposite wall was dark and cold. The fire must have died right after I'd fallen asleep.

The polished wood floor was littered with broken bow strings and heaps of clothing. My huge mahogany four-poster bed stood against the wall beside the door. A matching wardrobe, bursting with garments shoved haphazardly into its drawers, stood next to the bed.

The walls were a luscious shade of green with pink flowers and vines painted in a whorl pattern all the way up to the ceiling. Or at least that was what my mother had called them once. In my twenty-one years of life, I'd never seen a real flower before. They were one of the many things that had disappeared from our lands during the long winter.

Snow from the blizzard that had raged all through the night was piled halfway up the large window at the far end of the room. I could already see more menacing dark clouds gathering on the horizon. My heart dropped and I chewed my lip nervously. Blizzards, especially those that struck in the middle of the night, were an extremely bad thing.

Swallowing my anxiety, I rolled to my feet and resolved to get moving for no other reason than to make sure the storm hadn't meant disaster.

I crossed to the old green chair situated under the window and stepped onto it gingerly. It groaned and sagged under my weight, so I carefully placed a foot on the small bookshelf beside it. My sword, which had been leaning against the shelf, clattered to the floor as I peered over the mound of snow.

The world went dark as the fast-moving clouds swallowed the sunlight, casting an eerie shadow over the land. A group of farmers with bags and sacks slung across their shoulders rushed down the freshly cleared street towards the southern gate, shooting fearful glances towards the graying sky as they ran.

"Lumi! Let's go!" My mother's sharp tone made me pause. Unease gnawed in the pit of my stomach.

"Okay," I called hesitantly. My parents had left home without so much as a word to me more times than I could count. The fact that they were waiting could only mean one thing.

Recently, they had become obsessed with my marriage prospects. Many family meals had concluded with vicious shouting matches and me storming off. I had a sneaking suspicion they were waiting for me because they had a new suitor in mind and wanted to discuss it.

Dread prickled under my skin as I hopped down and slowly crossed to the washroom mirror. I took in my reflection and grimaced. My usually pin-straight black hair was a tangled disaster. I'd tossed and turned quite a bit in what little sleep I'd managed to get. Dark shadows circled my light blue eyes, and the freckles on my nose stood out starkly against my pale skin. My face looked like it had been spattered with dark paint.

I prodded a yellowing bruise on my cheekbone, wincing at the slight twinge of pain and glancing behind me at the object responsible.

A long ebony bow lay under my reading chair with broken bits of string dangling from both ends. My latest foray into teaching myself a new archery technique had gone awry, and the string had snapped, whipping me in the face as it went.

In the years I'd spent practicing, I'd lost count of how many times I'd been bruised or cut by a snapping string. Archery and sword fighting had started off as a way to emulate the heroes and heroines in the stories I loved so much growing up. But as I got older, it became an escape. It was the one piece of my life my father didn't control. The one little piece I got to choose. So, I spent a lot of time at the wall with the veteran guards, honing my skills.

I snatched a comb from the floor and tore it through the messy knots on my head until my hair once again fell freely around my shoulders. I pulled it back into a ponytail and gave the mirror one last glance before turning to the wardrobe and yanking on my favorite blue tunic and black pants. I was just buckling my belt when the door swished open.

"Lumi." Mother crossed her arms, her lips twisted in disapproval. Her blonde hair was wound into a tight bun at the back of her head. I'd gotten my full lips, small nose, and high cheekbones from her. Her face, however, was round and rosy. Mine was pale and much more angular. Her plump frame all but disappeared beneath the thick brown coat she wore over her favorite black dress with the hem that skimmed the floor. Her piercing gray eyes narrowed on me as she watched me pull on my boots.

"What are you doing?" she demanded.

"Dressing," I replied. I buckled a long sheath to my belt and grabbed my sword. The dull blade was slightly too large for the sheath, and it stuck as I shoved it roughly into place.

"Are you going somewhere?" Mother eyed me suspiciously. I shrugged and slipped a small dagger into my boot. I grabbed the bow and quiver from the floor before turning to face her. She was half a head shorter than me, so she had to look up at me as her frown deepened.

"Yep," I replied. I slung my bag over my shoulder, meeting her steely eyes. She opened her mouth to interrogate me, but no sound came out. Instead, she jerked her head towards the door and turned on her heel before marching out of sight.

I rolled my eyes and shot a glance out the window. For one wild moment, I considered jumping from it and running. But I knew if I did, my father would come looking for me. And I knew exactly where he'd cast the blame.

With a regretful sigh, I grabbed my coat before trailing reluctantly after her. I ambled down the hallway to the staircase leading to the entrance hall. My boots clicked against polished marble as I slowly made my way to the kitchen.

My mother had a taste for the obscenely opulent and my father doted on her faithfully. A ridiculous amount of ornate furniture dotted the room and fine art covered nearly every inch of the walls. The house was still. It was early enough that most of the townsfolk who cared for my father's manor had not yet arrived for their day's work.

I crossed the hall and slipped through a small door into the kitchen. The iron gray walls were covered in soot from the large coal ovens pressed against the back wall. A fire crackled merrily in the hearth to my left. One of the cooks was bustling about, cleaning. He spied me entering the kitchen and made himself scarce with a hasty bow to my parents.

They were seated at a small table, their plates already empty. I squared my shoulders as I sat across from them and forced a disinterested expression, digging into the potato bread and fish loaded onto my plate.

Their work bags were already leaning against a door in the corner of the room. My mother shot a glance at my father who was watching me with his square jaw clenched. I could feel the tension radiating off them. They were clearly prepared for a battle. Which probably meant my assumptions were right. I fought to keep my face impassive as irritation spiked through me and I braced myself for the inevitable. Finally, Father cleared his throat to get my attention.

My father had broad features and a crooked nose that had been badly broken once in his youth. His short hair and neatly trimmed beard were streaked with silver. I'd gotten his icy blue eyes and raven black hair, but not much else. My mother told me once that my grandmother was petite like me. I certainly hadn't gotten my build from him. My father was a massive man. He towered over me, with wide set shoulders and hands the size of my face. His expensive purple tunic and thick black coat were stretched tight over his broad chest.

Most of the villagers were absolutely terrified of him. He was the type of man that made a person nervous to breathe too loudly. Some villagers even swore up and down that he made the earth itself tremble in fear whenever he got angry. But despite his best efforts, my father had never managed to scare me.

He cleared his throat a little louder. I swallowed my last bite of bread and reached for another loaf from the platter on the table.

"Lumi," he began, his deep voice rumbling in his chest.

I paused mid-bite and met his eyes.

"Father," I replied tartly. He sat up a little straighter and placed his calloused hands on the table.

"Lumi, your mother and I are very concerned," he said. Mother crossed her arms tightly over her chest.

My temper flared. I swallowed the urge to jump straight into the fight they were waiting for and took a slow breath.

"Concerned." I arched an eyebrow, glancing between them.

"You're twenty-one now," Mother said tersely. "And you're still refusing to consider any suitable matches."

I groaned and rolled my eyes.

"Don't," Father warned. "We've given you several good options and you haven't bothered with any of them. It's time to grow up and settle down with a good husband."

"Does what *I* want matter?" I sighed, knowing full well that it didn't.

"Lumi, you have to consider the reputation of this family," Mother said. "Your father and I have worked hard to maintain a good rapport with the village."

"Oh, is that what we're calling it now?" I hissed, anger rising sharply in my chest. "Complete control over the village's food supply is a good rapport?"

"Enough," Father growled. I looked down at the table in disgust.

Years ago, my parents had been mildly wealthy farmers with a small standing in the community. They owned the farming caves at the base of the Fire Mountains and grew thermal crops like corn, wheat, and potatoes. Thermal crops were unique. They grew using energy from the volcanoes instead of sunlight. While they weren't as tasty as their sun-grown counterparts, or so I'd been told, they were essential to the village during the wintertime.

Then, twenty years ago, the world ended. My parents suddenly found themselves the most valuable members of our town and had spent the subsequent years building an absolutely ruthless dynasty. They bought the rest of the farmlands, the ore mines, and the fishing boats, making them the sole employers for the majority of Haven. Villagers who didn't work for them directly still depended on them to keep their own businesses running. "No" wasn't a word they were accustomed to hearing anymore. Anyone brave enough to say it had a bad tendency to disappear. All except for me. And I delighted in telling them "no" as often as possible.

"Your father and I have tolerated your obsession with swords and arrows for long enough," Mother said. She placed a hand on my father's broad forearm. "That and your choice in... *friends*." Her lips curled in disapproval, and I suppressed a snarled response. Tolerating my friends was the absolute last thing my parents had done. "It's time you choose a good husband and settle into the property in the north field. We've already spoken with Ovi, and—"

"No." Red hot anger seared through me. I gripped the edge of the table so hard, my knuckles turned white and shook my head. "Absolutely not."

"Why not?" Mother challenged. "I know his son has been seen hanging around with that cobbler's daughter recently. But no proposal has—"

"No," I repeated, meeting her eyes defiantly. "He's a womanizing pig. Sabine can have him."

"He is not a womanizing pig!" Mother jumped to her feet. "You've barely spoken three sentences to him! How could you make such a harsh claim?"

I looked away as the unwanted memory of rough hands where they shouldn't be shoved its way into my mind. Rough hands and cold snow. I crossed my arms over my chest and glared up at her.

"I won't marry Killian," I snapped. My father's jaw clenched as he stood to loom over me.

"You will do what's best for this family," he said coldly. "We thought you'd ruined your chances when you broke his nose for no reason—"

I smirked, recalling Killian's howl of pain as blood ran down his sniveling face. He had a nasty habit of touching me and, for whatever reason, had decided he had the right to do so whenever he wanted. Even after I told him no. On that particular day, I'd had enough and found a way to effectively let him know it.

My father bared his teeth and continued. "Ovi has assured us that if you come to the caves today and apologize—"

"Apologize!" I blanched and sprang to my feet, upending my chair in the process. It landed on the floor with a loud crack. "Apologize to that... and after he—" I gritted my teeth and took a deep, steadying breath through my nose. "Absolutely not!" I snatched the platter of bread from the table and dumped its contents into the bag on my hip. "I have somewhere to be," I spat.

"Where are you going?" Mother snapped.

"Out." I tossed the platter back onto the table and shoved my arms into my coat.

"With who?" Father demanded, his eyes narrowing on my bag.

"I am going out," I repeated.

"It'd better not be to see that creature," Father ground out.

I shot him a warning look. My nails bit into the skin of my palms as my anger threatened to bubble over.

"Who I associate with is none of your business," I retorted, turning to leave. Mother reached out to stop me, but Father placed a hand on her shoulder, and she paused.

"Now isn't the time, Celeste," he murmured.

"But Jasper!" Mother shot a look between us. Father shook his head, his eyes full of malice. I stood tall, squaring my shoulders, and defiantly meeting his glare.

"No," he said before turning back to her. "Come now, love. We are needed. I'll deal with him later."

I turned on my heel and marched into the entrance hall before they had a chance to stop me again, slamming the kitchen door behind me as I went. I leaned against the wall, breathing heavily for a moment as I did my best to settle my nerves. It was then that my father's words suddenly registered in my brain, and I froze.

Him.

Father said he would deal with *him*. Not *her*. He wasn't referring to me. I ground my teeth and stormed towards the front door, blindly snatching things from the entrance hall as I went and shoving them into my bag. I wasn't even sure what I was taking. I just wanted to steal some of their precious opulence and give it to someone who actually deserved it. I wrenched the front door open, grimacing at the blast of frigid air, and stepped out into the snow.

Bitterness gripped my chest as I stomped down the long drive to the road beyond. When I reached the gate, I paused and frowned back at the large manor.

The roof glistened with freshly fallen snow and the large windows were sparkling in the morning light, having been freshly cleaned the day before. The large double doors stood out, a dark blotch marring the pristine white marble façade that was bathed in the rising sun's warm glow.

To my right was a huge expanse of land that stretched away from the house. It had once been my father's fields. The barn that stabled his horses and cows had been taken down long ago and the plots where his meager harvests had grown had been barren for years. Now, the land was dotted with makeshift homes and shelters squished close together to fit as many people as possible in the space. Many of his cave farmers and house servants now lived in those crowded slums.

Haven's border wall stood proudly behind the manor. Constructed of huge stone blocks mined from the quarry, it circled the entire village and protected us from the dangers of the long winter. This segment of the wall cut through my father's land, slipping close to the back edge of the manor before sweeping off into the distance. Fresh guards were already arriving at the outposts situated every forty feet along the monolithic structure.

The wall towered over the house, but it was dwarfed by the mountain stretching up towards the cosmos behind it. The mighty peak loomed at the edge of the mountain range upon which so much of our lives had come to depend. Mother once told me that particular mountain was a volcano, but I'd never seen so much as a puff of smoke.

Most of the villagers feared that mountain, believing there was a demon that lived near the peak. The story went that it would race down the mountain in the middle of the night and steal cattle away. But once all of Haven's cattle had died off in the cold, the stories and the reported sightings had both stopped.

As I stood and stared up at the mountains, the small shacks around the manor began to stir with life. Soon, villagers and farmers would be emerging to start their day. I spat into the snow and gave the manor one last glare before turning away and heading up the road.

I drew my coat closer as the moaning wind picked up and whipped my hair into my face.

As much as it pained me, I couldn't stop myself from glancing towards the pretty house situated at the very edge of my father's land. It was a matchbox constructed of stone and wood compared to my father's luxurious estate, but the inside was cozy and full of warmth. The sweet little cottage had two bedrooms, a lovely kitchen and even a small library. I only knew this because it had been built for me.

On my twenty-first birthday, I should have moved into my small respite from the world and settled into a life all my own. But my father decided that he didn't want me to leave his house until I was, as he put it, "properly taken care of."

I knew what that really meant. He was afraid of who else might be in that house with me if I lived there alone.

A tired woman, uncomfortably heavy with child, trudged outside the cottage with a broom in hand and began sweeping snow off the front porch. That porch was my favorite part of the house. It wrapped around the front and afforded a perfect view of the village. She noticed my glare and gave me a shy wave. A small sleepy boy peeked out the door behind her, rubbing his eyes.

Anger squeezed my heart as I averted my gaze and sped away without returning her wave.

That house was supposed to be my paradise. A sacred place where I could go and hide from the rest of the world. In that house, I wouldn't have to be Jasper's only daughter and the greatest prize to be won in Haven. I wouldn't have to be the almost-princess to these terrified and downtrodden people. For the first time in my life, I would've been able to be myself, without any outside expectations or demands. My life would have been my own.

I swore and pushed the thoughts aside, yanking my hood roughly over my head. I kept my eyes trained determinedly on my feet as I trudged down the road that ran along the inside of the border wall and headed for the village.

Once, Haven had been a small place consisting of shops and farms centralized around the docks. The sprawling village stretching from the Fire Mountains to the Black Bay that unfurled before me was one of the last settlements still standing on the continent. As more cities fell to the cold or the ice demons roaming the lands, people arrived at Haven's tremendous gates in search of refuge and work behind its seemingly unbreachable wall.

Trade ships from the Western Lands bobbed along the docks, their white sails billowing in the harsh winds of the roiling sea. Dockhands rushed back and forth while shouting to each other and unloading cargo.

The Western Lands were the only ones who still traded with us. The rest of the world had nicknamed our continent the Forsaken Isle and feared that coming to our shores meant they might bring back our land's affliction with them. Not a soul from the Eastern Kingdoms had set foot here in eighteen years. The Southern Isles, once our most prominent trade partners and our closest neighbors, had closed their borders to everyone two centuries ago.

I had almost reached the fork in the road leading to the main square when a voice drifted down from the nearest sentry post, stopping me in my tracks. I glanced up and found two young guards leering at me.

I knew them, having babysat both of them when they were small boys. Barron and Robert had been best friends all their lives. Robert was rail skinny with mousey brown hair that stuck up everywhere. Barron was a half- head taller than his friend, with blonde hair and a toothy grin. I took a second to marvel at how young they looked. At seventeen years old, neither one of them fit properly in the armor they had been given. Robert's helmet was so large, it repeatedly slid into his face. He pushed it out of the way and chuckled as Barron called down to me again.

"Where are you headed, gorgeous?" Barron said, nudging Robert in the ribs. "We're awfully cold up here, you know. Think you might wanna come up here and uh... Keep us warm?" Their snickers died on their lips and the color drained from their faces as I pushed back my hood.

"Barron, what have we talked about?" I called up, frowning. Both boys blushed furiously and ducked their heads. "Do I need to come up there and remind you why we don't harass women as they walk by?"

"No ma'am," Barron said sullenly. He rubbed his right arm, clearly still remembering the last time we'd spoken about it. "We're sorry, Ms. Lumi."

Robert nodded emphatically in agreement.

"We're just so bored up here. Nothing ever happens," Barron sighed.

"You should be thankful for that. The guards from the shift a week ago weren't so lucky," I pointed out. I pulled my hood back up over my head. "But your boredom is not an excuse to act like a pig. Your mothers would be appalled. Don't make me go get them from the caves."

"No. No, ma'am. We're sorry," Robert chimed in, waving his hands in surrender. "We won't do it again."

"All right then," I smirked. I raised two fingers in salute and turned down the road leading off to the left.

The village was starting to wake up. People were emerging from their homes, shaking the snow from their boots, and hauling pots outside to the fires already roaring between the makeshift shelters.

I had heard once that Haven used to be renowned for having the best bakeries in all the land. The smell of bread and sweets had been so strong, it lured traders in from all over, making Haven a rich melting pot of cultures and goods. After the long winter fell, the cold had killed most of the crops and driven many bakers out of business. Their old shops had been converted into orphanages and shelters and the delicious smells had given way to the choking stench of dirt, grime, and smoke.

Shouts and laughter echoed around me as I entered the outer perimeter of buildings that marked the center. The miners and farmers had already left for their day's work. Those left at home were cooking and handing out bowls of potato gruel or attempting to corral young children. The older kids were shoveling snow and dirt into piles near the gutters. I glanced up at the graying sky and winced, knowing their efforts would soon be undone.

I paused at the blacksmith's shop on the edge of the square. Swords, daggers, and knives hung on hooks along the walls of the open shopfront. The wood floor was freshly swept and the orange glow from the forge inside illuminated the filthy windows.

The door swung open, and a large, muscled figure stepped out with several newly minted swords slung over her shoulder. Her blazing red hair was tied back in a thick braid. She turned and, spotting me, smirked, her brown eyes twinkling in amusement.

"Let me guess," she chuckled as she propped her newest work against the wall. She wiped her hands on her smudged apron before pointing to the sword sheathed at my side. "That needs sharpening. And from the looks of it..." She trailed off, her eyes taking in the bruise on my cheek. "I'd say you're in need of another set of bowstrings as well."

"Right as always, Anni." I huffed out a laugh and handed the sword over.

Anni held it up, letting the sunlight bounce off the dull steel as she examined it. She tested it, swinging it through the air with a frown.

"You know," Anni began, shooting me a sideways glance. "This blade is not the best."

"No. Absolutely not, Anni." I shook my head vigorously. "We've had this conversation before. This one is fine! Besides, you made it!"

"I know. But I tell you what..." Anni dropped my sword on the ground and grabbed a brand new one from the wall. The shining blade practically sang with lethal sharpness as she twirled it before me. "Try this one out. The grip is a custom-carved bone. Took me ages. And the jewel... I don't know. I just thought it needed something." She grasped the blade and gestured to me with the pommel. A gleaming blue stone carved in the shape of a snowflake was fastened to the grip guard. I glanced up at her and was about to shake my head when she sighed, "Just humor me."

I tentatively wrapped my fingers around the grip. It cradled my fingers perfectly. The blade was so well-balanced, it felt like an extension of my own arm. I took a step away from Anni and swung it through the air. It whistled around my head as it sliced brutally through the cold. I gave it one last look of longing before holding it back out to her.

"It's beautiful, Anni," I said. "But I don't know if I have anything to trade for it. You can see—" I reached for my bag, but she held up her hand.

"Sure, you do." She scooped the dull sword off the floor. "I'll take this."

"No. Abs—"

"Think of it this way," she said quickly. I sighed as my protest died on my lips. "I can't have Jasper's daughter walking around with *this*." She wrinkled her nose at the dull blade. "It'll ruin my reputation. But people see you with that beauty?" Anni smiled broadly. "Business will be booming."

"Anni, no," I reaffirmed.

She sighed again. "Come on, Lumi. You want it. I can see it on your face."

I glanced down at the sword and bit my lip.

"Don't argue with me and take it. Trade me for this." Anni beamed with triumph as she held up the dull sword.

I sighed in defeat. "Thank you, Anni." I smiled and sheathed my new blade at my side. It bounced off my leg comfortably, like it had always been there.

"No, no. Thank you," she winked. "I haven't named it yet so pick a good one. Just make sure your parents don't take this one."

My expression darkened. "They won't," I promised.

Anni nodded. "Let me get you those new strings." I reached into my pack and handed her a loaf of potato bread. She sniffed it deeply and sighed before retreating into her workshop momentarily, returning with a fistful of new strings.

"Might I make a suggestion?" she said. I raised my eyebrows at her before stuffing the strings deep into my satchel. "Let me look at that bow. It might be worn out and—"

I gave her a hard look.

"That obvious, huh?" Anni snickered. "I was hoping you wouldn't notice."

"Just like I wasn't supposed to notice how the grip on this sword just so happened to fit my hand perfectly?" I challenged.

She shrugged. "What can I say? If the daughter of the most feared man in Haven has one of my swords and my bows, my shop will be outfitting the wall before long. You'd be doing me a huge favor," she added slyly, cocking one eyebrow.

I frowned at her. My father's influence was not something I liked to wield for my own gain. It always felt wrong. But so many villagers held me in high esteem because of their fear of him. They showered me with gifts and free things, refusing my trades no matter how little they actually had. I hated it.

But Anni was the best blacksmith on the continent. Her work was unparalleled and yet business was scarce for her. Many didn't trust a female to craft their weapons. I knew her business would be impacted significantly if I were seen with one of her swords. Villagers would take it as a seal of my father's approval and flock to her doorstep. But with how painstakingly hard she worked on everything, accepting them for practically nothing felt too much like taking advantage of her. It was a conversation she and I had so many times. I touched a hesitant finger to the unyielding bow at my back. My frown deepened as I removed it from its holster to glare at it.

"Anni," I started.

She held up her hands. "I know what you're gonna say, but I swear. My offer is for purely selfish reasons. And only those reasons. Honest. I'm trying to take advantage of you to grow my business." Anni placed a hand over her heart with a mischievous wink.

I sighed through my nose and reluctantly handed the bow over.

Anni grinned and snatched it away, tossing it directly into the crackling fire outside her shop before I could change my mind. She turned on her heel and marched back into her workshop before returning seconds later with a beautiful white bow. She held it out to me proudly. I let my hands wander over it, noting the blue stone snowflake. I glared up at Anni and spotted the razor-sharp dagger she tried concealing in her other hand, which also sported a blue snowflake on the hilt.

"Anni," I said. She shrugged again before stooping and yanking the dagger from my boot, tossing the new one at my feet.

"There. Now I feel better. Thanks so much, Lumi. Make sure you tell people where you got them. See you later!" Anni cackled as she returned to her workshop and slammed the door in my face. I glowered at her door for a moment as her laughter subsided before looking back at the gorgeous white bow still clutched in my hand.

I plucked at the string, enthralled as the arms bent in eager response to my touch. I sighed and slipped the bow through the leather loop on my quiver, holding it in place.

I picked up the dagger. It was light, like the sword, and fit perfectly in my hand. Anni had outdone herself. I slipped the blade into my boot and glanced at the door before plunging a hand into my bag, withdrawing a solid silver candle holder and an ornate Eastern Kingdom vase. Items snatched from the entrance hall as I'd stormed out of my father's house. I set them to the side of the door and gave the grimy window one last smirk before striding away down the road.

CHAPTER TWO

LUMI

Fearful hisses and whispers followed me as soon as I left the blacksmith shop. I kept my eyes straight ahead as I walked quickly through the village streets. Several villagers paused, staring openly as I marched past, and I had to suppress the urge to start shouting at the gawkers. I was willing to bet my life that as soon as I was out of ear shot, one of them would run straight to my father and inform him of my whereabouts.

I was about to turn down the street headed towards the beaches when a loud scraping sound followed by a grunt of pain drew my attention. I looked around and found the bookshop owner struggling to push a heavy box up his cellar stairs. The box started sliding backwards, shoving the portly bookseller back down into the dark.

I raced over and wrapped my arms around the crate to halt its descent. Mr. Vanders yelped in surprise.

"Oh, Lumi! Thank you so much, my dear!" he panted.

Together, we wrestled the box up the stairs and into his dusty shop. Mr. Vanders straightened his back, wiping the sweat from his brow on a filthy handkerchief.

"Thank you," he repeated with a wide grin. "I thought I wasn't gonna get these books up here in time. The Western sailors always want books for their long journeys. And I hear they were just in the east! Hopefully, I can make some excellent trades this time around."

"Of course, Mr. Vanders," I said, wiping my hands on my tunic. "Is this the only one?"

"Well, now that you mention it..." His gaze flickered towards the cellar. "I actually have a few more. If you wouldn't mind?" Mr. Vanders trailed off hopefully.

I nodded before removing my belt and propping my things against his desk in the front of the shop.

"Not at all," I said, following him to the steps.

We worked together to drag the heavy crates into the shop. When the final crate was shoved into a corner, I stood back, stretching my aching muscles and wiping the sweat from my brow.

Mr. Vanders panted, surveying his shop excitedly.

"Thank you so much, Lumi. I don't think I could've hauled those last few up here without you."

"I'm always happy to help," I replied as I gathered my things.

"What can I pay you with? They were heavy so let's say... three?" He gestured around his shop. I glanced around at the dusty volumes and shrugged.

"Well, I'm not looking for any new books, but I happen to know your best customer. Just give me three from his list," I replied, fastening my belt. I glanced up to find Mr. Vanders frowning, his beady eyes darting between me and the door. My brows knit together, and a sense of dread crept up my spine. "What's wrong?"

"It's just—" His eyes shot to the door again and he lowered his voice. "Isn't there something *you* want? Anything at all?" My frown deepened.

"No. I just told you there isn't."

His voice dropped down to a fearful whisper. "Well. I mean, He's not... you see, Lumi, your father—"

My heart sank like a stone. I knew what Mr. Vanders was about to say and held up my hand to stop him. Searing rage flashed through my blood, and I swallowed, fighting to keep my composure.

"I said I'll take three from his list," I hissed. He looked as though he was about to protest, so I shook my head. "I'm not arguing. My father can deal with me if he has a problem."

Mr. Vanders regarded me anxiously. "But your father—"

"My father will never know," I replied, my voice edged with malice. "However, I can always tell him how you used me for labor and then wouldn't pay me." I let my threatening words hang between us for a few moments before holding out my hands.

Mr. Vanders stared at me for a long moment before ambling away, his shoulders slumping in defeat. He returned a few seconds later with a stack of five leather-bound books. I raised my eyebrows and he sighed.

"Two for your silence," he mumbled, before turning his back to me and grasping the edge of the nearest crate.

I slipped the books into my bag and walked out of the shop without another word. Tears burned in my eyes, threatening to overtake me as I made my way quickly down the road. My sweet, shy best friend must have been devastated when Mr. Vanders sent him away. Books were as essential to him as breathing. And now, because of my father, he was banned from the only bookshop left on the Forsaken Isle.

I knew Mr. Vanders wouldn't have willingly banned his best customer from his shop if my father hadn't instructed him to. But I was so damned tired of my friends being treated like shit, I had no sympathy left in me to care that Mr. Vanders only did it out of fear. He'd still done it. And while I hated using my father's influence for myself, I'd wield it like a battle axe for those I loved.

The road ended abruptly, and I paused before starting down the sloping dunes to the beach.

A vast sea of tents and shacks were crammed together along the sand. The white sails of the trade ships drifting across the Black Bay billowed like clouds in the distance. What was left of Haven's trade ships had not yet returned from their journey west. The rest had been beached years ago and converted into shelters for sailors fleeing the destruction of the port city in the north.

Villagers milled about the tents laughing, stirring large boiling pots suspended over crackling fires, and passing food to each other. Smoke curled in the frigid air outside almost every shelter.

Most of the villagers sitting around the fires looked up in alarm as I came into view. A few of them gasped and dove into the safety of their tent. Like I was going to awaken a monster.

I ignored them, holding my head up high.

I wove my way down the small path, stopping at an abrupt twenty-foot clearing in the shelters. A small wooden structure stood in the middle. People walking down the path gave it a wide berth without daring to look at it as they passed.

I frowned at the passers-by and stepped purposefully towards the crooked door of the shack.

"Do you think he'll eat her?" a small girl whispered nearby.

"Probably," came a tiny reply. "He's gonna burn her to a crisp and then swallow her whole."

I glanced around and spotted a boy and a girl huddled behind their tent. They clutched each other and watched me with wide eyes. I opened my mouth to say something, but a strong male voice began singing inside the shack. The children squeaked in terror and scrambled over each other as they fled.

I sighed and shoved the door open.

The shack consisted of one small room. The floor was a patchwork of broken wood slats and blankets that barely covered the sand beneath. An uncomfortable looking cot sat in the corner beside a crate stuffed with shabby, worn-out clothes. The roof was made up of long wooden strips. One of them was pushed back to vent the smoke from a blazing fire in the center of the room. It hovered a few inches above the sand, surrounded by a circle of mismatched stones. Standing next to the fire was one of my two best and only friends in the whole world.

Ash was a year older and half a head taller than me, with a stocky build and broad shoulders. The long hours he'd spent unloading freight for the trade ships had turned him from the scrawny teen I'd grown up with into a solid wall of muscle.

He had a handsome face with a slightly pointed nose and a sharp jawline that was covered in a shadow of stubble. His bright golden eyes widened in surprise and his lips parted with a gasp as I stepped inside and shut the door behind me. His strong hands were frozen in the act of bringing a large bucket of steaming water up to his chest.

It took a second for me to realize he was naked. His tan skin was covered in streaks of white soap and his chin-length, wavy brown hair was tied behind his head. The bucket was placed strategically to hide him from view.

"Well, hello," Ash said. His deep voice rumbled through his chest. He blushed furiously as I leaned against the door and made a dramatic show of looking him up and down.

"Nice," I winked.

He rolled his eyes and suppressed a smile as I strode across the room.

I yanked off my belt and quiver and leaned them against the crate before I plopped down on the cot and faced the wall. "I thought you'd be ready to go by now. I even got held up."

"I had to reheat the water a few times," he replied sheepishly. "Besides, I thought you'd at least knock or something."

"Oh please," I snorted over a loud slosh of water. "When have I ever knocked?"

Ash finished rinsing himself off as I pulled the remaining loaves of bread from my satchel. The bucket hit the ground with a dull thud. Ash sniffed and his stomach growled so loud I could hear it clearly from across the room.

My hands stilled. "Ash," I started. There was a rustling of fabric as he dried himself off. "When was the last time you ate?"

Several seconds passed before he answered. "Um… When was the last time you brought food over?"

"That was two days ago! Are you telling me you haven't eaten in two days?"

"Well, not with *that* tone of voice I'm not," he chuckled.

I whipped around and glared at him. Luckily, he'd managed to pull on a pair of faded brown pants and was yanking a stained blue tunic down over his chest. He noted the anger simmering in my eyes and cringed.

"You haven't eaten in *two days*?"

"Okay it hasn't been *that* long. I managed to stretch some out until yesterday," he said, shoving his feet into ragged black boots. The soles had been repeatedly stitched back on using old fishing lines. The frayed hem of Ash's pants stopped two inches from his ankles, and the sleeves of his tunic left his wrists exposed to the elements.

"Yesterday when?" I challenged, crossing my arms. He pressed his full lips together and looked away without answering. My heart dropped. "Dammit, Ash! Why didn't you tell me?"

"I didn't see you yesterday," he mumbled.

"And you don't know where I live?"

"Lumi, you and I both know your father would've killed me if I went anywhere near that house," he replied.

"What about Rowan?" I shot back. He ducked his head, poking at a loose plank with the toe of his boot. "You realize how he'd feel if he found out you had no food and didn't say anything?"

Ash blew out a long breath, pulling the string from his hair and running his fingers through it.

"I've caused him and his parents so much stress already. I don't want to bother them any more than I absolutely have to. Besides, my gorgeous best friend just brought me something to eat." Ash grinned and sat on the bed, tugging me down beside him. "So, it's fine now."

He gave me that bright, easy smile and my anger cooled.

I sighed and shoved the bread towards him. He grabbed a loaf and bit a piece off with a satisfied sigh.

"Don't think you've gotten out of this. I'm still telling Ro," I said.

"No," he groaned through a mouthful of bread. "No, please don't tell him."

"I'm going to. Then maybe you'll think twice about sitting here in the cold and starving."

"No." He grabbed my shoulders and met my eyes imploringly. "I'm sorry, Lumi. Please don't tell him!"

"Promise me then," I said firmly. "Promise me that you'll come find me or Ro."

"I promise," he replied. He released my shoulders and stuffed another bite into his mouth with a soft moan.

"I'm serious, Ash. If I find out you went without food again, I'll—"

"I promise! I promise!" He laughed and held his hands up in defeat. "No need for threats. I get enough of those as it is." He stuffed the last bite in his mouth with an appreciative sigh and reached behind me for his coat. My heart broke as I watched him pull it on and adjust it over his broad shoulders with difficulty. It stopped three inches from his wrists and didn't cover the breadth of his chest.

He caught me staring and waggled his dark eyebrows at me. "Like what you see?"

I rolled my eyes and stood, grabbing my belt.

"Whoa," he gasped. "That's not your sword."

"It is now," I replied darkly. "Anni suckered me into taking the whole set basically for free. Which I'm positive she custom-made for me."

I frowned and removed the blade from its sheath, handing it to him. Ash examined it carefully while I slung my quiver over my back and fastened my belt.

"It's gorgeous," he murmured. He took in the bow at my back as he handed the sword over.

"It really is," I sighed, slipping the blade into its sheath.

"It suits you," he said with a wink. "What did Anni name it?"

"She didn't. She said I could, but I haven't really thought of anything yet."

"Hmm..." His eyes dropped to the sheath on my hip. "What about Frost Breaker?"

"Ooh, I like that." I touched the blue snowflake lightly. "Frost Breaker," I rolled the name around on my tongue, smiling. "That's perfect. Thank you."

"I aim to please," he chuckled. "Anyway, we'd better get going." He reached up and slid the open panel in the roof back into place before stepping towards the door.

I cleared my throat as he threw it open wide.

"What?" he asked. He had one foot in the snow already, looking back over his shoulder at me.

I tilted my head at the fire still blazing in the center of the room.

"Right," he snorted. He turned halfway around and waved a lazy hand through the air, stretching his fingers wide. The fire sputtered and died out instantly. Panic gripped my chest and I flung myself at him.

"Ash, no! What are you doing?" I gripped the front of his coat and yanked him away from the door, pressing my body into his to keep him out of view as I peered around outside. Luckily, there wasn't a soul in sight.

"Well damn, Lumi," Ash chuckled, winking. I sighed and pushed away from him.

"What if someone saw you?" I wrung my hands anxiously.

"Oh relax," he replied breezily. "Everyone around here is terrified of me. They don't come anywhere near my door."

"And why do you think that is?"

"Because they can't handle all of this," he joked, gesturing down at his body.

"No, it's because they all think you're a monster or something." I frowned at him. "These people are looking for a reason to throw you out into the wild to freeze. Please don't give them one."

"I treasure you too, Lumi," Ash replied with a broad grin. That radiant and carefree smile never failed to silence my fears. I rolled my eyes and pulled him out the door, closing it firmly behind us.

"Let's just get going. Before you blow your house up again."

"I did that one time!" Ash cried indignantly. "Once! Ten years ago! Am I ever going to live that down?"

"Not a chance," I smirked. "I still remember how long it took your eyebrows to grow back."

Ash rolled his eyes and offered me his arm.

I slipped my hand into the crook of his elbow, letting him lead me away. A sudden, quick movement drew my attention, and I shot a glance to our left. Two women were standing outside of a tent with their heads bent, whispering to each other as we passed.

They spotted Ash and raced inside, peering around the flap nervously. Anger bubbled up inside my chest. I turned back to Ash and watched his face to see if he noticed. Thankfully, he was far too busy vehemently explaining exactly why his house burning down was not his fault.

"... no one said anything to me about that kind of wood being flammable. So how was I supposed to know?" he finished dramatically.

"Really," I snorted. "You didn't know *wood* was flammable? That's your excuse?"

"Hey, I was a little kid!"

"You were twelve!" I shot back, laughing.

"I didn't say I was a smart kid!"

I rolled my eyes and smiled. After a second, he met my stare and cocked an indignant eyebrow at me. "You're not supposed to agree with me on that."

"You burned your house down because you thought house wood and firewood were different," I teased.

He clutched his chest with his free hand in mock offense. "Wow, rude," he said, suppressing a smile as we crossed into the shopping district.

We were passing by the candle maker's storefront when the shopkeeper came out to set a wooden sign beside the front door. His face twisted in disgust when he spotted us, and he spat in Ash's direction.

Ash flinched but kept his eyes straight ahead. The shopkeeper shook a gnarled fist at him.

"Leave her alone, freak! Jasper will hear about this!" he shouted as he retreated into his shop, slamming the door, and locking it firmly behind him.

Rage surged through me. I moved to release Ash's arm and step around him, drawing in a deep breath to start yelling. Ash hadn't even glanced up at him. Instead, he caught my wrist and fixed me with his golden stare.

"Don't," he pleaded softly. "It's not worth it."

"The fuck it isn't," I snarled, trying to step around him again.

Ash's fingers tightened on my wrist.

"Please, Lumi. For me. Don't."

We stared at each other for a long moment, my anger giving way at the sight of the heartache glimmering in his eyes. I took several deep calming breaths before nodding and allowing him to place my hand back on his elbow to lead me away. I swallowed hard and glanced up at his face. His eyes were cast down at our feet. He ran a hand through his hair, his expression drawn and unreadable.

"Are you okay?" he asked suddenly. I blinked at him.

"Me? I'm fine. Are *you*?" When he didn't answer, I dug my heels into the snow, forcing him to stop and meet my gaze.

"Do you think I'm a ..." Ash trailed off with a huff, unable to say the words aloud.

I blinked away the tears blurring my vision and tightened my grip on his elbow in an effort to reassure him.

"Of course not," I asserted, pressing my cheek against his shoulder. "You know that."

He rested his chin on the top of my head for a few seconds before straightening and offering me a smile that didn't quite meet his eyes.

"That's all that matters to me," he said.

We continued through the village in a sullen silence. Every villager we passed had something horrible to say. Ash's muscles tensed under my fingers at every nasty word or gesture hurled in his direction. I kept glancing up at his face which he held carefully in an expression of indifference.

We finally arrived at an unassuming stone building situated on the far edge of a residential street. Ash glanced around before raising his fist and lightly rapping on the wooden door.

CHAPTER THREE

ROWAN

Stretched out in front of the fire with a book was my absolute favorite place to be. I loved the crackling flames and smell of smoke mixing with the rich scent of the paper. The cozy study had several armchairs to curl up in, but I relished the pull on my muscles as I let my favorite stories block out reality. I needed it after the morning I'd had. The deep red carpet at my back had come all the way from the Eastern Kingdoms. Its soft fibers had been flattened from years of me rolling around on it.

Someone cleared their throat nearby, drawing my attention away from the page. I flipped onto my stomach and propped myself up on my elbows, setting the book aside. My father poked his head into the study with a swift wink.

"They should be here soon," he whispered. Mother had already pulled his graying locks into a knot behind his head. I'd gotten his kind round face and narrow torso. But while his hair had once been solid black, mine was red and curly like my mother's. His lips were much thinner than mine and his face was covered in a thick, graying beard. He wore black pants and a black tunic with the sleeves rolled up, revealing two scarred wrists where his hands had once been.

Father's deep blue eyes sparkled with mischief as a knock sounded at the front door and he withdrew quickly. I sat up as the door let out a high-pitched squeak and opened wide.

"Hello, you two!"

Familiar voices drifted in as my father ushered my friends into the room. I hopped up, shoving my book into the deep pocket of my favorite green tunic.

"Hi guys!" I flashed a toothy grin and pulled Lumi into a tight hug. Something hard bounced off my knee and I glanced down at the white sword handle hanging by her side.

"That's new," I remarked, raising an eyebrow.

"Anni," she sighed with a deep frown. Lumi dropped her coat and quiver onto the floor, before plopping into a chair and removing her boots.

I chuckled. "Uh oh."

"Yeah. I tried to say no but she insisted. And if I don't take it, I feel like an ass. But I mean, come on. Look at this."

She held up her new bow. Like the sword, it was white and sported a glistening blue stone carved in the shape of a snowflake. "And there's a dagger too!" She gestured towards her boots with her foot. "She put all this work in and wouldn't let me trade for them. I left something at her door to make myself feel better, but it's not the same."

I grinned at Ash, who replied with a small shrug and hugged me. He was unnervingly quiet. His usually easygoing expression was dark and withdrawn, and that carefree smile was missing.

I shot Lumi a questioning look. Her gaze flicked in his direction before she shook her head ever so slightly in response. I furrowed my brow and turned, keeping one arm draped around Ash's waist. He laid an arm absentmindedly across my shoulders, too lost in thought to notice me gently prodding his ribs with the tips of my fingers. I bit back a sharp sigh of relief as sturdy muscle met my touch instead of bone. He had been eating at the very least.

"I know you hate it, Lumi," I said with a trace of humor. "But what's done is done. Besides, you needed a new sword. That last one was worn down so much, I doubt it could've sliced bread. And the bow you had sucked. I'm sorry but it did."

Lumi rolled her eyes. "I know, but..." She exhaled slowly and placed it back into the clip on her quiver. "I don't like taking advantage of my father's influence... For myself," she added with a strange smirk.

Ash slid away from me. He peeled off his tight-fitting coat and ragged boots before stepping over to the fire and placing his hands near the roaring blaze.

"So, what are you reading?" Lumi stood, lifting her eyebrows as she glanced down at the book in my pocket. I jerked a hand towards it without meaning to and Lumi's eyebrows shot up a little higher. "Haven't you read that one already? Twice?"

My heart dropped. I pressed my lips together, trying and failing to hide the disappointment swelling in my chest. I'd gone to the bookshop bright and early in the hopes of trading for brand new stories to get lost in. But Mr. Vanders turned me away and told me never to come back, slamming the door in my tearful face.

Mr. Vanders hadn't told me why, but I knew.

I glanced at Ash and swallowed hard, forcing a neutral, uninterested tone. She followed my gaze, her expression unreadable.

"Well...I mean, yeah, I *have* read it already. But sometimes it's nice to reread the classics."

"Classics," she repeated, grinning. "So that's not the romance novel with the arranged marriage and the assassin that's after the princess?"

"Romance novels can be classics," I muttered.

"Right. Of course," she said with mock seriousness. "Can I see it?" I handed the book over. She made a show of examining the cover before setting it on the bookshelf nearby, removing my bookmark and handing it to me. Before I could huff with indignation, Lumi reached into her bag and withdrew five large books, placing them in my arms one by one as I stared down in absolute shock.

She patted the top book proudly. "Since you're rereading the classics, I don't suppose you'd want these then?"

Emotions clogged my throat. I glanced pointedly over at Ash before meeting Lumi's eyes, pressing the books tightly against my chest and hoping she knew what this meant to me. Her smile widened and she winked to let me know she understood.

"Thank you so much, Lumi!" I said in as even a tone as I could manage. I turned away to place the books on my shelf, giving myself a much needed second to wipe away my tears and regain my composure. I carefully opened one of the new books and inhaled the smell of the pages before sliding it into my pocket. I was twirling the metal bookmark between my fingers as I turned back to Lumi, who was still beaming at me.

"It was no big deal," she shrugged. "Mr. Vanders needed a hand hauling book crates out of the cellar."

The ferocious gleam in her eye suggested that Mr. Vanders had been reluctant to give her the books meant for me. I nodded gratefully and turned towards the fire.

Ash was observing us carefully over his shoulder. Lumi and I stepped to either side of him and started warming ourselves too. He turned back, sighing deeply through his nose.

I shot a quick glance around and found his boots lying near the fire. The sight of the fishing line holding them together broke my heart. I leaned back slightly and caught Lumi's eye, tilting my head at his boots, and tapping the bookmark against my knuckles. She nodded and glanced up at Ash, who was still staring into the flames and hadn't noticed anything. I took careful aim and deliberately dropped my bookmark.

"Oops," I muttered, stooping down. Ash turned to look at me, but Lumi suddenly leaned into him, drawing his eyes. She glanced down as I took the sharpest edge of the bookmark and began slicing through the fishing line as quietly as I could. Ash raised his eyebrows at her. She met his gaze firmly and pressed herself against him.

"What?" Lumi challenged a little too loudly. "I'm cold, and you're basically a walking campfire." She threw her arms around him, forcing him to turn away from me.

Ash let out a breathless huff as Lumi buried her face in his chest and squeezed him tight.

"You're so warm," Lumi moaned, her voice muffled.

Ash held his arms out in confusion before patting Lumi gingerly on the back, wrapping her in a tentative hug. I suppressed a chuckle as I worked my way through the last stitch. I could almost feel the heat from the blush creeping its way up his neck. The last of the fishing line snapped in half, and I shot back to my feet.

"Found it!" I exclaimed, holding up the bookmark. Lumi released Ash and stepped around him to peer at it.

"It's so pretty, Ro! Where'd you get it?" Lumi said, winking at me.

Ash turned slowly, rubbing the spot where Lumi's lips had just been pressed with his fingertips and gazing at her with acute longing written across his face.

I raised my eyebrows at him, a slight smile tugging at my lips.

Ash's golden eyes shot to me. He swallowed hard and ran his hand through his brown hair, his expression darkening again as he turned back to the fire.

I'd seen that look on his face for years. Somehow, he always managed to hide it from Lumi. But he couldn't hide it from me. Not that I could ever get Ash to admit anything out loud, no matter how much I pressed him.

I fought the urge to sigh and turned the bookmark over in my hand. "My mother traded for it. It's all the way from the Winter capital in the Eastern Kingdoms." I tucked the bookmark in my pocket as my father swept into the room. He nodded at me, and I winked. He and I had a carefully laid out plan that I'd just set in motion.

"Ash, my boy!" Father boomed jovially.

Ash turned from the fire.

"I was wondering if you could help me?"

"Anything, sir," Ash replied.

"It's going to be a brutal night, you see. And I need more firewood brought in. That is, if you don't mind?" Father waved one arm at the foyer behind him.

"Of course," Ash nodded. He reached for his boots, gasping as he lifted one from the floor. The sole peeled away and fell with a resounding *thud* on the carpet. He stared down in bewilderment for a beat before his eyes cut to me with a fierce gleam.

I fixed my expression into a look of mild surprise and pressed my lips together. He let the rest of the boot drop and ran his fingers through his hair, sighing.

"Oh no!" Father said, peering over Ash's shoulder. "Well, not to worry, son. My lovely wife traded for some brand-new boots yesterday. Unfortunately, they're too tight for my old feet, and I can't slip them on easily," he added, indicating to his scarred wrists. "Let's see if they fit you."

Ash's fierce stare burned through my skull. He exhaled sharply through his nose and grabbed his shabby coat before turning to follow my father out of the room.

As soon as they started making their way up the stairwell, I blew out a breath and turned to Lumi.

"Smooth," I chuckled.

"Hey. I think I did okay considering you didn't warn me in advance," she said, sidling up to me. "Besides, did you see that look? He might be onto you. That fishing line was old, but it wouldn't have fallen apart all at once."

I shrugged. "If he'd just accept help instead of being so fucking hardheaded about it, we wouldn't have to do things like this." I glanced at the ceiling as footsteps clomped overhead. "Just wait," I added with a wicked grin. "I put fishhooks in that wood pile. They aren't sharp enough to hurt him, but that coat won't make it. That tunic either."

"Damn, Ro. That's devious." Lumi laughed. "But you don't think that'll give you away?"

"I don't care." I replied. "At some point he has to let us help him. Especially since he can't work at the docks anymore."

Footsteps thudded down the stairs again as Ash and my father headed out the door and into the snow. Ash's shoulders were tight, and his eyes were downcast, no doubt examining the shiny new boots.

"Did something happen? He's never this quiet," I asked.

"Someone spit at him on the way here," she said darkly. "And called him a freak on top of the usual cursing he always deals with. He's trying not to let it bother him, but... Ro, he actually asked me if *I* think he's a freak."

I clenched my teeth against the swell of anger in my chest.

"I don't understand these people," I hissed. "They're terrified of him, and it's based on what? A rumor of a rumor?" I shook my head and glanced at the door.

Lumi shifted, the top of her head grazing my cheek as she leaned on my shoulder.

Her voice wavered with shame as she mumbled, "Ro, be honest... is it bad?"

"Lumi. Don't do this to yourself." I pressed my cheek against the top of her head and slid an arm around her back. "You know that no one blames you, right?"

She didn't answer, wrapping her arm around my waist in response.

I sighed heavily. "It's not too bad. Mother is still very well respected. Jasper hasn't touched her reputation, and no one knows she's Cosmic too. People think she's using herbs and oils to heal them. They don't realize they're being healed by the power they're all so terrified of."

Lumi's whole body tensed at the mention of her father's name. I planted a small, reassuring kiss on the top of her head and continued.

"Father always has a hard time with the villagers. Who he is isn't exactly a secret. And having Ash here so often on top of it..." I trailed off, lulled into silence by the crackling flames.

"And you?"

"Just Mr. Vanders," I replied. "And I'd be devastated if Ash found out." I shot her a severe look.

"Of course," she said, her gaze flitting to the door. "Does anyone suspect you?"

"Not that I've heard. But unlike our adorable and very reckless friend, I am much more careful with my power," I added with a small grin. "And what about you? Any progress yet?"

"Nothing." She fought, unsuccessfully, to squash the disappointment that flared in her eyes. Her voice dropped to barely a whisper, and she glanced at the door again. "But on the subject of our reckless friend, there's something you should know."

I raised my eyebrows.

"Ro... Ash had no food yesterday."

"What?" I gasped, my stomach twisting in horror. "He had nothing?"

"Not until I brought him some this morning."

"Why didn't he come to us?"

Lumi shot me a dark look. "You know why."

"Dammit, Ash! Does he not understand what could happen? I get that he hates feeling like a burden but he's... Fuck!" I burst out, scrubbing my hands roughly over my face. "His power is the only thing he has for heat and if he runs out of energy in the middle of the night, or worse, in the middle of a blizzard!"

"I know," she replied. "It would be so much easier if he'd just let us *help* him—"

A soft snap sounded in the foyer. We whipped around and found Ash with a load of firewood clutched in his arms, wincing as he shuffled awkwardly into the room. My father was behind him, apologizing profusely.

"I'm so sorry, son! I have no idea where those fishhooks came from! I will of course replace your coat. And your tunic too! Come back upstairs. I'm sure I have... Oh no!" Father tread purposefully on a fishing line trailing from a hook that'd snared on Ash's pants and a giant hole appeared at his hip. "Quickly, son! Just drop the wood here before you lose your pants completely!"

Father brushed past him and hurried up the stairs. Ash dropped the wood in a heap on the floor, revealing the gaping holes torn in his tunic. Much of his muscled stomach and chest were visible, heaving from the effort of hauling the wood.

Ash didn't even try to hide it as he glared at me. But I was so angry, I didn't even flinch. I lifted my chin and glared right back at him. Challenging him to say a word. We stared each other down for a moment before Ash closed his eyes and looked away, dragging himself up the stairs after my father.

"He's definitely on to you," Lumi winced.

"He can kiss my ass," I seethed. "He could've died last night because he's so fucking stubborn."

I reached down and snatched his ragged boots off the floor, hurling them as hard as I could into the fire. They caught swiftly and filled the room with the smell of burning leather. Thick black smoke billowed up the chimney. I splayed my fingers wide, and my power surged forth. The flames leapt higher under my command, roaring like a wild animal trapped in a cage.

Lumi cleared her throat. I met her eyes and huffed, releasing my hold on the flames. They sputtered and returned to a soft, rolling crackle. Ash's boots were reduced to a pile of smoldering scrap. "I'm sorry," I mumbled guiltily. "You two are my best friends. My family. I worry."

She chuckled softly and hugged me. "I know," she said. "And I love you too. Both of you."

I hugged her back, my anger slowly ebbing as my father returned. He met my eyes with a swift wink.

Lumi stepped away and plopped into a chair, crossing her legs underneath her. Ash ambled sheepishly into the study a few moments later.

The vibrant purple tunic and black pants accentuated his form nicely. It'd been so long since I'd seem him in clothes that actually fit, it was almost shocking. He dropped his new boots and a bundle of new clothes on the floor near the entrance.

Lumi pressed a hand to her chest and looked him up and down dramatically. "Goodness. Don't you look dashing, sir," she said, grinning up at him.

"Thanks," he replied dryly.

Lumi smirked and looked away just in time to miss the fierce blush staining Ash's cheeks. My father settled into his favorite chair and began chatting idly with Lumi.

I strode purposefully up to Ash and wrapped an arm around his waist, looking up at him with a fierce challenge in my eyes. He spotted the charred remainders of his boots in the fireplace and glanced down at me with a cool expression.

"Fishhooks?" Ash hissed. "Really, Ro?"

"I regret nothing," I said with a wicked smirk.

Ash blew out a breath before raising his eyes skyward and shaking his head. He stared at the ceiling for a bit before he slumped and placed an arm across my shoulders.

"Thank you," he breathed. His fingers skimmed the purple fabric, and I patted his chest.

"Ash, we may not be blood, but you're still my brother," I replied. "I'm gonna make sure you're okay whether you like it or not."

Ash's throat bobbed with barely held-back emotion.

"And I'm sorry about your boots," I added, nodding towards the fireplace.

"Are you though?"

"No," I admitted. "They were hideous, and the world is a better place without them." I released him and walked over, throwing myself into the chair beside my father. Ash claimed the chair next to Lumi and slumped back. His eyes closed as he sank deep into the plush cushions.

Lumi smiled sadly at him before turning back to my father.

"You think all these storms are connected?" she asked, furrowing her brow.

"Unfortunately," Father sighed. He glanced out the window. The clouds had opened up, dropping thick clumps of snow on the world. "Storms like these are unnatural. I'm worried Winter is gathering her forces."

"So, the storms are a warning? You think she might attack Haven?" Lumi asked, paling.

"I believe so," Father replied grimly. "If rumors are to be believed, another city fell not too far east of here. She may be marching her demons this way."

Ash cracked an eye open in alarm.

"But the ice demons can't get over the wall," Lumi said. "Right?"

My father leaned back in his chair. "We can only hope to the Ethereal Two above that the wall holds. It's held out against her onslaughts so far. But the Lady of Winter is resourceful, and she's had twenty years to plot our downfall."

He glanced sadly at Ash. "That's why you three must be careful. Especially you, Ash. The people of this village mistakenly believe that our power can summon the spirits. If ice demons start attacking the wall, the village will be looking for Cosmics to blame. And fear can drive people to do terrible things. Trust me," he added grimly, looking down at where his hands should have been. "I know better than most."

Guilt flickered in Lumi's stare, and she looked away sharply.

"Kaelin," she gasped, tears welling up in her eyes. "I am so—"

"Ah, ah. None of that," Father said, cutting her off sternly. "What happened to me had nothing to do with you, my dear. You are not responsible for your father's actions. It was a long time ago, and I've made peace with my life since then. Besides... Despite what the villagers believe, I didn't lose my powers when he took my hands." A small gust of wind swirled around our ankles. "I have my gorgeous wife, my son, and my two adopted children," he added, his eyes sparkling. "I have no complaints." He glanced out the window at the formidable storm brewing on the horizon, and his face fell slightly.

"I count myself very lucky," he said. "My darling's reputation as the village doctor was the only thing that saved me from being executed like so many other Cosmic people. That's why you must be careful when and where you use your power. Jasper won't hesitate to execute you if he discovers who you are. Especially not after the demon that attacked the wall a few nights ago."

Lumi sucked in a sharp breath, pressing the heels of her palms to her eyes.

"So, everyone's gonna be really happy to see me now. Great," Ash chuckled sarcastically.

"That just means it's time to move back in with me!" I said, winking. Ash made a face at me and settled further into his chair.

My father got to his feet and bent toward Lumi. I didn't hear what he said, but after a second, she nodded, wiping her damp eyes. Father straightened and fixed Ash with a knowing stare.

"He's right, son. I'm afraid things are about to take a turn for the worse and you'd be much safer here with us."

Ash ducked his head without answering. It was an offer my father extended at least once a week. And it was one that Ash always refused. He'd lived with us for a long while. My parents took him in off the streets and raised him right alongside me.

Then one day, Ash found my father on the doorstep of the house getting screamed at by a neighbor. They accused him of all sorts of things and threatened to burn down our house for harboring a monster.

Ash was devastated. He built his miserable little shack on the beach and moved out on his own that very night, much to the dismay of my parents. Lumi and I had plotted several times to try and bring him back, but my father was adamant that Ash had to make the decision on his own.

Father sighed and glanced out the window. "You three do your best to stay out of trouble. My darling should be ready for lunch soon. I'll be back later." He gave Ash one last meaningful look before he turned and left.

I watched Lumi's face as the front door opened and closed.

"Are you okay?" I asked quietly. Lumi's eyes were bright with unearthly rage as she glanced back at me.

"I'll be okay," she replied.

"We're here if you need to talk," Ash said, rubbing his eyes vigorously.

I snorted and grabbed the cozy blanket draped down the back of my chair, shaking it out as I crossed the room and threw it over him.

"Wait... no. I'm not... oh." He tried to protest, but I gripped the back of his chair and pushed down. The wooden slats in the bottom shifted and snapped into place, reclining it back. His eyes fluttered closed and his whole body relaxed. A deep groan rumbled through his chest.

"Really," he mumbled. "I'm not... I..." He fell silent and drifted off hard.

"Damn," Lumi said. "He was tired."

"He probably doesn't sleep well on that shitty cot," I mused.

"Probably not," she agreed, shaking her head. "I hate that so much." She looked down at her hands clasped in her lap, gritting her teeth. "I hate what my father's done to him. What he's still doing to him. And... and what he's done to you. To Kaelin." She looked up at me, pain wrecking her beautiful face. "Ro, I am so sorry. I don't know how you can even look at me."

"Whoa now," I said angrily. She winced and looked away. "You are *not* your father, Lumi. I don't ever want to hear you say that again. Don't you start that shit on me too. I get enough of that guilty crap from him." I jerked my chin at Ash. "You're my sister. I can't live without you, and neither can Ash. So, stop it. Fuck! Since when am I the well-adjusted one in this family?" I said, shaking my head. She chuckled meekly.

"I guess you're right," Lumi replied, glancing over at our sleeping friend. Ash's chest rose and fell steadily. Lumi shot me a fearful look. "I worry all the time though... That my father will kill him," she admitted. I swallowed hard.

"I worry too." I passed a weary hand over my face. "Jasper doesn't strike me as a man who would have a problem killing someone. Especially not someone he seems to hate so much."

"No, he wouldn't," Lumi agreed. "I think the only reason he hasn't tried yet is because of me. I think he's hoping that once I'm married off, the husband he picked for me will keep me in check. Then he can do it and have all of Haven applaud him for saving them."

She let out a soft, frustrated sound. "I just wish I could do... something!" she burst out, staring down at her hands. "I wish I could make fire, a gust of wind. Anything! Then maybe they'd see he's not dangerous."

I swallowed hard. Her parents would never accept her as Cosmic. Their own daughter turning out to be Cosmic would be a scandal of epic proportions. One that they would absolutely blame on our sleeping friend. But I didn't have the heart to tell her that.

Instead, I blew out a breath and said, "We could get some practice in if you want."

Lumi nodded, jumping to her feet. We sat face to face in front of the fire and for the next few hours, we worked on her abilities.

First, I walked her through some air techniques. Nothing happened. Fire was next and still, nothing happened. By the time we'd gotten through earth and water unsuccessfully, the sun was deep into its afternoon descent. The blizzard had raged through the village fiercely, dumping snow onto the freshly shoveled streets. It had just blown itself out when Ash jerked awake and sat up, peering at us with bleary eyes.

"Why didn't you wake me up?" he yawned, stretching.

Lumi bit her lip, disappointment and frustration swirling off her like a storm.

"You were tired," I replied.

"Yeah, but..." He caught sight of her face and paused, glancing at me with raised eyebrows. I shook my head once in response before standing and helping Lumi to her feet.

"Come on," I said, hooking my arm around her waist. "I'm starving." We migrated to the kitchen and stuffed food into our mouths for an extremely late lunch.

Lumi was unnaturally quiet as she picked at her bread, leaving a pile of crumbs on the tabletop. Ash shot me a puzzled look. I splayed my fingers wide under the table, sending a small breeze trailing around his ankles. He looked back at his food with a subtle nod of understanding. After everyone had eaten their fill, I walked them to the door while they donned their coats and boots. Lumi strapped her quiver and sword in place before turning back to me.

"See you tomorrow?" I asked.

"Absolutely," Lumi said. "I'd rather be here than at home."

"Same," Ash said, chuckling.

"Awesome! Then I will see you in the morning!" I replied brightly. They both hugged me goodbye and stepped out into the snow.

CHAPTER FOUR

Ash

The fresh snow crunched under our boots as we walked side by side down the road. The blizzard had finally blown itself out and villagers were already sweeping their front porches or clearing the main road of snow. Delicious smells wafted through the air as dinners were prepared over open fires.

Several of them hissed, hurling the usual insults and curses as I passed. A few glanced up in horror and darted inside their homes.

I did my best to ignore them, focusing all of my attention on Lumi.

She appeared to be lost in thought, her eyes cast down to our feet. Sunlight wreathed her raven hair like a crown and made her pale face look like it was glowing. She must've felt my stare because she looked up suddenly, locking those breathtaking blue eyes on me.

"Are you okay?" I asked, offering my elbow to her.

She sighed without answering and took it, returning her gaze to our feet. I gently nudged her side, and she met my eyes again.

"You just—" I paused as a group of miners passed by on their way home from a hard day's work. People dressed in heavy armor yawned and stretched, heading in the other direction for their shift on the wall.

"You look like something's bothering you," I whispered, dipping my head closer to her ear.

She was about to respond when a scoff echoed from across the road.

I looked over and accidentally met the eyes of an old woman. She stood on her porch with a steaming plate clutched in her hands, glaring at me over the shoulder of a sturdy young man who was ascending the stairs. Her son glanced back. His lip curled in disgust, and he stepped quickly to the side, shielding his mother from me like I was about to sprout wings and start spitting fire. The old woman drew herself up and spat in my direction.

I hunched my shoulders and looked away quickly. Lumi jerked her arm away from me as she stopped walking, fixing her furious eyes on the pair. I stopped a few feet away, well out of reach of the man and the sword his fingers were twitching towards.

Lumi tracked his movement and grasped the hilt of her shining new blade, drawing it slowly. It whistled through the air as she twirled it at her side and spread her feet, bracing for a fight. The son drew his weapon in response and stared her down angrily, taking in Frost Breaker, the quiver full of arrows at her back, and then, finally, her face.

Recognition flashed across his face as he realized who it was that he was challenging. His eyes darted between us, and he swallowed hard, ramming his sword back into its sheath. Apparently, killing Haven's resident monster wasn't worth fighting Lumi and risking her father's wrath. He put an arm behind him, gently pushing his mother into the house. The old woman gave me one last vulgar gesture before letting her son sweep her inside and slamming the door behind them.

Lumi seethed, her chest heaving as she glared at the door.

"Lumi," I called.

She glanced around, bewildered to see me a few feet away instead of right next to her. I held my hand out to her.

She glanced towards the door. For one wild second, a raging fire danced behind her eyes. I read the murderous expression on her face and said softly, "Please, Lumi... It's not worth it."

Her eyes blazed as she locked them on me. I held my hand a little higher and met her gaze, defeated. She gave the door one last vicious glance before releasing a breath, sheathing her blade, and returning to my side. She leaned her head against my shoulder and laced both of her hands around my arm. My heart fluttered.

"Are you okay?" she asked quietly, her voice rough with emotion.

I made myself chuckle and nodded.

"One of these days, you're gonna have to stop trying to kill everyone who gets scared of me," I said with a weak attempt at a smirk.

She rolled her eyes and pulled me closer to her side, causing my breath to catch.

"Shut up," she grumbled.

"So, my fierce warrior queen," I teased, "you still haven't answered my question."

She raised her eyebrows.

"Are you okay?" I repeated.

"I'm fine." She plastered an obviously forced smile on her face.

"You're a terrible liar," I replied, cocking an eyebrow.

"Well, you're no master of deception either," she frowned. "I see those brand-new clothes you were given were left behind that chair. Real subtle."

"It was more subtle than Rowan 'dropping' his sharp, metal bookmark and you shouting to cover the sound of him tearing my boots up with it. Or his fishhooks," I said coolly, meeting her ice blue stare. "And what about the poking thing he does up my ribcage when he thinks I'm not eating? But I'm not supposed to notice any of that, am I? If I didn't realize what you two were doing, I'd truly be the idiot you seem to think I am."

Lumi flinched, looking away. My heart dropped into my stomach, and I regretted my harsh words instantly.

"We don't think you're an idiot, Ash. I'm so sorry," she said thickly, leaning her head onto my shoulder.

Guilt and shame wrenched through my gut and wrapped so forcefully around my chest that I almost couldn't breathe.

"We just worry. You won't let us help you, so we take drastic measures. But... I'm sorry we made you feel like we think you're an idiot. I hope you know how much you mean to us." She sniffed once and wiped her eyes on the back of her hand.

My breathing stalled completely. My chest felt like it was going to crack in half. I swallowed, forcing air into my lungs and leaned my head against hers. The sweet smell of Lumi's hair filled my nose as I sighed heavily.

"I'm sorry," I croaked. "I shouldn't have said that."

She straightened without looking at me and started walking again, pulling me along with her as she went. People skirted around us to avoid me. Lumi glared threateningly at each person who looked my way, so I maneuvered us off the main road and into the relative safety of an alleyway. We walked in silence for a long time before she suddenly huffed in frustration and stopped, jerking me to a halt.

"Why won't you let us help you?" she demanded. Her soft fingers tugged my chin, forcing me to meet her eyes.

My heart thundered against my ribs. I desperately wanted to give her an answer. I wanted to tell her how much she and Rowan meant to me. That I hated so many bad things happened to them because of me. Or how much it killed me that her father was pushing her to marry someone to keep her away from me. I wanted to tell her that I died a little more inside every time another villager stopped doing business with Kaelin because of me. My heart ached at the thought of everything I put them all through. But I couldn't bring myself to tell her any of that. Not if meant watching her face crumple again.

So, I gently pulled my chin away and started walking again.

"I do accept help," I replied.

"You do not. Not unless we make you," she replied fiercely.

"You haven't answered my question," I said. "Are you okay? You seemed upset at Rowan's."

"Don't change the subject."

"Too late," I said, smiling mischievously. "What's wrong?"

Lumi glared at me for a long moment before she finally relented with a deep sigh. "Fine. This conversation isn't over. But..." she trailed off, biting her full lip.

My eyes inadvertently darted to her mouth. I swallowed hard and forced myself to look away. "Ash... I have no proof I have any Cosmic powers like you and Ro," she burst out. "I've been trying for months now. You and Ro can just *do* it. I don't understand! Kaelin said I'm Cosmic... But then why can't I use a power I supposedly have?"

"Well." I cocked my head to the side in thought. The alleyway narrowed and Lumi had to release my arm to walk in front of me. "You passed the test, so you are definitely Cosmic. Maybe we need—" I stopped short as I suddenly sank thigh-deep into the snow.

Lumi kept walking, her light steps leaving small indentations in the surface of the snowbank as she wrapped her arms around her chest.

"I don't know what else to do! Nothing I try works for me. Ash, what if the test was a fluke? What if I'm—"

My foot caught on a rock under the snow. I let out a sharp cry, tumbling face first into the freezing snowbank. I pushed myself up and found Lumi staring at me in surprise. One look at my snow-caked front and she burst out in a bright, bubbly laughter that lit up her whole face. She doubled over, shaking and wiping her eyes.

"Are you okay?" she choked out.

"It wasn't that funny," I grumbled. I wiped the snow from my face and shook out my long brown hair.

"Oh no, sir. It was, in fact, hilarious," she giggled.

I had to fight against the smile threatening to overtake me. Hearing her laugh made my heart soar.

"You have to step lightly." She lifted a foot and waved it over the snow. "See? The snow is packed enough that you can walk on it if you don't stomp."

"Lumi, that's ridiculous," I said. I hiked a leg as high as I could and placed it gingerly on the snow. The second I shifted my body weight, my leg sunk back into the freezing bank.

"Well, I'm doing it." She turned in a circle for emphasis. "I'm telling you, walk lighter."

I rolled my eyes and shot a glance over my shoulder, making sure no one was watching as I rolled up my sleeves. Once I ensured we were alone, I spread my fingers wide and focused.

My power sent heat surging through my blood. It sparked and fire ignited in my hands. I willed the fire to grow, and it responded, filling the space around me. The snow melted instantly and revealed the dirty stone pavers underneath.

Lumi gasped, whirling around in horror to search for anyone lurking nearby. "Ash, no! What if someone's watching?"

"What's that?" I shouted, grinning at her wickedly as I took another step. The snow vanished before me.

Light danced off the surrounding brick walls, casting her features in sharp relief. Her face glowed like a goddess, and I couldn't help but stare, wishing I could tell her how beautiful she was. She dug her boot into the snow, taking advantage of my distraction, and kicked out hard. An icy slurry flew through the air and smacked me in the nose.

I swore and stumbled as the fire died instantly around me. I met her eyes, wiping the snow dripping from my face.

"That was a cheap shot," I grumbled, running my fingers through my hair.

"Well, be more careful next time," she chuckled. She looked up at the sky, her smile fading. A light flurry of snow was beginning to fall, and the sky was darkening all over again. "Come on. We better get going before it really starts coming down."

She hauled me out onto the street beyond the alley, frowning at the clouds and placing a hand absentmindedly on my chest. She looked down at her hand in surprise before glancing again up at me, searching my face. I willed my features into what I desperately hoped was a calm expression.

"Are you okay?" Her brows knit together in concern. "Your heart is going crazy right now." She pressed her hand into my chest, feeling the thunderous pounding of my traitorous heart beneath my ribs.

My mind scrambled for an explanation.

"I'm fine," I said finally, taking her hand and placing it into the crook of my arm again. "Lighting an entire alley on fire isn't easy," I whispered, ducking my head down beside her ear so I wasn't overheard. We rounded the bend and started down the sloping dunes to the beach. She must've believed me because she nodded.

"It's too bad Kaelin didn't try to send you home with food," she remarked.

"He offered while we were upstairs. But I already have some so..." I trailed off.

Lumi's fingers curled tightly around my elbow. "Ash, why did you lie?" she admonished.

I clutched my chest, gasping dramatically. "I didn't lie! How could you say that?" I cried, pretending to be offended.

We wove our way through the tents, avoiding eye contact with the villagers cooking outside over open fires.

"So, if I go in there..." she challenged, pointing towards my hut, "You swear to me that I'll find food."

"I swear," I winked. "You brought it, remember?"

"I only brought two! One of which you ate! You need food, Ash! Why'd you say no?" Lumi huffed angrily. "See? This is what I meant! Why can't we help you?"

I swallowed hard and met her eyes to find them brimming with tears. My heart lurched.

"Because I don't want to take from them," I said softly. "They already give me so much. And so do you. I mean... Look at these." I gestured down my body with my free hand. "All those clothes were new... They clearly traded for all this stuff. For me." I pressed my lips together in a frown.

"But you need to eat! If you run out of energy—" Lumi hesitated before glancing around to ensure no one was near enough to overhear.

I sighed, tucking her closer to my side as we entered the clearing around my hut.

"Don't worry," I reassured her. "I'll be perfectly— Oh shit." I froze. The wooden roof had caved in, dumping a heaping mound of snow into my home. The door had broken open and ankle-deep snow was spilling out of it. Lumi gasped and turned to me.

"I'll help you," she said, rolling up her sleeves. I shook my head and ran my fingers roughly through my hair.

"No... It's okay. It's getting late and your father will send out a search party if you're not home soon. If he finds you here, he might be unhappy."

She frowned. I could practically see the thoughts whirling through her mind as she came to the same conclusion.

"Go," I urged, rolling up my sleeves. "I promise I'll be okay. This will take me *maybe* thirty seconds to clean up."

Lumi hesitated for a moment before pulling me into a tight hug.

"Please," she breathed, "be careful."

"Always," I whispered. She gave me a long, anxious look, making herself turn and amble slowly back up the road. I watched her until she disappeared from view before turning towards my home with a grimace and shoved my way inside.

Snow caked everything in the small space. I frowned, groaning as I spotted the ruined bread, still lying on my cot where Lumi had left it. So much for my promise. I rolled my neck and held my hands out in front of me.

My blood ran hot, and fire circled my feet. Light danced on the metal slats of the roof. The snow melted rapidly, leaving behind small puddles in its wake. I maneuvered my power carefully, keeping a tight rein on the flames as they licked over my meager possessions. It took the better part of two hours, but I finally managed to clear the snow. I extinguished the flames and stood still, focusing intently.

The heat coursing through my blood was replaced by a deep chill. The puddles of water began to rise, and water seeped from all of my possessions, leaving them dry. The liquid floated through the air, sparkling like diamonds in the fading daylight. I guided a hand towards the bucket in the corner, and the water followed. It flowed inside with a quiet slosh.

I staggered a bit as I released my power and looked around. None of the wooden slats in the roof had fallen. Someone must have come in after we left that morning and pushed them aside to let the blizzard flood my home. I reached up with an exasperated sigh and put them back in their places before flopping down on the cot, exhausted.

My muscles screamed from the exertion of my power and a small headache had started to grow behind my eyes.

With no other alternatives, I propped myself up on an elbow and grabbed the bread. It disintegrated at my touch. I grimaced as I forced the mush down my throat. It tasted awful, but at least it was something. Immediately, the ache in my head eased and my muscles relaxed. I flicked a hand towards the circle of stones in the center of the room and a fire blazed to life, hovering a few inches above the sand.

I frowned at it and cocked my head, listening to the chatter and clattering of plates nearby. I could already feel the drag on my energy, but I couldn't risk going to scrounge for more food yet. The villagers were already terrified of me. Seeing me lurking in the shadows might actually give someone a heart attack.

So, I closed my eyes and laced my hands behind my head, letting my thoughts roam to distract me from the headache already starting to prickle behind my eyes again. They always wandered to the same place. A bright smile. Icy blue eyes. Raven black hair.

Lumi.

My heart ached with longing at the thought of my fierce warrior queen. My lips tugged upwards as I saw her in my mind, back straight, shoulders up, charging headfirst into trouble like she always did. I'd seen her stare down angry villagers like a general staring down combatants at war more times than I could count. She squared up to the most vicious man I'd ever met regularly, matching his ferocity with a fire all her own. Her father terrified everyone in Haven. Everyone except her.

My mind drifted back to the conversation we'd had on the way home and the doubt eating away at her. Every single cell in my body had screamed at me, demanding that I tell her how amazing she truly was. When her powers finally came in, and I was confident they would, she would be unstoppable. I wanted to tell her how she was everything to me. The words had danced on the tip of my tongue, fighting to break free and wipe the doubt from her beautiful face. I'd do anything to see that heart-stopping smile of hers. But I'd held my tongue. Because if I said all of that, she'd realize the truth. She'd see how hopelessly, desperately in love I was with her.

I couldn't let her see how my heart stuttered when she looked at me or how my skin burned at her touch. I couldn't let on how hearing my name on her lips stole the breath from my chest every single time. She deserved so much better than me. She deserved a castle, not some shack on the beach. But there was nothing I could do to make myself into a person who could give her the world. Nothing. Except leave. I closed my eyes, letting my mind flash back to the last time I'd worked on the docks.

My muscles had been screaming from moving the freight too heavy for anyone else. But it was honest work, and I needed a way to pay for food. So, no matter how heavy the freight was, I never said no to a job. They waited until I finished before telling me to go. Desperate, I'd begged them to reconsider. But Jasper's orders were law in Haven. Which meant I was sunk.

The captain of a western trade ship I'd frequently worked for found out and offered me a spot on his crew. He'd even agreed to hire Rowan. But as soon as I mentioned Lumi, he had shaken his head and said no, stating he didn't allow women on his ship. The thought of leaving her behind made my heart shatter, so I'd refused the offer.

He pleaded with me to reconsider. He told me he could guarantee a full stomach and a warm, safe place to sleep every night if I joined his crew. But I still said no. After that, he'd said if I ever changed my mind, he'd gladly take me aboard. Now, I was stuck in a tiny shack with nothing, forced to rely on the kindness of those I loved to survive.

Part of me knew that I should've accepted. I could've left all these hateful people behind and started over somewhere where no one knew my face. But every time I started to consider it, the image of tearful blue eyes came to mind and squashed the thought.

I couldn't leave her behind. A deranged part of my brain was still convinced she needed me here. Even if I was less than useless to her. To all of them. Nothing but a drag on the lives of everyone around me and the reason for every terrible thing that happened to them.

I sat up, running my fingers roughly through my hair as anguish and self-loathing shredded my soul. I shoved the thoughts away as best I could and gazed into the flickering fire. It had shrunk to barely an ember. I focused hard, willing the flames to grow, but was struck by a sharp pain in my chest. I gasped and released my hold on my power. The ember flickered and died, throwing my shack into near total darkness.

"Fuck," I muttered, closing my eyes. "Lumi's gonna kill me." I rolled off the cot and crept towards the door. The chatter from outside had finally died down. Hopefully, my unwilling neighbors had gone inside and left some scraps behind.

I opened the door and gasped as a wall of freezing air blasted into me. The sky had opened up again, sending a thick cascade of snow onto the world. I pushed the door shut again, struggling against the frigid wind tearing through the shack.

My breath rose like a cloud of smoke before my eyes as I panted with the effort of keeping the door shut. The wind howled ferociously and shook the wooden slats of the shack. Cold seeped into my bones. My teeth began to chatter as the chill sent pins and needles down my fingers.

The wind died down for just a second and I leapt from the door, throwing all of my weight behind the trunk at the edge of the cot. After a few moments of struggle, I managed to shove it up against the door and wedge it firmly in place. Every inch of me shook violently as I threw my coat back over my shoulder and shoved my feet into my boots. I rubbed my hands together, still shaking as the icy wind blasted through the cracks in the poorly constructed walls.

"Fuck, fuck, fuck..." I whispered, breathing hard on my hands. "Come on now, come on—"

I reached deep down into myself for the last slice of power I possessed. The whole world rocked. Stars bloomed before my eyes and sharp pain seared my body as my blood once again heated to a fever pitch. I blinked them away to find a small, crackling flame holding out against the cold and bathing the hut in warmth. I blew out a breath of relief. The world was still swaying slightly so I laid down and pressed a shaking hand over my eyes.

With no food to replenish my energy, my only other option was to try and get some rest. Otherwise, my fire would go out and I would be in serious trouble. Reassuring light danced behind my eyelids as I drifted to an uneasy sleep.

Rotting hands clawed at the door. I pressed myself against the wall and covered my mouth so it wouldn't hear me breathing. Suddenly, the scraping stopped and the monster outside the door screamed. It was joined by another. Then another. I squeezed my eyes shut as the horrible screeching filled my head, and a cold female voice hissed in my ear.

"You're nothing to me. Go die with your own kind." Rough hands seized me and jerked me away from the wall.

My eyes flew open, and I exploded from my cot, tumbling to the floor in a heap. Terror flooded my mind as I sat up, staring wildly around. It took me a few seconds to remember where I was. Finally, I stilled, trembling in fear as reality slowly set in. I was in my hut, I reassured myself with each heartbeat. I was nowhere near Trithica.

The sharp cold stole the breath from me and my whole body shook violently as I pushed myself up, reaching for my blankets and tossing them over my head. Complete silence had fallen around my hut. The blizzard had finally blown itself out, but my small fire had also died.

The cold had seeped through the shack and settled deep in my bones. I tried to flex my fingers, panic settling in my chest as I realized I could barely feel them. I looked down at my trembling hands and discovered with a jolt of horror that my skin was a pale gray.

"O-oh n-no…" I gasped through my chattering teeth. I closed my eyes and reached deep down within me. There was nothing. Not even enough power to make a spark. "F-f-fuck—"

My mind reeled with fear as I struggled to consider my options. If I stayed, Lumi would find me in the morning, frozen solid. I almost laughed as the thought crossed my mind that she'd kill me if I froze to death. But where could I go?

There wasn't a villager in Haven that would shelter me other than Rowan or Lumi.

I struggled to my feet and clung to the wall as my knees nearly gave out from under me. To get to Rowan, I would have to cross through the village, which was usually patrolled at night. If I went to Lumi, I could sneak along the border wall. But I'd also risk the wrath of her father, or worse. He might turn that anger on her.

I reached a shaking hand towards the door. I'd have to hope the blizzard drove the patrols inside for the night and do my best to get to Rowan's. If not… I'd have no choice but to risk Jasper's anger.

I threw the door open and stumbled out into the knee-deep snow.

CHAPTER FIVE

Lumi

The sound of a maid singing drifted through the front door as I crept towards it. Anxiety mounted in my chest, and I considered, for the millionth time, spinning around and marching back to the beach. I hated myself for leaving Ash, even if I knew he was right. My father would murder him if he found me there.

I mustered my courage and reached for the handle. As soon as my fingers brushed the cold metal, it was wrenched from my hand, and a burly man dressed in a thick coat and a scarf nearly slammed into me.

He stumbled back in surprise, clutching his chest. "Oh! Miss Lumi! There you are! Your parents sent me to get you." He gripped my elbow hard, yanking me over the threshold and steering me straight into the formal dining room.

Small, ornate lamps sent flickering shadows dancing across the dark green walls. The man released my arm and left me staring at the crowd sitting around our mahogany dining table. Servants paused clearing the table of the meal that had just finished. My parents were dressed in fine clothes, surrounded by equally dressed up people sipping tea.

"Finally," my father said. "Thank you, Frank."

The man who'd hauled me inside nodded and retreated quickly. I rubbed the spot where he'd grabbed me, scanning the faces that were glancing curiously in my direction. I recognized most of them instantly. They were my father's favorite followers. They did whatever my father asked of them without question and in return, they were granted special privileges. Mr. Vanders was a new edition to my father's favorites. He met my eyes before dropping his gaze to the table guiltily.

My mother cleared her throat and gestured towards the empty chair next to her.

I didn't move. My gaze flickered to the smirking face in the chair next to mine and I stiffened.

Killian.

He was leaning back, smoothing his light brown hair against his head. His cold grey eyes were roaming brazenly up and down my body. A thin scar ran from his eyebrow and down across his nose to the thin lips stretched into a cruel sneer. I had to fight not to smirk at it. Ash had scars on his knuckles to match.

Killian's lean frame shifted. He stretched his long legs towards my chair, wrapping a possessive hand around the arm.

My skin crawled at the thought of being anywhere near him and I had the sudden urge to punch Killian squarely in his stupid pointed face.

My father glanced around at the assembled group.

"That will be all." He waved his hand in a dismissive gesture.

Chairs scraped against the hardwood floor as the murmuring crowd got to their feet and filed out obediently. The servants grabbed trays and plates, whisking them off into the kitchen.

Killian sauntered by, brushing a finger down my cheek as he passed. I smacked his hand away as hard as I could without looking at him.

When the door closed behind the last straggler, my father set his cup down and stood.

"You weren't at the caves today," he said, crossing his arms over his chest.

"Nope," I replied.

Mother shot my father a sideways glance and placed her cup gently on the table before her.

"I remember telling you to come to the caves today," he said gruffly.

I shrugged. "You did."

"Then where were you?" he growled.

"Out."

"With who?" Mother demanded.

"I was just out," I replied, meeting her eyes defiantly.

"Well, I sent someone to that *thing's* hovel," Father hissed. "He was also out today. Any ideas where he might have been?"

Ice cold wrath plunged through my veins. I met my father's steely gaze and took a steadying breath, fighting to keep my expression neutral and uninterested.

"And why would I tell you that?" I said.

"Because we need to make sure you're not jeopardizing a good match for that filth," Mother chimed in.

"Do we have to do this? You know where I was. I'm sure at least a dozen villagers came to report where they saw me." I shook my head in disgust and turned for the door. "I'm going to bed."

"No, you're not," Father growled. He leaned forward and braced his hands on the table. "We're not finished with this conversation."

"Yes, we are," I hissed, clenching my fists. Rage simmered through my blood. "I'm an adult. Not your obedient little pet."

"If you want to be treated like an adult, stop acting like a petulant little brat!" Mother's voice pitched higher with every word. "Your father and I have spent years building a reputation in this village and you are determined to undermine it."

"A reputation? Is that what we're calling it? Well, if you're so worried about your precious reputation, then let me go live on my own."

"Lumi, I already told you no. I'm not taking that house from Garth and his family," Father sighed. "He's a good worker."

"Then let me build a house! I'll stay out of your hair and leave your all-too-important public reputation intact."

"It's not proper for a woman to live on her own," Mother retorted.

"And yet so many women in Haven do with no issue," I challenged, raising my voice. "No. This is about keeping me under your thumb so you can control who's in my life. Because you're worried that if I get my own home, I won't be living there alone." Mother's eyes flashed at my insinuation.

"That *creature*," she spat, "is a monster. I will not have it—"

"His name," I thundered, "is Ash."

"He's dangerous," Father growled.

I bared my teeth at him and dug my nails into my palms. "He is *not* dangerous! He's never hurt a soul in his life!"

"That's a lie and you know it," Father said, his voice dripping with venom. I clenched my jaw and said nothing. "He'd be more use dead. Then maybe you'd finally come to your senses and marry well."

"Marry who? Killian?" I shouted. "You're so worried about marrying me off, you don't care whether or not I'm happy?"

"And living with that *thing* would make you happy?" Mother screamed, her face turning red. "At least Killian has a future! A direction in life!"

"He's a pig who can't keep his hands to himself. Let Sabine be the wife he's unfaithful to."

"Enough," Father snapped, standing to his full height. "You are not to go near that creature. He has no future and he's dangerous—"

"Cosmic," I spat viciously.

My parents recoiled as though I'd struck them.

"People think he's Cosmic. But they can think what they want. It makes no difference to me. For all they know, *I* could be Cosmic." A thrill cut through my rage as the words tumbled from my lips.

My parents stared at me, too stunned to speak. Mother choked out a terrified gasp and covered her mouth with her hands while my father's rage froze in a mask of cold fury.

"Shut your mouth," he snarled. "You don't know what would happen if villagers heard you say that. Do not go within fifty feet of that thing *or* that freak Kaelin and his family. And you will never mention this again. Am I clear?"

I looked between my teary-eyed mother and my enraged father. The anger burning through me was stifling. I stood tall and met my father's glare.

"I know exactly what happened to the Cosmic people in this village. *You.*" I spat the word in disgust. "You can keep me trapped in this house, but I will not allow you to hurt my friends. And I will not stop seeing them to preserve your precious *reputations*," I hissed. "Ash has never done anything to hurt me. Unlike Killian, Ash would never, ever touch me without my permission. But you know what? Maybe I should just let him. Maybe I should go ahead and fuck him since you're so worried about it." Mother gasped in horror.

"You wouldn't dare," she hissed.

"No?" I sneered. "Maybe I have already. Or maybe I should go find him right now, drag him into the village square and let him splay me out for everyone to see. What would Haven think of your reputation then?"

Mother paled and fell silent. My father glared down at me with lightning crackling in his eyes.

"How dare you— Hey! Get back here!" My father barked after me as I turned on my heel and strode out of the room, slamming the door behind me.

My breathing turned ragged as I flew up the staircase, headed for my bedroom. One of my mother's personal maids spotted me and bobbed a quick curtsy.

"Evening, Miss..." She trailed off when she caught sight of my face as I stormed past. "I'll uh... I'll have dinner brought to you?" she called after me nervously.

I burst into my room and slammed the door before wrenching the bolt shut behind me. My chest heaved as rage threatened to completely overwhelm me. I leaned against the door and closed my eyes. I could hear my father thundering around, screaming at everyone in sight. I had to suppress the urge to throw the door open and scream right back at him.

My parents had never paid any attention to my friends before. As long as I stayed out of their hair, they hadn't cared where I was or what I did. Then one day, Ash made the grave mistake of walking me home. Father took one look at him and froze in horror. He ordered the docks not to let him work anymore and then warned the village that Ash was dangerous. All based on nothing but a glance. The rage boiling through me was so hot, I felt like I could spit lava.

A sudden idea struck me. I took a deep breath and held my palms out flat in front of me, squeezing my eyes shut. I pictured Ash with flames dancing around his hands in my mind, willing my anger to transform and burst forth.

After a few moments, I peeked through my lashes. My pale hands were still stretched before me, but no flames sparked from my fingertips. Disappointment edged my anger out of my chest, and I slid down to the floor with an audible *thump*.

I desperately wished something would happen. Anything. Ash could summon fire without even meaning to. Rowan had even lifted himself off the ground for a few seconds on a small gust of wind. But every time I tried to harness one of the elements, the only thing I summoned was a headache.

Bitter disappointment seized my heart again as I wrapped my arms around my legs and pressed my forehead into my knees. I fought back tears, focusing on the only shred of proof I had that I could be Cosmic.

Two years ago, Rowan, Ash and I had been seated around Kaelin's table. He'd placed a large black candle in the center. Ash had snapped his fingers around the wick, and it lit instantly. Kaelin said the candle was used to test children when they turned twelve. He'd said if we touched the wick and didn't get burned, it meant we were Cosmic. Children who were not Cosmic would feel the heat and be unable to touch the candle. Ash had demonstrated, placing a fingertip directly onto the wick without so much as flinching.

I'd reached out my hand, closing my eyes as I grasped for the candle. Something soft brushed my fingers and I opened my eyes to find I was touching the wick. The fire flickering around my skin felt like silk. Kaelin had smiled and announced I was indeed a Cosmic person.

Ash and Rowan had positively beamed at me.

The image of Ash's face sent a jolt of panicked guilt down my spine. I'd been so furious, I hadn't stopped to consider what my tirade might bring down on his head. My father was already looking for a reason to hurt him. My angrily declaring that I may or may not have been having sex with him was going to make it so much worse. Even if I admitted it wasn't true, it was already too late. The damage was done.

I opened my eyes and sighed before springing to my feet. Heavy clouds were blotting out the setting sun and thick snowfall was already drifting past the window.

I thought of Ash struggling to clear his hut before the blizzard rolled through and grew uneasy. The bread I'd given him would help replenish his energy, but I wasn't sure if it was enough to make it through the night. I crossed to the window and gripped the bottom, ready to throw it open and climb down the trellis to help him.

My father yelled something at a passing maid, and I froze. If I was caught sneaking off after what I'd shouted, I might as well throw Ash in the bay myself.

I blew out a long breath and released the window, deciding on a bath instead. As I stripped off my layers and propped my things against the wall, there was a soft knock at the door.

I wrapped myself in a robe and opened it tentatively to find a maid with a plate heaped high with food. I took it, mumbling my thanks. I re-locked the door, depositing the plate on my nightstand as I headed for the washroom.

I took a long bath that did nothing to ease my anxious fears as my thoughts kept straying to Ash. I desperately hoped he was all right. I had to repeatedly talk myself out of rushing to the beaches to check on him. When the water had gone cold, I hopped out and was drying myself when my father hammered on the door.

"Lumi! Open up!" The door rattled on its hinges. I threw on a sleeping gown and sat on my bed, watching the door shake and groan from his vicious knocking as I munched on my dinner.

After ten minutes, he gave up with a deep growl of frustration and stormed back down the stairs. I placed my half-eaten plate on my nightstand and lit a candle. The soft glow sent long shadows flickering along the walls.

I watched it carefully. Part of me screamed to place my finger on the wick. Like I did every time I lit it. It never burned me, but I never found it comforting, either. If anything, I found it disconcerting. I had definitive proof I was Cosmic, with no power to show for it.

I huffed out a breath as I settled back and snatched a book from the drawer beneath it instead. I opened to where I'd stopped the night before and let the story tear me away from reality, leaving my parents and the stress they caused behind.

I was jolted awake by a pinging sound echoing through my dark bedroom. I sat up and rubbed the sleep out of my eyes, peering around at the shadows.

The candle had burnt itself out. Wax had dripped down and cooled in smooth ripples on the surface of my nightstand. The only light in the room came from the moon and from the glow of the dying embers in the fireplace.

The book I'd been reading slipped from my chest and thudded to the floor as I stood. I winced and grabbed it, brushing the cover with my fingertips. Rowan had lent it to me, and he'd be unhappy if I returned it damaged. Once I'd assured myself it wasn't hurt, I placed the book gingerly on my bed.

Another sharp ping sounded from my right. I looked up just in time to see the pebble that had smacked the window drop out of sight.

I furrowed my brow and crossed the room to peer out the window.

A thick blanket of snow lay upon the world. The blizzard had finally moved on, leaving the air icy and clear.

I was about to turn away when a shadow moved in the corner of my vision and crept around the edge of the house. I squinted down at it, trying to discern a shape as it moved towards the back door of the kitchen.

Adrenaline surged through me as the figure tried the door and found it locked.

"Bandits." I shoved away from the window and leapt across my room, snatching my bow hastily from the floor. I took an arrow from my quiver and groaned. The shaft was broken in half and the arrowhead was missing. I cursed myself for having stuffed a broken arrow in my quiver and tossed it aside. I grabbed another one and was standing back up when a loud *thump* sounded from the window.

I looked up and found the remains of a snowball sliding down the glass. My heart started racing behind my ribs. I took a deep breath and crept across the room. Another snowball sailed through the air and plopped onto the window, spraying snow across the sill outside and frosting the glass with fresh ice. I paused to stare at the remnants of the snowball in confusion.

Whoever was outside was going through a lot of trouble to wake me if they wanted to rob my father.

I cautiously approached the window, gripping the bow tighter in my hands. Another snowball bounced off the glass and dropped out of sight.

A blast of frigid air rushed in as I shoved the window open. I notched the arrow and carefully aimed it at the shadow below. The razor-sharp arrowhead glinted wickedly in the moonlight. I pulled the arrow back as far as it would go. The figure looked up sharply as the bow creaked under the strain.

"Who are you?" I demanded.

The figure groaned and staggered back a step.

"Please don't shoot me. I'm already having a really bad night," a meek, shaking voice croaked.

Recognition flooded through me, and I stifled a cry. The arrow and bow clattered against the floor as I leaned out the window as far as I could.

"Ash?" I called. He stumbled into the moonlight. Even from afar, I could tell his lips were a sickening shade of blue.

His entire body was shivering violently. All the color had left his blanched skin. His arms were wrapped tightly around his torso and his feet were buried in the snow.

Horror seized my chest as he wavered and dropped to his knees.

"I-I n-need h-help," Ash gasped.

I pressed a hand to my mouth and slammed the window shut before flinging myself away from it and hurtling down the stairs. I flew through the kitchen like a banshee, wrenched the back door open, and hurled myself into the snow.

Ash was on all fours when I reached him. I grabbed him under his arms and hauled him to his feet. He managed two steps before faltering and falling into me.

I wrapped my arms around him, and half helped, half dragged him into the kitchen before kicking the door closed behind us to keep out the cold. I locked the door and threw Ash's arm over my shoulder, supporting him as we crept up the stairs. Luckily, the servants had already gone for the night, and no one saw us.

I pushed Ash into my room and had him sit in front of the fireplace. He flopped onto the warm floor without protest, still shaking uncontrollably. I locked the door firmly before rounding back on him.

"What happened?" I demanded. Ice clung to him just about everywhere. He must've been outside in the cold for a long while.

"I-I c-cleared out the s-snow. A-and then I t-tried to get some s-sleep... but then the b-b-blizzard came through. I was o-okay for a b-b-bit, but the snow r-ruined the bread you gave me and I... I ran out of e-energy. I couldn't keep the f-fire going. I'm so s-s-sorry. I don't wanna c-cause you trouble but—" Ash's voice shook as he struggled for breath.

Fear twisted in my stomach. I turned to the fireplace and grabbed a match, throwing on some fresh tinder before I reignited the fire. It sputtered back to life, filling the room with a soft warmth.

Ash sighed and edged closer to the heat.

"Why didn't you go to Ro? He's closer to the beach." I fought to keep the panic out of my tone. I was grateful he'd made it to me alive. Now I had to focus and keep him that way.

"I t-t-tried," he gasped through chattering teeth. "But the patrols wouldn't l-l-let me through. Said I might be up t-t-to something, so I had to creep along the b-border wall to get here."

My father's attempt to break down my door suddenly made more sense.

I shoved the firewood around in the grate, willing the flames to grow. Panic rose in my throat as Ash continued to shudder wildly. His skin was a pale gray, and his lips were still alarmingly blue. I touched his shoulder and found his coat was soaked through with half-frozen slush. The fire was melting the ice and water dripped from him onto the floor.

He wasn't going to get warm like this.

I sped over to my bed and yanked the thick blankets off before running back to Ash's side. I threw the blankets down next to him and gestured at his clothes.

"Take these off," I demanded. He raised his eyebrows in question, so I poked his tunic. "Your clothes. Take them off."

"W-wait, what? Y-Y-You want me to do *what*?" Shock creased his face.

"Don't argue with me, Ash. Just do it."

I helped him to his feet, and he dropped his shoulders, letting his coat slide to the floor. He tugged at the hem of his tunic with his quivering fingers, but he couldn't control them well enough to get a grip on the cloth.

I reached down and yanked it quickly over his head.

"Well d-damn," he said, surprised. He tried to huff out a laugh, but it came out as a wheezing cough. "That desperate to g-get me out of my c-clothes, huh?"

“If it’s gonna keep you alive, then yes.” I held his shoulders and looked away as he struggled to remove his boots and pants. He sunk back to the floor, and I tossed my blankets over him without looking away from the whorl patterns on the wall.

I glanced at Ash and saw him tuck the blankets around himself tightly. Panic squeezed my chest harder as he looked up at me with deep, dark shadows under his eyes.

“L-Lumi—“

“Hush,” I said, biting my lip in fear. Ash was still shaking, and the color hadn’t returned to his skin. “This isn’t enough.” My eyes flew around my room in a desperate hunt for something to warm him up. Anything. Suddenly, an idea hit me.

Without pausing to consider it, I threw my sleeping gown off, leaving me in my undergarments. Ash’s eyes went wide, his breath catching in his throat. I reached down and yanked open the blanket, relieved to see he still had his undergarments on as well.

“L-Lumi... W-what are you—“

“Just shut up,” I hissed, dropping my gown onto his crossed legs. He sucked in a sharp breath, eyeing me with a strange expression as I sat in his lap, facing him. I winced and gritted my teeth as my bare skin touched the hard lines of his icy stomach. I pulled the blanket around us and wound my arms and legs around him.

Ash wrapped his strong arms around my back and buried his face into the crook of my neck. I let out a small hiss when his cold nose brushed my collarbone.

“Y-you’re so w-warm,” Ash moaned, his breath tickling my skin. He tightened his arms around me.

His lips pressed against my neck and heat filled my face.

“Don’t get too excited,” I said quietly. “This is the fastest way to warm you up.” My blush burned hotter as he sighed deeply.

“I’d make a j-joke, but maybe now isn’t the best time,” he said.

I let out a hoarse chuckle. We held each other for a few long minutes before Ash’s shivering finally began to subside. Dizzying relief flooded through me, and I held him tighter.

“Do I at least smell okay?” I joked. I felt his lips curl into a smile against my neck and I suppressed a shiver.

“You smell phenomenal,” he chuckled. “Like I might not die.”

I shifted my hand higher up his back and was met with warm skin. I almost cried out in relief.

"Please, don't do that again," I said, leaning my head against his.

"Do what?" he asked.

My breath froze in my lungs as his words slid across my neck.

"Almost die," I whispered. Tears pricked behind my eyes, and I blinked them away before Ash could notice. His arms tightened around me, pressing me to his chest.

"I'm so sorry," he mumbled. "I promise I'll try not to die."

I closed my eyes, savoring the feel of his chest rising and falling steadily against mine. When his shivering finally stopped completely, I pulled him upright and looked him over. The color had returned to his face and his lips had lost their blue tint.

"I should probably let you go now. This would be hard to explain if your father walked in," Ash said grinning.

I rolled my eyes and stood.

"The door is locked. Besides, I'm not worried about my father." I helped him up. He was still a bit unsteady on his feet and swayed weakly against me.

"Well, I am." He looked away as I slipped fully out of the blankets and pulled the sleeping gown back over my head. "The last thing I want to do is cause you more trouble," Ash mumbled anxiously. "I should probably go." For a beat, I thought I'd misheard him. His fingers were just brushing the clothes piled on the floor when I stepped in front of him and grabbed his arm, forcing him to stand up.

"You're not leaving," I said sternly. He tried to pull his arm away and I stumbled against his chest. I stared up at him, eyes blazing in defiance and squared my shoulders. Our faces were inches apart.

He took a sharp breath and gulped.

"Lumi—" Ash started, shaking his head but I cut him off.

"You barely had the strength to stand up. You're gonna go back through the snow in soaking wet clothes? You won't make it!"

"Lumi, I'm fine. See?" He ground his teeth together and flicked a hand towards the fireplace. Flames jumped high up into the chimney before he released his power with a wince and the fire settled back into a crackle.

I arched an eyebrow at him.

"And that's supposed to convince me? I saw the strain on your face!" I huffed. He sighed and ran his free hand through his hair.

"I swear, I'm fine," he said.

"Oh, yeah?" I snapped, pointing at the grate. "All right. If you're so sure you're okay, then do it again."

He swallowed hard and looked away, avoiding my stare.

"Well, go on!" I said fiercely. "Prove me wrong, Ash! Do it again!" He looked back at me. We stared at each other for a long moment before he exhaled sharply and ducked his head.

"Okay, fine. I can't do it again. I nearly blacked out just doing that. But I have to go before your father—" he insisted, but I pressed a finger to his lips before he could finish.

"Just now, you promised you would try not to die. You're going to go back on it that fast? You go back tonight, you'll freeze."

He gripped my wrist and moved my hand away from his mouth.

"Your father will—"

"My father will do *nothing* to you," I growled.

"I'm not worried about what he could do to *me*, Lumi," he replied slowly. His eyes shone as he gazed back at me.

I met his stare, drawing myself up to my full height in defiance.

The tension in his shoulders eased slowly and he blew out a long breath, running his fingers through his hair.

His shoulders dropped. I released my grip on his arm and took a step back.

"Okay. I'll stay." He grinned slyly at me. "You know you're adorable when you're commanding."

I rolled my eyes and didn't bother trying to hide my blush.

"Shut up," I mumbled. I gathered up his wet clothes and hung them near the fire to dry.

"Thank you," he said quietly, watching me move about the room. I grabbed an extra set of blankets for my bed and tossed him a pillow.

"For what? Not letting you die? You're welcome."

"No. I mean, yes, that too, but... If anyone saw me come here..." Ash looked out the window. "I hate that Rowan and his parents struggle because of me. I don't want the same to happen to you."

"It won't," I replied, turning to face him. "And even if it does, who cares? You're my best friend. I need you in my life." I wrapped him in a tight hug. His heart raced beneath my cheek from the strain of using his power. "You and Rowan are the only ones who really care about me. So, you can't leave me, okay?"

Ash didn't say anything and instead just wrapped his arms around me. My cheeks heated up again as I stepped away. "All right, I'll stop being mushy now." I flopped onto the bed and patted the other side. "My bed is huge so you can take this side."

"That would be nothing short of blissful," he said, tossing the pillow next to mine and sliding onto the bed with a deep sigh. I flipped over to watch him settle in, throwing the blanket over himself.

"And I swear to the Ethereal, Ash," I said firmly. I propped myself up on my elbow and glared at him. "If you leave in the middle of the night—"

Ash chuckled and held his hands up in surrender.

"I won't leave." He winked at me and grinned mischievously. "I know you just want to see me naked again."

I made a face to mask my smile and flopped back onto my pillow.

"Shut up," I grumbled, closing my eyes.

"Seriously, though. Twice in one day? How does that even happen?"

"Guess I'm just lucky," I snorted. I peered through my lashes when no snarky follow-up remark came and found that he was already fast asleep.

Ash's head was tilted back slightly, exposing the strong column of his neck. He'd thrown an arm over his head, and his fingers were curled in his brunette locks splayed across the pillow. The blanket had slipped a little, revealing the hard-lined definition of his chest. I watched his stomach rising and falling steadily for a few moments, relieved to see the tan color of his skin had finally returned.

I smiled and rolled over, glancing at the door to double check that the bolt was secured before closing my eyes and drifting off to sleep.

CHAPTER SIX

Lumi

"Lumi!"

My father's voice boomed like thunder as he pounded on my bedroom door. I sat up in a flurry of blankets and reached over in a panic to wake Ash. But the bed was empty.

The door jumped but the bolt held fast. My father let out a growl of frustration and called out, "Lumi, unlock the damn door!"

"Hold on a second!" I shouted, glancing around anxiously.

"Open the fucking door!" He slammed his fist against the door so hard, it felt like the whole room rattled around me. I raced out of bed and threw it wide open before he broke it down. He met my stare for a split second before he pushed past me, scanning the area for anything amiss.

Panic sliced through me as my mind flashed to the clothes hanging up to dry on the mantle. I had no idea where Ash went, but a quick glance around told me where my bow and my sword were. I tensed and readied to spring for them.

After a few moments, Father gave me a hard stare and crossed his arms. I braced myself, waiting for the rage and shouting. He exhaled hard through his nose and said, "Get dressed and come downstairs. Now."

He turned on his heel and left, slamming the door forcefully behind him. I listened to the heavy thumping of his footsteps as he retreated down the stairs before I drew in a sharp breath and whirled around. The clothes were gone. I glanced around the room until I found a pair of eyes peeking at me from behind the bed.

"Well, that was terrifying," Ash said, pulling his pants on as he stood up. "Who knew your father was such a morning person?" He grinned sleepily at me as he scratched his bare chest.

I smiled in relief at the sight of his face filled with lively color.

His golden eyes were glowing in the morning light and his hair was mussed. He ran his fingers through it, shooting a quick glance out the window. "I better make myself scarce before he comes back."

"No. Stay," I replied. Ash blushed and looked away sharply while I changed. "He won't come back up here. Stay and eat."

"No, I—" His stomach growled fiercely, and he paused, rubbing his abdomen with a sheepish grin. "If you insist."

"I do insist," I said. I strode over and placed both hands on his bare chest, pushing him down to sit on the bed. "Just wait here, okay? I'll go grab something and be right back." My stomach clenched and a fresh wave of anxiety bubbled to the surface. Ash touched my wrist gently.

"Are you okay?" Concern filled his golden eyes as they searched my face. I huffed and waved my other hand, forcing a smile.

"Of course," I replied with more confidence than I felt.

"You don't think he knows, do you?" He glanced nervously at the door, and I shook my head.

"No. If he knew you were here, he would've torn my room apart. I'm sure it's fine." I tried to keep my tone lighthearted, but a horrible feeling twisted itself between my ribs.

Ash must've seen something on my face because he held my hand with both of his, circling his thumb over my wrist.

"I'm right here if you need me," he said softly.

I nodded and threw my bag over my shoulder, releasing his hands hesitantly. I shot him one last wary smile and stepped out the door before I lost my nerve.

Ash's words echoed in my mind as I headed downstairs, filling me with confidence. The thought of him racing to be at my side had me squaring my shoulders and breezing into the formal dining room with my head held high.

My mother and father were seated next to each other. They exchanged a quick glance as I sat in an empty chair on the other side of the table without acknowledging them. Father's eyes darted to my bag.

"Going somewhere today?" he said, raising an eyebrow.

"Out," I replied, filling my plate with toasted bread and cheeses from the Western Lands. I hesitated before loading some into my bag. My parents narrowed their eyes at me as I cleared the platter and fastened my bag before looking back up.

"Lumi," Mother began. She placed a delicate hand atop her husband's broad, calloused fingers. "We've been discussing things and we are very concerned."

"So you've mentioned. Repeatedly. But I don't need your concern." I brushed her off before stuffing food into my mouth. I ate as rapidly as I could, eager to escape back upstairs.

The clicking of heels echoed from the entrance hall as the maids arrived for the day. My heart stuttered when I heard the unmistakable sound of someone mounting the stairs, headed for the bedrooms above us. I gripped the edge of the table, readying to launch myself away at a moment's notice.

"Well," Mother pressed, obviously trying to say everything she wanted to before I disappeared to who knows where. "We've made a decision." My heart dropped into my stomach. I edged away from the table, gripping my bag tight.

"Enough is enough," Father sighed, exasperated. "You will accept Killian's proposal today."

"Not happening," I snorted.

"Lumi," Mother started. A knock at the door cut her short. A stout man wrapped in a thick coat slipped into the room.

"Sir," he said with a small bow. The man stepped closer and tossed something on the table before me.

The bolt from my bedroom door.

I fought to keep my face neutral as fear coiled in my chest. My father raised an eyebrow in question and the man shook his head. "No, sir."

"Keep at it," Father said, dismissing him with a wave of his hand. The man gave my parents another short bow and retreated. Father turned back to me, his eyes blazing. "Let's try again. You *will* go to the caves today. Killian has already been informed that you accept and you two will be wed. Today."

The world rocked beneath me.

"No," I breathed, eyes wide in disbelief. Shock rooted me to the spot, freezing my muscles even as my brain screamed at me to run. To yell for my fiery savior waiting upstairs.

"It's what's best for you. I know you and he have had your differences, but you can smooth things over once you're married," Mother said.

Married. The word hung over my head like a curse.

"You can't do this," I hissed.

"It's done," Mother replied. She reached to take my hand. My horror gave way to a blinding rage, and I launched myself backwards, crossing my arms over my chest.

"Don't touch me!" I snarled, backing into the wall.

My chair tipped and crashed to the floor. The nearby maids jumped, glancing over before ducking their heads fearfully and continuing their cleaning. I heard the smallest creak from above my head, like someone was shifting on their feet. I lowered my voice, scared my friend would come charging into this mess and get himself killed.

"You can tell that womanizing pig whatever you want, but I'd rather die than be his wife."

"Love, you're being unreasonable," Mother said. She rose to her feet with her hands held up as though she were attempting to soothe a frightened child. "We only want what's best for you. All these dangerous ideas in your head... Do you realize what would happen to us if people knew you thought you were different?"

"Cosmic," I spit with all the venom I could muster. "The word, Mother, is Cosmic. And they would do nothing to you."

They exchanged a glance. It was the truth, and they knew it. My father controlled not only the food supply, but all of Haven's trade and resources. No villager would risk starvation by crossing him.

"This is happening, Lumi. Accept it," Father said sharply.

"I am not a doll!" I snarled viciously. "You can't play with my life like this!" My anger boiled over, and I'd had enough. I marched past them into the kitchen and started wrenching open cupboards, stuffing every scrap of food I could find into my satchel. The door flew open and slammed into the nearby wall.

"What are you doing?" Father demanded.

Rather than answer, I dodged around him on my way back into the dining room. "You're not bringing *my* food to that creature."

"Stop calling him that!" I seethed, gritting my teeth, and whirling around to face him. "Ash is my best friend! Nothing you say is gonna change that!" There was a definite creak from above me that time. It sounded like a door being pulled ajar.

"Lumi, you cannot keep associating with that boy! He's dangerous!" Mother cried.

"No, he's not! He's never done anything to me! Unlike the piece of shit you're trying to marry me off to. Who touches me against my will and even tried to—"

I choked on the words as the memory flashed through my mind. I could still feel the cold ice pressed into my cheek. I could hear Killian's breathy laugh as he tried to wrench the clothes from my body, whispering how he couldn't wait to see Ash's face when he found us in the act.

I shook my head, brushing past them. "This conversation is over. You may have convinced everyone else to let Ash starve to death, but I won't allow it."

"You either stay away from him or he disappears," Father growled.

"Jasper, don't," Mother warned.

I froze, my hand poised over the doorknob. I took a deep breath and turned slowly to face them.

"If he disappears, then so do I," I hissed.

Mother gasped and covered her mouth with her hands. My father glared at me furiously but said nothing.

"And I'll make sure everyone knows what you did to your only child. What will happen to your precious reputation then? You might be willing to sacrifice my happiness for it. But is it worth my life?" Malice dripped from my every word.

Father clenched his teeth so hard, a muscle twitched in his jaw. Tears flowed down Mother's face, but I didn't meet her eyes as I reached for the door again. My fingers had barely brushed the surface when I froze. The visitor's words clanged through me like a bell and a sickening thought crossed my mind.

"You already tried," I hissed, turning back.

Father drew himself up to his full height. I huffed, clutching at my chest with a trembling hand. My whole body quaked with rage.

"That's what he meant," I said. "You sent him after Ash. That's why you burst into my room this morning. And the lock... You can't find him. But you tried."

He stayed quiet, his grey eyes crackling with anger. I shook my head and wrenched the door open.

"You sick fucking bastard," I snarled. Mother called after me, but I didn't so much as glance back at her. I flew up the stairs like a whirlwind and stumbled into my room, slamming the door, and pressing my back against it.

The world blurred as tears filled my eyes and rolled down my face in thick streaks. I covered my mouth with my hands. The sharp anguish in my chest became overpowering and deep sobs shuddered through me.

Strong arms wrapped around me, pulling me into a warm embrace. I wrapped my arms around Ash's waist and pressed my face into him. My shoulders shook as I openly wept into his chest.

"What happened?" Ash said frantically. He reached up to cradle the back of my head, slipping his fingers through my hair. His other hand tightened at my back.

I gripped his tunic, unable to form words as I soaked through the front with tears.

"Lumi, talk to me... Are you hurt? What—" Ash stopped short and his whole body went rigid as someone came rushing up the stairs.

"Lumi?" Mother's voice called from the other side of the door. "Love, please, we can talk about this. Lumi? I'm coming in."

I sucked in a gasp and shook my head vigorously. Without making a sound, he gripped me tightly and spun us around. He thrust his back into the door and pressed his full body weight against it.

The knob jiggled but the door remained shut.

"Did you block the door? Lumi, let me in!"

Ash shifted to keep his footing solid. His muscles tensed under my touch. The wood creaked and groaned as she pushed harder. Ash dug his heels in and fought with all his might to keep the door closed.

After a few moments of struggling, Mother finally gave up. I heard her exasperated sigh before she said, "We just want what's best for you. Be at the caves before noon."

I barely heard her retreating footsteps over my sobs. I sank to my knees and Ash followed, sliding his back down the door to keep me held tightly against him.

I curled into his lap and clung desperately to his warmth. He cradled me, stroking the length of my spine until I had shed every last tear I could muster. His hand stilled as I gulped several mouthfuls of air, the tears finally drying up.

"Are you okay?" Ash asked tentatively, placing his chin on top of my head.

I rubbed my swollen eyes and sniffed. "No," I croaked. "My parents decided I'm getting married today, and that I have no say in my future husband."

"I'll bet it's not me," he joked lightly.

I chuckled bitterly before letting out a deep, shuddering sigh.

"Killian." I shoved a lock of raven hair away from my face and looked up in time to catch a flash of white-hot anger blaze through his eyes.

A muscle jumped in his jaw and the hand with scars across the back flexed unconsciously.

I nodded. "I know. But they don't care. According to my parents, marriage will fix any minor issues we have to 'work out.'" My eyes ached from crying, and I rubbed them again with the back of my hand.

"So," Ash hissed through his teeth, "that's what they call what he did to you? A minor issue?" He huffed angrily and scrubbed a hand over his face. "So, now what? What are you gonna do?"

"I will not marry him," I said flatly.

"I mean about your parents. What happens when you don't show up to your own wedding?" A wave of fear swallowed me whole as I met his eyes.

"I don't know," I admitted. "But... My father threatened—" I tried to force down the lump forming in my throat.

"Me?" Ash guessed, raising his eyebrows. A fresh swell of tears welled up in my eyes and I blinked them away, nodding.

"I'm so sorry. It's all my fault," I whispered miserably. "My parents and I got into a screaming match last night. And I said I was going to—" I blushed furiously as he cocked one eyebrow, confused. I huffed out a breath and looked up at the ceiling, unable to look him in the eye as I blurted out, "I might have told them that I was going to have sex with you."

Ash froze. I winced and peeked at him. His cheeks were bright red, and his face was rigid with complete and utter shock. He blinked.

"Oh," he said, letting out a breathless laugh.

"I am so sorry," I groaned. "I was mad."

"No, no. I get it," he said. His golden eyes shimmered and there was a rough edge to his voice I'd never heard before. "I'm sure that went well."

"It went so well, my father sent people out looking for you last night."

"Oh. Great," Ash chuckled.

"I'm so sorry," I said, meeting his eyes again. "I really fucked up."

Ash cleared his throat, shaking his head. "It's really okay. I think we all knew it was only a matter of time before your father decided my ability to breathe was overrated."

"But why? The only thing you've ever done to me is make me happy! I just... I thought I mattered to them, but to treat one of my only friends like this..." I huffed and rested my head against his chest. "I thought it mattered to them if I'm happy, but clearly it doesn't." His heart was pounding against my cheek, so I sat up and met his eyes firmly. "My father's not gonna touch you," I said fiercely.

"Oh, I know," he chuckled. "You're terrifying."

I blushed and it suddenly dawned on me that I was still curled up in his lap. Our faces were only an inch apart.

"I guess it's out of the question for me to be your maid of honor," Ash joked.

"Shut up," I grumbled with a huff, rolling my eyes. I pushed away from him to hide the smile tugging at my lips in spite of myself.

"Am I at least invited?" Ash said with mock severity as he got to his feet. "Because if so, I simply must find something to wear." I gave his leg a gentle shove and he smiled before reaching out a hand to help me up.

"Just please promise me you'll be careful," I said. "I don't want you getting hurt."

"Especially not before you get the fabulous wedding gift I have planned," he said dramatically.

"Knock it off before *I* hurt you," I replied, grinning. He winked.

"Well, we should get going. I don't want to show up alone and I need to see if Rowan will be my date," he said. I shot him a dark look and he laughed, holding up his hands. "Okay, now I'm done. I promise."

I handed him my satchel and bent to pull my boots on, slipping my dagger into place and fixing my belt around my waist. Ash pulled his coat on, arching an eyebrow at me.

"Do you always plan on being attacked?" He gestured to the sword hanging at my hip.

"Today I am." I tugged on my coat and slung my bow and quiver across my back. "Besides, it's better to have it and not need it, then to need it and not have it."

"Fair enough." Ash glanced out the window and then back to me. "Think your parents are gone yet?"

"I don't care," I grumbled, taking his hand. I straightened my back and marched out of my bedroom, dragging him behind me. We breezed down the stairs and out the front door. Luckily, the maids were hiding from my father's rage, and no one saw us. Ash held the front door for me and together we stepped outside, gasping in the frigid air.

CHAPTER SEVEN

Ash

We marched past the farmlands in a companionable silence until we reached the edge of the village. My heart was still racing against my ribs and no matter how hard I tried, I couldn't stop my mind from wandering. I could still feel her bare skin pressed against mine. Her scent still clung to my hair. And when she'd said I made her happy, for a moment I felt like I could fly.

I swallowed, forcing my head back to reality as I shot her a quick glance.

Lumi's fingers were wrapped tightly around my arm and her head was tipped back, letting the freezing air caress her swollen eyes. Sunlight danced on her splotchy, upturned face. She reached up and traced her features with the tips of her fingers.

"I must look awesome," she groaned, leaning into my shoulder.

"I mean, you always look awesome. Just a little puffier," I teased with a grin.

She elbowed me in the ribs. I huffed out a laugh and the corners of her lips twitched upwards.

"You always know just what to say to make a girl feel all fuzzy inside," she replied sarcastically.

I opened my mouth to reply, freezing in my tracks as two hulking men stepped into our path. Lumi stumbled into me with a gasp, and I caught her by the shoulders, catching sight of two more men blocking the path behind us in my periphery. Ice plunged through my veins, and I pulled her closer to my chest. We were surrounded.

Every muscle in my body coiled, tensing for a fight. The men were sizing me up, balling their fists and cracking their knuckles as they stepped closer. Each one of them reeked of sweat, dirt, and fertilizers. I squared my shoulders, and Lumi gripped the front of my shirt.

She cried out as one of the men ripped her from my arms.

The other three surged forward and grabbed my elbows roughly. I twisted and fought to break their grips. They dragged me away from the last farmer, who was panting and wheezing as he struggled to keep a hold of Lumi. Sweat glistened on his forehead from the effort it took to wrangle her. His flabby arms cinched around her torso, pinning her arms to her side.

She flailed and kicked wildly, her foot connecting with every part of the man that she could reach. He ducked as she threw her head back in an attempt to smash his bulbous nose.

"Let go of me," she snarled.

Two of the farmers started trying to force me to the ground. The third man stepped beyond my reach, readying himself to jump into the fray.

I tensed and locked my knees, fighting with all my might to stay standing while desperately trying to break free. They grunted and shoved me down even harder, twisting my arms into agonizing angles in an attempt to force me to my knees. I jerked and thrashed, trying to shake them off to defend myself.

One of the farmers kicked the side of my knee several times. My power simmered in my blood, but I shoved it away, focusing all the energy I had on breaking the men's holds. Using it would be an instant death sentence, and I had to help Lumi.

"Bring him down, boys!" the fourth man said, dancing around us. "Don't let the freak get away!"

Lumi let out a small gasp of pain as the older man holding her squeezed tighter. Anger bubbled through me, and I thrashed harder. My skin burned under their tight grip and their hands rubbed my wrists raw.

"Stop fighting me, miss!" the older man grunted.

Lumi yelped as he clamped a fat hand around her wrist and twisted her arm behind her, forcing her up onto her tiptoes.

Red spots danced before my eyes. I managed to yank my arm away from the man on my right and swung wildly. My fist connected with the jaw of the man on my left. He let out a sharp cry of pain and crumpled face-first into the snow. The last farmer dashed forward and snatched my free arm. One of them swung, landing a sharp blow square in the center of my chest. Pain shot through my torso.

Lumi gasped and surged towards me, only to be yanked back to the man still fighting to hold her. He began taking small steps backwards, slowly dragging her away from the scene.

"Tom, get up!" the man on my left yelled. The man in the snow groaned and sat up, blinking, and shaking his head to clear it. The man on my right began kneeing me repeatedly in the side.

I yelled and twisted, struggling to break their hold on me. The man on my left cocked his fist back as far as it could go and threw all his weight behind a blow aimed for my stomach, knocking the breath from my lungs. My knees sagged as I fought for air and agonizing pain tore through me.

Tom got to his feet and reared back, slamming a fist into my jaw.

My head snapped sharply to the side. Stars bloomed before my eyes and darkness gathered at the edge of my vision as my consciousness threatened to desert me.

"No! Let him go!" Lumi screeched.

Every breath felt like I was being struck by lightning. Sharp blows rattled my bones as the three of them closed in and started to beat me mercilessly. I threw my fists out, landing several solid blows in return and sending them staggering backwards. I fought with everything I had. But it wasn't enough. One of the men kicked out hard, catching me in the back of the knee.

I staggered and hit the snow on all fours. The world swayed violently beneath me. The man holding Lumi pulled her back as Tom stood over me, slowly withdrawing a long knife from his belt.

Lumi's eyes filled with tears. She started thrashing desperately. "No! No!" she screamed.

I tried to force myself back to my feet, but none of my searing muscles could respond.

"Make it quick," the man on my right said. He drew back and rammed his knee into my side as forcefully as he could.

Something deep inside my abdomen cracked. The pain was so sharp, I could hardly breathe. He grabbed a fistful of my hair, forcing my head back and exposing my bare throat. The other man caught my arms and pinned them behind me.

"Hurry up, Tom!" the older man grunted. "Jasper said she has to see it!"

Tom flipped the knife and pressed the cold steel against my throat. I yanked on my arms, but it was no use.

I was a dead man.

"No!" Lumi screamed. She kicked out hard, connecting with her captor's knee. He swore and she fell forward, hitting the snow on all fours before surging back to her feet. Before she could take a single step, the man's arm whipped out and he backhanded her across the cheek. She cried out and fell face-first into the snow.

Tom looked away from me in surprise. In their shock, the man holding my head back released my hair and my arms dropped forward.

"What are you doing, you idiot?" Tom snarled and gestured at Lumi with the knife. "Jasper's gonna kill us if you left a mark on his daughter!"

Every aching muscle in my body froze as I looked down at Lumi, clutching her face. Burning wrath seeped through me. My power coursed through my blood and my hold on it faltered. Not that I cared.

A feral snarl ripped from my chest. I sat back on my heels, clenching my fists as a vicious heat blazed through my veins. Sparks began licking at my knuckles. The wind suddenly picked up with a howl. Ice formed around my knees and the ground beneath me trembled.

I locked eyes with the man who'd hit Lumi, baring my teeth like a wild animal. His face paled in terror. Every fiber of my being screamed for his blood. The other three men still had their attention fixed on him and Lumi. Any second, one of them would see the flames licking my wrists, but I didn't care. I would make him suffer for what he'd just done to her.

"No!"

The scream cut through the air like an arrow. My gaze shot to Lumi.

She sat up, meeting my eyes desperately.

The farmers, startled at her sudden outburst, all turned to her in confusion. She pressed her lips together, her eyes scanning my face as she shook her head once, silently begging me. Begging me not to unleash the rage that made my entire body tremble. Begging me not to reveal the power roiling inside me like the sea. I grit my teeth as she mouthed my name pleadingly. My heart stuttered, and the rage in my chest cooled at the sight of my name on her lips.

For one brief moment, the world faded away, leaving just the two of us. Lumi shifted slightly, tucking her feet underneath her and exposing the gleaming dagger clutched in her fist.

I understood then. My fierce warrior queen and my salvation. I took a deep shuddering breath and clenched my fists tighter, shoving them into the snow. A growl escaped my lips as I fought to smother the flames trying to dance their way up my arms. The shaking earth stilled, and the wind died down to a whisper, but my body started shaking violently. My power raged against my attempts to stifle it, fueled by the anger still surging through my blood.

I met Lumi's eyes again. She let out a quick sigh of relief before leaping to her feet, twisting deftly, and pressing the razor-sharp dagger to the neck of the man who had struck her. He yelped and threw his hands up in fear.

"Back up!" she snarled at the farmers. The men shot terrified glances at each other. "Step away from him," she said, punctuating every word by pressing the dagger tighter into the man's neck. A bead of blood formed at the tip and ran down into his shirt.

"Do it," he said frantically. I pressed my lips together, breathing deeply through my nose. Heat still thundered through my veins like a storm. The farmers didn't seem to notice the steam rising from where my hands were buried in the snow as they took a solid step away from me. My chest heaved. I sucked in desperate breaths, willing the tempest inside to quiet. But it refused to yield. Instead, it swirled harder against my hold, shoving to break loose. I realized with a jolt that it was only a matter of time before I lost my grip on my power.

Lumi turned back to the man she held at knifepoint.

"Tell my father that next time, his thugs will come back to him in pieces." She lowered her dagger. The terrified farmer stumbled back and broke into a run. The others followed quickly, shooting glares over their shoulders as they sprinted away. Lumi slipped the dagger back into her boot and rushed over to help me to my feet. I held up a trembling hand and she froze.

"No," I gasped frantically, gulping down air like I was drowning. "Stay back!" My power was about to boil over, and I had no way to stop it. I had to get away from her before I lost control. I stumbled to my feet and dashed into a nearby alley. My abdomen stung with the effort of holding back as I rushed deeper into the shadows. I turned a sharp corner and fell to my knees as my control failed at last.

The alley filled with blinding light as fire and wind swirled around me. The earth trembled, rattling the walls of the nearby shops. Power tore from me like a rampaging monster, crashing into the stone and spiraling up into the air. I pulled back on the overwhelming feeling in an attempt to smother it and regain control, wincing at a sharp ache that ripped through me in response. There was no way to stop the raging storm, so I bowed my head and let go. I unleashed it all. My power roared through the air as I knelt in the eye of the cyclone. The flames filled the small space, singeing the rooftops and blackening the stone walls of the buildings.

Finally, I collapsed. I was so thoroughly wrung out, I didn't hear Lumi as she approach. She knelt down, pressing her cheek to the ground to look at my face.

"Ash," she whispered, tilting my chin up with her finger. I met her eyes and gasped, horrified. A glowering purple bruise was smeared across her right cheek bone. "Ash, talk to me. Say something. Are you okay? Are you hurt?" Lumi gripped my wrists and tried hauling me to my feet, but I yanked her closer instead. I reached a shaking finger towards her face, stopping inches from her bruised skin.

"Look at what he did to you," I croaked, guilt giving way to the devastation crushing my heart. "Because of me." I released her and struggled to my feet. The world rocked violently, and I swayed.

Lumi shot up next to me, gripping my shoulder tightly.

"No," she said sternly. She stepped in front of me and looked into my eyes. "This was not your fault. Ash, look at me. This was not—"

"Of course it is!" I burst out, cutting her off. I scrubbed my shaking hands over my eyes. My chest felt like it was going to cave in. Shame cut through me like a knife, and I couldn't breathe. I jammed my fingers roughly through my hair, wishing with everything in me that I could wave a hand and stop existing.

"No," Lumi said firmly. "Don't do this to yourself. This was my father's fault. It has nothing to do with you."

"It has everything to do with me!" I moaned, covering my face with my hands.

"Ash—"

"He hit you!" I said, rounding on her. Concern filled her blue eyes as she looked up at my distraught expression. "He hit you because you were with me! All of this is my fault!" All the guilt and the anger I'd kept bottled inside flooded through me and the words tumbled from me before I could stop them.

"Everything! Your father is pushing you at Killian! Rowan can't get books anymore! His family is being shunned! And it's all because of *me*!" Anguish cleaved my heart in two as I looked away from her sharply.

"How... How did you..."

"Give me some credit," I said bitterly. "I'm not that dense. Rowan's face lit up like you handed him the world when he saw those books. And it's all my fault."

The silence stretched between us for a moment. Lumi reached for me, but I stepped beyond her grasp. Her touch, her sympathy. I didn't deserve any of it and it was too much for me to take. We stared at each other for a second before the pain in my chest became overwhelming.

Fearful murmuring voices floated through the air. Villagers were gathering in the square, looking for what caused the sudden earthquake.

Looking for me.

"What are you doing?" she demanded as I pulled away further. I gritted my teeth against the guilt and pain and pushed past her, striding back down the alleyway without stopping to think about what I was doing. "Ash?"

I pressed a hand against the wall, stumbling as I turned a corner and marched towards the sounds of the confused shopkeepers. Through the terrified whispers of volcanos and demons, I heard my name.

"Ash, stop! If they see you, they'll—"

"I don't care," I ground out. "Maybe someone will finally kill me. At least I won't hurt you or Rowan anymore. Or maybe I'll just go ahead and throw myself into the Black Sea. Save everyone the trouble," I muttered. Suddenly, I was jerked roughly to a halt.

Lumi grabbed my tunic and slammed me against the charred wall.

"Stop it." Hurt and anger warred in her eyes, and I immediately regretted my rash words. "Don't you *ever* say that again," she said fiercely. She pressed her hands against my chest, pinning me between her and the wall. Tears shimmered on her long lashes as she furiously stared me down.

I swallowed hard and pressed my lips together.

"You don't get to quit on me. On us."

My heart twisted and I blew out a breath, running my fingers through my hair. "No, I—"

"That's exactly what you're doing," she interjected roughly.

"No," I croaked. I placed my hands on her shoulders and tried to shift past her, but she dug her heels in, refusing to move. Her face was a breath away from mine. My head spun at the feel of her body pressed hard against mine and I cleared my throat. "You and Rowan—"

"Shut the fuck up, Ash," Lumi snarled.

I blinked, startled by her tone, and fell silent.

Lumi glared up at me. "Do you honestly think I'd be better off without you? You must've forgotten who my father is. He would still be shoving me at that pig whether you were here or not. Without you, I would be getting dragged off right now to be married against my will.

"And Rowan… How do you think he'd feel if someone he loves like a brother decided that his life would be better without him? How would Rowan feel if you went and got yourself killed over it? He'd blame himself. For the rest of his life, that guilt would tear him to pieces, and you know it."

I winced. Her words sliced through me like a blade.

"I—"

"Did it ever occur to you that we think you're worth it?" Lumi challenged. Her eyes burned into mine and I wasn't sure I was breathing. "Did you ever once stop to think that maybe, just fucking *maybe,* we deal with what these shitty people throw at us because we all love you? Maybe we want you in our lives? You don't get to decide we don't need you anymore, Ash. Because I've got news for you. We do need you. *I* need you. And you don't get to just… You can't just leave me here… and—"

Lumi's voice broke, fresh tears rolling down her cheeks and into the snow.

Anguish shot through me as I watched them fall. I never realized just how much I meant to them. They were my everything. But I'd never let myself consider that I could be anything more than a burden.

I squeezed my eyes shut and wrapped my arms around Lumi, pulling her into a tight hug. She stuttered out a small sob and draped her arms around my waist.

"I am so sorry," I whispered, my voice thick with swirling emotions. I pressed my trembling lips into her hair.

"You better be fucking sorry," she grumbled into my chest.

We held each other for a long while. An aching sensation crept into my muscles as she finally stepped back and wiped her eyes.

"Come on. Let's go before someone comes snooping this way," Lumi said.

I nodded and went to step forward. White hot pain tore through my chest, causing me to gasp and fall back against the wall.

"Fuck," I hissed, clutching my side. Lumi's eyes went wide with concern. I shook my head. "I'm okay," I panted. Pain sliced through me again as I shifted. I sucked a sharp breath through my teeth. "I'll be okay," I amended softly.

The adrenaline from the fight had finally worn off, leaving every inch of me throbbing and sore. I probed gently with my fingers and felt something in my ribcage give way at the touch. Something that wasn't supposed to give like that. I winced hard at the white-hot burst of pain that followed.

Lumi glanced around before grasping the hem of my tunic.

"Let me see," she murmured. She gently lifted the fabric, exposing my bare abdomen to the cold. I shuddered, wincing hard. She froze in horror. Unease coiled in my stomach at the look on her pale face.

I tried to bend down to see, but the resulting jolt of agony had me leaning my head against the wall and flinching with each breath.

"Is it bad?" I asked tersely. She didn't answer. Instead, she touched a finger to my skin and traced around a large spot on my ribcage.

"I really hope Rowan's mother is home," she said. Worry clouded her face as she pulled my tunic back down over my stomach.

"Oh good," I remarked dryly. I closed my eyes as another painful spasm shot through me. "That's not ominous or terrifying." Every breath sent a stab of agony through my ribs.

"We have to get you to Lucia," she said, gripping my elbow. "You're really pale."

"Hey now," I chuckled halfheartedly. "Just because I haven't had the time to sunbathe lately doesn't... Fuck—" I stood, crying out as the pain nearly brought me to my knees. Lumi watched me, concern lacing her features. Concern and a tinge of fear.

"I'm okay," I gasped, offering her a strained smile. "I've been through worse. Trust me." She frowned.

"Can you walk?"

"Well, uh..." I groaned as I tried to stand up straight. "I can try. But it might be a bit slow going." I took a shuddering step and my knee screamed in protest. "Very slow."

Lumi lifted my arm over her shoulder to support me, being extremely careful to avoid letting her body brush against the tender spot on my stomach.

Together we hobbled through the shadows in a tense silence, keeping to the alleys to avoid any other farmers that might be out looking for me. It took the better part of an hour for us to finally reached the residential streets. Lumi paused, letting me catch my breath a bit before steering me gently towards Rowan's front door.

"You look like you're about to pass out," she whispered.

"Oh, it's not fun," I said with a grimace. "But I'll make it. Listen..." I trailed off. She cocked her eyebrow at the guilt on my face. "Before we go in, please," I sighed. I tried to run my fingers through my hair and flinched from the pain, dropping my hand back to my side. "Please don't—"

"Don't tell our sweet, sugar roll of a best friend that you were going to walk out of his life for his own good without so much as a word?" Lumi said. I ducked my head low in shame. "Fine. But you ever pull that shit again, I'll tell him what else you threatened to do."

The thought of Rowan's devastated face made my heart ache.

"No," I moaned. "No, please don't. I'm so sorry. I promise... I'm sorry."

"Don't do it again. Or else," Lumi threatened, smirking up at me. I stumbled slightly and Lumi automatically shifted to support me. I cringed as she caught me, her shoulder coming dangerously close to the throbbing spot on my ribs.

"Oh, I won't, believe me," I joked through my clenched teeth. "I knew you were lethal but, damn, Lumi. You're a badass with that thing." I jerked my chin at her boot, and she blushed.

"Well..." she sighed, failing to hide the pride in her voice, "I've spent years training with the guards at the wall, so I should certainly hope I'd be able to handle a dagger."

I opened my mouth to say something, but the pain slicing through me knocked the breath from my chest. She tightened her grip and sped up her pace, practically dragging me through the snow. Rowan must have been watching from the window because he threw the door open with a wide grin.

"There you are! I was—" His face fell as his emerald eyes took in my pained expression.

I grinned meekly.

"What happened?" Rowan demanded as he rushed to my other side and slipped my arm over his shoulders. He wrapped an arm around my waist, his strong grip landing in exactly the wrong spot. My vision blurred as pain ripped through my side.

"Oh... you know... the usual. Someone tried to kill me," I chuckled softly as I blinked away the darkness gathering at the edge of my vision. Rowan paled and shot a horrified look at Lumi. She deftly nudged Rowan's hand to a better spot before turning to him, her expression murderous.

"My father."

"What?" Rowan gasped. "He hit you?" He nodded at her cheek.

"No," she replied. "But his goon did while three more tried to beat Ash to a pulp."

"Tried?" I croaked, trying, and failing to chuckle. "I feel like pulp, so I'd say they succeeded."

They managed to drag me into the foyer and settle me into a chair. Rowan started looking me over carefully.

"Look at his side, Ro." Lumi gently lifted my tunic. Instantly, his face went white. He stumbled back, swearing and covering his mouth with his hands.

"If people keep doing that, I might start panicking," I muttered. I leaned my head back against the plush chair as the throbbing intensified and the world started swaying. "Though... It's getting... kinda hard to... breathe," I added through several gasps.

Rowan scrambled towards the stairwell.

"Mother! Mother, help!" Rowan yelled, dashing up the stairs two at a time. Lumi let out a deep sigh of relief.

"Thank the Two she's still here," she whispered.

"It can't be that bad," I teased lightly, clutching the chair to stay upright.

Footsteps thundered down the stairs and a woman in her late fifties bounded into the room. The skirt of her dark gray dress was gathered up in her hands. She swirled towards me like a storm cloud with Rowan following close on her heels. She was a stout woman with Rowan's kind face and bright green eyes. Her vibrant red hair was coiled in a tight bun. She knelt in front of me, placing her hands gently on my shoulders.

"Hi, Mrs. Lucia," I whispered.

"Hello, Sweetheart," she said kindly. She raised my tunic and clucked her tongue. "Oh, you poor dear."

"Everybody keeps doing that. I'm starting to get mildly concerned," I grumbled. Pain speared me as she began prodding my side with her fingers.

"Someone certainly did a number on you, didn't they?" she said softly. She examined my side for a few moments before raising my pant leg and examining my knee. It was a swollen mess of purple and blue.

"Ah..." I tried to chuckle, but it came out as a wheeze. "I have that effect on people."

"Rowan told me what happened. You must be in a great deal of pain, my dear. I'm surprised you're still conscious." She stood, rolling back her sleeves.

"It's... getting really difficult to be," I admitted, my vision blurring slightly.

"And what about you," Lucia said, glancing towards Lumi. "I see you didn't get away unscathed."

"It's just a bruise," Lumi replied, her eyes never leaving mine. "Is he going to be okay?"

"He will be," Lucia said. "But he's getting paler by the second. We need to get him into a bath."

"Good idea. It might be too cold out for a swim right—" I tried to joke, trailing off with a groan as the world swayed faster.

"Now isn't the time for that charming wit of yours, son. Can you move on your own?" Lucia placed a steadying hand on my shoulder as I nearly slipped from the chair. I blinked at the ceiling and shook my head.

"I don't know," I said. She nodded and turned to Rowan and Lumi.

"You two help him into the washroom." She jerked her chin towards the door to the back. Rowan and Lumi flanked me and dragged me to my feet. I sagged between them. My stomach roiled with pain, and I groaned.

"Nope," I gasped, "Can't do it..."

"We got you," Rowan said quietly. They managed to help me stumble along through the study and into a large washroom where a white tub rested on large, clawed feet. Lumi and Rowan leaned me against a cupboard as Lucia entered the room.

"You two help Ash out of his tunic and pants. We need to get him into the water before he loses consciousness and can't hold himself up." Lucia set to work on the tub while Rowan and Lumi began carefully stripping my clothes off. Lumi smirked and leaned in, whispering in my ear.

"Just lucky I guess," she hissed. I rolled my eyes at her. If I could have, I would have blushed deeply as they shoved my pants down and tossed my boots aside. I caught sight of my reflection in the ornate mirror hanging on the wall and blanched. My torso, legs and arms were covered in round bruises. A large purple bruise colored my jawline where Tom had struck me, and my side looked as though someone had spilled black ink from my ribs all the way down to my hip.

"So that's what all the fuss is about," I grimaced. My voice sounded extremely far away, and a dull roar sounded in my ears. I swayed and the darkness crept further into my vision.

"Ash? Hey! Stay with me!" Lumi said anxiously. She placed her fingers gently on my chin and made me look into her eyes. "You have to stay awake for me. Okay? Stay with me."

I tried to smile for her as they supported my weight, dragging me over to the tub. They laid me down in the basin and warm water sloshed over me.

"All right, son." Lucia knelt down, placing both hands in the water. "I need you to keep yourself in the water, okay? This is going to hurt but I need you to try."

"Can't hurt... Worse... than this," I managed. I felt a twinge of fear as I took in her grim expression. "Can it?" I asked tentatively.

"Just hang in there for me, okay?" She shifted her focus to the water. "If you feel yourself passing out, I need to know."

I glanced fearfully at my friends. Rowan's jaw was set. He wrapped an arm around Lumi who had covered her mouth with both of her hands. The surface of the water suddenly started to churn, heating to a feverish boil.

The heat seeped through my skin and into my bones. I gasped, my body bucking against the fresh wave of pain. It felt like my very essence was set on fire. My breath came in short spasms, and I fought to hold myself under as Lucia had instructed. Her face was set with determination. Beads of sweat trickled down her forehead as she stared hard into the churning water.

The darkness dominating my vision was replaced with blinding white light as I felt several rapid pops down my side. Something shifted and snapped back into place inside my chest. I cried out and gripped the edge of the tub so hard I thought it might shatter in my hands, gasping at each zing of pain sent shooting down my nerves as whatever was broken mended itself at her command.

"Are you all right?" Lucia asked tensely. "Do you need me to stop?"

"No!" I gasped, shoving myself down deeper into the water. Everything in me screamed to escape, but I held firm. "I'm okay!"

Lucia nodded.

My arms shook as pain seared my chest. Something cracked hard and I nearly blacked out. But I focused with all of my might on the ceiling, fighting to stay awake.

After what felt like an eternity of agony, Lucia stood, and the water stilled. The pain receded instantly.

I whimpered as I slumped into the water and sucked in a deep breath. Air blissfully filled my lungs, and the searing throb was gone.

"I... can breathe!" I panted. I hauled myself over the edge and rolled onto the ground, my chest heaving. Exhaustion crept into my muscles and my eyelids grew heavy.

"Are you alright?" Lumi said anxiously. Her face appeared upside down above me. Rowan leaned in next to her. I gave them a thumbs up before letting my arm drop wearily onto my chest.

"Thank... you," I gasped as Lucia's face came into view.

"You're very welcome, love," she smiled. "You should rest and give your body a chance to regain its strength."

"Don't... have to... tell me... twice," I managed drowsily. I blinked slowly. My eyelids were suddenly much too heavy, and I closed them, quickly losing the fight to stay conscious.

"Let's get him to the spare room. Let him sleep for a while." I felt three sets of hands on me as they helped me to my feet. Next thing I knew, I flopped onto my back, my head finding a blissfully soft pillow. I let out a soft moan, finally yielding to the exhaustion and letting the dark swallow me whole.

CHAPTER EIGHT

LUMI

Ash's chest rose and fell with each easy breath. The bruising had faded from his body and the warm color had returned to his skin.

Rowan and I clung to each other as Lucia splayed a hand over Ash's sleeping form. The water seeped from the fabric of his undergarments and floated up into a shining ball at Lucia's command, leaving both Ash and the bed bone dry. She directed the ball and it sailed away, bobbing gently out of the room.

Lucia checked Ash's pulse and threw a blanket over him. She then laid his clothes on the chair in the corner and ushered us out of the room.

"Thank you, Mother," Rowan whispered. Lucia closed the door softly behind us. She turned and flicked her wrist, summoning a thin ribbon of water from the washroom. It slithered across my bruised cheek and a sharp zing shot through my skin. She flicked her wrist again and the water dissipated into a fine mist. I prodded my cheek gently. The bruise was gone.

"How did you do that?" I asked.

"Years of practice," she replied. "For the villagers, I usually add herbs and oils. But they're purely for show. The only thing they do is hide the fact that I'm Cosmic."

I glanced at Rowan. His face was still white, and his eyes looked hollow as he returned my glance.

"I thought he was going to die," he whispered.

"Me too," I admitted with a shaky voice.

"I can admit now that he was very close to it," Lucia said quietly. She glanced back at the closed door.

I tangled my fingers into the front of Rowan's tunic, and he gripped my arms in horror. Lucia met our eyes with a weary expression.

"His injuries were much more serious than I let on," Lucia said. "His ribs were in really bad shape. Several of them were broken into splinters. There was severe internal bleeding and one of his lungs was also punctured. I didn't want him to panic so I didn't tell him. He's lucky you were with him, Lumi. Those injuries were fatal."

Rowan and I clutched each other harder. Lucia looked out the window, smoothing her rumpled skirts and rolling down her sleeves. "His body will finish the healing process as he sleeps. For now, I have to go. Mrs. Johns is having her baby today and I have to go see how her labor is progressing." She met Rowan's eyes. "Check his pulse if he's not up in three hours. If anything seems amiss come get me." She hugged us both, grabbed her coat, and rushed out into the snowy day.

Horror, rage, and relief warred with each other in my heart as I buried my face in Rowan's shoulder. His breathing turned shallow. I couldn't get the image of the horrible bruise on Ash's side out of my mind. Or the image of the knife pressed against his throat.

Panic gripped my chest tighter. I needed to see him. Needed to feel his heart beating. I pulled away.

"I-I need to—" I stammered, gesturing wildly towards the bedroom.

"Me too," Rowan nodded, taking my hand. "I need to make sure he's breathing."

We rushed back into the dark room, closing the door softly behind us. Ash hadn't moved an inch from where he'd settled.

I crawled onto the bed and let out a small sob as I rested my head on him. His heart thumped strongly against my ear.

I listened to it for a long while before I looked up at Ash's face again. He was still sleeping peacefully, completely unaware of my presence. I sighed, relishing the feel of his strong chest rising and falling under my head.

I slipped off the bed and Rowan sidled up beside me, taking my hand in his.

"He almost died today," I whispered. A single, furious tear rolled down my cheek. "My father almost killed him."

"You can't blame yourself, Lumi," Rowan murmured.

"I don't."

"Yes, you do," he replied softly. "I can see it in your face." I looked away and closed my eyes against the flood of images battering my mind.

"They tried to beat him to death, Ro." I clutched Rowan's hand tighter. "He fought back but they forced him to the ground and held his head back... One of them had a knife." My voice broke. "My father told them I had to watch Ash die. I was so fucking scared." My voice trembled.

"How did you get away?" Rowan asked. I shifted my foot towards him. He glanced down at the hilt visible in my boot and looked back up at me sharply. "You killed them?" Rowan gasped.

"I wanted to," I replied bitterly. "But I knew he would get blamed if they died. And his life would be harder than it is already. I managed to scare them off. Which was lucky..." I jerked my chin at Ash. "He almost lit the whole square on fire. He barely held it back and as soon as they ran away, his power overwhelmed him. I've never seen him lose control like that."

"Well, they were trying to kill him," Rowan said.

"That's just it though," I replied. "He didn't touch his power until one of them hit me."

Ash's face twisted with vengeful fury and the vicious snarl that ripped from his chest flashed rapidly through my mind.

I looked at Rowan. "I've never seen him that angry."

"Only after you got hit?" Rowan said. He furrowed his brow and stared down at Ash's sleeping face. A knowing look danced in his eyes for a moment before he smothered it.

"After they ran off, he ducked into an alley. I don't know what he did, but he must have unleashed a lot of pent-up power. When I found him again, the walls were black, and the ground was shaking." I glanced at Ash. "I knew he cared about us, but for him to lose it like that only after I got hit..."

"Yeah. I'm sure he does care... About *us*... Deeply," Rowan said slowly, staring at me with a strange expression. I furrowed my brow, and he shook his head with a deep sigh. "Well... Thank the Two you were with him," Rowan said, leaning in close to me.

"We have to do something," I told him. "He can't go back to the beach now. When my father finds out he's not dead, he'll send someone else."

"I agree," Rowan nodded. "But getting *him* to agree is gonna be the tricky part."

"I'll handle that," I replied firmly. "He's not gonna say no. Not this time."

Shouting from the foyer suddenly drew our attention. We left Ash sleeping peacefully and crept towards the sound.

"Your kind isn't welcome here!" an angry voice shouted from just beyond the front door.

Rowan and I peered cautiously around the corner. Kaelin had his back to us. A large basket hung from the crook of his elbow. His tone was calm and patient as he faced the furious man standing in the doorway, almost nose-to-nose with him.

"Jonathan—"

"I know you're causing all this trouble!" the man spat, cutting him off. "The wall was attacked last night! And then I see you coming out of the candle shop with *that* after the strange earthquake hit the village this morning?"

My heart sank. Rowan glanced at me, and I jerked my head back towards Ash in answer.

"You still worship the spirits! You call them here!" the man screamed, his face turning red. "I'll bet that's why that little freak is always here! You're teaching him!"

"Jonathan, be reasonable," Kaelin sighed. "The spirits aren't summoned by anything, let alone a simple candle."

"So, you don't deny it!" Jonathan pointed a finger at Kaelin. "I knew it! I'll make sure everyone knows what you really are! And I'll tell Jasper! He'll finally have you chucked out! You and that little freak with you!" He spat at Kaelin's feet before storming off.

Kaelin sighed and turned, jumping as he caught sight of us peering nervously around the corner.

"Oh!" He stepped further into the house, placing an arm across his chest. The door closed behind him on a phantom wind. "Goodness, you scared me! I'm sorry you had to hear that. He's had it out for me for years. Never misses an opportunity to curse at me." He stepped closer and peered at us with a frown. "Where's Ash?"

Rowan and I exchanged dark looks and stepped back around the corner.

"We were attacked on our way here," I told him. Kaelin paled. "I only had a bruised cheek. But…" I swallowed fearfully, glancing over my shoulder.

"Oh dear," Kaelin murmured. "Is Ash all right?"

"He is now," Rowan said. "Mother said he wouldn't have made it if she hadn't gotten to him when she did. Luckily, Lumi managed to drag him here before Mother left for the day. He's asleep in the spare room."

"Thank the Two," Kaelin said, sighing in relief. "Who attacked you?" His deep blue eyes fixed on me.

"Farmers," I said bitterly. Hatred seared my heart.

"I see," Kaelin replied quietly. There was no need to explain further. He met Rowan's eyes with a determined expression. "Perhaps it's time we were a bit more insistent, son. Today's attempt failed, but the next one might not."

"Oh, trust me," I replied firmly. "He won't say no this time."

Kaelin sighed. "Good. Now let's go take our minds off the unpleasantness of today. You two can help me with something special while he rests."

We followed him into the study. The fire was already blazing in the grate, bathing the cozy room in a comfortable warmth.

"What's that?" Rowan said, pointing to the basket. Kaelin faced us and, with a sad smile, held out his arm.

Rowan slid the basket from his father's elbow and peered inside. He cocked an eyebrow, withdrawing a large black candle and setting it on the table near the fire.

"This," Kaelin said sadly, "is a mourning candle. We light it to honor our missing spirits and keep their memory alive. If you would please, Rowan."

Rowan placed his finger and thumb around the wick and snapped. A little flame crackled to life under his touch, dancing merrily.

"Thank you, son," Kaelin nodded. "Today, we honor Lord Spring. His cycle should've started yesterday. Spring was a kind soul. He was quiet, gentle, and patient. He was an excellent cook, and he loved his garden. He grew thousands of flowers in every shape, size, and color you could dream of. When he was on the throne of the World's Tower, the air was sweeter, and the world was filled with life." Shadows gathered in his eyes. "Soon, the Festival of Flowers should have started," he said quietly.

"What's that?" I asked, sitting in a chair by the fire. Rowan claimed the seat next to mine as Kaelin smiled wistfully.

"Oh, it was a lovely festival to honor Lord Spring. The villagers would pick children to serve as the Flower Kings, Queens, Princes, and Princesses. The whole community would get together and make royal outfits and lovely flower crowns for the court. Then the children would judge the pastry contests and march in the Parade of Flowers." Kaelin's eyes misted over with nostalgia and his shoulders slumped.

"I'm sorry," he sighed. "I don't mean to get emotional. I worked for Lord Spring for a long time, and I miss him dearly. He was a good friend. He was a lot like you, son. I think you and he would've liked each other."

"Were there festivals for the other spirits?" I asked in an attempt to distract him from his sorrow. He smiled broadly.

"There were. There was The Great Feast to celebrate Lord Fall's generosity and goodwill. The whole community would gather and eat as one family. Sharing food and stories. Then there was the Fire Festival. Lady Summer was a vain, indulgent creature. During the Fire Festival, villagers would eat the spiceberries that used to grow at the mouth of the volcanoes. They were a powerful aphrodisiac and a pregnancy inhibitor. You can imagine what those celebrations were like," he chuckled.

"Children were taken on a camping trip by the elders and young adults still too young to get involved in the other celebrations. And for the serious and stoic Lady Winter, villagers celebrated First Frost. There was a decorating contest and a gift exchange. Lady Winter loved her books... So, on the first night, the villagers would gather in the town square and swap books in her honor."

"Oh!" Rowan sat up excitedly. "Is that where the Book Keeper came from?"

Kaelin nodded, smiling.

"The Book Keeper?" I asked.

"It was this legend about a spirit who loved books," Rowan beamed. "You'd put books on a high wall in town square. Then the spirit would come at night and swap them for new ones. I used to do it with someone in the village when I was a kid. I don't know who it was, but..." He shrugged. "It's nice to know there's a kindred soul out there. Or at least there used to be. They stopped one day, and I never heard from them again."

"Unfortunately, the festivals were all abandoned. People thought celebrating the festivals or worshiping the spirits would summon Winter's ice demons," Kaelin said. "The same fear that drives these people to exile, maim, or even kill Cosmics." He sighed and turned. "Ah, well. Thank you for listening to an old windbag reminisce about the past. I think though that I need a nap. Should Ash need something, please come get me." He gave us one last smile, ambling from the room. We watched him go before Rowan turned to me.

"Ash is probably gonna be out for a while. We could get some practice in if you want," he suggested.

"Sounds like a plan," I replied, slipping down to sit on the floor.

Rowan sat in front of me and began trying to help me summon a ball of wind. I tried everything I could think of to muster control of the power I supposedly possessed. I willed it. I demanded the wind bow to my whims. I even begged.

Still, despite all I tried, I didn't summon so much as a slight breeze. We sat there for a long while, stopping only when we were interrupted by a shuffling sound from the hall outside the study.

We turned and leapt to our feet as Ash sidled into the room. His pants were slung low on his hips. The toned muscles of his abdomen and chest were no longer peppered with dark bruises and his side was unblemished. He blinked at us, still bleary-eyed and drowsy.

"Ash," Rowan gasped. "Are you all right?"

Ash nodded slowly and I had to fight the sudden urge to fling myself into his arms.

"How long was I out?" His deep voice was still husky from sleep.

"Only about three hours," Rowan said. "Are you sure you're okay? We can wake you later if you need more sleep."

"I'm all right," Ash said, stretching his body cautiously.

Unable to fight it any longer, I leapt forward and wrapped my arms tightly around him.

"Ash, I'm so sorry," I whispered.

"You have nothing to be sorry for," Ash said into my hair as Rowan appeared on his other side, burying his face in Ash's shoulder. He wrapped his arms around us with a deep sigh.

"We were so scared," I mumbled.

Rowan nodded, tightening his grip. Ash pulled us both closer.

"Me too," he rasped.

The three of us stood there, holding onto each other for a long time. We only let go when Ash's stomach rumbled loudly.

He chuckled, running his fingers through his hair as we stepped back to wipe our eyes. "Sorry," he said sheepishly, rubbing his abdomen. "But uh... I'm starving."

Rowan grinned and shot a glance at the sunlight trickling in through the window.

"Well... It's actually a nice day today," he said casually. "How about a picnic in the west fields? Might not be a bad idea to head out in case someone comes here looking for you."

"A picnic sounds good. Just as long as no one tries to kill me." He glanced at our anxious expressions and winced. "Too soon to joke about?"

"Are you sure you're up to it?" I said, wringing my hands.

"I'm okay," he replied. "My fierce warrior queen can always save my life again." He winked at me and grinned.

I valiantly fought—and failed—to suppress a smile.

"Awesome! I already have some food in the bag behind that chair. To the west fields," Rowan beamed. Ash turned, disappearing for a moment.

"So, Ro... Why the west fields?" I asked grinning as Ash returned with is coat in hand. His tunic and boots were already on.

"Um," Rowan mumbled.

"It wouldn't have anything to do with a certain miner who comes in for lunch every day, would it?" I smirked. Rowan blushed and started plucking at a string stuck to his powder blue tunic.

"Right," Ash said, catching on with a wink to me. "The blonde one with the dimples and the big arm muscles. What was his name? Michael?"

Rowan's blush deepened as he looked away and did his best to mask a grin. "His name is Heath. And I have no idea what you mean."

"Of course not," I chuckled. "All right, let's go so Rowan can ogle his boyfriend."

"Ugh, I wish," Rowan sighed. "He hasn't talked to me in a while. But I guess a little ogling wouldn't hurt."

Ash and I exchanged a look behind Rowan's back. Ash frowned, recovering smoothly as Rowan turned back to us.

"Are you kidding?" Ash said incredulously. His bright smile was fixed convincingly back on his face. "I'm gonna ogle him too!"

"Oh yeah? But I thought you liked your men brunette and really, *really* chatty," Rowan teased, slinging his bag across his chest. Ash shot him a dark look as he yanked his coat up over his shoulders.

"Seriously? That was forever ago. Am I ever going to live that down?" he grumbled.

"Two years is not *forever* ago and no you absolutely will not live it down," I replied, grinning.

Rowan and I laughed our way through the foyer with Ash still grumbling behind us. We trooped outside into the afternoon sunlight and set off arm in arm towards the west fields.

CHAPTER NINE

LUMI

"Let me get this straight," Rowan said incredulously. The sun shined weakly on our heads as we turned at the fork in the road, following the path leading along the inside of the border wall. Most of the villagers were inside preparing lunch, leaving the road blissfully deserted.

He shook his head and laughed in disbelief. "Your father sent farmers to drag you off to your own wedding against your will in broad daylight? And what were they gonna do with Ash after they murdered him in the middle of the square?"

"No idea," I said darkly. "My father's insane if he thinks I'm going along with this stupid fucking plan of his."

"What now?" Rowan asked with a sidelong glance at me. I exhaled sharply.

"I'm not sure. I won't marry that pig. If they try to force me—"

"I won't let that happen," Ash snapped fiercely. His eyes were fixed on our feet crunching through the snow.

"We," Rowan added. "We won't let that happen."

Ash nodded. "We," he agreed.

Warmth spread through my chest. I wrapped my arms around their waists and tugged them close. "I treasure you both, too," I grinned.

"You know," Rowan said slowly. "You could always stay with me. Father already suggested it and Mother thinks it's a great idea." I shook my head.

"If I leave that house, my father will lose his mind," I sighed. "And if he found out I'm living with you, he'd do something horrible. After he comes to drag me out by my hair, that is."

"I'd like to see him fucking try," Ash growled viciously. His face was a mask of cold fury. I glanced at him as he raised a canteen to his lips to take a swig.

"See?" Rowan winked. "It's all settled. You take the spare room on the first floor and Ash is taking the one upstairs."

Ash sputtered and choked on his water. He gave Rowan a pained look, wiping his mouth on the back of his sleeve.

"Ro," he began, but Rowan shook his head.

"Nope. I'm not arguing with you. I'll tell Father when we get back home. He and Mother will be so relieved." His face broke into a wide grin.

I gave Ash a long, pointed look. He blushed and ducked his head.

Suddenly, a bloodcurdling scream shook the air around us. We gripped each other tightly, skidding to a halt and looking around fearfully.

Terrified villagers peered out of their windows. I drew my sword, looking up as another scream sounded high above us and freezing in horror. A giant creature was vaulting over the side of the wall. It slid down, its sharp claws leaving deep gashes in the stone.

"Guys, run!" I shouted.

Rowan grabbed Ash's arm and dragged him away. He reached for me, his fingers grazing my sleeve as I surged forward with Frost Breaker gleaming wickedly in the sunlight. My feet pounding against the ground as I ran toward the creature. Every nerve in my body buzzed sharply.

The creature hit the ground on all fours and straightened, whipping its head towards me. Shadows dripped from its black, eyeless sockets, curling into the air, and dissipating like smoke. It was the size of a horse, with a catlike body made entirely out of jagged shards of gray ice. Large spikes ran from the base of its round skull down to the tip of its tail. Its long legs ended in razor sharp talons, each one larger than my hand. Serrated teeth stuck out of its wide mouth at odd angles. Clasped tightly in its jaws, screaming for his life, was Barron.

The terrified guard flailed in the creature's mouth as tears streamed down his bloodied face. He caught the creature in the neck with his boot and it shook him violently in return.

I closed the distance rapidly, swinging my blade in a wide arc and bringing it slicing down on the beast's muzzle. It reared back, dropping Barron in a bloody heap. He hit the snow face first and fell silent.

The creature roared loud enough to shake the icicles from the buildings nearby and launched itself at me, its massive jaws snapping as it swung a clawed foot out. I dropped to my knees, barely avoiding losing my head. The claws sailed past my face, missing my skin by inches. It swung again and I slashed at the beast's legs, catching it in one of its joints. The sharp blade sliced through the leg completely. Thick black shadows leaked from the severed limb and pooled on the snow. The creature's screams echoed off the wall as it staggered back in pain.

I rolled to the side and braced my legs beneath me as it shrieked furiously and attacked, its jaws opening wide as it tried to catch me around the ribs.

I dodged, barely avoiding its swiping claws, and snapping teeth. My heart was pounding frantically behind my ribs. I whirled and gripped the sword with all my might, launching myself towards the creature as it again opened its massive jaws and rammed Frost Breaker upwards. The blade sank deep into the roof of the creature's mouth.

It let out a shrill cry and ripped itself away, its arms flailing wildly. Sludge and smoke poured from the wound, splattering the snow with long black stains. I swung with every ounce of strength I could muster. Frost Breaker whistled as it sliced through the air and straight through the creature's neck, severing its head. A sudden silence fell before a warm blast of air ripped through the clearing. The creature exploded in a shower of ice fragments and dust, throwing me off my feet.

A ball of bright, golden light hovered in the air above me. It floated on the breeze for a moment before streaking off into the sky like a shooting star and vanishing.

Dazed, I struggled to my feet and brushed the dust and ice from my shoulders with shaking fingers. A thousand questions swirled through my mind as I sheathed Frost Breaker. All around me, terrified villagers came streaming out of their homes, chattering nervously.

"How'd an ice demon get over the wall?"

"Are there more?"

"I thought we were safe here!"

I turned and found a small crowd gathering around the motionless guard. A man pressed two fingers to his neck and waved others over frantically.

"He's alive!" he gasped. "Bring that cart!"

Several young men rushed out of the crowd. They lifted the limp Barron into a cart that had been emptied of its contents and wheeled over.

My stomach churned at the sight of the pool of blood left behind in the snow.

Several villagers murmured my name, gesturing at the sword sheathed at my side. I took a step backwards into a strong pair of hands that gripped my arms and pulled me away.

I whirled around in a blind panic and found Rowan. Together, we wove our way quickly through the frightened villagers and ducked into an alleyway, out of sight.

Ash was waiting in the shadows. He rushed forward and seized my arms as soon as I was within reach.

"Lumi!" He crushed me against his chest in a tight hug. "Are you okay? Are you hurt?" I stumbled slightly as he frantically held me at arm's length to scan me for injuries.

"I'm all right," I said, sounding much calmer than I actually felt. My insides were still quivering from the adrenaline. I wiped the sweat from my brow and looked back towards the clearing.

Ever since I was small, I'd heard the vague stories of the ice demons terrorizing villages. My young imagination had conjured up images of formless shadows lurking in the night. Never had I dreamed they were as monstrous as the creature I'd just faced. My heart hammered against my ribs at the thought of those wicked claws swooshing by my face, missing me only by inches.

Ash hugged me close again.

"I'm sorry, Lumi."

"For what?" I replied, bewildered.

"I should have stayed and helped you!"

"Ash…" I shook my head and pulled away. "If anyone saw you, they'd blame you for the demon and they would've killed you. Besides… I think I did okay."

"You were incredible!" Rowan exclaimed. The voices grew louder as more people arrived on the scene.

I heard the faint murmur of my name circulating through the crowd. Ash's name came up as well and was whispered in fearful tones. It was quickly followed by words like 'river,' 'banish' and 'monster.' Then came my father's name. My heart lurched hard, and I gripped him tighter.

Rowan glanced back towards the crowd, placing a hand on Ash's arm. "Let's get out of here."

My mind started racing as we sprinted through the shadows to put as much distance between us and the growing crowd as we could. Panic, pride, and shock swirled in my stomach. An ice demon. I'd fought a real demon and survived.

We burst around the corner of the last building and found ourselves overlooking the docks. The sails of the trade ships snapped in the wind rolling in from the Black Sea. Merchants had set up shop and were bartering and trading with the villagers that milled around the stalls. Sailors dressed in strange clothes stood grouped together in tight clusters for warmth, frowning and shivering from the cold. Rowan took a deep breath and looked back the way we came.

"We need to let that crowd clear out before we try to head back home. Might as well look around here for a while," Rowan said, eyeing a cart stacked high with books.

Ash sniffed the air and groaned. "I wouldn't mind finding out what that delicious smell is."

I nodded and reached a hand into my bag, handing Ash a shiny silver trinket to trade. He hesitated and I shot him a severe look before firmly shoving the stolen object into his hands. Whatever it was, my parents wouldn't even notice it was gone.

Ash sighed and mumbled his thanks. He yanked the hood of his coat up over his head and tugged it low over his eyes, hiding most of his face from view.

"Come on," I said, stepping forward. We slipped into the mass of shoppers and ambled from stall to stall examining their wares.

The air was thick with a delicious blend of exotic spices and herbs. Ash breathed in deeply and turned, following the wafting smell of warm food. One stall in particular caught my eye. It was covered in strange, brightly colored objects. Rowan stepped up beside me and grinned.

"They're flowers. Real ones," he said.

"Wow," I whispered, leaning in to examine a deep red one. Rowan winked and retreated to the book cart. "They don't look like the ones painted on my wall."

"Beautiful, aren't they?" A kind-looking man sidled up to me.

"They are," I agreed. "I've never seen a real flower before."

"Never?" The man's brow furrowed. "That won't do. Every lovely lady needs a flower." He nodded towards a deep red bloom. "That's a rose. Here." He plucked it from the bucket of water and handed it to me.

I reached for my bag to offer a trade, but he waved me off.

"No, no. Just take it. It won't last in this cold, and I won't be able to keep them alive for much longer anyways. Enjoy it while you can, okay?"

"Thank you, sir," I breathed, cradling the soft bloom to my chest. He winked and turned to address a woman who had strolled up to his stall.

I brought the flower to my nose and breathed in, savoring the sweet scent. The petals tickled my cheek as I brushed them across my face. I'd never seen such a vibrant color in all my life. The rose was at such odds with the bleak world around me, it felt like I was cupping a small bit of magic in my hands.

I looked up, excited to show the gorgeous flower to my friends. I had only walked three steps towards Rowan and the book cart when an arm shot out from the crowd and clasped painfully around my wrist.

I yelped and twisted to find Killian sneering down his pointed nose at me.

"Ah, my blushing bride. I've been looking everywhere for you!" Killian drawled. He yanked me closer to cup my cheek, forcing me to look up at him.

A lecherous hunger shone in his eyes as they roved up and down my body. I tried to jerk away but he squeezed, holding me in place as he plucked the rose from my hand and tossed it into the snow. "Your father was most insistent that we be wed tonight. But now that I've found you, why wait? I'm sure he'd oblige me. Come." He barked out the last word as though I were a disobedient dog.

"Let go of me, you fucking pig!" I spat.

Killian arched his thin eyebrow as I tried to shake his hand loose.

"Is that any way to address your new husband?" He clucked his tongue at me. "I would've thought Jasper's daughter would know her place better than that. But I've never minded a challenge. I'll straighten out that wicked tongue of yours." Killian pulled me closer and leaned in to kiss me.

I jerked away and discreetly lifted my foot to unsheathe the dagger from my boot.

"Let her go." Ash's deep voice was dangerously quiet. Killian jumped and whipped around nervously.

Ash loomed behind Killian, his golden eyes flashing with wrath as he stared hard at my assailant. The hood had slipped from his head. People gasped and stepped fearfully away from him.

Killian's smug grin slipped from his lips ever so slightly. He loosened his grip on my arm and took a small step backwards before once again plastering a self-assured expression across his pointed face. His eyes darted around, noting the merchants and villagers watching us.

"She's not your concern anymore. Or hasn't she told you yet? She's mine now," Killian said smoothly. "So why don't you crawl back to your little hole in the ground before you get hurt."

"I'm not going to tell you again," Ash's voice was barely above a whisper. But the crowd had gone silent, so Killian didn't miss a single word. He clenched his fists in an effort to leash his fiery rage.

"And if I don't?" Killian sneered, drawing me in close again.

I lowered my foot as slowly as I could so Killian wouldn't notice the movement. The cool hilt of the dagger rested against my palm.

"Then we will make you." I whipped my head around to find Rowan on Killian's other side. The cold wrath in his eyes sent a chill up my spine. Killian tightened his bony grip, making me wince.

Ash gritted his teeth and let out a low, vicious growl. The gathered villagers gasped at the sound and fled. Sweat gathered on Killian's upper lip as he took a step backwards, calculating his odds.

"She belongs to me now," he said, his voice edged with panic. "And if either of you come near her again, I'll have you executed." He met Ash's glare and smirked. "You hear me, you fucking freak? She's mine now." He locked eyes with Ash as he reached down and cupped my breast roughly.

I slashed upwards, driving the dagger straight into the flesh near Killian's elbow. Warm blood seeped onto my hand as Killian cried out and collapsed to his knees.

"You stupid bitch!" he screamed.

I twisted the hilt of the dagger still lodged firmly in his flesh. He howled in pain, and I crouched, bringing my face close to his.

"I am not yours," I said, venom dripping from every word. "I never will be. Touch me again and I will remove your tiny little cock."

Killian shrieked in agony as I twisted the dagger again and ripped it free.

"I'm gonna tear you apart, you stupid fucking bitch!" Killian snarled, tears of pain streaming down his pale face.

Ash moved towards him, but I held out a hand, pressing my palm to his chest to stop him. A dark fiery hatred burned in his golden eyes. He met my gaze for a brief moment before exhaling sharply and taking a small step back, running his hand through his hair. I patted him once and turned back to the squirming pig in the snow, leaning a little closer.

"Try me and see what fucking happens," I hissed. I wiped my dagger on Killian's pant leg and turned on my heel, striding away as he rolled around on the snowbank beside the path. Ash and Rowan fell in step behind me, flanking me like knights guarding their queen.

We strode silently through the crowd without making eye contact with anyone. The people parted fearfully around us without saying a word. They were even too scared to throw the usual insults at Ash. I kept my dagger in my hand just in case anyone had any ideas about attacking him as we passed. But no one even looked at him. Killian's screams of pain receded into the distance as we marched purposefully up the road and back to the village.

We slipped into the shadows and darted through the alleyway until we made it back to Rowan's home. He let out a low whistle, turning to watch as I stowed the blade back in my boot.

"Whelp," he said, "This day has been... Insane. Are you okay?"

Ash and I nodded. Rowan sighed and shook his head.

"I'll see you tomorrow. Okay? Unless you need me." He gave me a meaningful look and I nodded grimly in response. He patted me on the arm reassuringly before turning to look up at Ash. "I'll have the room ready for you by morning." Ash looked like he was about to say something, but Rowan shook his head. "Someone tried to kill you today, you stubborn ass. I'm not arguing with you this time. You either come here, or I'm moving in with you on the beach."

"Ro, you don't want to live down there," Ash said, grimacing.

"Then pack your stuff tonight," Rowan replied firmly. He locked Ash with a hard stare, silently daring him to say something. Ash sighed and pressed his lips together without another word.

"Thank you. I'll see you in the morning," Rowan said. He trudged up to the door and shot one last look at us before slipping inside and closing it softly behind him. We stood side by side in silence for a moment, staring up at the house.

"Are you okay?" Ash asked finally.

"Of course." I waved a dismissive hand.

He arched an eyebrow as if he didn't believe me. I shrugged and did my best to ignore the exhaustion creeping into my bones.

"I'll be okay," I sighed. "Come on. Let me walk you back for my own peace of mind."

I took his arm, leaning my head on his shoulder as we started back down the road to the beach.

Once or twice, I thought I saw something stir in the corner of my vision. My hand never left the hilt of my sword.

Ash glanced down at my hand and chuckled darkly. "I swear." He sounded as drained as I felt. "If anything else happens to us today... I don't know what I'll do." Ash pinched the bridge of his nose and sighed before saying, "So what will you do now?"

I chuckled, tilting my head back to look at him. He avoided my gaze, keeping his eyes focused on the street ahead.

"I honestly have no idea," I said through a humorless laugh. "My father will be furious, that's for sure."

Ash snickered.

"It'll probably only be a matter of time before someone else is chosen for me," I sighed.

"And what do *you* want?" Ash said.

I considered his question for a long moment before I replied.

"I just want to be happy," I said softly. "I want my own house where I make the rules. Somewhere with a room for you, so I know you're safe and warm at night. I want to be able to walk the street with you and not have someone try to kill you. I want to sit next to the fire of *my home* with Rowan and discuss books. I want to help train guards at the wall, so they stand a chance. Unlike poor Barron. I want..." I trailed off.

My mind filled with images of fire dancing in my palms and wind whipping around my feet. My heart sank. That was what I wanted most, deep down. My heart's true desires were things that seemed impossible. I sighed through my nose and looked back to the road.

"I don't think that's too much to ask," I finished quietly.

"No," he agreed. "It's not." He eyed me carefully for a moment.

I blew out a breath, steadying my nerves enough that my smile would appear genuine.

"I'll figure it out," I said with a shrug. "I always do."

"Well, you know I'm always here for you," Ash said.

"I know you are," I smiled.

We rounded the corner and made our way down the sloping dunes towards the beach. As we wound our way through the tents, I spotted a man creeping along the path. Alarm bells sounded in my head, and I gripped Ash's arm to hold him back.

He opened his mouth, but I pressed a finger to his lips to silence him. The suspicious man paused at the edge of the clearing around Ash's hut. Panic seized my chest as the man stood up on his toes and craned his neck to survey the surrounding area.

I shoved Ash off the path and dove after him before the man spotted us.

"What are you doing?" Ash whispered.

I shook my head and motioned for him to follow me. The sounds of gleeful cackling and crunching wood filled the air as we drew closer. I searched the shadows for any sign of another person nearby. There was no one else in sight. The man lurking along the path must be the lookout.

We crept to the edge of the clearing and peered around a tent. My stomach clenched in horror, and I pressed my fingers into my mouth to stifle a scream. Ash peeked over my shoulder, his face paling.

"No," he gasped, sinking to his knees as he covered his mouth with both hands. His home was being destroyed.

The roof had been caved in and a group of men were kicking their feet through the brittle walls, leaving gaping holes in the wood. Every one of his few possessions had been thrown out onto the sand and maliciously covered in water. The frigid air had frozen most of his things into a solid block of ice, destroying his belongings.

I knelt beside Ash and held him by his trembling shoulders as we watched the men trample on his life. A battered, old music box sailed through a hole in the broken wall and crashed to the ground, splintering into a thousand tiny pieces. Ash groaned and placed a shaking hand over his heart.

One of the men stepped out of the hut and cackled wildly as he pulled the front of his pants down to urinate on a pile of Ash's clothes.

"Any sign of him?" the cackling man called over his shoulder.

"Not yet," a voice called back from somewhere close to us.

Ash and I shrank back into the shadows.

"Ash, they're looking for you," I whispered in his ear, horrified. "We've got to go before they find you and—" I trailed off. My heart shattered at the devastation on his face. He was looking up at what was left of his home with tears shining in his eyes. A wooden keepsake box smashed to the ground beside the remnants of the music box. It sprang open, spraying letters and scraps of papers across the snow.

I wrapped my arms tightly around his chest and he reached up to grip my wrists, clinging to me like a drowning man might cling to a rope.

"Lumi," he whispered raggedly. "That was everything I had." He met my eyes, his face broken in despair. "I have nothing. And there's a blizzard coming." He shot a fearful look at the darkening sky. "What do I do now?"

My heart ached as I pulled him to his feet and took his hands tightly in mine.

"You come home with me." My voice cracked as I struggled to keep my emotions in check. "You come with me before they find you here. Please."

He squeezed his eyes shut to smother the tears rising there as I pulled his hood low over his face and led him away. We darted back through the sea of tents, doing our best to avoid the eyes of the villagers as we passed.

I strained my ears to pick up any sound of shouting or pounding footsteps chasing us as we ran.

We avoided the main path and scrambled on our hands and knees up the snow-covered dunes until, finally, we reached the place where the road bent out of sight of the beach.

I laced my fingers with his and started quickly up the road towards the farms. Ash followed a step behind me with his eyes cast down at the road. After a few feet of silence, he sighed and sped up his pace. I glanced at his devastated face and wrapped my arm around his waist.

"Ash, I am so fucking sorry," I said, leaning into him. "Are you okay?" He didn't say anything for a long time, watching the ground as we walked.

"I'll be alright," he said finally, barely above a whisper. He pushed his hood away and ran his fingers through his hair. "This isn't the first time I've lost, well, everything." I opened my mouth to offer some words of comfort, but nothing came out. Instead, I held him a little tighter, leaning in close as we stomped through the snow towards my father's estate. After a few more moments of silence, I felt him tense beside me. He shot me a wary look and opened his mouth.

"Lumi," Ash started.

"Don't," I warned, sensing the words before they left his lips. "Don't say it."

"You know as well as I do—"

"I don't want to hear it," I said, squaring my shoulders as the buildings along the road gave way to sprawling farmlands.

"Lumi..."

"Don't, Ash," I said firmly. He sucked in a breath and fell silent for a moment before he gathered the nerve to continue.

"If your father is home..." Ash looked over and caught sight of my fierce expression before he held his hands up in surrender. "All right. I'm sorry. I'll shut up," he said meekly.

Arriving at the front gate, I swung it open and strode down the drive with my head held high. I marched up to the front door and ripped it open before storming into the entrance hall like a queen leading her troops into battle. Ash stayed close to me as I crashed through the door of the formal dining room like a cataclysm.

CHAPTER TEN

Ash

"Father!" Lumi strode through the door like a general into her war room. "If you so much as think about—" She stumbled to a halt upon realizing the room was empty.

"For what it's worth, you looked very formidable," I chuckled.

She shot me an annoyed look and crossed the room to peer out the window. The sun was only just beginning its descent towards the horizon and gray clouds were gathering over the mountains.

I peered back into the entrance hall, but there wasn't a soul in sight. The manor was unnervingly quiet.

"Where is everyone?" I asked.

"My parents must still be at the caves," Lumi said, frowning. "The servants are probably eating. They usually take their dinner breaks in the kitchen." She waved a hand at the small door behind her.

"I should probably keep my voice down then," I joked. "Don't need someone—" I stopped short at the sound of a sharp gasp coming from the kitchen. Panic seized my mind, and I dove to the floor behind the dining room table.

The long green tablecloth billowed as the kitchen door burst open and several people rushed into the room. Lumi plastered a bright smile on her face, tucking her bloodstained fingers behind her back as a female voice gasped.

"Oh!" the voice exclaimed. "Miss Lumi! Are you all right?"

"Of course," she replied, shifting nervously on her feet. "Why? What's wrong?"

"We thought we heard someone in here with you," another female voice said cautiously.

Lumi shook her head.

"Nope. Just me talking to myself. No need for the rolling pins. Or the knife," she added, swallowing hard.

My heart pounded against my ribs. I pressed a hand over my mouth so they wouldn't hear my breathing.

"Your father is at the caves, Miss," a male voice said. "But Ovi's son was here looking for you."

"Was he?" Lumi said with exaggerated surprise, her false smile never wavering. Anger flashed through my chest. "Well," she continued, "I'm sure whatever it was can wait until tomorrow. Enjoy your dinner."

A brief moment of silence was followed by the sound of footsteps retreating back into the kitchen. As soon as the door closed behind them with a soft *thunk*, Lumi sagged. I stood up.

"Great," I sighed. "Now everyone wants to stab me."

Lumi peered into the entrance hall and removed her bag from her shoulder.

"Coast is still clear," she said before handing me the bag. "There's food in here. I'm going to grab some water for us, and I'll meet you upstairs." I nodded swiftly and crept from the room. The sun cast a deep orange glow across the marble floor of the entrance hall as I snuck up the stairs and pushed open the door to Lumi's room.

I couldn't help myself as I inhaled deeply and closed my eyes for a moment, letting her scent sweep over me. I flicked a hand towards the empty fireplace and excited flames jumped to life in the wood piled over the hearth. I placed her bag on the bed and turned around in a circle.

Bowstrings still littered the floor and a round sharpening stone sat on her nightstand. Dull swords were propped against the wall next to her small bookshelf, brimming with worn novels and small trinkets. Despite the gilded cage her father tried to keep her locked up in, her room was still so very much her that I couldn't help but smile.

Soft footsteps crept up the stairs behind me and I pressed myself against the wall out of sight. The door opened with a small *click* and Lumi entered before kicking it closed behind her. A large pitcher of water and a cup were clutched in her hands as she glanced around the room until she spotted me.

"Come on." She jerked her chin at the bed. "Let's eat." She handed me the cup and I took several satisfying gulps.

"Ah," I moaned, smacking my lips. "That's good. Thank you."

She opened her bag and threw me a loaf of bread as I plopped down next to her.

"I can't believe they haven't come home yet," Lumi muttered.

"Maybe they're avoiding you?" I suggested while tearing off a chunk of bread with my teeth.

"Maybe." Her shoulders sagged as she pulled another loaf of bread from her bag and began absentmindedly picking at the crust.

I paused mid-bite and eyed her carefully. "Are you sure you're okay?" I said.

Lumi blew out a breath and rubbed her palm over her eyes. Exhaustion was written all over her beautiful face. She glanced down at her other hand and flexed the fingers still stained with Killian's blood.

A shameless, feral pride roared in my chest at the sight, but I swallowed the feeling and focused intently on her face.

"I don't know..." Lumi looked up and blushed slightly. "I guess if I'm really honest with myself... I was really looking forward to a fight," she chuckled. "I was hoping to march in here with you and let my father have it. Show him that he can't keep me from you. Or Rowan. Show him that he can't decide my fate for me." She huffed. "He may have this entire village twisted around his fat little finger but I'm my own person. And after everything he did to you today..." She shook her head. "I was ready. But now I guess I have to wait."

My breath caught in my throat as she fixed those blue eyes on me.

"Well," I began, furrowing my brow. "Maybe that's not such a bad thing? I mean, is another fight *really* what you need right now? I know you're angry. I would be too. But maybe it's a good thing you can have some time to collect your thoughts." I shrugged and cocked a sly eyebrow at her. "That way you'll know exactly what you want to say and can absolutely tear him limb from limb."

She sighed and covered her face with her clean hand.

"I guess you're right. But I didn't mean a literal fight. I meant an argument."

"Well, all I'm saying is that I know your father is a very formidable man. After today, though," I said, "I'm more convinced than ever that you could take him in any kind of duel."

Her lips curled into a small smile.

I brought another piece of bread up to my lips right as she gasped and sat bolt upright. Her movement was so fast that I jumped and nearly threw my bread across the room in surprise.

"Hold on!" she hissed. "What do you mean you *would* be mad? You should be *furious* right now! He tried to have you killed today! Twice, in case you forgot! And is still actively trying!"

"True," I mused, tipping my head thoughtfully. "But I'm still breathing, thanks to you. And now I'm in his daughter's room— which is the absolute last place he wants me to be— and I'm eating his food so..." I trailed off with a grin and winked, drawing a weary chuckle out of her.

"Fair enough," she sighed.

I smiled broadly and took a large gulp of water to wash down the bread.

Lumi slipped off the bed and stood. "You get cleaned up first." She pointed to the washroom. I glanced at it before looking back at her, cocking an eyebrow.

"Are you trying to tell me that I smell?" I said.

Lumi pressed her lips together, wrinkling her nose in response.

I clutched my chest. "Oh, my poor, poor pride," I cried dramatically.

She rolled her eyes, and I couldn't help but laugh. "All right, fine. But just so you know I don't have anything to—"

My eyes fell to the floor as my thoughts crashed back to my shattered home.

"I'm sure my father has something," Lumi suggested. "Mother buys him so many new clothes, I doubt he'd notice anything that might be missing." I shot her an incredulous look.

"Lumi, your father is massive," I said flatly.

"Yeah, but he wasn't always. And my parents never throw anything out. They don't want anyone to have more than they do. Go get washed up and I'll be right back." She turned on her heel, disappearing out the door.

I ambled into the washroom and ran a scorching bath. Jasper had his luxurious home constructed with the absolute best of everything, including an intricate system of pipes that drew heated water from deep down near the thermal vents in the nearby volcano. And while every home in Haven had eventually been given this feature, Jasper's water somehow seemed to run warmer than anyone else's. And there was never a shortage of hot water for a nice long soak.

I took my time, savoring the heat on my aching muscles. Lumi had a wide variety of soaps, so I picked the one that looked like she'd used it the least. It smelled like a crackling fire and smoke. I scrubbed the suds deep into every inch of me, relishing the feeling for a moment before I ducked under the water, rinsed myself off, and hopped out.

I borrowed Lumi's comb to tame my long brown hair and was drying myself off when I heard the door open and shut quickly. I threw the towel around my waist and peeked out, grinning. Lumi waved frantically at me, her eyes wide with panic as the sound of feet crashing up the stairwell met my ears. Fear shot through me like lightning.

I dove under the bed. Lumi ran into the washroom just in time for the door to slam open.

"Lumi!" Jasper thundered.

My heart pounded as his broad boots stomped into view, followed closely by the clacking of Celeste's heels. I shrank back until my feet hit the wall behind the headboard.

"Lumi! Are you... Oh!" His feet turned sharply towards the window, embarrassment lacing his tone. He shifted and I saw Lumi's bare legs in the doorway to the washroom.

I blinked, my mouth going dry.

"Excuse me?" Lumi cried indignantly. "I'm trying to take a bath!"

Both of her parents were shifting their weight from foot to foot awkwardly, unsure of what to say next. I was painfully aware that the moment they peered under the bed, I'd officially be a dead man.

My foot slid up the wall, bracing to spring away when a slight breeze tickled my skin. I glanced back and saw that the massive headboard sat about a foot away from the wall. Lumi's pillows were so huge and fluffy, I hadn't noticed before.

A crazy, near impossible idea struck me. I slipped back to lay parallel to the headboard and reached up with a hand and a foot, grasping the top edge and hoisting myself up between it and the wall. The towel was still around my waist, caught between my knees and out of view from under the bed. I braced my other hand and foot on a small lip in the wood, holding myself out of sight and thanking every lucky star in the night sky that Lumi's bed was so monstrously huge.

"We—" Celeste stuttered. She cleared her throat and tried again. "We wanted to make sure you were all right." She stepped towards Lumi, who took a solid step backwards.

"I'm fine. Especially now that Lucia had a look at the bruise on my face from where father's friend punched me," Lumi spat.

"Someone hit you?" Celeste gasped in horror.

"Lumi," Jasper started in a low, concerned voice.

I took slow, silent breaths as my muscles started shaking with the effort it took to hold myself up between the wall and headboard.

"I don't want to hear it," Lumi spat. "Because it was nothing compared to what they did to Ash. They almost killed him. Lucia said that had I not been with him, he would've died in the snow."

A small slice of fear gripped my chest. Lucia hadn't told me that. Or let on that I was in that bad of shape. The pain had been blinding and I knew they were sent there to end my life, but I didn't realize they very nearly succeeded in actually killing me.

Jasper let out a growl of frustration. He must have opened his mouth to speak because Lumi cut him off.

"Don't you dare," she hissed, viciously. "Don't you dare say it. He's my friend. And I will never forgive you for what you've done to him." The floorboards creaked and I realized with a jolt that her parents were searching her room.

I squeezed my eyes shut and held my breath as Celeste's heels clicked near the bed. After a moment, I heard her voice from a place that was much too close for comfort.

"Nothing here," she sighed.

Celeste's heels clicked away, and a dizzying feeling of relief flooded my veins. Sweat trickled down my skin as my muscles started screaming in exhausted protest. A rustling sound filled the air. It sounded like someone was tearing through Lumi's wardrobe.

"Just what the fuck do you think you're doing?" Lumi snapped.

"Where is he?" Jasper demanded.

I grit my teeth, willing my breaths to stay even and silent.

Lumi scoffed. "You think I would tell you if I knew?"

"I have men watching Kaelin's and his little hole in the sand," Jasper snarled. "The two of you left Kaelin's together and he hasn't gone back to the beach. Which means you either brought that filth into my home or you know where he's hiding. Where is he, Lumi?"

"Fuck you," she replied.

Jasper made a quick move like he was headed towards her, and I tensed. My power slid through my blood, waiting to be unleashed. The floorboards creaked like Jasper was turning in a circle and scanning the room for any sign of me.

Panic squeezed the air from my lungs as I remembered my clothes piled on the washroom floor.

"Lumi," Celeste said in a firm tone. "That boy is dangerous. You have to end this nonsense right now and move on. Killian—"

Lumi let out a cruel laugh.

"What is that?" Jasper demanded.

"You know exactly what it is," Lumi seethed. "Maybe now he'll learn to keep his hands to himself."

"What have you done?" Jasper thundered.

"What he deserved!" Lumi screamed back. "I will not allow anyone to touch me like that without my permission. Ever! And the scar on that pig's arm will remind him every time he sees it!"

Jasper stomped toward the washroom.

"What are you going to do? Hit me? Go on then, *Father*," she shouted, spitting the word at him in disgust. "Do it. Leave a mark on my face and show everyone who you really are."

Her fearlessness amazed me as she faced down the most terrifying man I'd ever known. My fierce warrior queen.

"Lumi, that's enough," Celeste screeched.

"I will find that *thing*," Jasper hissed. The very air around the room seemed to quiver at his rage. "He can't hide from me forever. And once I do? You won't even recognize his face when I'm through with him."

I swallowed hard and held the headboard a little tighter.

"Is that so?" Lumi's voice was low and dangerous. "Well, it should be easy to find him. Because as many times as I fucked him today? I'll bet he still smells like me."

I nearly lost my grip on the headboard as my heart started hammering against my ribs. The heat surging through me had nothing to do with my powers as I struggled to keep my breathing even.

Jasper let out an angry sound, striding from the room and slamming the door behind him so hard that the window rattled.

"Lumi. Your father and I are just—" Celeste began, her tone severe. But Lumi was having none of it.

"I'm done talking," she said firmly. "Get out."

"You can't talk to—"

"Get out!" Lumi shouted. There was a long, tense silence.

"One day," Celeste said, "when you have your own children— when you're married and happy—you'll thank us. When that day comes, your father and I will accept your apology."

"Well, with any luck... Those children will have bright golden eyes," Lumi spat. "And long brown hair."

Celeste drew a sharp breath as though Lumi had struck her and sped from the room, shutting the door behind her without another word.

My breath caught in my throat as I listened to the footsteps retreating down the stairs. A soft rustling sound reached my ears, followed by a huff of disbelief.

"Ash?" Lumi whispered. "Where are you?"

The bed shifted and suddenly, light flooded into the space between the wall and headboard.

"Ash!" Lumi's face appeared at the edge of the mattress. "How are you doing that?"

"Panic," I grunted. I released my grip, letting myself drop gently to the floor and sliding out from under the bed. "Lots and lots of panic." I held the towel to make sure it still covered me as I stretched out on the floor and gulped in large mouthfuls of air.

My skin was slick with sweat. I pressed a hand on my heaving chest and looked up at her, arching an eyebrow as a faint smile crossed my lips.

"Why is it that," I said through ragged breaths, "every time we hang out... I end up in some... compromising position? Usually naked. Huh? Why is that?"

Lumi rolled her eyes and chuckled as she dropped some clothes onto my chest. I blushed and glanced at the ceiling, swallowing hard as Lumi hopped off the bed.

She was in only her undergarments. I tried to keep my gaze fixed on the ceiling above her head. I really did try. But I failed. My treacherous eyes dragged their way down and slowly back up her curved figure. My fingers twitched, desperate to touch that soft, exposed skin. Salacious urges filled my head, sending flashes of intense heat through my blood. I blinked and forced my gaze determinedly to her face as she turned to look at me.

"Stay quiet. I'm going to get cleaned up."

I nodded and forced my eyes frantically to the vaulted ceiling as she walked into the washroom and closed the door behind her.

My heart was still thundering in my chest like a war drum, and I blew out a breath, passing a shaky hand over my face. My mind reeled from what she spat at her parents. The thoughts her words had stirred up did nothing to help my pounding heart slow. I shook my head, shoving the images currently setting my blood on fire away as best I could.

I hopped up and used the towel to wipe the sweat off of my skin before I threw on the clothes Lumi had given me. They fit my body nicely, much to my surprise. I laid back down just in time to hear Jasper and Celeste screaming at each other. They screamed at every servant who crossed their path. Then they screamed at each other some more. Jasper kept referring to 'that creature,' which I assumed meant me. They were beginning to discuss putting up a bounty when Lumi came out of the washroom fully dressed and her hair twisted into a braid.

I pressed a finger to my lips, tapping my free hand against the floor. She cocked her head and listened to her parents arguing in the dining room below us.

"They've been screaming since they left," I whispered.

"What are they saying?" Lumi whispered back as she sat down on the bed.

"From what I could gather," I started, sitting up. "Your mother is livid you got hit. They are both pissed the farmers didn't manage to slit my throat. And they still want me dead, so that hasn't changed. A few people have gotten screamed at because they can't track me down. They're terrified I'm going to father their grandchild before they manage to kill me, which is incredibly insulting because I would make some damn cute babies," I joked.

Lumi blushed and looked away sharply.

"They also started discussing putting a bounty on my head," I sighed. "They haven't decided on anything yet, but from the sound of it... It's going to be a big one."

"I'm sorry," Lumi winced.

"For what? Oh..." I trailed off, grinning. "For what you said? No, I get it. Heat of the moment, right?"

"It was probably awkward for you to hear all that." Lumi rubbed her arm nervously.

I waved a dismissive hand and shook my head. "No. I understood what you were doing. And it worked. I've never heard him so mad before."

"I just," Lumi hesitated before continuing, "don't want to make you uncomfortable."

"Not at all," I grinned. "Don't worry about me."

She smiled meekly and patted the bed. I hauled myself up from the floor and plopped down next to her. Out of the corner of my eye, I noticed her watching my face carefully as though she were still looking for any sign of discomfort. So I looked over with mock seriousness.

"Well," I said, placing a hand on my chest. "I don't know about you, but all that sex today wore me out."

"Oh shut up," she grumbled, fighting to suppress a smile.

"Was I at least good?" I joked.

She laughed and shoved me lightly on the arm. Hearing her laugh was like seeing the sun come out.

"Oh, the absolute best I've ever had," she giggled. "I couldn't get enough."

"Yes," I hissed, pumping my fist in the air and she laughed harder.

"All right, all right. Knock it off," she said before, trailing off in a deep sigh. I looked out the window and saw thick clumps of snow falling past the glass.

"Guess I'm not going anywhere tonight." I jerked my chin at the window. She glanced over and frowned.

"Where else would you have gone?" she said, crawling up to stretch out on the bed. She looked back at me and patted the pillow next to her head. My breath hitched for a second as I obliged.

"Honestly?" I said, laying down next to her and lacing my hands behind my head. "Nowhere. I wasn't going to fight you this time."

"Good," she smiled lazily. "Life will be a whole lot easier once you accept that I'm right all the time."

I chuckled and sighed. "You're absolutely sure that your dad isn't going to miss these clothes?" I glanced down at her and she snorted.

"Not a chance," Lumi huffed. "They were stuffed so far back in his wardrobe that I doubt he even remembers they exist. They were wrapped around a bunch of Mother's jewels and an old book. And I have never seen that man read anything. Ever. So, I think we are fine."

"What does someone like your father even read about anyways?"

"No clue," Lumi shrugged. "It's a big purple book. That's all I saw."

"Very descriptive," I chuckled.

"Well excuse me." Lumi shoved me playfully. "I was a little too busy trying to make sure you didn't get caught naked in my room by the man trying to kill you."

I sighed and rolled my eyes.

"Guess I really can't say no to Rowan now, can I?" I said quietly.

"No, you can't." She watched my face carefully. "What other choice do you have, Ash?" I swallowed hard.

A trade ship flashed, unbidden, across my mind. I sighed through my nose and looked over. Those gorgeous blue eyes were all too easy to get lost in.

"None," I breathed, looking away. I hoped Lumi wouldn't hear my traitorous heart pounding against my ribs. "At least I can travel light." My face fell as I remembered the shattered remains of my father's treasure box scattered across the sand.

A weight settled on my shoulder, and I glanced down. Lumi had placed her head there. She splayed a hand out over my chest, and I wrapped an arm around her back, pulling her in close to my side.

"I'm so sorry, Ash," she whispered.

"I'll be okay."

"Maybe we could go back tomorrow and try to salvage something?"

"Nah," I sighed, running a hand through my damp hair. "There were bad memories attached to some of that stuff. And it's not like—" I cut myself off, unwilling to let the dark memories come flooding to the surface. My breath caught in my throat, and I swallowed hard, fixing my eyes on the canopy above the bed.

"Like?" Lumi whispered. I glanced at her, sadly.

"The life I had before you and Ro isn't something I want to remember," I said. "And some of those things... I kept them because they were all I had. But they were a constant reminder of my parents and all the parts of my life I wish more than anything I could erase from my head."

The memories slipped dangerously close, so I refocused my thoughts on Lumi. I let myself dwell on the feeling of her warm body pressed tightly against my side.

She drew in a sharp breath, and I glanced at her. I could practically see the questions swirling in her mind. But she hesitated.

Watching her face as she struggled to find the words she wanted to say, I was suddenly struck with how close we were. I could count her long eyelashes and the freckles peppering her cheeks. She gazed up at me with those startlingly blue eyes, and my mind went utterly blank. My heart felt like it might beat its way out of my chest.

"Um... Ash..." Lumi whispered nervously. "What happened to your parents?" I blinked, struggling to force my brain to focus.

"Huh?"

"It's just... In all the years I've known you, you've never even mentioned them," she mumbled quickly. My face fell ever so slightly, and I sighed. But before I could answer her question, she looked away, sucking in a wavering breath. “I’m sorry. We don’t have to talk about this.” Tears sparkled in the corners of her eyes.

“What? No. Don’t be sorry. I’m actually kind of surprised it took this long for you or Ro to ask.”

“We didn’t want to hurt you,” she sniffed. “You look so unhappy any time your past comes up.”

“There’s very little you or Ro could do that would hurt me,” I said quietly. She blinked hard as I rolled and wrapped both arms around her, pulling her against my chest. “But… It’s, ah… It’s not a particularly good bedtime story,” I admitted.

Lumi pressed her head into my chest, soaking up my warmth.

“I promise I will tell you. Just… not tonight. Okay?” I said.

Having her pressed in tight was something I wanted to cherish. I didn’t want to ruin this moment by summoning up the ghosts of the past.

Lumi nodded with a deep sigh. Her breath skittered across my neck.

“Do you know any good bedtime stories?” she joked. I smiled and propped my chin on her head.

“I do actually. It was one of my favorites growing up. Kaelin tells it better though.”

Lumi sidled impossibly closer, and I suppressed a shudder.

“So,” I began. “There was this princess. She held a dangerous and awesome magic. One that let her transform into a powerful black dragon. The dragons ruled a magical land. But the Phoenix Emperor and the Fae King got together and decided they wanted the dragon’s kingdom for themselves. And so…”

Lumi’s body settled against mine, her breathing deepening as I told her about the adventures of Ada, the dragon princess and her best friend Milo, the unicorn warrior. I talked and talked until she shifted, and I caught sight of her gorgeous face. She was sound asleep, cuddled as close to me as she could get.

I lay there for a long while, holding her close. She’d saved my life. In the span of a short few hours, she’d saved me from freezing to death, from being murdered, from dying in the snow after I was beaten within an inch of my life, and from her father’s rage. My fierce warrior queen and my salvation so many times over.

She inched even closer, wrapping an arm around my waist with a deep, content sigh. I could feel her heart beating against me as her fingers sleepily trailed across my back.

I thought about the blood that had stained those fingers and anger flashed through me.

Rowan should've let me kill him that night.

We'd been stargazing on the steps of Rowan's house while he was inside making us something for dinner that he'd learned about from the book he was reading at the time. He had yelped and we'd stepped inside to check on him. Lumi had left her drink on the railing. We'd come back and, after one sip, she started shivering violently and said she felt like she was about to puke. I'd wrapped my coat around her and jumped up to get her a blanket, mentioning to Ro what was happening on my way back through the house. Ro had frowned and raced outside to check on her. But she was gone.

He found them in the alleyway.

Killian had apparently planned to get caught and playing it off like we discovered them about to begin. But Lumi was fighting him off with everything she still had. Whatever he'd tried to drug her with hadn't been strong enough. By the time I found them, Rowan had cracked Killian across the head with the scalding hot pan still in his hand.

I've never felt a boiling rage like I did that day. Rowan helped an unsteady Lumi to her feet and brought her back to the house. As he passed, he'd locked eyes with me and patted me once on the chest before he stepped away, leaving me alone with a cowering Killian.

I lifted my hand and examined a long thin scar running across the back of my knuckles. A worthwhile souvenir of what I'd done that night.

Rowan had returned, watching for a long while before putting a hand on my wrist to stop me. He fished the bottle of whatever it was that Killian had used on Lumi out of the sniveling coward's pocket and kept it, with the promise of handing it over to Jasper should he ever come sniffing again. I'd delivered one last blow and we'd left what remained of Killian there in the snow.

Despite my seething hatred, I never touched my power that night. His burned remains would've raised too many questions and brought trouble down on Kaelin and Lucia's head. But because I didn't summon my fire, Killian was now the only person in Haven who believed I was powerless. He once sneered at me that he knew what everyone else didn't. And that I may have everyone else fooled into thinking I was a dangerous Cosmic, but he knew the truth about me. I didn't bother to correct him.

My mind flashed back to the memory of him twisting her arm until she winced, and I ground my teeth together furiously.

Next time, I promised myself. Next time, I'd unleash it all and damn the consequences. I was going to make sure he never touched her against her will ever again.

Lumi frowned in her sleep and rolled, pressing her back into my chest. I realized my body was tense and blew out a breath, shoving the angry thoughts away and settling into the softness of her pillow.

I tried to move away a bit, but she caught my wrist and tugged me closer, wrapping me around her tightly. Her legs tangled with mine and she slipped her head back under my chin, soaking in as much of my warmth as she could. She hummed in contentment and snuggled into me.

The smell of her hair filled my nose and I smiled, letting myself relax into the mattress. It was hard to be upset about anything when Lumi was safely in my arms. I sighed, clutching my warrior queen to me, and wishing with all of my soul that I could stay like this forever. Even though I knew I couldn't. In the morning, I would have to find a way to get to Rowan's house without being seen by the people out looking for me. Until then, I let myself savor the moment and drifted off, holding the woman I loved close to my heart and pretending that she was mine.

CHAPTER ELEVEN

LUMI

A sudden gasp and shouting startled me awake. Ash's arms were ripped away from me. He was hoisted up into the air, his legs swinging wildly as he was slammed into the wall.

I looked up in horror as my father gripped the front of Ash's tunic.

He kicked and flailed against my father's iron grip. When that failed, he reached out a hand. Fire sparked at the ends of his fingertips, but it sputtered and died swiftly.

I went to jump up and help, but my hands were tangled in the blankets on the bed. I tried to yank them free, but the harder I pulled, the more tangled in blankets I became.

I cried out in terror as my father reached for the dagger in his belt. The razor-sharp blade glinted wickedly. I lunged, but the sheets had wound their way around my waist.

My father glanced back at me with a cold expression before he drove the dagger through Ash's chest. Blood seeped into the fabric of his tunic, spilling onto the floor. My father wrenched the dagger out and rammed it into Ash's stomach.

His body sagged as my father repeatedly punctured his flesh. Over and over and over. Ash took one last shuddering breath, whispering my name before the light died in his eyes and they lost focus.

A dull roar filled my ears. I sobbed, helpless, and screamed.

My father released Ash's body. It slid down the wall before slumping into an unmoving heap.

"Lumi."

I struggled to break free of the sheets as my father drew closer, calling my name softly. Blood dripped from his dagger, splashing on the floor.

"Lumi. Lumi. Lumi."

"Lumi, wake up."

I cried out, my eyes flying open in a panic. Dazzling sunlight blinded me. My heart was racing, and I struggled to take in air against the panic tightening around my chest like an iron band. I tried to sit up, but something strong had wound itself around my stomach to hold me down.

"Easy." Ash's deep voice brushed against my ear. "Breathe, Lumi. Just breathe for me."

I stilled at the sound of his voice and took in a long breath. Ash's arms were wrapped around me, and my back was pressed into his chest. Sharp relief filled me as I felt his heart beating near my shoulder.

Ash yawned, his languid breath trailing across my neck, and shifted slightly to hold me just a bit tighter. "I've got you," he murmured sleepily.

I let out a small sob and buried my face in my hands. The image of his blood splattered on the floor had burned itself into my mind. I rubbed my eyes vigorously, blinking away the nightmare and squinting at the bright sunlight filling my room.

Ash sighed deeply, pulling me a little closer. I laid there for a few moments, clutching his wrists, and letting the sound of his steady breathing calm the swirling terror.

"Are you okay?" Ash whispered drowsily.

"I think so."

"Said my name," he said through another yawn. "A lot."

"He killed you. And... and I couldn't..." My voice cracked. He stilled for a moment, his breath catching in his throat.

"I'm okay," Ash murmured. After another few moments, he released his hold on my waist. "Sorry. You were flailing around, and I didn't want to get hit in the face."

"It's okay," I said, reluctantly letting go of his wrists as I sat up. Ash flopped onto his back and stretched his arm across his face to block out the light.

"You keep letting me sleep in a bed like this and I'm going to get spoiled." His voice was deep and gravelly from sleep. His lips curved into a drowsy smile.

"Well, luckily Rowan's bed is just as comfortable as mine," I said, standing up to stretch.

"I bet he's an awesome cuddler," Ash chuckled and rubbed the sleep from his eyes as he sat up and crossed his long legs underneath him. His hair stuck up at odd angles and his clothes were heavily wrinkled from sleeping in them. "In all seriousness though." He looked up at me awkwardly, wringing his hands in his lap. His golden eyes seemed to glow in the bright morning light. "I didn't... me being here last night... I don't want to make you uncomfortable." He rubbed the back of his neck, blushing.

I rolled my eyes. "Ash..."

"I know. I know. I just don't want you to feel like I'm crossing a line."

"You're not," I replied. The sincerity in his eyes made my heart flutter strangely. "You know me better than that. I'd tell you if I was uncomfortable."

"I just don't want to do anything to lose you. You're my *best friend*." Ash's voice wavered slightly on the last two words.

"And you won't," I reassured him. "Besides, if you're here with me, then I know you're safe and warm. I sleep a lot better when I know you'll still be alive in the morning," I added, smiling. He ran both hands through his hair.

"Lumi, I don't deserve you." He turned his gaze to the fire, his expression unreadable. Something dark and sorrowful laced his tone and I felt the sudden urge to hold him.

A noise from downstairs caught my attention. Ash heard it too, cocking his head to the side.

Voices—lots of them—mingled into an unintelligible hum as people streamed through the entrance hall below. I glanced at Ash before crossing the room and pulling the door open slowly. A cacophony of shouts and yells blasted through the thin opening.

"What's going on?" Ash whispered. I shrugged and was about to step out when I felt his hand on my arm.

"It sounds like every farmer in the village is down there," he hissed. He darted back into the room and snatched his boots from the floor.

"What are you doing?"

"It sounds like all your father's cronies are downstairs instead of out looking for me. This might be my only shot at getting to Rowan's. I'll meet you there, okay?" He threw his coat onto his shoulders and headed for the window.

"Okay." Worry gnawed at me. I threw my hair up into a bun as Ash pulled the window open. "Just... promise me you'll be careful." My heart lurched and a strange feeling twisted around my stomach as he looked back at me.

His bright smile was dazzling in the morning light. Mischievous and carefree, like nothing bad had ever happened to him. The sun streaming through the window caught his handsome face and made his eyes glow like molten gold.

My cheeks heated as he hitched one foot out the window and braced himself against the sill.

"I promise," he said, his smile widening. He turned and slipped out the window, disappearing from sight. I darted over and closed the window quietly before leaning my forehead against the icy glass. He climbed down the side of the house, peering around to ensure no one was near before dropping to the ground and dashing out of sight.

I watched for a few seconds, breathing a sigh of relief when no one appeared from the shadows to charge after him.

My mind reeled and I pressed my hand to my chest, startled to find my heart was pounding.

In all our years of friendship, Ash had smiled at me at least a million times. But this swirling feeling inside me was new and confusing. I could still feel his arms wrapped tightly around me. I could still smell him in my hair. I pushed away from the window and strode across the room, shaking my head to clear it.

What was happening to me? I shoved the strange feelings away and left, closing the door swiftly behind me.

The myriad of voices bouncing off the walls was overwhelming as I descended the stairwell. Farmers were packed tightly together in the entrance hall, chattering anxiously. I took in all the collected bodies, each one clad in a heavy coat and thick boots. Many of them had large empty sacks slung on their backs.

I spotted Killian sulking near the door. His arm was wrapped in bandages and bound to his side by a sling. A few feet away from him were the men that had attacked me and Ash. Their heads were bent close together, whispering and glancing around at the growing crowd that pressed in on them. A surge of vindictive triumph swelled in my heart at the sight of the bruises on their faces. I had only made it halfway down the stairs when the dining room door swung open.

My parents emerged, dressed in heavy winter gear. Mother noticed me on the stairs and frowned.

"Listen up!" Father boomed over the crowd.

Silence fell at once. A servant pulled out one of the dining room chairs and placed it in front of my father. He stood on it, towering over everyone like a king addressing his court.

"I've already received some reports from town square that they've arrived and are in bad shape. We'll split up into four groups."

I crept to the bottom of the stairs and slipped through the crowd as covertly as I could, my curiosity outweighing my desire to get away from my parents.

Father cleared his throat and pointed to the far corner of the room. "You all will go with Ovi to the eastern caverns. Over here, with Jasmine to the western caves. Over here, with Celeste to the central system. The rest of you come with me to the lower caves! Once there, we will give you your crop assignments. If you're harvesting, get the crops to the runners as fast as you can. Runners. As soon as your carts are full, you go. These people are starving. Pull up as much as you can and replace as you go! With any luck, we will have enough. Let's go!"

The room instantly came alive in a flurry of movement. I tried to step out of the way and stumbled backwards, colliding with something solid. Large, calloused hands gripped my shoulders and prevented me from being knocked off my feet as the farmers shoved their way past on their way out into the snow.

"Whoa there, little lady. Careful or you might get trampled!"

I cringed at the sound of the gravelly voice behind me.

"Hello, Lumi," Killian's father said in my ear. "I need to have a word with you."

I stiffened and turned to face Oleander. Ovi, as my father had always called him, was a sturdy wall of muscle with gray hair and a slightly crooked nose. His kind brown eyes were fixed on me with a penetrating stare.

My mother sidled up to us and crossed her arms, frowning at me.

"Hi, Ovi," I said weakly. He frowned, glancing down at my mother with raised eyebrows.

"I was just telling your mother about how Lucia was able to save Killian's arm." He arched a bushy eyebrow at me. I swallowed and said nothing.

"Quite the wound you gave him," Ovi continued. "Lucia said the dagger must have gone all the way through."

"Ovi, I assure you," Mother said, snatching me by the wrist. "She will beg for his forgiveness right this instant."

I blanched and opened my mouth to argue but Ovi shook his head and pulled my hand from her grip.

"She will absolutely not apologize to him," he replied firmly.

Mother blinked and took a step back. A few people nearby glanced in our direction before hurrying off.

"What do you mean?" Mother said, flabbergasted.

"I mean, no. She will not be apologizing to him. In fact," he turned back to me," I would like to sincerely apologize, Lumi."

My mother sputtered in surprise, but he held up a hand to silence her.

"I hadn't gotten to tell your mother why you stabbed him. And rightfully so."

Utter and complete shock jolted through me. I pressed my lips together and waited.

"I had stepped away for a moment in the market. He'd come with me because he said he was looking for you. I returned and found him touching you in a way that was very disappointing. I was going to handle the situation, but you took care of it for me. I was appalled when he grabbed your... Well... I am so embarrassed." He blushed before continuing. "I didn't think his behavior could get any worse than that. But when I brought him to Lucia and explained what happened, she off-handedly mentioned something disturbing. I want to know if it's true and I'd like for you to be honest with me."

I knew exactly what he was talking about and nodded, bracing for what he was about to say. Ovi drew in a deep breath. "She mentioned that the last time she treated Killian for an injury, she also had to treat you the night before. For... something put in your drink." He raised his eyebrows at me, and I nodded once. Ovi's face fell.

"I'm so sorry, Lumi. I am so disgusted. Please know that my son will never bother you again. I thought I raised my boy better than that. I've made it clear to him that his actions are an embarrassment. I value your family's friendship too much to tolerate him touching you like that." The pain that flickered across his face made my breath catch.

"I don't hold his actions against you, sir. I know you too well," I added with a smile. He returned the grin and clapped me gently on the shoulder.

"As I said, he's not going to bother you any further. You should have seen his mother's reaction. I don't think he'll ever stop sulking." He chuckled and shot a glance at the stocky woman talking to my father. "I do have one last question, and I'd like you to answer this one honestly as well," he said, shifting his weight between his feet. "Your ah... *friend*... was very angry."

He gave me a meaningful look and I knew what he meant. I shook my head.

"He won't do anything. Not unless I ask him to," I replied.

"Ah. Well, thank you for not asking," he said, relieved. "Despite his awful behavior, I would like to keep him around. See if I can't turn him into someone respectful. But I will speak to your father and put an end to this engagement. Which, by the way…" Ovi turned to my mother angrily. "I was under the impression both Killian *and* Lumi wanted to be married."

My mother's eyes filled with horrified tears as she finally realized I'd been telling the truth.

I fought to keep the triumph from crossing my face as I looked back at Ovi.

"Thank you, sir. And no, I do not want to marry him. But for what it's worth, I would've at least liked being your daughter in law."

He smiled kindly at me.

"I appreciate that. Now, Celeste," he said, grasping my mother by the elbow. She looked up at him, her face still stuck in a horrified expression. "We're going to have a chat with Jasper. Come now." He led her away.

Elation filled my chest. The entrance hall had all but emptied as I turned and bounded back up the stairs to my room.

I grabbed my things and got ready as quickly as possible, fearing that my parents would come looking for me. For what, I wasn't entirely sure. But whether it was to apologize or to scream at me, I didn't care. I would deal with them later.

I leaned over to pull on my boots and caught the rich scent of fire and smoke coming from the pillow next to me. I straightened my back and frowned at it as the strange fluttering feeling twisted my stomach again.

A dark brown strand of hair was curled on the pillow, and I picked it up, rolling it against my palm. My mind drifted and I found myself wondering what running my fingers through his hair would feel like. What it would be like to pull his head back and expose the strong column of his throat. I could run my fingers down it to his chest and—

I sucked in a breath and dropped the hair on the floor, mortified. His smile flashed before my eyes, and I shook myself physically and mentally.

"Stop it, Lumi," I scolded myself. "What's going on with you?" I forced my mind back on track as I rushed to finish preparing for the day.

I threw my belt on and ran a finger on the hilt of the dagger concealed in my boot, ensuring it was tucked safely away where it should be. Frost Breaker bounced off my leg as I departed from the room.

I raced down the stairs and practically flew through the entrance hall. Someone called my name in a firm tone, but I continued out the door and dashed down the drive, hurtling through the gate before whoever it was could catch me. The guards on the wall jeered at me as I streaked by, running full tilt down the icy road. Villagers raced by in a blur of faceless shadows as I shot past.

"Whoa! Lumi!"

I stumbled to a halt, panting as I looked around for whoever flagged me down. Anni stood in front of her shop, bundled up in a large black coat. She locked her front door and stepped into the snow.

"What's the rush?" She cocked an eyebrow at me.

"I—" I stopped short and frowned. It was only then that I realized I had no idea why I was running.

"What? Did your little boy toy steal something from you?" Anni chuckled and shoved her broad hands into her pockets.

"Boy toy?" I stammered, my heart twinging with fear.

"Yeah," she said as she strolled down the road towards the town square.

I jogged over to her side and slowed, matching her pace.

"The gorgeous one with the dark hair I always see you with. The one everyone is terrified of for some reason. He went flying by here a little bit ago." She met my eyes and I gulped.

"Was he alone?" I asked tentatively. Suddenly, I realized exactly why I'd been running.

"He's not cheating on you, is he?" Anni shot me a sharp look.

"It's not like that. He's just a friend."

She gave me an incredulous glance.

"Honest," I added. "My father doesn't like him, though..."

"I gotcha." Anni looked down and nodded lightly in understanding. "In that case, then yeah. He was alone."

I huffed out a long breath, relieved.

"Good."

"Can I ask you something?" she asked, furrowing her brow. "Why are people so afraid of him? I've never seen him so much as raise his voice, but everyone dodges around him like he's a fire-breathing monster."

"Because my father told them to be," I replied in a low tone. "Among other things."

We passed a group of anxious people who were all holding pots and plates heaped with food. A man standing in the center of them was barking out instructions.

"I'm sure you already heard what happened," I said quietly.

"That Tom and his boys almost beat him to death or that you drove your shiny new dagger through a certain little asshole's arm?" Anni smirked.

"Oh... Well..." I wrung my hands and paled.

Anni chuckled. "At least now I know why I got so much business last night. Oh yes..." she added, noting my bewildered expression. "I had ten women come in wanting daggers for self-defense. So, thanks for that. I'm honestly surprised nobody has stabbed that little prick before now."

"I can't say I regret it, but I probably shouldn't have stabbed him," I said, wrinkling my nose at the thought of him.

"Yes, you should have," she replied, glancing behind us. "Looks like he's headed in the same direction."

I blanched and looked back. Killian stood at the side of the road, scanning the crowd. I yanked my hood up and whipped back around.

Anni glanced at him in disgust. "Want me to punch him for you?"

"I'm very tempted to say yes to that," I replied grimly.

We rounded the corner into the town square, and I gaped at the chaotic scene before me.

Anni turned and patted me on the shoulder. "I have to go help. See you later, Lumi."

I nodded vaguely as she strode off.

The town square was packed with at least three hundred terrified people. They were all filthy, exhausted, and had the same hollow look in their eyes. Children clung to their parents as if they were adrift at sea. Somewhere in the crowd, a baby wailed inconsolably.

Several of Haven's villagers waded through the petrified newcomers, handing out food, soap, and blankets, among other things. The rest of them were collecting the newcomers' meager possessions and loading them onto a cart nearby. My father would have his goons search through them as soon as they were done in the caves. My eyes darted from face to terrified face until I spotted one I recognized well.

Lucia knelt before a small boy who had deep gashes in his cheek and arm.

The little boy watched me approach, his eyes wide with terror. I smiled and held my hands up harmlessly.

Lucia turned and nodded grimly to me. "Hello, love," she said. Her usually vibrant eyes were dim from exhaustion.

"What happened?" I whispered.

Lucia stood and patted the boy reassuringly on the shoulder. She reached into her pocket and withdrew a small vial of bubbling water, handing it to his parents.

"Rub this on the area gently to clean it. It will dull the pain and start the healing process."

The parents nodded but were clearly dazed from whatever they'd experienced. They clung to the injured boy who had started crying silently.

Lucia pulled me along with her until we were out of earshot.

"Winter claimed another town in the north," she said tersely. "They have been traveling for days. They were hit with three blizzards. And when her storms didn't get them all, Winter sent her ice demons after them."

I looked back at the boy huddled against his mother. Nausea rose in my stomach as my mind flashed to the snarling beast that had climbed over the wall. For a child to face that...

"This," Lucia whispered, gesturing to the huddled mass around us. "Is all that made it here. They started off with two thousand."

"Two thousand?" I gasped looking around. The crowd suddenly seemed so tiny. "Is there anything I can do to help?"

"No, you go on to the house," she said, nodding her head behind me. "There's someone here that has been looking for you."

I turned and spotted the back of Killian's head. He was still scanning the crowd, adjusting the strap of the white sling holding his arm higher onto his shoulder. I glared and, for one wild moment, I wished the earth would split open and swallow him whole.

"I already had to stop Ash from lighting him on fire today," Lucia sighed. "Go. Rowan is waiting for you."

"Are you sure?" I tore my eyes from Killian and took a small step back, ignoring how my heart did a quick flip at the sound of Ash's name.

"Go on, love. I'll see you later." Lucia smiled and turned back towards the injured little boy.

I looked around at the terrified refugees for a moment. My heart felt like it was being wrenched from my chest. These people had lost so much in so little time. It was a miracle they'd made it at all.

Killian moved in the corner of my eye, and I looked over. He had spotted me and was trying to maneuver his way through the crowd.

I turned, shot him a quick glare, and dashed away.

CHAPTER TWELVE

ROWAN

I watched from the window as Lumi came dashing up to the front door, glancing behind her. I grinned maniacally and raced over, flinging the door open before she could knock.

She stumbled back a step at my sudden appearance.

"Fuck!" she hissed, clutching her chest. "You scared the shit out of me!" I grabbed her arm and pulled her into the house, slamming the door behind her.

"She's here!" I called over my shoulder.

Ash looked up from the large black coat he was buttoning.

"Finally," he winked. "I thought Ro was going to pace a rut in the floor."

I rolled my eyes at him and turned to face Lumi, practically vibrating with excitement. She glanced between us, taking in our thick coats and heavy winter boots, before looking at the wall where three large bags were packed and waiting. Nearby was another pair of boots and my mother's heavy purple coat.

"What's going on?" Lumi asked.

"Last night I was thinking about what my father told us about the spirits. I was curious, so Father gave me this."

I reached into my pocket and took out a small black book.

"It's a journal he kept while he worked for Lord Spring at Nature's Palace." I flipped to the page depicting a hand drawn layout of the castle and shoved the book under her nose, tapping the page with my index finger.

She peered down at it before looking back up at me.

"A storeroom?" Lumi tilted her head, puzzled.

"You saw the refugees, right?" I asked.

She nodded, her eyes clouding with worry. "My parents brought all the farmers into the caves to gather what food they could. But I don't know if there's enough to go around."

"I think I found a solution for that." I tapped the book with my fingertip again. "Father said this storeroom was always full of food. No one's been brave enough to go up to the palace in ages, so chances are there's something there we can salvage to feed everyone." She frowned and met my eyes incredulously.

"Ro, it's been twenty years. If there's anything there, I doubt it would still be edible."

"Normally, I'd agree with you," I said, rapidly flipping through the pages. "But look here. Lord Spring told Father about an enchantment that was placed on the palace by the Ethereal Two. It kept the temperature perfect, and the food stored inside permanently fresh. Father says in this passage here that all of the enchantments on the palace are tied to the heralds. And since Winter is still alive—"

"That enchantment might still be in place too!" she exclaimed, understanding crossing her face.

"Exactly!" I said, shutting the book. "The three of us can go check it out. And even if there's no food, there might be something else we can salvage."

"It's worth a shot," Ash threw in. Lumi nodded and reached for the purple coat.

"What's with the bags? We shouldn't be gone that long," she asked.

"You never know. I packed for whatever I could think of, just in case," I replied, shrugging. "I have food, a map of the Fire Mountains, supplies for in case we get snowed in. And a bunch of other stuff."

She looked back at the bags and nodded, impressed.

"Well, all right then. Let's go!" Lumi grinned. She looked around, pulling the heavy coat on over her own. "Where's your father?"

"He went to see if he can help with the refugees," I said, my smile faltering. "I heard him and Mother talking this morning. Were there a lot of people?"

"No, not really," Lumi replied quietly. Sadness filled her blue eyes. "They started with two thousand people. Only three hundred made it here."

"That's still three hundred more than Haven's food supply was ready for," I said, helping Ash slide his bag onto his back.

"How much food do you think might be up there?" Lumi asked. She leaned over and attached her bow and quiver to her bag. Ash helped her pull the bag up over her shoulders and she tugged a wool cap low over her ears, stuffing her raven hair up into the back.

"I have no idea," I replied, tossing a cap to Ash. "I asked Father about it, and he said the store room was always full. So hopefully quite a bit."

Ash helped me pull the last bag onto my back before he turned and looked out the window.

"Looks like a blizzard followed them here," he said. "We'd better get moving before it starts coming down again."

I bounced on the balls of my feet, unable to contain my excitement. I'd read so many adventurous stories in my life. My nerves buzzed at the idea of embarking on one of my very own. I flung the door open wide and whirled around to face my friends.

"We'll be there and back before the blizzard hits. Now, come on guys!" I said dramatically, pulling my knit cap down over my riot of red curls. "Let's go on an adventure!"

They smirked at each other and followed as I bounded out into the sunshine. We passed crowds of villagers clogging the road, all headed in the opposite direction to lend a helping hand to the refugees.

Everyone seemed too preoccupied to even hiss and curse at Ash, but we decided not to push our luck anyway. We ducked into the alleyway and made our way quickly to the outer edge of the village. The border wall stretched high above us, and we slipped along its shadow.

"We have to be careful," Lumi whispered over her shoulder. "If the guards spot us, they'll stop us from leaving."

She trailed a hand along the stone as she walked, keeping her eyes on the guard post closest to the gate. The sun vanished behind a cloud and the sky turned an ominous shade of gray. Lumi held up her hand and pressed her side against the wall. We stopped, straining our ears to hear the voices spilling over the edge of the guard post.

"Damn, it's cold out here," a male voice grumbled. "I need to step in for a second. Come on."

"We're not supposed to leave our post. Especially not after what happened yesterday," a second, much younger voice said.

"Demons don't come from the mountains," the first voice snorted.

"That's not what I've heard," the younger voice replied defensively. "What about the demon that used to fly over town?"

"That demon wasn't real. Just nervous people out too late at night. And even if it was real, it hasn't been seen in at least twelve years. Come on. Your nose is turning blue."

There was a heavy sigh, followed by the sound of a door opening and closing.

Lumi stepped from the shadows and craned her neck to get a better view into the guard post.

"Clear," she whispered.

We scurried along the wall, pausing only when we arrived at the large iron gate. It stretched halfway up the structure, ending in a point high above our heads. Lumi glanced back at the post to be sure the guards had not returned, gripping the large handle with both hands.

"We have to go fast," she said. "See the rust on the hinges? It's going to be really loud." She threw her weight against the handle. The door jerked slightly, but it stayed closed. She threw her body against the gate again, but it still didn't open.

"What's wrong?" I whispered.

"Shit," she hissed. "Hold on." She dropped her pack and threw everything she had at the door. But it still refused to budge. "It's frozen solid. I can't get it to move! I'm not strong enough."

"Here," Ash said, stepping around me. He stood directly behind Lumi and braced his hands on either side of hers. She blinked, heat filling her pale face. I pressed my lips together to suppress a wicked smile. I'd seen that look on Ash's face so many times before. But I'd never seen it on Lumi's. This was new. And very, very interesting. She bit her lip and swallowed hard as he adjusted his grip around hers, practically cradling her in his arms.

I glanced at Ash to see if he noticed her reaction, but he was too busy focusing on the handle to see the color growing in her cheeks.

"Ready?" Ash said.

Lumi nodded once. She glanced over at me as I arched an eyebrow, not bothering to hide the smirk on my face anymore. She frowned and looked away quickly.

"Okay," Ash braced his body against Lumi's back and the brilliant red flush crept down her neck. "On the count of three. One... two... three!"

Together, they shoved downward. The ice freezing the hinges shattered under the strain of their combined weight. The gate cracked open, and they stumbled backwards. Ash dropped, landing hard on his ass. Lumi swayed slightly and flailed her arms in an attempt to catch her balance before she fell straight into Ash's lap.

"Oh! Oh no!" Lumi gasped, whipping around to face him. "Did I hurt you?"

"I'm okay," he said, wincing. "Are you all right?"

"I'm fine," she replied. They stared at each other for a beat and the air between them was suddenly charged with delicious tension. My smirk grew wider as I stepped over their tangled legs and took hold of the gate.

"Do you two need a minute?" I teased.

They jumped and looked away from each other, both blushing profusely and rushing to their feet.

I suppressed a snicker as he helped her slide her pack onto her shoulders again before releasing her quickly and stepping away. They avoided looking at each other and sidled up on either side of me.

My hopeless romantic soul sang with glee. I could see the story unfolding as if it were on the pages of a book. Part of me wanted to press the issue, but this development might be too new. The last thing I wanted to do was push so much that I frightened off whatever was brewing between them.

Besides, we still had a quest to complete.

A horrid metallic screech split the air as I yanked the gate open, and we piled through it. I rammed the gate closed behind us and we dashed away. The shouts of the guards followed us as we sprinted up the pass.

We stopped running as we rounded a corner and entered the outermost range of the Fire Mountains, each of us panting and clutching our chests. The thermal caves were barely visible in the distance to our left. A group of farmers came rushing out, each one pushing a cart filled with crops from the underground fields. Lumi followed my stare and frowned.

"We have to hurry," she said, glancing back down the road behind us. "If those guards saw my face, they'll tell my parents, and my father will send someone after us."

"Which will be especially true if they saw me with you," Ash said.

I raised my eyebrows at him.

"Oh, there's a bounty on my head now," Ash explained, chuckling. "I don't know how much but I'm sure it's a good one."

"Really?" I glanced between his easy smile and Lumi's thunderous expression. "What did you do this time?" I joked.

"Her," he shrugged, jerking his chin at Lumi. I stumbled a few feet and whirled around in shock. Ash broke out in a loud, cackling laughter while Lumi pinched the bridge of her nose with a groan.

"I got mad," Lumi sighed, shooting Ash an annoyed look that only made him laugh harder. "My father was threatening to find Ash and kill him. So, I said he could follow my scent because Ash and I had spent the day fucking.

And then I..." She trailed off with a huff, embarrassed. "I may have implied I was trying to have Ash's baby." Her voice dropped to barely above a whisper as she stared hard at the snowdrifts lining the road.

"So now," Ash said, still laughing, "Jasper is trying to murder me before I give him the most adorable grandchild ever." He winked at Lumi, who's whole face turned red.

For a moment, I could've sworn I saw a look of acute longing written across Lumi's face. The same look I'd caught Ash giving her for years.

"You should've seen him, Ro," Ash continued. He was grinning at me, totally oblivious to the way Lumi had just looked at him. "He was livid."

We reached a fork in the road. I paused and consulted the hand drawn maps in my father's journal.

"So why did your father draw all these maps?" Ash gestured to the book in my hands.

"He made them for Mother," I replied. "She was so busy with her medical apprenticeship, she rarely got to come up this way and visit him. So he documented everything for her when he had to be away."

"That's adorable," Ash chuckled. I nodded in agreement.

"Right? I wish I had someone like that. Now let's see... We need to go that way."

I pointed towards a sharp incline. The path was difficult to make out thanks to the many years of snow obscuring the landscape. Large boulders lined the pass on either side and acted as a barrier between the road and the precarious slope beyond.

"That's quite a climb," Lumi said, trailing her eyes along the buried pass. "All right guys. Let's do this." We started up the road in silence, pushing through the snow and ice as we trudged higher and higher up the mountain.

Ash and Lumi occasionally shot each other glances that the other always managed to miss. I walked a few paces behind them, observing and grinning to myself. I'd read enough romance novels to see what was happening between them. And I was absolutely loving every second of it.

Ash flexed his gloved hands unconsciously, his thumb rubbing the spot that had touched hers. He pulled off his cap and tousled his long hair. Lumi's eyes were drawn to him as he stretched his arm up over his head.

It was utterly adorable how oblivious they both were, and I decided to try slowly wriggling the truth out of them. I loved them both more than life itself and wanted them to be happy. They both deserved it. Not to mention how much it would sate my match-making heart to help them admit their feelings.

We clambered up the path until we encountered a particularly deep patch of snow. Ash and I sank thigh deep immediately, but Lumi inexplicably stepped across the surface, leaving nothing but light footprints behind.

She turned and spotted us, chuckling.

"Guys, you're stomping," she chided. "You have to step lightly. Like this." She took a few steps backwards, lifting each foot carefully to demonstrate.

I shot her an annoyed look. Ash growled in frustration as he plodded another step forward and sank deeper into the snow.

"We're never gonna make it up the mountain through this before the blizzard hits!" Ash glanced over his shoulder before ripping his gloves off and shoving them in his pockets.

I followed suit and we splayed our hands out over the snow. Heat coursed through me, and a ring of dancing fire blazed to life. The snow around me melted rapidly. Ash opted to blast the snow out of his path. Flames sprang from his palms, slicing through the snow and clearing it from the road.

"You're making this harder than it needs to be!" Lumi raised her voice over the roar of the flames.

I released my hold on my power and turned to her. Ash took a few steps forward and ended up stumbling on a rock. His concentration faltered and his flames sputtered out.

"How are you even doing that?" I demanded, pointing at her feet.

"Easy, I'm not crashing through the snow like a brute," she chuckled.

"Lumi, that's ridiculous," Ash said flatly.

"I'm telling you guys," she smirked. "You have to step lighter."

"No," he replied. He glanced around angrily before lurching to the left and making his way slowly towards the boulders lining the side of the path. "That's not it. I could step lighter than the tiniest fairy and I'd still sink."

"Just try," she insisted.

"Fine," he grumbled, rolling his eyes. Ash took a deep breath and raised a foot carefully, stretching it out above the glistening surface. Slowly, he lowered his boot and shifted his weight forward. His boot sank rapidly, knocking him off balance and sending him reeling forwards into the snow.

Lumi snorted as he struggled to shove himself back to a standing position.

"You see?" Ash said, wiping the snow from his face. Lumi's shoulders shook and she pressed her hands over her mouth. "I don't know how you do that but it's impossible."

"You stepped too hard," Lumi replied through her laughter. His eyes flashed.

"I did *not* step too hard!" he hissed indignantly. He made his way to the boulders and heaved himself up on top of the nearest one. "We can just do this!" He hopped to the next one, his face widening in a triumphant grin. "Come on, Ro. We'll get up the mountain in no time like this. Leave Lumi to her weird snow curse."

"It's not a snow curse!" Lumi rolled her eyes. "And that seems like a terrible idea."

"It's a brilliant idea," he said confidently.

I shook my head and winced as he leapt to the next boulder.

"Yeah, no. Fuck that," I said. "I'm not boulder hopping up the damn mountain."

"But this will be so much faster," Ash insisted. He crouched, preparing to make the next leap.

"Absolutely not. That's too dangerous for me," I said.

"And it's way too dangerous for you, too," Lumi said firmly.

Ash rolled his eyes. "Would you chill? I know what I'm doing." He leapt forward and landed awkwardly on the next boulder. He flung his arms out and tried to maintain his balance as he swayed around, but it wasn't enough. He tipped backwards and cried out as he fell off the boulder and out of sight. Lumi and I exchanged amused glances.

"Oh yeah. You know exactly what you're doing," Lumi snickered.

There was no return jab.

"Ash?" Lumi called.

Silence pressed in around us. We shot each other terrified glances and raced over to where he fell, heaving ourselves up on our hands and knees. We looked down with a gasp of horror. A gaping hole had opened up on the other side of the boulder. It dropped into an icy tunnel that went straight down for a few feet before twisting to the left and continuing to who knew where.

"Ash! Ash!" Lumi called into it. Her voice was all that echoed back at us. "Shit, shit, shit," she muttered. She stood up and wrung her hands. I watched the decision cross her face and she glanced around, measuring the distance between the boulder and the hole.

"Wait, what are you doing?" I exclaimed as she bent her knees and prepared to jump.

"I'm going down after him," she said tersely. "There's some jagged rocks sticking up. I'll climb down and pull him back up. Then I'm gonna kick his fucking ass." Her icy blue stare fixed on me. I looked over the edge into the hole and groaned, my stomach lurching in fear.

"I swear. If we die... I'm going to find him beyond the veil and beat the shit out of him. Wait for me," I muttered, stumbling to my feet, and clutching her hand. She nodded, swallowing hard.

"Ready?" she said, gripping my hand tight. "Jump!"

We pushed off the boulder. My stomach dropped as I sailed through the air. I cried out as we cleared the rim and disappeared into the icy darkness.

CHAPTER THIRTEEN

LUMI

Rowan's hand was ripped away from mine. I threw my arms and legs out, snagging on some rocks jutting out from the side of the hole to halt my fall. I snapped out a hand to grab Rowan's coat, but he hit a patch of ice and spun out of reach. His eyes were wide with terror as he stretched a hand out toward mine, only missing my fingertips by a fraction of an inch. He yelped, skidding around the bend, and dropping out of sight.

"Rowan!" I screamed.

The tunnel opened before me like the maw of a giant beast waiting to devour me whole. I heard Rowan cry out from somewhere far below me, his voice growing further and further away by the second.

I steeled my nerves, sucking in a deep breath before I wrenched my limbs from the wall and dove down into the tunnel after him. I hit the bottom, my bones rattling from the impact. The sides of the shaft were coated with ice, sending me sliding around the bend and down into the darkness below.

My knees and elbows knocked hard against the sides of the tunnel. I tucked into a ball and started spinning like a top. Bile stung the back of my throat, and I squeezed my eyes shut tight. Suddenly, I collided with something hard and slammed to a stop with a grunt. I lay still, fighting to contain the rising nausea. Something shuffled near my head, and I opened my eyes only to find a bright light hovering before my face.

"Oh no," I moaned. "I'm dead."

"Not quite." Ash's face appeared a few inches from mine. He'd pushed his sleeves up, exposing his muscled forearms. Fire danced in the palm of his hand. He smirked and reached out his other hand to help me up. "Glad you could join us, but you're squishing Rowan."

The ground beneath me moaned and shifted. I yelped and let Ash haul me to my feet. A ruffled looking Rowan sat up, rubbing his abdomen.

"I'm so sorry. Are you all right?" I winced, helping him up. He groaned as he stretched out his lean muscles and dusted himself off.

"I'm okay," he said, shaking out his red curls. His cap was nowhere to be found. He looked up into the darkness and frowned. "Where the fuck are we?" I followed his gaze to find nothing but an eerie darkness overhead. Our field of vision ended at the edge of the fire's light.

"I don't know," I said, squinting up at the ceiling in an attempt to discern anything beyond the shadows.

Rowan sighed and waved a hand at Ash. "Bring the light over here."

Ash stepped closer to him as Rowan shoved his hand into his pack. He rummaged around for a few seconds before he withdrew a large map.

"I found this in Father's study," he explained. "It's a map of the caves. Servants used them as shortcuts down the mountain when they went on supply runs. Let's see..." He glanced around and frowned. "Ash, can you make the fire bigger?"

"I can try," he replied. He cupped both his hands together, focusing hard on his palms. The fire popped and grew to a towering column of flames that threw light on the cavernous room around us.

The ceiling was over fifty feet high and sparkled like stars under the influence of the fire's light.

Rowan looked up and nodded. He muttered to himself as he paced back and forth around the room, glancing this way and that before lowering his eyes back to the map. While Rowan walked around the cavern in search of a way out, my attention wandered to Ash.

The flames threw his face into sharp relief. His intense eyes gleamed in the light and his full lips were pressed together tightly. A muscle jumped in his sharp jaw as his arms trembled under the strain of holding his power. A lock of his dark hair fell over his forehead, and I suddenly felt the urge to brush it away from his handsome face. Sweat trickled down the strong column of his neck. He flexed his arms and the flames blazed brighter.

He glanced in my direction and locked eyes with me, arching one dark eyebrow. My heart started pounding frantically in my chest and I sucked in a sharp breath, blushing deeply.

"Are you all right?" he asked, grinning slyly. "You're looking at me funny."

"I'm fine," I mumbled. "I was just—"

"Okay, okay. I get it," Ash chuckled. "I'm sorry I fell down the hole. But I promise I won't light myself on fire."

"Right." I turned away so he couldn't see the strange look that was undoubtedly on my face.

What was going on? A small voice whispered across my mind in response, and I swallowed hard. *Perhaps,* it said, *you were being more serious than you thought when you said those things to your father.*

I shook my head and tried to distract myself from that voice by examining our surroundings.

We stood in a large chamber. There were several tunnel openings, each one leading off in a different direction. In the far end of the room was a large pool of water.

I stepped over to it and peered into its murky depths. Something large shifted and eyes flashed just beneath the surface. They stared up at me for a moment before disappearing, the movement of whatever it was disturbing the surface of the pool. I gasped and stumbled backwards until I hit the opposite wall.

Rowan stopped in the center of the room. He tilted the map before glancing up at the tunnels while muttering to himself.

"Ro," Ash hissed through a clenched jaw. "You might want to hurry... I... I can't..." His arms shook with the effort of sustaining the flame. Sweat trickled down his brow. He sucked in a deep, heaving breath and swore as the fire sputtered and dimmed. His shoulders tensed and a deep growl rumbled up from his chest as he forced the flames back to their full height.

"I got it," Rowan said, striding back to him. "We're good."

Ash gasped and released his power. The flames dropped to the size of a small ball and danced in his palm. He panted and wiped his brow with the back of his arm.

I jumped as I caught myself staring once again and ripped my eyes away from his face.

"All right, look." Rowan and I crowded around Ash's flame. I helped stretch the map under the light as Rowan traced a finger across the paper.

"We're here," he said, indicating a large chamber in the center of a web of crisscrossing tunnels. "And if we go *that* way,“ he pointed towards one of the openings, "it should lead into the tunnel system that will come out over here." He jabbed his finger at an opening in the cave system. "If I'm right, that should bring us to the road that leads up to the palace."

"All right then," I said, straightening and hitching my pack further up onto my shoulders. I handed him the map and he pocketed it. "Lead the way, Ro."

Rowan grinned and opened his palm, fire springing from his fingertips. His flames cast long, eerie shadows on the icy walls as he led the way into the dark.

Anxiety needled my chest as I wrung my empty, useless fingers. I reached back and pulled the bow from its holder before nocking an arrow. The weight of it held at the ready in my hands was comforting as we moved silently through the cave.

We had to tread carefully to avoid the dark patches of ice slicking the stone floor. My eyes darted around, peering into the shadows for any sign of movement.

Rowan paused at a fork in the tunnel. The right side was open, but the left was blocked by a tightly packed wall of jagged stones.

"Shit," he sighed. He slipped the map out of his pocket and examined it closely. Ash stepped closer, holding his flame above his head.

"Shit," Rowan said again, smothering his fire. He stowed the map in his pocket and threw his hand up in the air.

There was a faint scraping sound, but the stones stayed firmly in place. Rowan clenched his teeth. Sweat rolled down his temples as he shoved more and more of his power at the wall blocking our way. But no matter how hard he tried, the rocks didn't budge.

Rowan let out a huff and slipped his hand into his pocket, yanking the map open again.

"What's down that way?" Ash nodded towards the open tunnel.

"A dead end," Rowan replied, furrowing his brow as he stared down at the map.

"Is there another way?" I asked. Rowan frowned and sighed through his nose.

"Maybe." He held the map up for us to see and traced his finger along a tunnel. "If we go this way instead, we should be able to cross through this cavern here and circle back."

Flames reignited in his palm, and he turned, leading the way down the open tunnel. It twisted and turned sharply. I was starting to feel disoriented when the light sputtered behind me, and I turned to find Ash wiping a shaky hand across his brow.

"Are you okay?" I asked nervously. He met my gaze with a weak smile.

"I'm fine," he said. "Just running a little low."

"Same here," Rowan huffed. His hands were trembling slightly, and his flame had dropped in size.

Fear squeezed my lungs. If their fires went out, we'd be lost in the dark with no way out.

"We're almost there," Rowan said as he turned a corner in the tunnel. Even his voice was shaking. "It should be around this... Fuck!" He tossed the map onto the ground and scrubbed a hand angrily over his sweaty face.

I looked around the corner and saw that the tunnel opened up into a large chamber. Beyond it was another tunnel that had collapsed, leaving only a tiny sliver of open space near the ceiling. Ash stopped at my side and swayed slightly, looking around the icy room.

"Guys, look here!" he said suddenly. He darted towards the opposite wall and held his dwindling fire up high. "Look at the stone!"

Rowan and I stepped over to him and peered up at the ceiling where he was pointing. There was a large, round hole in the rock directly above us. Ice had formed over the opening, plugging it up like a stopper in the sink.

It was barely perceptible, but I recognized the faint glimmer of light above the ice.

"Snow," Rowan breathed. Ash and I looked at him as his face broke into a relieved smile. "It's snow!" He pointed at a large pile of snow a few feet in front of us. "Hold on." He clenched his fist, extinguishing the flames, and stretched his hands out wide, gritting his teeth. He faced his palms away from each other and pushed them apart slowly.

Light flooded through the hole, casting a dim glow around the room. Through the ice, I could just make out the branches of a tree swaying in a light breeze.

"Think you can break through?" I asked. Rowan and Ash exchanged a dubious look.

"I don't think I have that kind of power right now," Rowan said, dropping his hands.

"I definitely don't," Ash sighed, extinguishing his flame. As soon as the light faded, his shoulders slumped. "We need to eat first. I can maintain a little fire in the meantime, but we definitely need to rest before we try to break through that ice."

"Sounds like a plan," I nodded. Rowan dropped his pack and stepped away from the hole. I moved to follow him, catching the toe of my boot on something hard that jutted up through the snow dusting the ground. I cried out and fell forward. Ash's arms shot out to catch me before my face hit the stone.

"Whoa! You okay?"

"Yeah... Yeah, I'm fine. I just..." I looked down to see what had caught my boot. Fear jolted through me. An arm was barely visible in the snow. Its hand was stretched out, frozen into the shape of a claw. I screamed and flung myself at Ash, leaping off the ground and into his arms. He stumbled back a step, supporting me with one hand pressed to my side. His other arm managed to catch me just under my knees as I threw my arms around his neck and buried my face in his shoulder.

"What is it?" Ash shouted frantically. He clutched me protectively to his chest and I screamed again. "What happened? Lumi, what happened?"

"A dead body!" I cried into his collarbone. "I just tripped over a dead body!"

"A what?" Rowan gasped, kneeling down. He brushed a hand across the snow pile, revealing a face frozen in perpetual fear. He swore and stumbled back, landing hard on his butt, and scrambling backwards.

Ash looked down before throwing his head back and laughing. The deep, beautiful sound rumbled through my chest as he placed me back on my feet and wiped his eyes. My arms were still wound loosely around his neck as I glared at him, frowning.

"Guys," Ash choked out. "It's just a statue." He splayed his fingers and swept his hand off to the side.

The snow scattered on a phantom wind, revealing a male figure carved out of dark, cloudy ice. The statue's eyes and mouth were wide, and his arms were outstretched as if he were reaching out for someone to save him from whatever horror he was facing. I released Ash and knelt to examine the statue's face.

"What an odd thing to find down here," Rowan said as he crawled up next to me.

"I don't know guys. Could be dangerous. We'd better get out of here before whoever killed him comes back," Ash snickered.

"I'm glad you think our terror is so funny, you ass," I spat over my shoulder.

Ash held his stomach as his whole body shook with deep, rolling laughter.

"Oh, it was hilarious," he managed to say, sighing deeply. He caught my eye and gave me a wicked grin that made my heart flutter.

I forced myself to glare at him before turning my attention back to the statue.

"He'd be gorgeous if he didn't look like he was about to die," Rowan said. The statue had been given a straight nose and a razor-sharp jawline. His gaping lips were full, and his wide eyes might have been round, but it was hard to tell from the expression on his face. Loose curls bounded down his forehead and his ears came to a point at the tip.

"I really like the jawline," Rowan smirked, tracing a finger along the statue's face. I took a closer look at the long, flowing robes, noting the strange shapes on the hem.

"Oh, look! Roses!" I gasped. "I saw some at the market."

"Interesting," Rowan said, touching a curl on the statue's forehead. "Whoever did this must have been a very skilled artist. The detail is extraordinarily lifelike."

"You two go ahead and ogle the statue. I'm going to eat," Ash said. He flipped his wrist and a small ball of fire appeared next to me, dispelling the shadows, and bathing the statue in a bright light.

"Thank you," I said before turning back to stare at the roses. My heart dropped slightly. I desperately wished I still had mine.

Ash muttered something I couldn't hear, and Rowan chuckled.

"What's the matter, Ash? Jealous of that jawline?"

He frowned at Rowan, who was still running a hand down the statue's chin, and bit off a chunk of bread, rolling his eyes.

"My jaw is square, too," he mumbled around his mouthful of food.

"Yeah, but not like that. This man's jaw could cut glass," Rowan sighed, taking the bread Ash offered him. "Too bad he's not real. I'd let him ruin my life."

I chuckled and arched my spine backwards to stretch out my aching muscles. Ash tossed me a loaf of bread from his pack, and I sunk my teeth into it with a moan.

Ash's small fire hovered next to me and glowed brighter with each bite of food he took. Once we'd finished eating, Ash stood up and stretched his arms over his head. I tried to think of something to distract myself with as he ran his hands through his hair. But I caught a flash of the toned muscles on his stomach and my mind went blank. He tugged his coat back down over his hips as he and Rowan began talking about the best course of action to tackle the ice. I tried to listen to what they were saying, but my thoughts kept straying back to my dark-haired friend.

My stomach fluttered as I shot a glance at Ash. He caught me looking and smiled slightly, amusement dancing in his golden eyes for a moment before he turned his attention back to the hole above our heads.

My heart stuttered and I leaned back, bracing my arms behind me as I looked up at the ice. What was happening to me? I'd never felt odd fluttering feelings like these before. About anyone. Not even in the few relationships I'd had. And now I had this strange feeling every time I looked at Ash. It started right after we were attacked and had plagued me ever since. I felt that slice of fear again as I thought of the huge bruise staining his side and looked back in his direction.

Ash ran his fingers through his hair and nodded at something Rowan was saying. Sharp relief pushed away the fear as I watched his chest expand with air, reminding me that he was alive and well.

Suddenly, something clicked in my head. The clouds swirling in my brain cleared and everything came sharply into focus. I could've smacked myself for not even considering it. Of course, I was feeling strangely around him! Of course, I was hyperaware of his every movement! He'd almost died! Several times! All those strange feelings that kept bubbling up were just the relief that I hadn't lost one of my best friends.

I smiled and was mentally patting myself on the back for solving my own internal mystery when something ice cold suddenly dragged itself across my wrist. I jumped and looked down. Horror struck me like a blow to the gut and I screamed, leaping to my feet, and stumbling right into Ash's chest. He wrapped his arms around me protectively as I pointed to the spot where I'd just been sitting, words failing me.

Ash's fire hovered above the statue's outstretched hand. The heat from it had melted some of the ice, revealing bright pink fingers.

And they were moving.

CHAPTER FOURTEEN

Ash

I stepped forward, crouching slightly as I placed myself in front of my friends. The ice cracked and shrank under the heat, revealing a palm and a forearm. I rammed my sleeves up to my biceps. Power flared through me as the fire spread from my open palms and crawled up to my elbows. The small floating ember crackled and grew to a roar in response to the swell in my blood.

Rowan's power ripped a jagged stone from the wall. It hovered beside my head, ready to strike.

A loud creak sounded near my left ear. I glanced over and found the wicked glint of a razor-sharp arrowhead, carefully aimed over my shoulder.

"What the fuck is it? An ice demon?" Lumi hissed.

I shook my head.

Deep cracks ripped their way up the ice and it splintered further, exposing a slender arm. The shivering hand braced itself against the ground. It shoved hard and the ice shattered around a shoulder.

I raised my hand to recall the flame, stopping as Rowan grabbed my wrist.

"Wait!" he whispered. "What if it needs help?"

"What if it tries to kill us?" I hissed.

"It's not an ice demon."

"That doesn't mean it won't try to kill us!" I retorted. Rowan shot me a pleading look.

"Just trust me, okay?" he said, releasing my wrist. "Something in my gut says it needs help."

I gave the creature a wary look and turned back to him, arching an eyebrow. He met my eyes imploringly. My common sense screamed at me to recall the fire and leave the creature encased in ice.

"Trust me," Rowan repeated.

We stared at each other for a moment. Finally, I let out a low growl and turned back.

"Fine." I flipped my wrists out and four more hovering fires appeared. They bounced away, gliding over to surround the creature. "But if we get eaten, I'm going to be really pissed at you."

"Seconded," Lumi added. She adjusted her bow to aim carefully between the creature's eyes.

I stretched my hands out in front of me and willed the fires to grow. The heat coursing through my blood turned lava hot as the flames leapt toward the cavernous ceiling. I clenched my jaw tight and tensed my shoulders, holding my power in place. The heat from the blaze washed over my face, and beads of sweat rolled down my neck. After a few tense moments, a sharp crack split the air followed by a ragged gasp.

A shadow moved behind the fire. Something sat up and stumbled out of the flames before it crashed to its hands and knees before us.

Lumi adjusted the arrow as the figure bowed its head. It wheezed painfully, taking in deep drags of air.

A strange, dizzying sensation suddenly washed over me. The world swayed as my energy was swiftly drained away. I fought to keep control of the flames, but my strength failed me, and my power sputtered and died. My muscles grew heavy as bursts of light popped before my eyes.

Rowan groaned and stumbled back a step. The stone slipped from his control and crashed to the floor. He dropped to all fours, clutching his head.

Lumi staggered and fell to her hands and knees, releasing the arrow.

It shot forward and raced towards the creature's bowed head.

Without looking up, the creature snatched the speeding arrow out of the air, catching it inches away from its hair. It tossed the arrow aside and clutched its chest with a gasp.

I hit the ground hard as the world rocked violently underneath me. Bile rose in my throat.

The creature took a long, shuddering breath and pushed itself to its feet. It was a man.

Curly green hair fell down across his forehead. He had a sharp jaw, a slightly square face and a straight, pointed nose. The man's dark green eyes darted anxiously between the three of us sprawled out before him. He wore long, flowing robes of green and gold. There were a few long streaks of dirt and grime smudged into the fabric and several of the red silk roses sewn into the hem were missing. His bright pink skin flushed as he panted, trying desperately to catch his breath.

The world continued to spin, and I shut my eyes. Somewhere close by, one of my friends retched and the other groaned.

"I'm sorry," the man croaked. His lilted voice rang through the air like a soft melody. "I'm really, really sorry. I don't like to do that, but my power hasn't returned yet and this is an emergency."

The world had finally stopped moving and my strength was slowly returning. I pushed myself up onto my elbows to meet the man's gaze.

He offered me a slim hand and I hesitated before taking it. He pulled me to my feet with an unnatural swiftness that sent my stomach churning once more.

Lumi was lying flat on her back with her fingers curled into the snow and her eyes shut tight. Rowan was on all fours, wiping his mouth.

I wobbled and glanced back at the man.

His face broke out into an expression of pure relief. "Thank the Two! I thought I was done for." The man walked over and helped Rowan to his feet. "My power is still locked from me so that means it's not too late! We have to get back before something terrible happens and Winter does something she will regret. Which way do we go from here?"

Rowan and I shot each other a confused look as the man pulled Lumi rapidly to her feet.

Lumi groaned and swayed into me. I took her hand, placing her carefully behind me. She wrapped her fingers around my elbow and peered cautiously over my shoulder at the stranger.

"Is it just the three of you?" he asked, his full lips twisting into a frown.

"Who are you?" Lumi demanded.

The man turned around sharply, staring at her like she'd grown another head.

"What do you mean 'who are you'?" he said slowly. He sucked in a deep breath and the dizziness once again tore through me. I swore loudly.

Lumi gripped my arm tighter, and Rowan doubled over, gagging.

The man released the breath and the swirling immediately subsided.

"That's what I thought," the man muttered. "But I don't recognize you. Didn't you come from the palace?"

I shifted half of a step to the left, ensuring Rowan and Lumi were both behind me.

Rowan placed a shaking hand on my back to steady himself.

"No, we didn't come from the palace," I said roughly. Fire began to lick my wrists. "And she asked you a question. Who the fuck are you?"

The man blinked and stared at us, dumbfounded. A small jolt of panic spasmed across his face.

"Are you... Are you new?" he stammered. "You must be new. Where's Kaelin? He will explain everything. He's—"

The man faltered, furrowing his brow as Lumi and I turned in unison to look at Rowan. He paled, eyes widening as understanding dawned on his face.

"Lord Spring?" Rowan gasped weakly.

Lord Spring rounded on him, beaming.

"Yes! Yes, of course it's me! Now hurry! We have to get back and..." He trailed off, frowning as we continued to gape at him. "What?" he demanded, panic rising in his tone. "Why are you looking at me like that? We have to hurry! Where's Kaelin?"

"Kaelin," Rowan said, his voice trembling, "is my father."

Lord Spring stared at him for a moment before he shook his head.

"No," he snorted. "That's impossible. Kaelin has worked with me for years. His son was just born a few months ago. In fact, he was going to leave after I returned to go and get the boy so I could... finally..."

Lord Spring trailed off. His dark green eyes darted around the cavern, looking around for the first time. The color drained from his face as he stared up at the icicles hanging from the ceiling.

"No," Lord Spring whispered softly. His eyes were wide with fear as they shot back to Rowan, truly taking in his face for the first time and noting the features he undoubtedly recognized. "No," he said again, his voice cracking. "Please..." He met all of our eyes desperately. "No..."

"I'm so sorry, Lord Spring," Rowan said. "But it's true. Kaelin is my father, and Lucia is my mother."

Lord Spring staggered back a step and shook his head in disbelief.

"That can't be true," he gasped, clutching his chest. "It can't. You... You have to be at least... How old are you?"

Rowan cleared his throat and stepped around me. I tensed as he stepped within arm's reach of Lord Spring, who watched him as he approached, his pink features twisting with despair.

"How old are you?" Lord Spring whispered, trembling. Lumi removed another arrow and drew back her bow as Rowan tentatively placed a hand on Lord Spring's arm.

"I'm about to turn twenty-one," he replied softly. "You... You've been missing... For twenty years."

Lord Spring froze in horror.

"That... that can't be true," he croaked, shaking his head. "Please... Please tell me it's not true." His gaze snapped to me, taking in the fire burning around my clenched fists. Then his eyes slid to the razor-sharp arrow Lumi had aimed at his heart. He stumbled back another step and clutched his chest tighter, balling his robes up in his fist. His face crumbled in anguish, and he let out a ragged breath.

"But..." he hissed, shaking his head again. "No. If she took the throne then my power would've come back! I'm still powerless! It can't be true!"

"I'm so sorry, Lord Spring," Rowan said again. "But it is true. It's been winter for the last two decades."

"This can't be happening," Lord Spring gasped. Tears filled his eyes. His knees gave out from underneath him, and he dropped, burying his face in his hands. "No, no, no," he choked around his sobs. "Oh, Winter... What have you done?"

Rowan knelt down beside Lord Spring tentatively and wrapped an arm around his trembling shoulders.

"I'm so sorry," Rowan whispered. Lord Spring shook his head and leaned over, sobbing into his hands.

"She did it," he said through his anguish. "She actually did it. Winter, what have you done?" He straightened and looked up at us, tears glazing his face. "What happened to the world? Are the humans all right?"

We exchanged nervous glances.

I swallowed and rolled my shoulders, extinguishing the flames. Lumi lowered her bow and returned the arrow to her quiver.

"Haven still stands," Lumi replied, stepping around to stand beside me.

"Haven? Just Haven?" Panic edged Lord Spring's words.

"There's a city still standing to the north. Maybe two. But... Most of the survivors made their way to Haven a long, long time ago," Lumi said, toying with the ends of her raven black hair. Her icy blue eyes shot to me briefly as Lord Spring's breathing stalled.

"Survivors?" Agony laced his voice. "But the Cosmics... Are you three not from the academy in Trithica?" Lord Spring pressed.

The world around me screeched to a halt. My skin felt clammy, and my chest heaved in a burst of panic. I blinked, fighting to push away the sudden flood of awful memories. The clock tower. Swirling flames. And screaming. So much screaming. I clenched my jaw, wincing as they shoved their way to the forefront of my mind.

"Trithica fell... many years ago," I said quietly, unable to keep the pain out of my voice. From the corner of my eye, I saw Lumi turn to stare at me. I saw the questions burning in her mind, but I pressed my lips together and looked determinedly ahead. I couldn't face the monsters clawing at me from the shadowy corners of my memories.

I clenched my fists, willing my breaths to come steady and even, pushing hard against a past I could not afford to let myself think about. Or else I'd lose myself to the dark. My pulse pounded and panic edged its way into my mind. Horrible screams and claws scratching at wood echoed in my ears. I was losing my grip on my fear, so I forced myself to look at Lumi.

Confusion and concern were written all over her beautiful face and I let myself stare into her eyes for a moment. Reminding myself where I was. The panic eased slightly, and I turned back towards Lord Spring as he wrung his hands.

"But... but the Cosmics... Are they...?" Lord Spring whispered, trailing off fearfully. He met my eyes, reading the anguish on my face. He let out a shuddering sob, his face wracked with despair as he bowed his head and wept in Rowan's arms.

Lumi shot me a glance before she approached Lord Spring and crouched in front of him.

"Twenty years..." Lord Spring took a deep breath and looked up at her while wiping his streaming eyes. "How did you ever find me?"

"We kind of... stumbled into you," I said, grinning at Lumi. She scowled in return.

"What happened?" Rowan said.

"I came back from the Tower and Winter was angry." Lord Spring sniffed loudly. "She was crying and said..." Lord Spring sat up straighter and his eyes went wide as he looked around at us.

"Wait... how did you free me?" he said urgently.

Lumi and Rowan looked up at me. I let my power swell and flicked my wrist. The little ball of fire reappeared and hovered before them.

"I summoned this for light," I explained. "It was above you and the ice started melting."

"Cosmic fire?" Lord Spring stared at the ember in confusion. "But... That shouldn't have..." Suddenly, he surged to his feet and rushed towards me.

I flinched, stumbling backwards as he seized my shoulders in a tight grip. Panicked flames momentarily erupted across my palms in defense. I had to shake my hands out to smother them.

"Please," he said desperately. "Please, you have to come to Nature's Palace with me!" He turned, not releasing his hold on me to address Lumi and Rowan. "Winter said Summer and Fall were there when I saw her last. She must've frozen them somewhere in the palace! And if you were able to free me from her ice, maybe you can free them, too!"

"If we free them," Rowan said slowly, "the world can be put right again."

"Well, we were headed there anyway," Lumi said, meeting my eyes.

I nodded and stepped out of Lord Spring's grasp, prying his fingers from my shoulders.

"We have to get through that first." I pointed up at the ceiling.

Lord Spring turned to examine the hole.

"That ice is too thick to break outright. But you two..." Lord Spring waved a hand at Lumi and Rowan, who stood. "You two could summon a breeze. Hoisting you up..." He jerked his head at me. "And then you could summon a blaze to melt the ice."

Lumi shuffled her feet awkwardly, looking down at the ground and wringing her hands. My heart wrenched at the sight of her crestfallen face. "I'm not... Well... I don't think I'm Cosmic," she admitted miserably.

"Yes, you are," Lord Spring said, confused.

When she shook her head, he turned his focus entirely on her and drew in a slow deep breath.

She paled and swayed into Rowan, clinging to him as her knees sagged.

"Stop it," I spat fiercely. Fire simmered in my blood, itching to tear through me. My nails dug into my palms, and I had to struggle to rein in my power. Lord Spring blinked and ducked his head apologetically.

"I'm sorry," he said to Lumi. She took in a shuddering breath and straightened.

"What did you just do?" Rowan demanded, glaring.

"I can siphon off Cosmic energy," Lord Spring replied sheepishly. "It's unpleasant, as you know. I hate doing it, but it is definitive proof that you are, in fact, Cosmic. If you weren't, there would be nothing for me to take and you wouldn't feel anything."

My anger evaporated in an instant and I shot Lumi a wide grin, arching my eyebrow. Wild hope danced in her eyes.

Lord Spring tipped his head thoughtfully. "Though, you do seem somewhat disconnected from your power," he said. "There's a block, but I'm not sure where it came from. You have to get past it first and then your power will come easier."

"A block? How do I get around it?" The hope dissipated from Lumi's expression.

"I don't know," Lord Spring admitted. "But right now, we need to focus on getting out of this cavern. I don't know what happened to my power, but the little I have left isn't enough to do much of anything." He turned to Rowan, who blushed inexplicably. "Can you hold him by yourself?"

"I can try," Rowan mumbled. He turned to me, rolling up his sleeves. "Ready?"

I nodded and bent my knees. Rowan spread his hands wide. Snow lifted from the ground, swirling in the air as a cyclone of wind barreled towards me, whipping my tunic up to my chest. I shivered as the icy blast stole the heat from my bare skin. Lumi pressed her lips together and looked away sharply. I arched an eyebrow, silently daring her to laugh.

Rowan furrowed his brow as the air began spinning faster. My feet left the cavern floor, and I tipped forward, throwing my hands out for better balance. Rowan's face turned red with the effort. He lifted me four feet into the air and groaned, his arms shaking.

"I can't get you any higher than that," he panted. "Hurry."

I nodded and stretched my hands above my head, waking the fire in my blood. Powerful flames surged from my hands and blasted upwards in two powerful streams. The ice began to crack and drip and, after three minutes, I'd burned a sizable hole in the first few inches of ice. Rowan gasped and I wobbled hard.

"Shit," Rowan hissed, trembling. I dropped suddenly and he stumbled back, clutching his stomach.

I landed hard on my feet.

"Sorry," Rowan panted.

"No worries. You good?" I said.

He nodded and braced himself again. "Ready?"

"Uh... Guys?" Lumi said. We stopped. She stepped between us and pointed at the ground. "Wouldn't it be easier— and faster— if you piled rocks here and then you both stood on them to melt the ice?" Rowan and I turned to stare at each other, dumbfounded.

"It would be," Rowan said, chuckling. "But we didn't think of that cause we're idiots."

"Lumi, we'd be so lost without you," I grinned. She blushed furiously and rolled her eyes.

"Yes, I know," she replied, suppressing a smile.

I turned towards the pile of stones blocking the passageway and reached out. Rowan mimicked my movements and together, we pulled several large stones towards us. They bounced and rolled across the ground before stacking themselves into a neat pile.

"After you," Rowan winked. I scrambled up the pile and reached back to haul Rowan up after me. He sidled in close and stood shoulder-to-shoulder with me.

"Please be careful," Lumi warned. She wrapped her arms around her chest as she eyed the pile of rocks. I caught Rowan's eye and winked.

"I fall down a hole one time and now she thinks I'm not careful," I said with a dramatic sigh. A snowball sailed through the air, colliding with the side of my head. I gasped as freezing cold snow slid down my neck and into my tunic. Lumi grinned, wiping her hands on her coat asI shook the snow out of my hair and shot her a look.

"If you two are done flirting," Rowan said loudly. He smirked at me, and my stomach flipped. I pushed my hair out of my face and rolled my eyes at him.

"All right. Ready?" I grumbled.

Rowan nodded.

We stretched our hands above our heads and summoned twin blasts of fire. Light filled the cavern as the flames roared and water began raining down on our upturned faces. We turned our heads away as we continued to burn through the ice.

"Fuck, that's cold," I gasped. The icy chill crept into my bones as water continued to stream from above. Rowan shivered violently beside me.

"Almost there," Lord Spring called anxiously.

"There!" Lumi yelled. "Stop, stop, stop!"

Rowan and I released our power at the same time and the dull roar of flames echoed away to nothing. I wiped the water from my eyes and looked up, squinting at the weak sunlight streaming through the freshly made hole.

"Okay," Rowan said. He flicked a hand towards me. The water vanished from our skin, hair, and clothes, streaming down to the floor.

I called my fire, sending heat surging through my blood to chase away the lingering chill from my skin.

"Now..." Rowan furrowed his brow. "We can both fit through, I think... Lumi, I put some rope in your pack."

She nodded and bent down to dig through her bag.

"Got it!" She stood and tossed the rope to me. I caught it and slung it over my shoulder.

"Okay.... Now what, Ro?" I asked, looking back up into the light.

"Now," he said, stretching his hands out before us. "We lift the rock we're standing on and climb through the hole. How's your energy?"

I shifted my weight, feeling the movement of my muscles. Nothing ached... Yet.

"I'm okay for now," I replied, stretching my arms out to mirror him.

The stone jerked violently under our combined commands and nearly threw us off.

"Whoa..." Rowan gasped, clutching my arm. "Okay. Let's try again. On the count of three this time. Ready? One... two... three!"

We heaved together, feeling the weight of the stone press against our power. It shuddered beneath our feet before rising slowly into the air. We gritted our teeth, shifting in unison to guide the stone up to the hole. It eased into the opening, jerking slightly when we hit the ceiling of the cavern.

"I've got it, Ro," I panted, my arms shaking. "You take the rope and climb up. Hurry." The weight pressing against my powers doubled as Rowan released his hold on the rock.

He slipped the rope off my shoulder and scrambled up into the snow.

My muscles began to scream. I grunted, fighting to keep the rock steady. "Stand clear!" I called down into the cavern.

Rowan reached out with both hands and instantly the weight of the stone eased. I released my power and leapt onto the ledge next to him. The added weight caused him to slide towards the hole and he dug his heels into the snow, carving deep trenches behind him as he was dragged back towards the pit.

I reached out, snatching his coat and yanking him backwards as he released the stone from his power. It fell and hit the rocks piled below with a resounding *crash,* demolishing the stack.

"Are you okay?" I called out, peering over the edge.

Lumi and Lord Spring emerged from the shadows and craned their necks to look at me.

"We're fine," she said.

"Grab the bags," Rowan called. She disappeared momentarily, reappearing with the bags and her quiver. She handed two of them off to Lord Spring. Rowan tossed the end of the rope down and called out, "Grab on!"

Rowan and I heaved, yanking the rope up slowly. Finally, Lumi and Lord Spring emerged from the hole, and we pulled them up over the edge.

While Rowan and I panted and caught our breaths, Lord Spring stood slowly. He looked around at the frozen landscape in absolute horror, thick tears streaming down his face.

CHAPTER FIFTEEN

SPRING

My soul shattered. I stared in horror at the frozen landscape as my new companions caught their breath. The trees of the once mighty forest were shriveled and barren, their twisted branches stretching high like the claws of a beast.

Not a single flower or blade of grass swayed in the bitter, howling wind. No birds swooped through the frigid air. There was nothing. Just snow and ice as far as the eye could see. The rich, luscious color had been erased from the world. I looked up at the towering mountain behind us. Through the mists, I could just barely see the spires of my home peeking over the cliffside.

"Lord Spring?"

I looked down and found Kaelin's son standing before me. The soft smile on his kind face eased the ache in my chest as I wiped my eyes and gestured to the barren trees.

"This was a beautiful forest once," I told him, my voice breaking with emotion. "It was so green and full of life. I feel like I just saw it. So much time has passed in the blink of an eye."

The kind one placed a tentative hand on my shoulder.

"I'm so sorry."

I sighed, grief giving way to a heavy guilt weighing on my heart. "No. *I'm* sorry. I should've been here to stop this. This is my fault."

"Winter did this. Not you," he said in an attempt to comfort me. "You're not responsible for her actions." He smiled kindly at me, and my breath caught. Shame stained my soul as I stared at his shy, trusting expression. I knew better, but I couldn't tell him the truth. Not if it meant watching that kind smile slip away.

I could see it now. His round face so resembled my beloved gardener's. And he had his mother's vibrant red curls and bright green eyes. I looked away from him, overwhelmed by a deep sadness.

The other two sat nearby and watched us carefully.

The dark-haired male's golden eyes burned into me as I met his searing gaze. His companions might be willing to trust me, but he certainly wasn't. He edged forward, placing himself between me and the pale female beside him. I could feel the thrum of his power from where I stood. It rolled through him like wildfire, intense and chaotic. There was something about the way his power raced through him that tugged at the back of my mind, but I couldn't remember why.

The raven-haired female glanced between us and laid a comforting hand on his elbow. He shot a quick glance at her before he blew out a long, calming breath. The hum of his power dimmed drastically under her touch.

She turned her bright blue eyes towards me, her fingers toying with the end of her long, bound hair. Her power was muted, trapped behind a thick wall and out of her reach. The little bit of it that trickled around the wall was barely noticeable. But I could feel the depth of her abilities behind that barrier. Once she figured out the way around it, she'd be formidable.

I looked back to Kaelin's son. Of the three Cosmics before me, he was by far the most powerful. The power swirling in his chest was almost immeasurable and ran deep through his blood. I wasn't surprised. His mother was the most powerful Cosmic in human history. It made sense that he would have inherited that power. But unlike his fiery companion, his power was calm and quiet, making me wonder if he realized how strong he actually was.

"Rowan," I guessed, raising my eyebrows at him. "That was what Kaelin told me his son's name would be. Or Malachi."

"Rowan," he nodded. "And these two are my family. Ash." He nodded to the dark-haired male. "And Lumi." She inclined her head.

"Family? Kaelin had more children?" I was dumbfounded. I turned to examine their faces and Rowan chuckled lightly.

"Not by blood," he clarified, his smile widening. "But my parents raised both of them. Which would be why Ash is fighting the urge to growl at you."

Ash arched one eyebrow, frowning.

"I do *not* growl," he grumbled, crossing his strong arms over his chest. Lumi grinned and patted him on the elbow.

"You do actually," she said. She wiped a speck of ice from her freckled nose and glanced up and down the road. "We need to get moving. Those storm clouds are coming in quick."

A sudden jolt of panic seized my heart as I looked up. Dark gray clouds were barreling through the sky, blotting out the sun.

"We have to hide," I hissed quickly.

They turned, watching me in surprise as I backed into the shadow of a nearby tree.

"Why? It's just a blizzard." Lumi furrowed her brow, gesturing up at the sky.

"No." My voice dropped to a whisper. "No, it's not. Winter can see through them. Heralds can create a storm and throw their sight into the clouds from the tower. We have to hide!"

"Wait! She can see us?" Lumi gasped.

I nodded and shrank further back into the shadows.

"She might be looking at us right now," I whispered. "But I can't tell for sure. If I reach out, she will sense me, and she already tried to kill me once." I gulped, looking fearfully at the roiling clouds.

"What's she gonna do, kill you with snow?" Ash snorted, arching an eyebrow at me. I shook my head and pressed myself harder into the tree trunk.

"No. But she can summon giant chunks of ice to crush me!" I hissed. The faces around me paled.

"I'm sorry. She can do *what*?" Lumi asked shrilly.

"She can summon an ice storm," I whispered.

"Are you sure?" Ash asked skeptically. "If she can create a storm like that, I feel like she would've sent one to flatten Haven already."

"Yes, I'm sure!" I snapped. They exchanged a glance.

"Well, we can't stay here and wait her out," Ash said, scanning the horizon. "Those clouds are going to open up any second."

"We'll just have to risk it," Lumi nodded in agreement, watching the clouds.

"Here," Rowan said suddenly. He rummaged through his bag, pulling out a long black coat. "Put this on."

I took it gratefully and slipped it on, pulling the hood low over my eyes.

"Thank you," I said, steeling myself. "All right... I know a short cut to the palace. Let's go."

Rowan and Ash led the way, clearing the road with their fire as we trudged up the mountain.

I directed them off the main road and towards a narrow strip of path, barely visible between two large rocks. As soon as we shoved our way between them, I stumbled to a halt with a gasp. The pass had once been a clear shot all the way to the palace gates, but there must have been a landslide at some point. It was now a maze of snow, boulders, and debris.

"Well," Lumi sighed. "Looks like we're climbing."

"Just what we needed," Ash grumbled, running his fingers through his hair.

We began climbing over boulders and fallen trees on our way up the steep pass. Halfway up the mountain, Rowan shot me a sideways glance.

"Lord Spring?" he began.

"Please," I said, panting as he helped me up a particularly large rock. "Spring is fine."

"Spring," he repeated, a faint blush staining his cheeks. "Do you know why Winter hates humans so much?"

We crested over the ridge and stood at the edge of a long drive that cut through the trees. Nature's Palace stood starkly against the harsh sky, towering over the last stretch of the Great Forest. Guilt burned me. But before I could respond, movement to my left caught my eye and I paused.

Ash tensed, fire enveloping his clenched fists as he stared off into the trees. I followed his gaze and spotted a monster. It prowled through the snow on four sets of lethal claws, sniffing at the air like it was searching for something. It was nothing but jagged shards of ice and vicious teeth. A spiked tail swished through the air as the creature turned its dark and empty sockets towards us, still sniffing wildly. Black smoke drifted from its skull and dissipated in the icy air.

"Shit," Lumi whispered. "Ice demon! Hide!"

"A what?" I asked, bewildered. Rowan gripped my sleeve, pulling me behind a large tree. Ash pushed up his sleeves and the fire spread up to his elbows.

He took a step forward, but Lumi snatched the back of his coat and yanked him out of sight behind a boulder. She pressed him into the stone with both hands, glaring up at him. He ducked his head to hide the blush staining his cheeks and smothered the flames.

We peered around our hiding places at the beast stalking through the gloom. Something familiar tugged at my heart, calling to me. I focused on the sensation and let out a small gasp as images flooded my mind. Each one was laced with a thick, seeping darkness.

I saw a familiar creature, joyously leaping through the sunlit trees, chasing the shadow of a great silver dragon gliding overhead. I saw a tender kiss. I felt unending despair and bitter hatred. And the last image was my face, streaked with dirt and staring back in anguish. The black ichor swirling through the memories seemed to pause and turn. Almost like it was looking at me.

I sucked in a breath as the darkness suddenly lunged, reaching out to ensnare my mind.

The shadows edged into my thoughts, and I reached deep down into the well of my power. A small spark had regenerated there, and I summoned it, stretching it into a vast mental shield that forced the shadows out. The darkness slithered across the surface of the shield, trickling towards the Cosmics around me, drawn to their power.

Panic seared my nerves. I reached a tendril of power out, snaring each one of their minds and yanking them under the safety of my mental shield. They blinked and shifted but kept their focus on the prowling monster.

The image of the silver dragon swam through my brain, and I was struck with a sudden, horrible realization. My stomach jolted as I looked back at the creature.

"Calliope," I breathed, horrified. I stepped out from around the tree, pressing a hand to my mouth.

"Spring, what are you doing?" Rowan whispered frantically. My heart thundered in my chest. Calliope didn't notice me. She turned, dashing through the trees and out of sight.

"That was an ice demon," Lumi said, releasing Ash. "They serve Winter."

"No... Her name is Calliope," I choked out. Anguish closed around my throat, making every breath burn. "She was my friend. She was the patron spirit of the Great Forest. Calliope," I sobbed. "What has she done to you?" I looked around, wiping my streaming eyes. "We have to hurry." We stepped onto the road and started quickly towards the palace.

"You knew that ice demon?" Ash said.

"She's a spirit, not a demon," I said, more sharply than I meant. He glared at me, and I cringed. "And yes, I know her... But she didn't always look like that," I replied with an apologetic expression. "When one of the major spirits stays attached to the tower for too long, their energy becomes corrupted. That corrupted energy then feeds back into the tower and spreads. Minor spirits use that same Cosmic energy. Winter has completely corrupted it, so the minor spirits have lost their minds." I glanced in the direction where Calliope disappeared and quickened my pace. "I only hope we can still fix this."

"How do you know for sure that she's your friend?" Lumi asked. Her eyes carefully scanned the tree line as we raced down the road.

"I felt her," I said. "She's still in there... But I also felt a darkness. Which I think might have been Winter... Or what's left of her, anyway. I got away before she could sense me there. When I became Spring, I was warned not to stay at the tower for longer than my cycle. We *all* were."

We rounded the bend and started up the long drive. The palace seemed to have dimmed. Its luster and opulence were muted by the ice clinging to its facade. We bounded through the iron gate of the outer wall and entered my gardens.

I gasped in shock and slammed to a halt.

My gardens were barren and icy. The gnarled remains of my orchard trees sat piled in a corner near the wall and all of my beautiful flowers were gone.

I clasped my hands over my mouth. I had suspected as much, but seeing my beloved gardens reduced to nothing was still a powerful blow to the chest.

"Spring!" Rowan came up beside me and grasped my arm. "We have to keep going." As he spoke, a glob of snow landed in my hair. Lumi and Ash were already at the front doors, waving us over frantically.

I nodded, swallowing hard, and let Rowan lead me towards the palace.

Ash threw his weight against the heavy oak door to open it, slamming it shut again behind us as we crossed the threshold. The ache in my chest only got sharper as I stood in the entrance hall, looking around at my home.

It was destroyed. The furniture was smashed, and debris littered the floor. The banister of the great staircase was in splinters and the tapestries and artwork decorating the walls had been shredded by vicious claws.

"It looks like someone was looking for something," Ash remarked.

Fear rolled up my spine as the image of Winter plucking the stones from the crowns passed through my memory and I remembered another warning we'd been given all those years ago.

"Oh no," I gasped. I dashed up the stairs, vaulting over the debris and broken glass as I whirled into the altar room.

The statue of the Ethereal Two had been shattered, but the plinths were still standing.

I dropped to my hands and knees and began sifting frantically through the wreckage. I had to be misremembering. My memory had to have been warped from spending all those years frozen solid. “No, no, no, no, no...” I moaned. The others stepped carefully into the room, watching me with uncertainty.

“What are you looking for?” Lumi said, glancing around at the mess.

“Crowns,” I replied quickly. “Three of them. They have to be here somewhere. She wouldn’t... She wouldn’t... I have to be wrong. Please, please, please... Let me be wrong,” I repeated, more to myself than to anyone.

“Like this one?” Lumi asked suddenly.

I looked up to find her holding a familiar circle of golden roses. The facet in the front was empty.

“No!” I cried, springing to my feet, and seizing the crown. “No, no, no.” They exchanged bewildered glances.

“What is it?” Rowan asked.

“Winter took the stone,” I said. Understanding hit me like a boulder crashing down a mountainside and I sucked in a sharp breath. “That’s where it went. Oh no.”

“Where what went?” Lumi asked. I pressed a hand to my thundering heart.

“My power,” I said. “When she took the tower, her power pushed mine out. But I was already frozen, so it didn’t come back to me like it should’ve. It must have returned to my stone instead. Which means I’m just about powerless until I get my stone back. But, if Winter has it...”

“There’s two more over here,” Ash called. He held up a crown of sunbeams and a crown of leaves. Both of the facets were empty. My shoulders slumped as I realized what this meant. What Winter planned to do. Suddenly, the ransacking of the palace made horrifying sense.

“No!” I moaned. “She took them all... Winter has the stones.”

“What stones?” Lumi asked. The trio dropped their bags and began stretching out their sore muscles. I scrubbed my trembling hands over my face in disbelief.

“The stones,” I stammered. “They’re part of our heraldship. They only respond to their spirit. But she took them all!”

“Why would Winter want them if she can’t use them?” Rowan asked.

“Because if she has all of them, she could use them to rule the world... Or destroy it,” I said quietly. They stared, wide-eyed and gaping.

“I’m sorry?” Lumi stuttered. “What do you mean she could destroy the world with them?”

I didn’t answer. Instead, I seized Ash by the wrist. He tensed as I began to pull him towards the door.

"Please," I begged, tightening my grip. "I need you to free Summer and Fall. We have to set the world right!"

Ash shot his friends a wary look before relaxing just enough to allow himself to be pulled through the door.

We raced back into the hall and down a long corridor. Along the way, I glanced into each room. They were all destroyed. All but the library, which was as pristine as it had been when I last saw it.

Rowan and Lumi were right on our heels as we reached a spiral staircase and began climbing up the tower to Summer's private room.

I pushed the door open and reeled back in shock. My sister's room had been destroyed as well, but not in the same way as the rest of the palace. There were giant icicles embedded in the furniture and deep scratches gouged the stone walls. The oversized bed was nothing more than a heap of splinters and shredded fabric. Shards of ice littered the golden carpet. I stepped into the room, looking around.

"She has to be here," I said desperately. I threw open the doors to Summer's wardrobe and sifted through her fine robes and gowns. I turned towards the remains of the bed and found my new companions still standing in the doorway, staring at the floor.

"Please," I begged. "Help me! We have to find her!" They looked up at me, each one paling.

Ash bent down to the ice littering the floor and picked up a large chunk, holding it up for me to see. It was a finely manicured hand, frozen with its fingers curled into a claw.

My heart ripped in two.

"No!" I sobbed, tears clouding my vision. "Summer... No!" I staggered forward and reached out a trembling hand.

He handed the ice to me. A large, ornate ring sat on the middle finger. It was a yellow diamond surrounded by rays of sunshine cast in gold. My breathing turned ragged as I looked down at the ice. I spotted a small, pointed ear and half of a nose. Wrapped around a small cylindrical piece was a thin bracelet, made of red, orange, and yellow twine.

I choked out a gasp. It had been made by a small child and given to Fall to bring him good fortune. He hadn't taken it off since.

"Fall," I sobbed. "No..." I whipped to Ash. He stumbled back a step as I ran to him and shoved the hand back into his. "Please!" I cried. Panic and desperation gripped my heart. "Maybe... Maybe we can still save them!"

Ash's throat bobbed. He glanced at the others for a beat before fire sprang from his palms. He cupped his hands around the piece of my sister and focused. His flames formed a ring that rotated slowly.

The ice melted and I saw a flash of yellow skin before it turned gray. The piece crumpled and slid through Ash's fingers like sand and drifted down to the carpet.

All that remained in his palm was her ring. There was no saving them. Summer and Fall were truly gone. A hole tore its way into my chest as I cried out in anguish for my friend. For my sister. And for the broken world I had been too cowardly to save.

CHAPTER SIXTEEN

Ash

Lord Spring's chest heaved violently. He collapsed, kneeling over the remains of his fellow spirits as he sobbed heavily into his hands. My heart broke for him.

Lumi and I exchanged glances. Her eyes misted over as she reached a nervous hand up to toy with the ends of her hair. I didn't even want to imagine the pain of losing her or Rowan. And from the look on her face, I could tell she was thinking the same thing.

I placed a comforting arm around her shoulder, and she leaned closer, pressing her cheek against my chest. Rowan knelt beside Spring.

"I'm so sorry," he murmured.

Spring looked up at him, brushing a green curl from his streaming eyes.

"They're gone," he sobbed. "She killed them. Summer and Fall are gone." He looked up at each of us in turn. "It's too late," he breathed. "I don't know what to do now. I can't set the world right without them." He looked back down at his fallen friends and let out another sob. "Please. Will you help me?" He looked up at me in despair. "I can't leave them like this. Please..." He stopped short, pain twisting his face.

Sorrow wrapped around my heart, and I nodded, understanding what he couldn't bear to say. I stepped away from Lumi and drew a deep breath, letting the heat of my power flood my body. A circle of fire burst forth and spun itself around the carpet. The ice vanished rapidly, leaving only a pile of crumpling dust in its wake.

Rowan stood and tapped Lumi on the shoulder, jerking his chin silently towards the window.

She nodded and jogged over, throwing it open wide. He nodded to me, and I released my power, noting the small ache blooming behind my eyes. Rowan slowly swept a hand out in front of him. The dust was caught by a phantom wind and swirled out the open window.

"I should've been here to save you," Spring whispered, watching as the dust rose over a distant peak and disappeared from sight. "I could've stopped this. This is all my fault." He stood and ambled slowly from the room. Rowan started after him but stopped short.

"Should we follow him?" he said, wringing his hands.

I shook my head. "I think he might need some time alone," I said softly, meeting Rowan's bright green eyes.

He nodded and heaved out a sigh. "Then I guess we should go find the storeroom. Hopefully, it's not destroyed like the rest of the palace." He withdrew the leather notebook from his pocket and flipped through the pages.

"Which way do we go?" Lumi asked. Rowan frowned, rifling through the pages again.

"I saw it here somewhere... But I can't... Oh, here it is. Okay." He flipped the book around for both of us to see and tapped his finger on a diagram of the palace's interior. "We're here in Summer's private residence. If we go back down this way and pass through the servant's quarters," he dragged his finger down a long corridor, "then the storeroom should be here. Follow me."

He stowed the book in his pocket and led the way from the room. We wound our way back down the tower and emerged into a long corridor.

"This way," Rowan said, pointing.

We trouped silently down the hall, passing the door to the entrance, before continuing to a steep staircase that led down into darkness.

"The servants' quarters are down here, and the storerooms should be just beyond that," Rowan said. Flames sprung from his hand, and he lifted it high above his head. Light flickered off the stone walls and floor, dispelling the gloom before us.

I lifted my hand and summoned a second flame. Lumi gripped my arm, pressing closer to my light. A thick silence hung in the icy air as we crept down the stairs. The only sound was our breathing and the soft scrape of our boots against the stone steps.

"Okay." Rowan looked back at us as we reached the bottom, whispering like he was trying not to rouse a sleeping monster. "The storerooms are just... Fuck!" He turned towards the hallway and swore loudly, stumbling back into me and knocking me off balance. Both of our flames died, plunging us into darkness. The soft hiss of a sword being drawn echoed in the quiet.

"What happened?" I whispered, gripping Rowan's shoulders to hold him steady.

"There's someone there," he replied fearfully.

I stepped in front of him, tensed and ready for a fight as flames licked my palms.

Shadows danced around us and retreated, revealing a figure standing just beyond the sphere of light.

"Who are you?" I growled. The flames grew, illuminating the person peering around a door frame.

His face was frozen in shock. The ice covering his body sparkled in the fire's light. Horror clenched my gut as I held my hands out, letting the fire burn brighter. Several more frozen people came into view. Each one had the same shocked and terrified expression, caught in the act of fleeing from an unseen threat.

I held my hand up higher, revealing more doorways and even more people. Even the stone walls and floor were coated in a thick black ice. A terrifying moment flash frozen and preserved for all time. A few of them lay on the ground with icicles protruding from their abdomens.

"Were these the servants?" she gasped, returning her blade to its sheath.

Rowan lit a fire in his hands. His face had turned ashen and gray.

"She killed them too. But why?" he breathed as he stepped forward, carefully approaching one of the figures stretched out on the floor. The figure's eyes were closed, and her face was blank. Rowan held his fire up to get a better look at her.

"She has a sun around her neck." Rowan gestured to a necklace just visible under the ice coating her chest.

Lumi and I crept forward. She slipped on the ice and clutched my arm tighter for support. I ignored the jolt through my stomach at her touch and knelt closer to another figure sprawled on the floor. Four icicles protruded from his chest. I peered closer and found a small sun hanging from a chain around his neck.

"He has one too," I said, straightening.

"So does he," Lumi added, pointing to a figure slumped against the wall. "They all do. The ones that..." She trailed off, indicating vaguely to her chest.

"They must've been Summer's personal servants," Rowan said. He glanced around at the prone figures. "But if she was going to kill everyone anyway, why'd she stab them first? And why just Summer's personal servants?"

"Something must have happened," Lumi replied.

"I think," I said slowly, lowering my hand, "it might be time to get some answers from Spring."

"I think so too," Rowan nodded, looking towards the end of the dark hallway. "Let's go check the storeroom and then we can go find him."

We crept past room after room of frozen victims. In one of them, two people were twisted together in a passionate embrace. They were pressed against the wall, intensely focused on each other, paused forever in the act. In another room was an older man sitting in a chair, reading a book. The servants further down the hall must not have heard the commotion. Many of them were frozen performing everyday tasks such as eating, sleeping, and dressing.

The ice coating the floor ended at the final doorway. We peered inside and found a mess. There was nothing left but chunks of splintered wood and shattered glass littering the floor. Three frozen bodies were pinned to the wall by thick, black ice. Each one of their faces were twisted in agony and fear. And each one wore a sun pendant.

"Definitely time for some answers," Rowan muttered, eyes wide. We crept past, stomachs churning with horror and rounded a sharp corner, stopping short as we found the storeroom.

"Okay," he said. "This is it." Rowan glanced back at us and heaved the door open. Like the rest of the palace, the storeroom had been destroyed. Crates and barrels had been smashed and strewn about the room. If there was anything even remotely salvageable, it was buried under debris.

"Shit." Rowan's shoulders sagged. "Come on. Let's look around. Maybe there's still something here we can take back with us."

We spread out and began picking through the rubble. As I kicked over a small pile of wood, my eyes fell upon three small vials. I picked them up and examined them a little closer. The red liquid inside shimmered in the firelight and the glass was extremely warm.

"Whoa," I said, holding them up for Rowan and Lumi to see. "These feel really hot."

"It might be spiceberry wine," Rowan said, glancing over at me. "Those are the berries Father told us about, remember?" I shook my head.

"He was passed out for that," Lumi reminded him, turning in a slow circle.

"Oh right. I forgot." Rowan hopped over the debris and took a vial from my hand, wincing as the scorching glass touched his skin. "Oh yeah. This is spiceberry wine for sure. It's a strong aphrodisiac and it prevents pregnancy. People drank this during the summertime festival." He handed it back and turned away.

"Wonder what it tastes like," I muttered. Rowan and Lumi both had their backs to me as I slipped the bottles into my pocket to try later.

We searched the storeroom for a while longer. Finally, Rowan scrubbed a frustrated hand over his face.

"I can't believe there's nothing here," he sighed.

Lumi nudged a piece of wood over with her boot. "Someone went through every box. They must've had the same idea as us."

"Maybe... but why smash the crates?" I replied, scanning the wreckage. "If they had the same idea then they would've taken the crates and everything inside. But they destroyed everything instead." My mind drifted to the smashed furniture upstairs. "I definitely think someone was looking for something."

"Looking for what though?" Lumi asked. "It certainly wasn't the food."

"No idea," Rowan shrugged, brushing a red curl from his forehead. "But I think it's time to go find Spring." He gave the room one last forlorn glance before leading us back out into the servants' quarters. We made our way back in dejected silence, carefully avoiding the frozen bodies on the floor until we emerged into the entrance hall. Snow was falling past the windows in a thick flurry.

"We can't go back out in that," Lumi remarked. "Guess we're stuck here."

We found Spring in the room at the top of the stairwell with the smashed stone. He was sitting with his back pressed to the wall, leaning his head against it. His long legs were curled into his chest, and he'd braced his forearms on his knees. We entered, shivering at the bitter wind tearing through the broken window.

"I'm sorry in advance," he said.

Before we could respond, the world tilted, and the sickening dizzy feeling overtook me. I hit the ground on all fours, blinking and fighting the urge to vomit. Suddenly, the sensation vanished. I looked up to find the pile of stones blocking the hole in the glass.

"Sorry." Spring ducked his head apologetically. I struggled to my feet and glared at him as Lumi groaned and rolled onto her back. Rowan was face down on the floor with his hands pressed over his mouth. I reached down and helped them to their feet.

"You owe us some answers," I said forcefully. Spring inclined his head.

"I do," he agreed. He watched as Lumi dug some food out of her backpack while Rowan and I set up a roaring fire. It crackled to life and bathed the room in a comfortable warmth. We ate in silence. Spring leaned his head back and stared up at the ceiling. Dark shadows danced behind his eyes. The silence seemed to stretch on forever as he struggled to find the right words.

"Why don't you start from the beginning?" Rowan suggested finally, sidling over to sit in front of him. Lumi sat next to Rowan, and I slid next to her. Spring nodded and heaved a deep, mournful sigh.

"Winter," he began, his voice still thick with emotion, "wasn't always like this. She was kind once. She cared about our people." He closed his eyes, his face twisted in a pained expression.

We all exchanged glances as Spring opened his eyes and fixed them firmly on the ceiling again. Like he couldn't bear to look at us. "The four of us were chosen six hundred years ago by the Ethereal Two as the seasonal heralds. The previous heralds were... Let's just say they 'displeased' the Two. I was never sure exactly what happened. But we were Cosmic servants here at the palace and one day they were just... gone. The Two chose the four of us to replace them. Winter, Fall, my twin sister, and me." He swallowed hard.

"For a long time, we coexisted pretty peacefully. Or most of us did anyway. My sister is... was," he corrected himself with a grimace, "a vain creature. She loved expensive things. The shinier and rarer, the better. For the most part, we let her be. She knew exactly how to shut me up and Fall was always too kind to say anything to her. Winter was the only one who tried to rein Summer in.

"My sister hated being told no when she was after something. She could usually charm anything from just about anyone. Humans would fall all over themselves trying to please her. They fought and, in some cases, killed to be the one to present her with what she wanted. Almost everyone she met instantly fell under her thumb.

"Except Winter. And after years of refusing to cave to her wishes, Summer started trying harder to irritate Winter. It became something of a game to her. She tried her best to get under Winter's skin, but she never got the rise from Winter she was hoping for. Until she..." His breath caught in his throat. "She took something from Winter. Something irreplaceable."

"What did she take?" Rowan asked quietly.

"Her heart." Anguish twisted Spring's face. "Winter and Fall were in a serious relationship. They fell for each other shortly after we were given the heraldship and they were inseparable for centuries. Summer made it her mission to seduce him out of nothing but spite. She told me that she felt nothing for him. She just wanted to prove to Winter that no one could deny her what she wanted. I am ashamed to admit that I didn't say a word. I thought there wasn't a chance in this world Fall would betray the one he loved."

"But he did," Lumi surmised, raising her eyebrows.

Spring blinked hard and nodded. "For decades, she flirted and favored him with attention every chance she got. And I really thought he'd eventually snap and tell her to back off. But one night, we had a feast. Winter was at the World's Tower, and I was reading in the corner of the banquet hall. I guess they forgot I was there. Summer had been plying Fall with the finest wines in her collection when he drunkenly confessed his desires. They made love on the spot. I happened to look up from my book and found them on the table. So, I ran.

"I'm embarrassed to admit I did nothing to stop it. I should've gone straight to the tower and told Winter what happened. But he was drunk. I just knew he'd be horrified when he sobered up and it would never happen again. I was so sure, I talked myself out of going. Fall and Winter were together for six hundred years. I thought that meant something. He wasn't going to throw away a love like that for a night of passion with someone who didn't care about him.

"But then, I went to borrow a book from Winter's library and found my sister's dress on the floor. I heard them in Winter's office, and I realized... I was wrong. For the rest of Winter's cycle, Fall and Summer were constantly together. I found them having sex three more times before I started hiding to avoid the situation. I should've told Winter then. But... I didn't... I didn't want to be the one to break her heart. I realize now I was just being selfish." He rubbed his eyes with the heels of his palms.

"I thought once my cycle started, it would be over. Winter would be back home, and I could mark the whole thing up to a huge lapse in Fall's judgement. But they didn't stop. I wish I could sit here and tell you that I had no idea what happened while I was away. But my sister's second greatest joy in life was making me squirm. She visited the tower every chance she got to keep me updated on her little scheme. And I still didn't say a damn word. Summer absolutely loved that Fall kept choosing her over Winter. And Fall... I guess he didn't love Winter like she loved him. Like I thought he did.

"It was an open secret. Everyone in the palace knew it. Everyone but Winter. Summer made sure that she and Fall were very indiscreet and... Finally... During the last days of my cycle, Winter learned the truth from a minor spirit. I'm guessing it was one of Summer's personal servants that tipped her off. They were just like my sister, vain and entitled."

My mind flashed to the servants below us. To the bodies pinned to the wall or frozen with ice protruding from their chests.

Spring drew a shuddering breath and continued.

"I made it home and found the palace completely empty. Summer didn't show up to the Crossroads Temple when she was supposed to, so I was late. I found Winter here in the altar room. She said she confronted my sister... Who laughed. It was always a game to her, but she didn't realize she'd pushed Winter too far this time." He pressed his lips together, the memories swimming behind his eyes drawing a deep sob from his chest.

"She was furious. Winter said I betrayed her. And... She's right. I did. But she said as retribution for her stolen happiness, she would take everyone else's. She said humanity had helped me teach my sister that she could have anything without consequence. Then she trapped me in the ice and threw me out that window. I blacked out and the next thing I knew, I was surrounded by you three." He looked down and met our eyes, clasping his hands tightly in his lap.

"I'm so sorry," he moaned. "I could've stopped all of this, but dealing with my sister has always been difficult for me. I took the worst job in the world just to get away from her and yet still somehow ended up with her constantly in my face for six hundred years. She knew how to keep me in check and I'm ashamed to say I never tried to change that. No matter what she did to me. I just gave in with the hope that if I did, she'd leave me alone. But now, Summer and Fall are dead, and the world is doomed. Because of me."

We sat in stunned silence until Rowan frowned and sat up straighter.

"So," he said, his green eyes blazing. "Before, you said there are stones connected to the heraldship?"

"Yes," Spring replied. "They are the heralds' connection with the major cosmic energies and our powers. The power of the heraldship is too much for us to hold all at once. Our stones bridge that gap and give us access to all of our power when we need it. And when we're cut off from our power, the stone holds it for us. Right now, most of my power is locked to it and I'm next to useless. I can draw from your energy, but only in small amounts without hurting you. And I can't use your energy to replace mine. I can only borrow yours, but it will dissipate if I don't use it right away."

"Why?" Rowan said, tilting his head thoughtfully.

"The energy is different," Spring replied. "Cosmic people don't draw their power from the major cosmic energy like spirits do. They are born with a connection to the minor cosmic energy making up everything in our world. Which is lucky." Spring frowned deeply. "Winter's extended stay at the tower has corrupted the major energies. It drove the lesser spirits crazy and turned them into monsters. If you used the same energy, you'd all have lost your humanity a long time ago. As a herald, I can still use some of the Cosmic energy I was born with, but it's what kept me alive for the last twenty years. I have next to nothing left of it."

"You said she took the other stones," Lumi said. "If she can't use them and thinks all of you are dead, why did she take them?" Spring fell silent for a moment.

"There is a book," he began, his pink cheeks growing pale. "It was written by a faithful follower of the Two, thousands of years ago. It describes the cosmic energies in vivid detail and every possible way to use them. I've only ever seen it once." His eyes misted over. "When I performed the ritual to become Spring. After that, we weren't even allowed to be in the same room with it."

"Why?" Lumi asked.

"It describes a dangerous ritual," Spring said, meeting her eyes. "The cosmic energy can become so corrupted that even the Two would be affected. Chances are they've warded themselves against Winter by cutting themselves off from her influence. But the book details a ritual that uses all four stones. It renders the cosmic energies inert for just long enough."

"To do what? To kill them?" Rowan asked. His panicked tone sent unease creeping through my gut. Lumi reached out, lacing her fingers through mine for comfort.

"Not only kill them, but replace them," Spring said grimly. "She would take their powers and gain the ability to reshape the world however she wanted."

"Humans," Lumi whispered, horrified. "That's why the palace was wrecked. She was looking for the book. To destroy us." Her fingers tightened on mine in fear. I stroked my thumb across the back of her hand reassuringly.

"We won't let that happen," I said. She met my eyes and my heart stuttered.

"Ash, it's been twenty years," Rowan croaked, pressing a shaking hand to his lips. "She probably already has the book."

"No," Spring replied firmly. "If she had the book, you'd all be dead."

"Then where is it?" I asked, still stroking the back of Lumi's hand with my thumb. She glanced down and I released her hand quickly, running my fingers through my hair instead.

"I don't know," Spring admitted. He brushed a green curl from his eyes and tucked it behind his pointed ear. "All I can tell you is it was written by a spirit. He was a collector of rare and exotic books. Winter used to trade with him. I think he was even the inspiration for a human book trading ritual."

Rowan's face lit up like starlight.

"Oh!" he exclaimed, "The Book Keeper! Right?"

Spring let out a startled laugh and a smile tugged at his lips.

Rowan blushed furiously. "S-sorry," he muttered, shrinking back. "I just... grew up loving that story."

"Don't apologize. You're absolutely right. He came to be known by humans as the Book Keeper," Spring said, grinning. "He earned his nickname traveling to human villages to collect books for Winter during First Frost. I've never actually met him, but she and the spirit had a close relationship. But he never shared the book with her. At least, not that I know of anyway. I'm not even sure where it could've ended up."

"That must be why Winter never tried to crush villages with an ice storm," Rowan mused. "A book thousands of years old like that would be destroyed under the rubble if someone had it."

A sudden idea struck me.

"Could the Book Keeper tell us where it is?" I asked, sitting up straighter. Spring frowned.

"If Winter's corruption took an Eternal like Calliope, I doubt the Book Keeper would've fared any better," Spring said.

Rowan looked crestfallen.

"But maybe there's still something? Something where he lived that could give us a clue?" I pressed. "There has to be a way to stop her."

Spring furrowed his brow. "We'd need to remove her stone from the throne. It would lock her power to the World's Tower," he said. "And she must be so corrupted by now, she probably wouldn't survive losing her power." He shook his head. "But even if her stone were removed, I would have to take her place and there's no one to take mine. We'd be right back to where we started."

"You said you were chosen," Rowan said slowly. A wild light danced in his eyes. "Why you?" Spring stared at him, understanding dawning on his face.

"Because I was Cosmic once," he whispered.

"And the book has the ritual," Lumi said, catching on in the same instant I did.

"We could do it," I said, meeting Rowan's eyes and then Lumi's. "We could perform the ritual! We could take the heraldships and set the world back right!"

"The Two would have to accept you first," Spring added quickly.

"Right... But we could at least try," I pressed. "And it's not like there's that many of us left."

"What do you mean?" Spring said in surprise. We exchanged a quick glance.

"Humans have not been kind to the Cosmic," Rowan said sadly. "They think our power summons Winter's ice demons. Many of us have been killed."

Spring sucked in a sharp breath. "Kaelin," he said fearfully. "Is he...?"

"No," Rowan replied sadly. "But his hands were removed."

"*Removed*?" Spring paled.

"Humans think that if we have no hands, we have no power," Rowan explained.

Spring leaned forward and clutched his chest.

"My mother and father have gone through a lot to hide the three of us from the people of Haven," Rowan added with a swift, apologetic glance in Lumi's direction. She looked down, fury flashing briefly across her expression.

"Oh no," Spring whispered. "Then..." He looked back up at us. "You three may very well be the last hope the world has." His statement hung heavy in the air between us. I looked at my friends and we stared at each other for a long, tense moment.

"We have to try," Rowan said finally, his green eyes bright with excitement.

"But what about your parents?" Lumi said, wringing her hands.

"My parents will understand," he replied. "What about yours?"

Lumi huffed out an angry breath. "I don't really care what they think." Her eyes were like chips of ice as she met mine. "But, if we do this and I don't come back, you know who my father will blame."

"I don't care," I said as sincerely as I could. "Let him think I stole you. It will keep his anger away from Kaelin and Lucia if he has it all focused on me."

"Still," Rowan said, looking worriedly towards the snow-covered window. "I wish there was a way to get a message to them. Just to let them know we're okay. If we really are going through with this, we can't go back. Jasper will weld the gates shut behind us."

"After he murdered us for kidnapping Lumi," I added. She scowled at me before turning back to Rowan.

"Do we have enough food?" Lumi asked, toying with her hair nervously.

"I packed enough for at least three weeks," he said. "In case something happened. I wasn't joking when I said I packed for every scenario I could think of. We have rope, tents, sleeping bags, spare clothes, soap…" he shrugged sheepishly.

"Damn, Ro. Way to be prepared," I whistled. He nodded absentmindedly, shooting another look out the window.

"They're gonna be worried sick," he mumbled.

"What if we leave something here?" Lumi suggested. "Kaelin knew where we were going. We could leave a note somewhere where he'd see it explaining everything."

"Good idea," Rowan sighed, rubbing his eyes. "I hate the idea of making them worry but at least it's something."

"It's been a long day and this storm isn't letting up anytime soon," I said, stretching my aching muscles. "We should probably get some sleep."

"Agreed," Lumi said. Rowan waved a hand at the bags.

"We have the tents. Or we could just use the sleeping bags," he offered. The thought of putting up a tent seemed physically impossible, so we decided to leave them and rolled out our sleeping bags instead.

"I'll see you in the morning," Spring said. "I don't need to sleep, so, I'll keep watch."

"Do you want a book?" Rowan asked shyly.

Spring blinked and smiled. "Sure," he said. "If you don't mind?" Rowan dove a hand into his bag before withdrawing a stack of books and handing them over.

"Help yourself," he mumbled, blushing.

Spring's handsome smile widened as he took them. "Ooh, I love romance. Thank you." Their eyes met and Rowan's blush deepened. He muttered a quick goodnight before sliding into his sleeping bag and turning away. Lumi and I exchanged curious glances before settling into our own sleeping bags.

"Goodnight, Ash," Lumi yawned. Light from the moon illuminated her face as she grinned sleepily at me. My breath caught in my throat.

"Night, Lumi," I said.

She sighed and closed her eyes, exhaustion claiming her almost instantly. I forced myself to roll over, focusing on the ceiling. But inevitably, my thoughts drifted back to her perfect face. I chanced a look in her direction and couldn't help staring, wishing desperately that I could run my hands through that gorgeous raven hair. My heart started pounding, and I made myself look away sharply, glancing back over to Spring.

He had a book propped open on his knees but was peering over it at Rowan, examining him closely before he glanced over at me.

I cocked an eyebrow, frowning, and he blushed.

"I know you don't trust me," Spring began.

"Not particularly," I agreed.

"I won't hurt you," he promised.

"I'm not really all that worried about me," I replied. "But Ro and Lumi are my everything."

"You have my word. I don't mean any of you harm." He held up his palms in surrender. I narrowed my eyes before sighing and running my fingers through my hair.

"Fine, but just remember... You try to do anything to either one of them, you will answer to me," I said threateningly before closing my eyes.

"Understood," Spring said. I heard the rustle of a page turning and settled further into my sleeping bag. My mind drifted back to running my fingers through raven hair and kissing full lips. I sank into a deep sleep with a smile on my face.

CHAPTER SEVENTEEN

WINTER

My footsteps echoed off the walls of the World's Tower as I lazily paced the length of the throne room. This space had once been open and light, made from the finest marble and stone. But twenty years under my control had turned it into an icy fortress. Icicles the size of grown men hung from the ceiling and large columns of ice stretched their way up the walls. A black throne stood in the center, facing the large balcony that overlooked the land.

My land. As far as the eye could see, there was nothing but bleak desolation. A masterpiece, reflecting my heart upon every inch of my glorious kingdom. My eyes were closed, and my consciousness was drifting, flitting between the minds of my thralls prowling the land.

Most of them were searching tirelessly. It had been many centuries since I'd seen the *Book of the Cosmics*. But I knew it was still here. If it wasn't, the kings in the east or the commanders of the west would've used it to end my reign long ago.

Most of the human settlements had already been ransacked with no luck. So, I had directed my thralls to start searching the wilderness. They rutted about in the frozen tundra and sniffed the roots of every tree. Any trace of the spirit they once were had long been suffocated and now, they were mindless drones, bound to my every whim.

I stopped in the mind of a thrall in the farthest corner of my land. It was snarling down at a terrified human woman. She screamed, throwing her hands above her head as my thrall slashed out, dragging its long claws across her chest. Blood sprayed the snow and the woman fell silent.

My thrall was surrounded by other demons that had finally breached the walls of the port city far to the north. They were ripping through the human settlement, destroying buildings, and tearing the pathetic creatures to shreds. Screams of anguish and pain filled the air. The creature spotted another human and went bounding after it, its teeth gnashing furiously. I smiled as it clamped its jaws around the man's neck and moved on, still flitting from mind to mind.

I paused in the mind of another creature. She was dragging her snout through the snow of the Great Forest in an attempt to detect any trace of something buried there.

I sighed in frustration. Part of me yearned to go back to the caves— back to the place the book should have been— and make him suffer even more.

The Book Keeper swore he'd given it away to some human. It took inflicting a great deal of pain for me to learn that he'd given the book to the headmaster of the Cosmic Academy in Trithica. Or so I thought.

I'd marched straight there to claim my victory, only to discover the headmaster had ended his life to spare the world from me. And my book was nowhere to be found. I'd destroyed the academy in retribution and my search began in earnest. I huffed, about to turn away from my thrall's mind when something tugged at the end of it. Something familiar.

My spine stiffened. I reached out with my power, sensing an entity inside her mind with me and attempted to trap it. It felt me and retreated quickly, leaving behind only the slightest trace it had been there at all. I examined the trace of its power, unease twisting my heart.

There was no way.

I opened my eyes, reaching out across the land with my power. Far off in the distance, something weak flinched away from the touch of my power before it threw up a wall, shielding itself from me. I pushed against the shield, but it wouldn't budge. I pushed again, my face going blank with shock as a rich floral scent filled my nose.

Roses.

It wasn't possible. He was dead.

My ragged white dress billowed around my legs as I strode out onto the balcony, bracing my hands on the railing as I stared off towards the mountains in disbelief.

The towers of Nature's Palace were barely visible, peering over the mountain like a frightened child. I pushed again against the shield. It shuddered but stayed in place.

It couldn't be. I had to be imagining things.

In my impatience, I'd tried for years to figure out the joining ritual by myself. And after two decades of trying, I was no closer to joining the stone than I was the day I took the tower. But in that time, I'd seen the spring emerald, the fall amethyst, and the summer diamond almost every single day. If they were still attached to a herald, the would be glimmering softly. But each one of them had a blinding glow that rivaled the stars, indicating that their spirit was dead, and the connection was severed.

I reached out again, sure that I was imagining things. The smell of roses was like a punch to the gut, and I gasped.

"Spring," I breathed in disbelief. "You're alive."

I sent these words towards the wall wrapped around his mind. His power was nothing but a mere trickle of what it once was and he was expending his strength as fast as it regenerated by holding his wall around not only himself, but someone else.

My heart hammered against my ribs. It wasn't possible. I froze him. He should have been dead. My ice had already proven its lethal power against his bitch of a sister. But I could feel him in the distance, shrinking away from what my power had become. There was no force in this world that should have been able to free him from my ice. And yet...

"My brother is coming."

The sultry voice behind me made white hot rage blister through my blood. I turned towards the throne and found Summer leaning back with her long legs draped over the arm.

She was dressed in her favorite black nightgown, just as she had been the last time I saw her. The gossamer cloth swooped down low in the front and slits climbed up the sides almost to her hips. Her full lips were stretched into a malicious smirk. Her golden hair tumbled freely past her small shoulders and her bright yellow skin shone even in the dim light. Her sunny yellow eyes were fixed on me as I turned fully to face her.

I'd always hated her beauty. She had the kind of face men and women fell all over each other for. She lifted her chin defiantly as I glowered at her.

"You're dead," I spat, striding back into the room. "I killed you."

"You killed *him* too," she purred, nodding towards the corner behind me. I turned and blanched.

Fall was leaning against the archway I had just walked through. His eyes were fixed on the wall and his mouth was turned down in a frown. He was shirtless, wearing only his black sleeping pants. The weak sunlight framing his body made it look like he was glowing. His square jaw was covered in the dark shadow of orange stubble. His long orange hair was tousled as though he'd just been sleeping. He crossed his muscled arms over his broad chest and cast his deep brown eyes to the floor. His skin was a patchwork of red, orange, and yellow that swirled across his body like the fall leaves shifting in the winds.

"Fall," I gasped.

My heart still fluttered at the sight of him, but I couldn't bear to utter his name. His true name. He didn't look at me, turning instead to scan the horizon.

"Fall..." I whispered again. I had not seen him in twenty years. Part of me wanted to reach for him. The other part of me wanted to rip his throat open all over again.

"You're wasting your time," Summer chuckled. I turned back to her as my power thrummed against my bones in my anger. "He won't speak to you," she added, smirking.

"Thanks to you," I snarled.

Summer tipped her head back and laughed. "You're so ridiculous," she said, her eyes gleaming. "Still blaming me for all your problems."

"You stole my heart from me," I snapped. "Ripped it from my chest and stomped on it."

Guilt washed over Fall's handsome face. He turned away further.

"Oh, grow up." She rolled her eyes. "It's not my fault he wanted some warmth in his bed for once."

"Stop," Fall sighed. The sound of his voice sent a jolt up my spine. He stared at her mournfully. "Don't do that," he begged. Summer glanced at him and settled smugly into the throne.

"Fall," I said loudly. He flinched slightly but didn't turn to look at me. I bristled. "So, after everything... You'll talk to her, but you won't even face me?"

"Would you talk to the unhinged person who murdered you?" Summer mused, tracing idle circles in the air with her bare toes. "Look at yourself, Kiora."

"Do *not* call me that," I hissed through my teeth.

"You really let yourself go." Summer tossed her wavy hair over her shoulder. "Your lovely white hair has turned all black and scraggly. Your skin is so gray, and those black eyes are unnerving. Though not as unnerving as your new... *features*." She wrinkled her small nose at me.

I traced a fingertip along the shard of ice protruding from my cheek. I had a patch crawling up my neck and another stretching across my forehead.

"Your handiwork," I sneered, gesturing at my frail, thin body. "Funny how taking what doesn't belong to you has consequences."

"Oh please," she snorted. "I didn't take anything from you." She smirked wickedly, curling a golden strand around her finger. "He gave it to me. Repeatedly."

"Mirela, please," Fall groaned, burying his face in his hands. My rage boiled over and I clenched my fists.

"You're not real," I hissed. "You're dead. Shattered and strewn all over your bedroom floor."

She curled her perfectly manicured fingers around the arms of my throne and got up slowly, her eyes locked with mine.

"It's over Kiora," she sneered softly. "My brother is coming. And he will take his vengeance."

"Please," I snorted. "Your brother is a sniveling coward." I summoned my power and formed a long ice spear in my hand. Her eyes flickered to it before sliding back to mine.

"Do you see?" She gestured incredulously to the spear. "You have truly lost your mind. What're you gonna do? Stab a ghost?" Summer spread her arms wide and gestured at her chest. "Go on then. Stab me, Kiora. Again."

I curled my lip in a sneer.

"Oh, don't worry. This isn't for you," I purred, twirling the spear at my side. "This is so your brother can join you beyond the veil."

Summer's back stiffened. She drew herself up to her full height, eyeing me hatefully. I met her gaze, forcefully driving the spear into the stone at her feet.

"You're nothing," she spat. "The corruption has destroyed you. When my brother arrives, you will be no match for him."

"Your brother is weak. And I have his stone. I have *all* the stones. And soon, I will have the *Book of the Cosmics*," I said triumphantly.

Summer's shining yellow skin paled. "You can't," she gasped. "Kiora, you don't know what joining the stones will do."

"I know exactly what it will do," I said, stepping closer to her. "It will kill those wretched so-called 'gods' that have neglected this world for several millennia. And when I take their place, I will destroy your precious pets. I will resurrect my love, and I will wipe every single trace of your existence from this world. Not even the rats will remember you." Wild delight danced through my heart as she backed up fearfully.

"Kiora."

I turned, startled at the deep rasp.

Fall gazed at me with a heartbroken expression. "Please," he begged. He took a hesitant step towards me. "Please, you can't do this."

I frowned at him. "I don't have a choice. I have to do this," I said, reaching back to wrench the spear out of the floor.

"You don't," he replied desperately. "You don't have to do this. You could remove your stone from the tower and let yourself heal from the corruption. Spring can help you. Find him and let him help you get better, Kiora. Please. You could help him rebuild the world and move on."

"Rebuild the world?" I snorted. "For who? Those groveling worms that would have gleefully burned it all down for her?"

I pointed an accusing finger at Summer, who now stood beside Fall. Rage blinded me as she casually touched his arm. I met his eyes again.

"You'll see. I'll unite the stones and destroy the Two. Then I will remake you with no memories of this wicked *bitch*." Summer bristled but I ignored her. "You and I will wipe the world clean and start over."

Fall winced and opened his mouth, stopping short as Summer chuckled darkly.

"You can try all you want," she sneered, letting her fingers trail down his chest. He frowned at her hand but didn't stop her. "You can destroy every trace of me. But no matter what you do, you will always know the truth." Her eyes were bright as she leaned closer, dropping her hand to his stomach. Fall still did nothing to stop her.

I clenched my fist around the spear.

"That no matter how much you loved him... He was really mine." She grasped between his legs. He let out a startled groan and closed his eyes, leaning into her touch.

My vision turned red, and I hurled the spear at them. It shattered against the floor, scattering shards of ice across the stone. Tears burned my eyes as my power shot rapidly around the room in my rage. Ice embedded in the walls and the ceiling.

My breathing turned ragged as silence fell. I was alone.

I pressed a hand to my throat. A crack had ripped open in the skin above my collarbone and black chunks of ice were beginning to grow from the gaping hole. Rage still simmered in my veins as I strode out onto the balcony and closed my eyes, unleashing the full force of my powers. I sensed Spring at Nature's Palace and pounced.

My power descended upon his shield like a predator cornering its prey for the kill. It bowed against the onslaught but held firm. I let my power slither over its surface, searching for any kind of cracks or weaknesses, but there was nothing.

His natural power would regenerate on its own, but without the power attached to his stone, the process would be very slow. He was redirecting his energy to the shield the moment it was usable, but even that had it's limits. The moment he fell asleep or lowered his guard even for a second, he was finished.

"You can't hide from me forever," I whispered to him, withdrawing my power. As I retreated, I felt a shudder under the shield.

He would be coming for his stone. And then he'd come for mine.

I sent an order into the minds of my thralls. All over the isle they increased their efforts. Those that I had sent to the north to attack the human town froze in their tracks before scattering to search for the book.

I opened my eyes again and sent my power into the sky. Storm clouds gathered above the tower and began rolling towards the mountains. I sent a new order to the thrall still prowling through the forest. It was the same one where I had first sensed Spring.

"Calliope," I said. She stopped in her tracks. "Spring has returned. Go to the castle and kill him or bring him to me. I don't care which."

She turned and begin trotting up the pass. I smiled and pulled out of her mind, looking up to watch my storm race towards the palace. Spring may have survived all those years ago, but he was clearly too weak to fight off an attack.

This would be over quickly.

CHAPTER EIGHTEEN

Rowan

Bitter cold seeped into my bones and I sat up, shivering and rubbing the sleep from my eyes.

Spring looked up from the book he was reading and fixed his intense green stare on me.

"Did I wake you?" He whispered. I shook my head.

"No. But it got very cold." I glanced around and saw that the fire had gone out. "What time is it?" I asked through chattering teeth.

Spring lowered the book and glanced out the window. Thick snowfall was still dropping past the glass and the sky beyond was an angry gray.

"I'm not sure but I think it's morning," he replied. I nodded and looked back as he stretched his long legs out from underneath him, revealing his bare feet.

"Aren't your feet freezing?" I asked. He chuckled and shook his head.

"A little but I'm okay. I hate wearing shoes." He shot me a meek grin. "There's nothing like feeling the grass beneath your feet. That's why I always garden barefoot."

"Really? I'll have to take your word for it on that one," I replied. "So, gardening huh? What else do you like to do?" He held up the book and I grinned. "Me too! I like to change it up with the genres every once in a while, but I'm a sucker for a good romance with a happy-ever-after."

"Oh, absolutely," he nodded, sliding his feet back into his shoes. "The world has enough heartache in it already. I need a happy ending when I'm trying to escape reality."

Lumi stirred in her sleep and rolled over, edging closer to Ash. He was sound asleep on his back, one arm thrown over his head.

Lumi tucked her shivering form tightly into Ash's side, placing her head on his shoulder and sighing deeply at the warmth. He groaned and flicked a hand without waking. A large ball of fire blazed to life, bathing the room in a comfortable heat.

He rolled over to settle closer to Lumi without realizing it, draping one arm across her back, and tangling his fingers in her unbound hair.

"Speaking of needing a happy ending," I said.

"I was going to ask you about that. They seem uh... close," Spring remarked, raising his eyebrows at me.

"Oh yeah," I snickered. "They are 'close.' But I haven't gotten either one of them to admit it out loud."

Spring pressed his lips together to suppress his smile. "That's adorable."

"And incredibly frustrating," I sighed.

"I can imagine." His handsome face broke out in a grin and my heart fluttered.

I cleared my throat, dropping my gaze back to my sleeping friends. "Hopefully, I can help them admit to their 'closeness'."

"That's very kind of you," Spring said, closing the book with a soft snap.

"I just want them to be happy. They both deserve it."

"Why not tell them yourself?" he mused.

"Oh, that's no fun. Besides, Ash wouldn't believe me if I told him. He's been through a lot and doesn't think very highly of himself most of the time." I shot Ash a mournful look. "And even if Lumi told him, I don't think he'd let himself believe it right away."

"And what about you?" Spring asked. He leaned forward and braced his forearms on his knees.

"Nope. Not me," I grinned, shrugging. "Someday maybe. I'm still waiting for the right man to sweep me off my feet."

"Oh?" Spring replied, his eyes bright.

"Yeah." I averted my eyes briefly. "So, uh... What about you? Was there someone special before all this?" I asked, gesturing towards the window. He snorted and shook his head firmly.

"No," he replied. "No one special. Just men I wish I'd never met."

"Oh, me too. Nothing but a bunch of regrets. Where's that handsome storybook prince when you need him, right?" I joked. He chuckled and looked up at me with a small grin.

"Yeah," he agreed, a soft glimmer filling his eyes. "I'm still waiting for my chance to be someone's storybook prince."

"Oh," I said quietly. Heat crept down my neck and flutters filled my stomach. We stared at each other for the span of a heartbeat.

"One day though," he murmured, keeping his eyes locked with mine. "One day I'll find him. And maybe... Maybe he'll let me sweep him off his feet."

I sucked in a soft breath, blushing furiously at the boldness of his statement. He blinked and rubbed the back of his neck sheepishly, like he couldn't believe he had just said that out loud. I was suddenly hyper aware of him. His hands. His gorgeous green eyes. The movement of his chest as he drew breath.

I cleared my throat and stood with a casual stretch to avoid meeting his stare. His pink cheeks darkened, and he looked away as the hem of my tunic rode up slightly, exposing my stomach to the cold.

"So," I began, yanking my tunic back down quickly. "Are you hungry?"

"No, I'm okay. I don't need to eat," he said, waving a hand at the three of us. "It's a long trek to the tower and I don't want to take from your food supply."

"You don't have to eat at all?" I asked.

"Not if I don't want to," he replied. "But I do know my way around the kitchen. I like to..." Spring paused, grimacing. "Well... I used to summon all kinds of fresh fruits and vegetables. And the chef would help me make the most delicious dishes. She and I would cook and sing for hours."

"You sing?" I asked, raising my eyebrows.

His face fell and shadows danced behind his deep green eyes.

"I..." Spring swallowed hard and passed a hand over his mouth. "I *used* to," he mumbled.

The pain on his face broke my heart, so I cast my mind around for a change of subject that would bring that handsome smile back.

"Fresh fruits and vegetables, huh? I've never had anything fresh before. They don't do well on the ship-ride over from the Western Lands. I've always wanted to try a strawberry, though," I remarked, rolling my sleeping bag back up and attaching it to my pack.

"What?" Spring gasped, pressing a hand to his chest in mock horror. I was relieved to see the glimmer returning to his eyes. "You've never had a strawberry?"

"No," I said, grinning. "I don't even know what they look like."

"Oh, absolutely not." Spring hopped to his feet. "No, I have to fix that immediately." He stretched out a hand and met my eyes. "May I?"

"Really? You can make one?" Excitement bubbled in my stomach, and he grinned again.

"I can. But I need a tiny bit of energy to do it." He held his hand out further and I took it eagerly. As soon as my fingers brushed his, a small jolt ran up my arm and my heart started racing.

A small wave of nausea rocked through me and was gone in an instant.

Spring flipped my hand over and, in it, I found the strangest thing I'd ever seen. I stared at it in wonder, tracing my finger along the yellow seeds peppering its glossy red surface.

"That's a strawberry? It's not what I expected," I gasped, eyes wide in awe.

"What were you expecting?" Spring chuckled lightly, his lilted voice filled with glee.

"I..." I trailed off, holding the strawberry up for a better look. "I'm not sure." I looked up at him and his smile widened. "What do I do now? Do I have to peel it? And are these little seeds okay to eat?"

"No peeling," he said. "And yes, the seeds are fine. You don't eat the green part, but you can just bite right into it."

I hesitated slightly before raising the fruit to my lips and sinking my teeth into its soft flesh. My mouth was instantly flooded with the sweetest, most delectable taste I had ever experienced. My eyes fluttered closed in sheer bliss as I took another bite.

"Do you like it?" Spring asked through a wide smile. I nodded and inhaled the rest of it.

"That was the most incredible thing I've ever tasted," I moaned, smacking my lips.

"Well don't worry," Spring grinned, tucking his hands into his pockets. "Once I reclaim my power, I'll make them for you whenever you want." He blushed a bit. I felt a low heat simmering in my stomach.

"I'd really like that," I grinned, looking down at the tiny green leaves in my hand and running a finger along the velvety surface. "I've never seen anything so green in my life."

Spring took the leafy stem from me and rolled it between his fingers. "That's my fault," he said, anguish dripping from his tone. "But I'm going to fix it." He tossed the leaves into the fire.

My heart lurched. "Winter destroyed the world, not you. It's not your fault." I reached out and touched his arm gently. Darkness flickered behind his green eyes as they slid to me.

"If you knew the whole truth, you would feel differently."

I opened my mouth to respond but a groan from behind us drew my attention.

Lumi let out a soft sigh as her eyes fluttered open. She blinked and stretched, accidentally brushing her cheek against Ash's shoulder. She looked over, startled, before sitting up. She met my stare and blushed furiously.

"Morning," I smirked, arching an eyebrow at her.

"Hi," Lumi muttered. She scooted further away from Ash as he began to stir. He opened his eyes and slowly sat up, stretching his arms over his head.

"Morning, Ro," he said, looking up at me with a sleepy grin.

"Morning, Ash," I chuckled. "Did you sleep okay?" Lumi shot me a dark look.

"I did actually," Ash said. His deep voice was still gravelly from sleep.

"Your cuddle buddy didn't bother you too much, did she?" I asked, pressing my fingertips into my lips to stifle a laugh.

Ash looked confused for a moment before he blinked, blushing. A smile tugged at the corners of his mouth, but he forced his expression, with great effort, to remain neutral as Lumi turned to him.

"I'm sorry. I was cold," she muttered, embarrassed.

"Right. Of course," Ash said, trying so hard to sound unaffected. "No problem. Hope I didn't smell."

Lumi shook her head and stumbled quickly to her feet. "No... No, you smelled fine," she mumbled as she strode over to the window.

I shot Spring a glance, raising my eyebrows and grinning broadly. Humor danced behind his eyes.

Ash got to his feet. He brushed a hand over his face before he froze, pulling back in surprise. A few long black hairs were tangled around his fingers. His golden eyes went molten before they shot up and met mine. I cocked my head to the side, and he huffed, shaking the hair loose.

"You okay over there?" I asked.

"Huh? Oh yeah. I'm fine," Ash mumbled, running his fingers through his hair.

"Well," Lumi sighed heavily. "I don't think we're going anywhere anytime soon. This blizzard is a bad one."

"It's for me." Spring's voice came out small and hollow. "She is sending me a warning."

"A warning?" Ash asked.

"Yes," Spring nodded. "She knows I'm alive. And she has my stone, so I'm basically useless."

"We'll get it back," I assured him. He smiled meekly at me and nodded.

"All right, well... First things first," Spring said. He trailed off, fidgeting nervously. "Are you absolutely sure that this is something you want to do? Once you take the heraldship, there's no going back."

Lumi, Ash, and I glanced around at each other.

"Well," Ash said through a yawn. "I mean it's not like I have... well... anything. So..." He shrugged.

I let my mind drift to my parents. A deep ache squeezed my heart followed immediately by a sharp sense of thrill. I'd miss them so much. But a sense of adventure hung in the air around us and I yearned for it. The thought of a real quest to save the world was invigorating. Like I'd jumped headfirst into one of my books.

"I'm ready," I said with a nod.

I looked over at Lumi and saw her eyes fixed intently on Ash's small flame, her expression unreadable. She was silent for a long moment before finally, she sighed and looked up.

"I want to do this," she said fiercely. "My father won't ever hold any power over me again. And... I feel like I was meant for this." She trailed off and met our eyes. "You know what I mean?"

"I do," I said. Ash nodded in agreement.

Spring let out a slow breath and sat with his legs crossed underneath him.

"Then our first order of business has to be the book. We can't perform the heraldship ritual without the *Book of the Cosmics*," he said, clasping his hands in his lap. "We know for a fact Winter doesn't have it. And by the looks of it," Spring gestured to the wreckage around us. "I think it's safe to assume the book isn't here either. So, where is it?"

"Well, we know it's not in Haven," Lumi said. Spring raised his eyebrows at her, and she turned to him. "My father has every person searched and checked for powers before he lets them in. And he confiscates all their things. That way, he can give them new stuff and the refugees are in his debt before they can blink. If a book came through the gates that had anything to do with Cosmics and spirits, he'd have lost his mind over it."

"We talked about the Book Keeper last night," I interjected. A joyous balloon swelled in my chest as I pictured a good-natured creature surrounded by towering piles of tomes.

"We did." Spring frowned and my balloon deflated just a bit. "But there's almost no chance the Book Keeper stayed uncorrupted for all these years."

"It might still be worth a look," Lumi chimed in.

"I really doubt the book would be there. And it would've been the first place Winter searched," Spring replied.

"Maybe. But there might be a clue or something. It's at least worth a shot," Lumi pressed. Spring tilted his head thoughtfully.

"You're right, it is worth a shot. And I honestly don't know where else we could possibly start. All right then." Spring nodded once and stood, motioning for us to do the same. "Follow me."

We grabbed our things and followed Spring from the room and back into the corridor. We stepped over the wreckage strewn about the hall as Spring swept quickly past an open door. He ducked his head to avoid looking inside. Ash paused, furrowing his brow at Spring before he peeked into the room. His golden eyes went wide.

"What is that?" he asked, pointing.

Spring froze in his tracks. He turned back, clenching his jaw tight as anguish filled his handsome face.

"Something horrible," he hissed. He said it so quietly that only I heard him.

Lumi and I peered over Ash's shoulder. The shelves lining the walls of the small room were covered with shining round ovals in every color imaginable, displayed proudly on little wooden stands. It reminded me of the kaleidoscope I'd had as a child. Each oval gleamed like a bright light were fixed on it. There were some smaller than my thumbnail, some larger than my head and every size in between.

Lumi stepped inside the room and ran a careful finger across a brilliant yellow oval. A distant recollection tugged on my memory. Something I'd read long ago, but I couldn't remember what it was.

"It's warm!" Lumi exclaimed.

A sudden realization hit me, and my gut twisted in horror. The passage of a book floated across my mind, and I turned to Spring, desperately hoping I was wrong. He seemed to read my mind and nodded glumly, closing his eyes. My stomach dropped through the floor. I turned back to the room, shock and horror ripping apart my heart as Ash picked up a tiny purple oval.

"This one is too," he mused, holding it out to Lumi.

She took it and turned it over in her hand to examine the glimmering surface closely. She went to hand it to me, frowning as she caught sight of my expression. "What's wrong, Ro?"

"These," I said, gesturing to the walls around us, "are dragon heart scales."

A soft exhale escaped Spring's lips. He stepped up to my side and stared around the room with unfathomable guilt burning in his eyes.

"What's that?" Lumi asked, still tracing a finger across the tiny oval. "Some kind of gemstone?"

"No," I said, my voice cracking as I looked down at row after row of tiny scales. "It... it covers a dragon's most vulnerable spot and can only be removed... once the dragon is dead," I finished quietly.

Lumi gasped and whirled around, staring in horror at the gleaming ovals. There must have been at least a hundred of them.

"The size," I croaked, eyes fixed on the tiny flash of purple she had clutched tightly in her fist. "The size shows the dragon's age when they died. The bigger the scale, the older the dragon was."

She opened her palm, sucking in a sharp breath as her eyes filled with tears.

"So, this..." Lumi trailed off.

"Was probably a hatchling," I finished.

She wiped away tears and placed the tiny scale back on the shelf.

Ash rounded on Spring, fury twisting his expression. His golden eyes burned like molten metal. Wind hissed at our feet and fire wrapped itself around his clenched fists. "Why?" he snarled. Spring winced but didn't answer. "Why are these here? Displayed like sick fucking trophies!"

"Because that's exactly what they are," Spring whispered. His voice broke with despair. He wrapped his arms around his chest and let out a small sob.

Despite my horror, I felt the sudden urge to hug him.

"Sick twisted trophies. And the beginning of the end." He turned and strode from the room, unable to bear it any longer. Lumi continued staring at the shelves.

"There's so many little ones," Lumi whispered, stifling a sob.

Ash drew in a deep breath and shook out his hands, extinguishing the flames with a soft hiss. The wind swirling around our ankles died swiftly as he pulled her into his chest. She leaned into him, clutching the front of his tunic, still staring around the room.

I shook my head to clear the seeping horror numbing me and let out a short breath.

"Come on, guys," I said roughly. "Let's get out of here."

We left the room, pulling the door closed firmly on the awful sight. Spring was just outside the door with his back pressed to the wall. His head was leaning backwards against the stone, eyes fixed on the dark ceiling.

"I'm so sorry..." he gasped. "I'm sorry you had to see them. Sorry that they're even here in the first place."

"Why are they here? What happened?" Ash demanded angrily.

"Another of my many transgressions," Spring replied bitterly.

"You killed them?" I gasped. I couldn't imagine such a seemingly gentle soul slaughtering so many dragons for sport. He met my eyes and pressed his lips into a hard line.

"I may as well have," he whispered. He stared at me for a moment before shoving away from the wall and striding down the corridor.

We glanced at each other before following closely on his heels.

"What did you mean?" Lumi said. Spring didn't respond. He quickened his pace, unwilling to meet her eyes. He rounded a corner and threw a set of double doors open wide.

I froze in awe.

"I think Ro might have died from bliss just now," Lumi smirked, nudging me gently in the ribs. Ash clapped me on the back and stepped around me, following Lumi into the biggest library I'd ever seen.

Enormous wooden bookshelves stretched all the way up to the vaulted ceiling. Every bookshelf was stuffed with books and had large rolling ladders. The shelves were clustered together in groups, and each group had its own set of plush chairs and unique décor. One section had lush red armchairs and portraits of couples in various compromising positions. Another section had dark gray chairs and portraits of gruesome crimes.

"Winter's personal library," Spring said, gesturing around the large room. The warmth had not yet returned to his voice. "She would have kept what we're looking for in her office." He strode to the back of the room, passing a section with white armchairs and paintings of famous people and events.

On the very back wall, there was an open archway that led into a small, cozy space. A dark wooden writing desk sat in the corner, overladen with papers and quills. A large, ornate marble fireplace sat behind it, and an opulent mirror gilded in silver and gold hung on the wall next to the archway, reflecting the black chairs arranged in a semi-circle before the fireplace.

Spring walked to the desk and began rifling through the papers.

"And what exactly are we looking for?" Lumi asked, dropping her bag onto the floor. She turned in a slow circle to take in the room's opulence.

I put my bag next to hers. Ash flicked a wrist towards the empty grate before tossing his bag aside. Flames shot up, throwing soft light, and bringing a bit of warmth into the windowless room.

"We are looking for the map," Spring muttered. "Winter learned the way by heart, but before that, she had a map of the cave systems near here. It showed the way to the chamber where the Book Keeper lived. She would've kept it here."

"Is that why the room isn't destroyed?" Lumi asked gently touching the ornate mirror.

I looked around in surprise and realized she was right. Everything in the room, as well as the library beyond had been left completely untouched. It was like Winter had just stepped outside for some fresh air not two minutes ago.

"She knows every single item in this library. And these books are her prized possessions. She would've told her ice demons not to touch this room," Spring said. "Ah! Here it is."

He held up a piece of paper with a flourish and opened it for us to see. "See here... This is the palace. We need to go this way." He traced a finger down a long path that led into the mountains and tapped his finger on a large open cavern situated underneath a high peak. "This open space is the cavern where the spirit lived. But there might not be anything left there."

"What choice do we have?" Lumi asked, eyeing the map closely.

I took it from Spring to examine the crisscrossing passageways.

"None," Ash concluded, looking over my shoulder. "We have to start somewhere."

I glanced at him. His face was pale and sweat glistened on his brow.

"We probably need to eat first," I said, folding the old map delicately before slipping it into my pocket. "Then we can head out. It doesn't look like it will take long to get there."

We spent the next few minutes in a circle on the floor, eating. Spring disappeared for a few moments, returning wearing a fresh green tunic and black pants. I had Ash take a break and conjured a fire to replace his. We sat around it and munched on our bread and dried meat. Ash swallowed a large mouthful and locked eyes with Spring.

"Before we go anywhere else with you, I want to know why those dragon scales are here," he said, his expression hardening. "What did you mean, the beginning of the end?"

Spring's shoulders sagged. He fixed his gaze on the fire and was silent for a long moment with his hands clasped in his lap. Finally, he drew in a soft breath.

"My second greatest regret in all my life is that I didn't tell Winter about Fall and Summer. The first... is those scales. Two hundred years ago, the four of us met with the Council of Dragon Elders."

"Dragons?" Lumi asked. "They were here?"

"Yes," Spring replied, a haunted look filling his deep green eyes. He clenched his hands so tightly, his knuckles turned white. "This was once known as the Isle of Fire. The Southern Isles were connected to the mainland and dragons lived here alongside the humans. They helped humans farm the land and keep warm in the colder cycles, and the humans fed and housed them. We brokered a new set of human and dragon laws for shared goods. And as a thank you... the head of the council offered us a sacred gift. The heart scale of a great dragon king. Full-blooded dragons don't die of old age, like humans. But they can be killed." Spring's expression twisted and he looked down, running his shaking hands over his face.

"Summer was enamored with it. She said she'd never seen something so beautiful. And her human followers at the time were... to say *obsessed* with her feels too mild. They did anything they could to get her attention. So..." The words caught in his throat. Lumi, Ash, and I exchanged horrified looks.

"They started killing dragons," I breathed.

Spring nodded. "They did. Several of the dragons living on the mainland were hunted and killed. Her followers even attacked the Isle of Fire's royal family and drove them into hiding. Then they ransacked their palace to bring Summer something special. They literally ended the reign of the dragon king, just to give Summer a shiny treasure." He swallowed hard.

"Each time a human brought Summer something new, she showered them with her affection. Going so far as to take a few of them to her bed. This drove them into a desperate frenzy and led to the humans climbing into the mountains and desecrating the dragons' nesting grounds. Summer was beside herself with glee. She didn't care where the gifts came from, only that they kept coming. I am ashamed to admit that I didn't do enough to stop her," Spring said. His eyes were hollow and distant.

"Fall was at the World's Tower for his cycle. I was never good at standing up to my sister. But I overheard her talking about how shiny a hatchling's heart scale must be and I tried to tell her off. But she shut me up. Very, very quickly." He gulped and pressed his hands into his eyes.

"I was such a coward," Spring whispered miserably. "Winter was the one who finally put a stop to it all. I arranged safe passage off the isle for the dragons and helped them flee to safety. Then I sank the pass between the Isle and the South.

"Summer was livid. She blamed Winter for the loss of her shiny trinkets and made it her mission in life to exact her petty revenge. In my cowardice, I hoped things would simply work themselves out." Spring pressed his hands harder into his eyes, as though he was trying to squash the painful memories flickering behind them.

"When Summer seduced Fall and they started their affair, I didn't say a word. Not to Winter or to Summer." He dropped his hands and drew his knees up to his chest. "I just wanted my life to be quiet. Simple. But my cowardice allowed all of this to happen." Spring fell silent. Tears began to sparkle in his eyes.

Ash blew out a long breath and glanced at Lumi who was worrying at the end of her braid.

Spring shook his head and squared his shoulders. "But... I will set the world right again. And once I do that... I will atone for my mistakes. If you three are still willing to help me." He looked tentatively at us, clutching his knees closer to his chest.

"I am," I said softly.

Spring's shoulders relaxed a bit as Lumi and Ash nodded.

I stood up and brushed the crumbs off my tunic before flicking my wrist to snuff the fire out.

"Looks like the blizzard blew itself out," Ash said as he stood and stretched, glancing up at the window just barely visible through the office archway. We pulled our bags on over our shoulders as Spring got to his feet.

"Follow me." He strode towards the door, pausing only to thread an arm through mine.

The place where he touched my arm sent bolts of lightning up my shoulder. My cheeks heated.

"We can use some of the cold weather gear from the coat room off the main hall. But before that..." Spring's green eyes sparkled as he led me into the library and up to the nearest section.

It was the red section, with paintings of couples and lovers strewn about the walls.

My blush intensified as I caught sight of Lumi arching an eyebrow at Ash. He grinned back, chuckling.

Spring stopped in front of one of the shelves and ran a long pink finger down the line of tomes, pausing on a large book. The beautiful red leather cover was embossed with golden roses and hearts.

He pulled the heavy book from the shelf and, as he turned to me, I could've sworn I saw his pink cheeks darken slightly. He held out the book and I took it, glancing up at him curiously.

"It's... ah... an older print. But it's a five-book collection. So... I thought you might like them. It's my favorite romance series." I touched the soft cover with my fingertips and smiled up at him. His face had in fact darkened slightly and he rubbed his chest sheepishly with his free hand.

"Thank you! I'm excited to read it," I said a little too cheerfully as I stuffed the book into my bag. He released my arm and nodded.

"I hope you like it." He cleared his throat and gestured towards the door. "Follow me." He turned on his heel and led us quickly from the room.

Spring's fingers brushed the spot where our arms touched, and my heart fluttered. I couldn't keep the grin off my face as we made our way back to the entrance hall and into the coat room.

It was a small space, crammed with all kinds of luxurious clothing.

Ash selected a thick black coat with deep pockets sewn into the sides. Spring sighed as he slipped into an inconspicuous looking brown coat that had large buttons up the front. Lumi donned a bright purple coat, and I pulled on a thick red one.

As we turned to go, Spring dashed into the corner of the room and returned with gloves, hats, and scarves. We yanked them on, groaning from the blissful and soothing warmth of our new clothes.

"All right," Spring said, wrapping his fingers around the straps at his shoulders. He had found a backpack, which lighten our own loads quite a bit. He stopped in the entrance hall and made a slow circle, taking in the intricate details of the columns and the vaulted ceiling before he sighed deeply and turned back to us. "Let's go."

CHAPTER NINETEEN

LUMI

We left the palace grounds and trudged carefully up the long road that wrapped around the mountainside. Ash and Rowan were behind me, struggling to push through the fresh snowfall. Even Spring was having a bit of trouble navigating his way through it. I shoved my hands deep into my pockets and looked down at my feet as they left small indentations in the snow's surface, failing to suppress a smile.

Ash saw my face and shot me a warning glare. Before I could respond, Spring glanced up at me and smiled.

"See?" he exclaimed. "I told you that you have Cosmic powers."

"What makes you say that?" I said, confused.

"You didn't think that was normal, did you?" he said, jerking his chin at my feet. When I didn't answer, he shook his head. "Loose snow doesn't support a person's weight like that. Your powers are manifesting to hold you up."

"What? I'm using my powers?" I gasped. "How? I…" I looked down, trying to sense any flow of power coursing through me.

Suddenly, the ground beneath me shifted and I dropped thigh-deep into the snow.

"I knew it!" Ash exclaimed triumphantly, smacking the snow, and sending a fresh spray of powder into the air. "I fucking knew it! I told you your power is there!"

A balloon of hope swelled in my chest and was popped swiftly by creeping anxiety.

I really was Cosmic.

Even with Spring pulling the energy from me, I hadn't let myself believe it until now. But now that I knew I had them, why couldn't I use my power on command?

As if he could read my thoughts, Spring cocked his head to the side, tucking a long green curl back under his wool hat.

"You still have a mental block. But whatever it is, it's shrinking," Spring said. "I can sense your power swelling behind it. Once it shrinks enough, your power will flow much easier."

"I wish I knew how to make it shrink faster," I muttered. He winced apologetically.

"I think you just need to let the fact that you have them sink in. And try using them as much as possible. It's like a muscle. The more you use it, the stronger it becomes," he replied.

I frowned and hopped up, sinking back down into the snow immediately.

"Right," I said, chewing on my bottom lip.

"You'll get it," Ash said, reaching over to grasp my shoulder. "I know you will. And I'll help you, okay?" He flashed a brilliant smile, and I had the sudden urge to lean into him.

Get a grip, Lumi. I shook myself mentally and took a deep breath.

"Okay," I said meekly.

We pushed forward, struggling through the snow. Rowan and Spring fell in step beside each other and started quietly discussing romance books. Their excited murmurings and soft laughter was the only sound in the air around us.

My thoughts drifted back to Haven, and everything we were leaving behind. My father was probably storming around his mansion in a towering rage by now. And I knew, as surely as I knew my own name, he'd send someone to bring me back. Especially when he realized Ash was missing too. And when they found us...

I shot Ash a startled look as the realization hit me and found him watching me.

"Are you all right?" he asked, frowning.

"I'm fine," I replied quickly, plastering on a sweet smile. He wasn't buying it.

"Liar. What's wrong?"

My face fell and I shoved my hands back into my pockets. "I was just thinking about my parents," I admitted.

Ash nodded thoughtfully and sidled closer as we reached the stretch of forest crawling up the mountainside. The snow between the trees was tightly packed and frozen over. We clambered up on top of it and kept walking, making our way much faster now that we didn't have to wade through loose snow.

"You know," he began cautiously, "it's okay to miss them. They *are* your parents—"

"*Excuse me*?" I shot him a furious scowl and he raised his hands in surrender, wincing.

"Ooh damn, I'm sorry. I read that all wrong. What's on your mind then?"

"You," I mumbled.

He stumbled a step and blushed furiously. "Huh? Me?"

I sighed and kicked a solid clump of snow off into the trees. "I was just thinking about how they're going to react to all of this. Knowing my father, he'll blame this on you. And if they find us..." Worry clamped itself around my throat, choking the words off before they could cross my lips.

Ash scoffed, tugging off his cap and running a hand through his long brown hair. "I'm not worried about that."

"You're not?"

"Nah. They won't find us. And even if they did, I know you'll save me," he added with a wink.

"But, what if I can't?" I said anxiously. The image of Ash's beaten body forced its way to the forefront of my mind before I managed to shove it and the ensuing panic back down.

Ash waved a hand, unaffected. "Nah," he said again, grinning. "I'm convinced there's nothing my fierce warrior queen can't handle."

A strange warmth twisted around in my abdomen and my cheeks heated. I met his intense stare and my breathing stalled. I blinked and looked away quickly.

"I'm glad at least *one* of us has faith in me," I sighed. "But if they overpower me—"

"No one's gonna touch you," he hissed fiercely. His face darkened and he clenched his fists.

His sudden change of demeanor surprised me. His eyes gleamed as he shook his hands out and huffed.

"Anyways..." He shot me a sly grin like nothing had just happened. "So, you think about me a lot?"

I rolled my eyes and opened my mouth to retort when something hard knocked against my shins, tangling around my feet, and sending me sprawling. I hit the ground as footsteps sounded all around us. Someone placed a knee in my back. They grabbed my wrists, wrenching my arms roughly behind me and binding them with thick rope.

"Let her go!" Ash growled. A large hand closed painfully around my arm and forced me into a sitting position.

Three men struggled to push Ash away as he kicked and punched every inch of them he could reach. The man who'd just tied me up rushed over to help subdue him. Another man had grabbed Rowan, twisting his arms behind his back, and pressing a dagger tightly to his throat. Spring glared at the man with a simmering rage. The dagger pressed to his own throat didn't even seem to register in his mind.

I yanked at my arms, wincing at the bite of the rope burning my skin.

"There you are," a cold voice hissed. "I was beginning to worry." Killian stepped out of the tree line, leering down at me. A long saber rested across his shoulders. Ice plunged through my veins. His pointed face lit up with glee as he waved a hand at the men restraining Ash.

"Let him go," he ordered.

They shot Ash a fearful glance before stepping back, out of his reach.

"I don't appreciate you kidnapping my wife," Killian sneered, meeting Ash's burning stare.

"I will *never* be your wife, you fucking asshole," I spat fiercely. He shot me a malicious grin in response.

"You already are," he purred. "Your father declared us married just yesterday. The village magistrate took care of the paperwork for him and made it official. You're mine now. And I'm taking you back home, where you belong." Shock and horror twisted my stomach into tight knots. He winked and turned back to Ash. "My father-in-law wants your head on the end of a sword. And I'm more than happy to oblige."

He pointed the tip of his blade at Ash, who glared back. His golden eyes flashed dangerously in the sunlight. Panic sliced through me. I jerked my feet, trying to dislodge the rope wound tightly around my boots.

"I've been waiting for this for a long time," Killian drawled, twirling the blade menacingly. He seemed almost bored as he circled around behind Ash, who had started trembling. "I'll do the gentlemanly thing, of course, and let you defend yourself," he sneered.

Killian was so busy gloating, he didn't notice the wild gleam in Ash's eyes. Or the snow melting around his feet.

He stopped in front of Ash and raised his sword. "So go on, freak. I'll even let you make the first move." He punctuated the statement with a swipe of his blade.

Killian clearly thought he had the upper hand and had caught Ash unarmed. Ash's glinting eyes slid to me, his chest heaving in anger. I met his stare and shook my head firmly.

"Ash... Don't," Rowan warned, sensing the same thing I did. Sensing what was about to happen. The man holding Rowan jerked his arms and he cried out in pain.

Spring let out a low, angry sound.

"Oh, don't worry," Killian snickered, grinning at Rowan. "Your stupid mother can't save you from me this time. You'll be joining the freak beyond the veil." He waved the sword dangerously close to Ash's chest.

Ash didn't flinch. He locked eyes with Killian, his handsome face splitting into a terrifying smile. Killian's confident demeanor slipped just a fraction as Ash began slowly rolling his sleeves up to his elbows.

"Ash, please. Don't do it. It's not worth it," I pleaded.

Killian shot me a bewildered look before glancing back at Ash, whose eyes never left his pale face.

"Ash! Ash, please!" I called loudly. He didn't look at me.

"He's not even armed!" Killian cried shrilly. "What's he gonna do? I'll run him through the minute he—"

A low, vicious growl rumbled through Ash's chest, cutting Killian off. I swallowed fearfully. I was losing him to his rage. I glanced at Ash's fists, relieved to find that they weren't engulfed by flames. Yet.

"Ash," I said again. He still didn't look at me. "Ash, It's not worth it. Ash, don't—"

"Like fuck you aren't worth it," Ash growled through his clenched teeth.

I blinked. Killian shot me a quick glance, leveling his sword at Ash's heart with a smirk.

"She's mine, freak. She's married to me. You lose," Killian hissed, taking a step forward.

"I should've killed you," Ash snarled. His eyes practically glowed with wrath. "I let Ro stop me, but I should've just fucking killed you." His whole body shook with rage.

I realized with a jolt that it wasn't his anger making him tremble. It was the power roaring in his veins, fighting to break free. And judging from the snow melting around his feet, Ash was losing that battle quickly.

I shot Rowan a fearful look and he gulped. Killian misread Ash's trembles as fear and smirked triumphantly, taking another step forward. He now had Ash within arm's reach.

"Oh... Don't worry about Lumi," Killian smiled viciously. "As her husband, I'll make sure she knows her place. Once you're dead."

The tether holding back Ash's anger snapped and he bared his teeth.

"I let you live once against my better judgment," he seethed, locking eyes with Killian, and splaying his hands wide at his sides. "I won't make the same mistake twice."

He rolled out his shoulders and the ground beneath our feet began to tremble. Wind whipped around us. Killian paled, his eyes darting around fearfully. Flames erupted from Ash's clenched fists and crawled up to his elbows.

"It's true! Cosmic! He's Cosmic! Kill him! Kill him!" Killian shrieked. Ash strode forward as Killian staggered away in terror.

Several of the men bleated in fear and took off, sprinting back down the road.

Spring wrapped his fingers around the dagger pressed to his throat. The thin blade crumpled like paper under his grasp as he yanked it away and cocked back, slamming his fist into the man's nose. The farmer staggered and dropped into the snow.

The man holding Rowan squeaked and ran.

"No! Come back!" Killian screamed. The remaining four men drew their daggers and circled Ash.

Rowan turned to Spring. "I have to help him! Cut her loose," he said. He jerked his chin at me before spreading his hands wide.

A rock came hurtling out of the trees and smashed into the nearest assailant. He fell to the ground, unmoving. Fire crawled across Rowan's hands. He sent a fireball at another attacker who'd rounded on him, the man's eyes wide with fear.

"Two!" he gasped. "There's two Cosmics!"

Rowan began flinging balls of fire, driving the men back as Ash sent a stream of flames straight at Killian.

Killian barely managed to dodge the blast, inadvertently jumping right into the path of the onslaught of stones Ash sent barreling towards him. They struck him hard in the torso, sending him flying backwards.

Spring knelt and began sawing at the ropes tied around my wrists as Ash slammed a fireball into Killian's chest.

Rowan sent two men soaring into the trees with a strong gust of wind. They crashed through the branches and hit the ground hard.

The last one screamed and ran, leaving Killian alone.

Killian's eyes were wide with terror as he scrambled across the snow, barely missing volley after volley of flames as Ash struck with unrelenting fury. He summoned a wall of fire and sent it roaring towards a screaming Killian, who managed to dodge it and broke into a run, streaking off towards the tree line.

Ash lifted a fist and a large stone ripped itself from the ground. It slammed into Killian, sending him careening backwards. He landed hard in front of Ash, wheezing and clutching his chest. His sword sailed through the air and vanished into the trees.

Spring swore and yanked at the ropes binding my hands as Rowan dashed over to start untangling my feet.

I looked up at Ash, my heart thundering in my ears. I knew what his rage was driving him towards. And I knew that what he was about to do would destroy him.

I had to stop him.

I yanked at the ropes desperately. Killian tried to drag himself across the ground on his elbows, wheezing as Ash advanced on him. His face was as cold as death.

"You can't... You can't... Kill me!" Killian wheezed.

"Watch me," Ash spat. His flames burned brighter. He splayed a fiery hand wide, and the large stone stopped above his head. "You're never going to fucking touch her again."

Killian surged to his hands and knees in a desperate attempt to scramble away. He made it two feet before Ash sent the boulder crashing down. It caught Killian's legs, and a sickening crunch filled the air. Killian screamed and fell back as the stone drifted high above his head, dripping blood into the snow.

Spring managed to untie my hands and I scrambled frantically to help Rowan untangle my feet. I had to stop him. Everything in me was focused on getting to Ash before he did something that would mar his heart for the rest of his life. We wrenched the rope away and I was finally free.

I sprang up, racing to Ash as he raised his fist again. His golden eyes burned with hatred as he fixed them on Killian's anguished face. I slid in front of him and threw my arms around his heaving chest.

"No!" I cried, pressing my face into him. He stumbled back in shock. "Don't do this!" I clutched the back of his coat and felt him falter at my touch.

Ash's heart pounded against my forehead. The flames died from his fists as he took a shuddering breath, but the boulder still hovered dangerously over Killian's head.

"Please," I murmured against him. "You're not a killer. And I'd never forgive myself if you became one for me. Please, Ash, put it down." I looked up to meet his eyes. They swirled with a dark rage and flashed dangerously as Killian whimpered in the snow behind me. I cupped his jaw with both hands, bringing his focus back to me.

"I'm not gonna lie to you," I whispered. "And tell you that I don't think he deserves it. He does. But I know you so well... You're such a good person and if you do this, it will break you. It will destroy your heart and I can't let that happen... Please, Ash... For me. Put the boulder down. For me..." I trailed off, holding my breath.

Ash's jaw clenched under my palms. His golden eyes closed as his shoulders dropped and the fury finally eased from his expression. Slowly, he let his fist fall. The stone wobbled before crashing to the ground beside Killian with a resounding thud.

I breathed a deep sigh of relief and pulled him into me. He pressed his forehead into my shoulder, and I wound my arms around his neck, holding him tightly.

"I'm sorry," he croaked. I shook my head.

"It's all right, Ash. You're okay," I whispered.

Killian hissed and I turned to stare down at him, keeping a careful hold on Ash as I did so. Killian glared up at the back of Ash's head, his eyes streaming with tears of pain. I avoided looking down at his legs and the dark stains in the snow.

"I'll fucking kill you," he spat at Ash. "I'll make you watch as I break her and when I'm done, I'll fucking gut you."

Ash tensed against me, and I clutched him tighter, glaring at Killian.

"You come anywhere near me again and he won't get the chance to kill you. I'll do it myself," I hissed.

All but one of the men had vanished. The last one was just sitting up, groaning, and rubbing his sore head.

I jerked my chin at Killian. "Take him to Lucia," I commanded. "Tell my father I'm not coming back. And if he—"

A vicious roar split the air and cut me off. Ash straightened as we locked eyes in fear. The roar sounded again. Only this time, it was much closer.

We spun around. Standing on a nearby ledge just inside the tree line, was a huge ice demon. It ground its icy jaws together, its swishing spiked tail leaving deep gouges in the trees around it.

"Calliope," Spring gasped.

The ice demon opened its massive maw and screeched before charging down the slope at us. Ash grabbed my hand, and we sprinted down the road. The last attacker streaked past us, leaving Killian in the snow.

Killian screamed as the ice demon came bounding through the trees at him. I glanced back just in time to see the demon's jaws close around Killian's chest. There was a loud crunch and his screaming stopped, his body instantly going limp.

It chomped down again. Blood sprayed the snow as his body was shredded by the demon's jagged teeth. The creature whipped its head and flung Killian's lifeless body into the trees.

Ash released my hand as we caught up to Rowan and Spring. The ice demon roared and charged after us, closing the distance rapidly.

"Run!" Spring shouted, gripping Rowan's sleeve. We took off, sprinting a few feet when I suddenly realized someone was missing. I slammed to a halt and whipped around to find Ash staring down the rampaging beast, hands blazing. He turned and waved at us to keep going.

"Go!" he shouted. He turned back and ran straight at the monster. Terror stole the breath from me as he slung his hands up, sending a large wall of fire barreling towards the demon. It lowered its head and charged through the flames, snarling as it bore down on him. Blood dripped from its jagged teeth.

Ash stumbled back, throwing blasts of fire into the demon's face. It tried to dodge his attacks but was struck on the snout and roared in pain.

"Ash, run!" Rowan screamed, pressing his mouth into his hands.

"We have to help him!" I shouted, reaching for my bow.

The creature screeched again as Ash brought a rock crashing through the snow from underneath it. The boulder slammed into the demon's chest and cracked the spikes jutting from its collarbone.

He threw his hands out and a gust of wind tore past him. The creature rolled to the side and slashed outward with its wicked claws. It caught the front of Ash's coat, lifting him off his feet and slamming him into a tree. The creature opened its massive jaws and leaned in to rip off his head. Blinding terror froze me to the spot.

"No!" I screamed, reaching out without thinking. A sharp cold zinged down my arms. For one horrifying second, everything seemed to pause.

Suddenly, a loud crack broke the air. A huge spear of jagged ice sprung from the ground and slashed upwards through the demon's chest. It tore its way through the creature, bursting out between its shoulder blades. The demon let out a terrible wail and dropped Ash into the snow. It flailed for a beat before it burst violently into a cloud of snow and dust.

A warm gust whipped through the air, throwing us all off of our feet. The force of the impact knocked the air from my lungs as I landed hard on my side. I wheezed and rolled onto my back.

A glowing green orb danced gleefully in the air just above my head. It twinkled once before it rose into the sky and vanished.

Rowan propped himself up on his elbows with a groan. Spring helped him up as I scrambled to my feet and raced to where Ash was still laying on the ground in a daze. I slid onto my knees next to him and ran my hands across his chest.

"You're not hurt. Oh, thank the Two," I gasped in relief, tears prickling in the corners of my eyes.

"I'm okay," Ash said. He sat up and patted his chest lightly, looking up at me in awe. "Lumi that was inc—" Before he could finish, I threw myself into his lap, locking my arms tightly around him. His heart raced against mine as he slid his arms around my waist and pressed his forehead into my neck. "I'm okay," he repeated softly. "I'm okay."

Everything fell away, leaving just the two of us locked in a tight embrace. I relished the feel of his heart beating and the steady rhythm of his chest rising and falling with each breath. In that moment, nothing else mattered. He was alive.

My heart thrummed and I found myself never wanting to let go of him. I wanted to hold him this way until the world stopped spinning. The realization hit me like a stone crashing through the surface of a placid lake. It rocked through me, stealing my breath.

Ash had almost killed someone for me. And then he'd almost died to save me. To give us time to escape. The fluttering in my stomach returned, followed by a deep, intense feeling. One I realized I'd been fighting for a long time. I wanted to look into his eyes. I wanted to run my fingers through his hair. I wanted... *Him*.

I'd shoved the feeling away for so long, explaining it away in my head. But I couldn't ignore it anymore. I was hopelessly in love with him. The truth set my heart pounding against my ribs and my head spinning. I loved him.

"Lumi?" he whispered softly, snapping me back to my senses.

I pulled away, clearing my throat, and standing quickly to hide my burning face.

Ash brushed the snow from his hair as Rowan came sliding across the ground, clutching the sides of Ash's face.

"Ash, are you okay?" Rowan's voice pitched. He scanned Ash for signs of blood or broken bones. "Are you hurt? What the fuck were you thinking? Are you all right? Say something!" Ash reached up and covered both of Rowan's hands with his.

"Ro, I'm fine," he replied. Rowan sagged in relief. Spring appeared beside me and gripped my elbow.

"We need to go," he said tensely, glancing around us. "Winter will know Calliope is dead and send more demons this way. Come on." He reached down and hauled Rowan to his feet. Ash hopped up and dusted himself off.

I pulled him into another tight hug.

"You almost killed him," I breathed. Ash winced in my arms. "You almost killed him to protect me."

He let out a breath and held me close. "Lumi, I'd do anything for you."

"Like risk your life?" I hissed.

"I just—" he began, but I cut him off.

"Please, don't do that again," I whispered into his chest. I fought against the overwhelming urge to press my lips to his throat. My heart screamed at me to reach up and kiss him. To tangle my fingers in his thick brown hair. I had it bad for him, which meant I was in trouble. He rested his chin on the top of my head, blissfully unaware of my inner turmoil.

"I won't," he promised. His deep voice sent a shiver down my spine. I was in so much trouble. "I just wanted to give you guys a head start," he added sheepishly.

"Well maybe don't next time," Rowan said flatly.

Rowan caught sight of my face as I pulled away from Ash. He arched an eyebrow and shot me a sly grin. It was hard to take him seriously with his red curls poking out from the rim of his cap, but I blushed anyway. He tilted his head to the side as though he were about to say something, stopping short as a distant screech reached our ears. It was answered by a terrifying chorus of screams and snarls, sending a deep chill through my bones.

"We have to go now!" Spring cried, yanking Rowan towards him.

We broke into a run, dashing up the road as the screeches and wails grew closer.

"Hurry!" Spring urged. From the trees around us, we heard creatures galloping and crashing through the ice and snow. Their roars grew louder, surrounding us.

"Shit!" Rowan panted, "There must be hundreds of them!"

"We're almost there!" Spring called.

We picked up the pace, sprinting full tilt up the road as eyeless sockets and gnashing teeth appeared between the tree trunks. One of the demons reached out and barely missed snagging Rowan's collar by inches. He dodged to the side, pointing as we rounded a bend.

"There, there, there!" he gasped. "That cave opening! Quick!"

We plunged into the darkness of the cavern. Ash turned and threw his hands high above his head.

"Ro! Help me!" he yelled. His arms shook with the effort of the power he was trying to use.

Rowan glanced at him, his face white with fear and threw his hands up as well, gritting his teeth.

I turned and stifled a scream.

Like an avalanche crashing down the mountainside, hundreds of ice demons were clawing and climbing all over each other to get to us. We'd outrun them but they were closing the distance between us rapidly.

A loud crack sounded above our heads, and I looked up at the opening. Ash and Rowan were trying to bring down the stone ceiling and cave it in to block the demons. I stretched my arms over my head and focused with all my heart.

"Please," I whispered. "Please, please, please." The screeching grew louder, but I kept my focus on the rock. A strange, heavy feeling suddenly flooded my arms and the rock above the opening shuddered. I saw the creatures in my periphery. Another heartbeat and they'd be tearing us to shreds. I shoved the panic threatening to drown my senses away and threw every ounce of will I had into the strange sensation coursing through me.

A deafening crack echoed in my ears and the rock crumbled. It rained down on the creatures that were just stepping inside, crushing them with a final shriek.

Ash grabbed the straps of our bags and flung us backwards, diving out of the way as more stone came thundering down, plummeting us into pitch black darkness.

Silence fell, punctuated by ragged breaths and gasps.

I was flat on my back, my mind reeling as I stared up into nothing.

"Fuck," Ash hissed, his voice echoing off the stone walls. "Everybody still alive?"

"Ugh... I think so," Rowan groaned.

"I am here," Spring said. I opened my mouth to respond but no sound came out.

I was consumed by shock and disbelief. I had done it. I had actually used my power on command.

"Lumi?" Ash gasped. The fear lacing his tone brought me back to my senses.

"Still breathing," I said numbly.

"Good." Ash blew out a sigh of relief. "Everyone close your eyes. This will be bright," he called.

I heard a rustle of fabric and squeezed my eyes shut just as light flared on the other side of my eyelids. Slowly, I eased them open, adjusting to the brightness of the flame held high over Ash's head.

He turned and let out a low whistle. I rolled my head to the side to survey the damage. The opening of the cave was buried under a large pile of jagged boulders.

As we watched, the rocks at the top of the pile shuddered followed by a loud roar.

"Come on," Spring said from behind us. "We have to get deeper before they break through."

We leapt to our feet and scurried off into the shadows. The sounds of the demons faded quickly as we retreated deeper into the cavern.

"They'll try to follow, but I doubt they can see very well in the dark," Spring said quietly. "The farther we get, the safer we should be."

Rowan dug the map out of his pocket and held it up under Ash's flickering light. He examined it closely, tracing a finger across the thick parchment.

Ash made a face as he scanned the surrounding area.

"Ugh," he groaned, running his fingers through his hair. "Another cave."

"We need to go this way." Rowan pointed towards a tunnel curving off to the left. "There's a stream running through a chamber a little way in. We can cross it, so the demons lose our scent before we double back around to the spirit's chamber."

"Brilliant idea!" Spring exclaimed, beaming at Rowan. "You are extraordinary."

"Th-Thanks." Rowan blushed furiously and ducked his head.

Ash caught my eye with a smirk. The firelight dancing on his fingertips illuminated his face, making his golden eyes glow.

I wasn't sure I was breathing. My heart flipped as he winked at me and turned back to Rowan.

"After you, Ro," he said, sweeping his arm towards the tunnel.

Rowan muttered something I couldn't hear and trudged ahead, lighting a fire in his palm as he passed. Spring followed on his heels and Ash turned to me, offering me his arm.

I slipped my hand into his elbow and let him lead me into the tunnel. I had to fight the urge to lean in close to him as I studied his face in my periphery. The handsome set of his sharp jaw. His lips. The way his hair fell around his face. I was definitely smitten. More so than I'd ever been with anyone in my life.

His body brushed against mine and my heart flipped.

"Ash?" I glanced up at him, swallowing hard as I met his eyes. "Would you really have..." I trailed off.

A dark shadow passed over his face and he looked away sharply. "I would have," he confessed softly. "Without blinking." He met my eyes again. "I meant what I said. I'd do anything for you."

A lump formed in my throat as he let out a long sigh.

"But I'm so sorry if I upset you. It's just... It killed me that he was allowed to walk around like nothing happened. And then he—" He sucked in a sharp breath and gritted his teeth.

I leaned my head against his arm, and he glanced down.

"You're not upset with me?"

"Not even a little."

He relaxed under my fingers.

We reached the small stream cutting through the stone floor of the tunnel and paused. Ash crossed it and reached a hand back to help me over.

I took his hand, stifling a gasp at the jolt of lightning I felt at his touch. He smiled at me and tucked my hand back into his elbow as we followed a muttering Rowan through the shadowy tunnel.

I shot Ash a sideways glance. He'd never shown any feelings towards me other than friendship. But I found myself wondering if there might be more to us. If there *could* be more. He met my eyes and grinned sheepishly.

"Thanks for saving my life," he said.

I blinked. "Wha— Oh, right. It wasn't a big deal," I mumbled, blushing. Luckily, my face was hidden by the flickering shadows, and he didn't seem to notice.

"No big deal? Are you kidding? You were amazing!" Ash said excitedly. "I told you that you had power. You just had to get out of your own way. Guess you found your way around whatever that mental block was, huh? Wonder what it was..." He tipped his head thoughtfully and I shrugged.

"I'm not sure," I said quietly.

He shot me a sly grin. "And you saved my life again. For like, what, the millionth time in a week? What would I ever do without my fierce warrior queen?" He arched one eyebrow and I made myself roll my eyes, fighting to hide the balloon swelling in the pit of my stomach from his compliment.

"Shut up," I mumbled, and he laughed. I looked down at our feet as my heart fluttered. Part of me wondered if I should tell him. I thought about grabbing his face and planting a kiss on those full lips of his. But before I could dwell on the thought too much, Ash stopped suddenly. I stumbled into him as he threw his head back, staring at the ceiling in astonishment.

Rowan had stopped ahead of us and was tapping the map, his eyes cast up to the dark ceiling above us.

Ash nudged me and jerked his chin upwards. I looked and gasped at the deep blue gems that sparkled overhead like stars.

Rowan nodded and consulted the map again. "These are the markers," he exclaimed. "That means the Book Keeper's cave should be just up ahead!" He was practically vibrating with excitement as he gestured for us to follow him.

Spring smiled as he watched Rowan hurry off ahead. We followed the curve of the stone tunnel, only stopping once we reached the entrance to a large chamber. Rowan let out a long, startled gasp as he stepped forward, mouth open wide in shock.

The round chamber was huge. It was as if an entire mountain had been hollowed out. The stone ceiling must have been at least a hundred feet overhead. The walls were lined with floor to ceiling bookshelves, which were stuffed with thousands upon thousands of books. On the wall between the shelves were large iron torches, each one host to its own blazing flame. In the center of the ceiling was a gigantic circular window.

"Whoa," Rowan said. "Look at all these books! I've never seen so many in my life!" He stepped further into the room and spun around to face us.

Spring frowned up at the nearest torch.

"What's wrong?" Rowan asked, shaking his hand to extinguish his flame. Ash did the same and absentmindedly patted my hand on his elbow.

Spring's frown deepened.

"The fires," Spring said, pointing. "If no one's been here for twenty years, how are the flames still lit?"

Ash and I exchanged a quick glance.

"No clue," Ash said, turning to Rowan. "Any ideas? Ro? Ro, are you all right?"

Rowan had paled, staring above our heads in absolute horror.

I moved to look, freezing as a deep thunderous growl rumbled through the air.

CHAPTER TWENTY

ROWAN

Vicious purple eyes glared down at me from an alcove cut high in the cave's wall. I let out a frightened squeak as they shifted.

Lumi and Ash stepped into the cavern and froze, staring upwards. Spring covered his mouth with his hands.

"It can't be," he whispered, shrinking back into the tunnel.

"Who are you?" A deep voice rumbled like thunder through the still air. There was a rustling sound as an enormous creature leapt from the alcove and landed with an earthshaking crash in front of us.

Flames licked Ash's palms and Lumi drew her bow as they backed away slowly.

I pressed my back against a nearby bookshelf, trembling in fear as I met the eyes of a giant, furious dragon.

Cat-like pupils darted between the three of us and torchlight gleamed off his shining purple scales. He had a pointed snout and razor-sharp claws that clacked against the stone when he moved. Deep purple spikes started from the base of his large skull and ran down his spine to the long tail swishing behind him in irritation.

"Who are you?" the dragon repeated angrily. He tilted his head and glared at Lumi's arrow, aimed carefully between his bright violet eyes. "You'd better put that away, princess. Before I snatch that pretty little head from your shoulders." His tongue flicked over his long, pointed teeth for emphasis.

"I'd love to see you fucking try," Ash growled, putting himself between us and the angry creature. He locked eyes defiantly with the dragon as flames roared across his shoulders.

"A Cosmic?" the dragon crooned, sounding almost amused. "I thought you all were dead. I do love Cosmic humans. They have a much more satisfying crunch." He inhaled deeply, eyes widening in delight. "Three Cosmic humans! Well, isn't this just my lucky day! And just in time for dinner."

"Wait!" I seized Ash by the wrist. He shot me a wary look and I shook my head firmly at him. I kept my hold on him and pressed a finger to the shaft of Lumi's arrow, pushing it down to aim at the ground. "We mean you no harm."

"Ha," the dragon said dryly, rolling his eyes. "That's adorable. Darling, the most damage you and your little friends could do is get stuck in my teeth."

"Oh yeah?" Ash hissed, wrenching his wrist from my grasp. His flames flared brighter, coming dangerously close to the shelf behind us. The dragon noticed and snarled.

"You hurt my books and I won't bother to kill you before I rip you to pieces," he growled viciously.

Ash stretched out a burning hand, stopping inches from the ancient looking tomes. The lightest touch would send the dusty books up in flames.

Panic sliced through me as the dragon reared back and let out a horrible roar. Ash didn't flinch.

"You threaten my friends again and I'll set this whole room on fire," he seethed, glaring up at the beast.

"Oh," the dragon hissed, flaring out his enormous, leathery wings. "I will enjoy this." He lashed out, his claws gleaming wickedly.

Lumi drew back her bow and aimed for the dragon's eye while Ash braced for a fight, fire blazing around him.

Without thinking, I stepped in the way, throwing my hands up. My power swept through me, and a gust of air washed over Ash, extinguishing his flames. The dragon paused and eyed me carefully, his claws inches from my face.

"Lumi," I said slowly. "Drop the bow."

"Ro." She shot me an incredulous look.

"Trust me," I pleaded. She hesitated before lowering the bow, letting it drop to the stone with a loud clatter. The dragon withdrew, still watching me cautiously.

"Aren't you a curious one?" he murmured. "Why are you here?"

I glanced at my friends who were watching me with flabbergasted expressions. I had no idea why, but everything in me was telling me not to fight him.

"I..." I began, unsure of how to put my strange intuition into words. "I think we're here to see you."

"Is that right?" the dragon mused. "And what could you possibly want with me?"

"You might be able to help us," I replied. "We came here looking for someone." I gestured towards my friends and then towards Spring. The dragon turned and froze, locking eyes with the terrified spirit.

"Vallath," Spring said weakly, shrinking back into the shadows. The dragon's eyes went wide with shock.

"You..." he growled. A terrible sound ripped from his throat as he rounded on Spring, snatching him up and slamming him into the nearest wall. "How dare you show your pathetic face here! I should rip you in half for the audacity!" The dragon's teeth snapped inches from Spring's face. Ash started forward, but I grabbed his arm and held him back.

"Vallath... I... I'm so..." Spring trembled, holding up his hands in surrender. Vallath's earth-shaking screech cut him off.

"Oh, don't you fucking *dare*," he seethed, pressing Spring harder into the wall. "There is no amount of sorrow or regret you could ever feel that would absolve you. And I won't give you that satisfaction before I smash your head like the bug you are."

"Vallath, wait!" I yelled, dropping to my knees. The raging dragon's eyes slid down to me. "Please!" I gasped, holding my hands up. "He's trying to right the world."

"Bullshit," Vallath snorted. "Do you know what this sniveling weasel has done? What he let happen to my kind?"

"He told us," I said, my voice edged with panic. "But we need him. Winter is trying to destroy the humans."

"You think I give a shit?" Vallath challenged viciously. "Why should I care that the species who tried to exterminate my kind will be exterminated themselves?"

"Because there's still some good in the world that's worth saving. But we can't do that if you kill him. Please," I begged.

Vallath watched me for a long moment before he shot a furious look at the spirit clutched in his claws. "He told you everything?" he asked.

Spring paled further.

"I... yes, he did," I said, darting a glance to Spring, who avoided looking at me.

"He told you he's the reason the humans found the nests? That he led the humans straight to them?" Vallath snarled. My heart stopped.

"He... he didn't tell me that..." The image of the tiny scales floated in my mind, and I blanched, not wanting to believe it.

Spring pressed his lips together in shame.

"I didn't think so," Vallath growled, "Still think he's worth saving?"

I paused and looked up at the spirit clutched in Vallath's grasp. Shameful tears rolled down his face.

"Yes," I said. "Please, don't hurt him."

Vallath glared down at me and released Spring, letting him fall heavily to the ground. He laid in a heap, staring up at the dragon.

"I didn't know," Spring sobbed. "I promise you, Vallath, I didn't know anyone was following us. I swear on my life I never would have gone if I knew."

"But you didn't stop them." Vallath glared at him. "Did you?"

"I tried. I swear to you I tried. But I wasn't fast enough." He rolled to his knees and bowed his head before the furious dragon. "Vallath, I'm so—"

Vallath growled viciously, cutting him off. He glared at the spirit for a moment before shifting his eyes back to me.

"What do you want, curious one?" he said.

"We came here looking for the Book Keeper," I told him.

"Congratulations," he sighed before turning to walk away. "You found him. Now, leave."

Lumi, Ash, and I glanced at each other in surprise.

"Wait," Ash said, straightening up. "*You're* the Book Keeper?"

"Oh good. Turns out you're not a complete idiot after all," Vallath said sarcastically as he retreated deeper into his cavern. His spiked tail swished menacingly behind him as he went.

I jumped to my feet and went after him, rounding a corner into another large chamber filled with books. My fingers itched to flip through their pages, but I focused my attention on the dragon glancing over his shoulder at me.

"What do you want?" he sighed, turning to glare as Ash, Lumi, and Spring appeared behind me. "Here to try your hand at killing the last dragon of the Forgotten Isle? Or is it the Forsaken Isle now? There've been so many names, it's hard to keep track. Well, you're in luck. I'll be dead soon anyways. All you have to do is wait."

"No." Lumi shook her head. "We came for a book."

"A book?" Vallath asked flatly.

Lumi nodded and the dragon snorted.

"Darling, this isn't a library. Now, out." He pointed the tip of his wing off to the right.

"We came for the *Book of the Cosmics*," Spring said quietly.

"The *Book of the Cosmics*." Vallath's eyes went wide and shot to him, stunned. "And why would you think I had that?"

"Because you're the Book Keeper," I replied, unable to keep the awe from my voice. "You're renowned for your legendary collection."

"Not anymore," Vallath sighed, looking around sadly. "You're wasting your time. I don't have it."

"Do you know where it is?" Lumi pressed.

"Gone," Vallath replied simply.

"It's gone?" Ash repeated. "How can it be just gone?"

"Why are the gorgeous ones always so stupid?" Vallath rolled his eyes at the ceiling. Ash opened his mouth to reply but Vallath cut him off. "It's *gone*," he repeated firmly. "When Winter lost her mind, I knew she'd come here looking for it. So, I burned it and told her it was given away. You can imagine how thrilled she was," he added bitterly. "She destroyed a huge portion of my collection as retribution. And then just because she was feeling spiteful, she froze my fire gland instead of just killing me outright." He reached up, tapping a claw on a chunk of black ice protruding from between the scales on his chest.

"Her ice is creeping across my lungs and soon I won't be able to breathe anymore. I lost my ability to fly twelve years ago. I can't shift into my human form. I've been living off the disgusting mud fish in the caves because I can't go hunt for food. I am effectively stuck here until I suffocate. Away from my kind." He turned his violet eyes to the window above our heads. "The book is gone," he said, turning away and heading off into the stacks.

"Well... Maybe we can help you?" I called after him. My heart ached. I couldn't even imagine being trapped here for so long, just waiting for death. "There's gotta be something we can do."

"That's not how it works, curious one," Vallath sighed. "Winter is a herald and she's currently in power. There's nothing anyone can do to help me. And there's nothing I can do for you."

Lumi and Ash exchanged panicked looks. We were sunk. Without the rituals outlined in that book, there was nothing we could do to return balance to the world.

"Now what?" Ash said, wringing his hands.

"I don't know," I whispered. I glanced frantically around the room as though a solution would magically reveal itself and we'd be saved. My gaze landed on a large green book on a shelf near the floor. The title stamped on the spine had a deep gash torn across it. I stared at it in shock.

It used to be mine. One of the many I'd placed on that high wall, hoping to find something special there the next day. It hadn't been an unknown villager I was trading with all those years ago. I smiled sadly.

"It was you," I murmured without thinking.

Vallath turned to look at me, cocking his head to the side.

"What?"

"That one," I said, pointing. "It was mine." I glanced up at Vallath and was surprised to see the shock written across his scaly face.

"What do you mean?" he hissed, turning to face me fully.

"I-I just... I mean..." I took a tentative step back.

His long, curved claws scraped against the stone floor as he approached me.

"I used to put books on the wall in Haven when I was a kid. I thought someone in town did it with me... but... I guess it was you."

Vallath stopped in front of me. My heart pounded and I quailed under his intense violet stare. He stood up straighter, his long neck curving above me.

"It was *you*?" he growled softly. "You were the only one who still... You?"

"I... I guess so," I squeaked. My hands began to tremble, and I clenched them tightly. He and I stared at each other for a moment.

Then, Vallath flared out his massive wings and flapped once, shoving away from the ground, and flinging himself into the air. He soared up to the cave's ceiling and seemingly vanished into thin air. The coloring and the angle of the ledge where he now stood camouflaged it perfectly from anyone on the ground. He reappeared seconds later and glided down to the ground. He examined me closely and held out a tightly curled claw.

"For you. *And only you*," he said fiercely. I nodded once and held out my hands. Gently, he placed a black box in my outstretched palms. I carefully brought it to my chest and opened it, revealing a brown leather tome. The front cover was embossed with two gold figures, twined together in a loving embrace.

I gasped, touching the book with a shaking finger.

"Is this...?" I trailed off, meeting his eyes.

"No." Vallath tucked in his wings. "That is not the *Book of the Cosmics*. That is the meticulous notes handed down from the Two themselves, before the final draft was penned.

We all looked up at him in surprise.

"I'm full of all kinds of surprises," Vallath said, grinning. "I gave the *Book of the Cosmics* to the headmaster of Trithica academy a long time ago. Winter eventually figured it out, but when she went to find it, the book was already gone. I honestly have no idea what happened to it, but I'm assuming the headmaster destroyed it. Which is such a shame." He shook his head.

"It was such a lovely book," he sighed. "The rich purple leather was hand crafted into the cover by the finest tanner in all the lands. What you hold now is all that's left. And Winter has no idea it exists. My apologies for lying to you. But I wasn't sure I could trust you. And given what Winter plans to do with it, I wasn't eager to share the information with *another* herald."

He looked down at the book. "It has not seen the light of day in a few thousand years, so be careful with it. And..." Vallath's hot breath swirled the dust around my feet as he stooped down to meet my eyes. "I meant what I said. That is for you and you only. From one fellow book lover to another. Once you have what you need from it, I expect it back."

"You have my word." I closed the box and clutched it tightly.

"Good," he replied. He plopped down and stretched out his wings.

My fingers trailed across the lid of the box in awe. I was clutching a priceless treasure. No human alive had ever laid eyes on its pages. The thought of being the first one sent a shiver of excitement down my spine, and I was itching to dive in and soak up its knowledge.

Vallath watched me closely, something resembling a smile stretching across his mouth.

"How did you find it? Winter's been searching for twenty years," Lumi said. Vallath winked at her.

"Yes, but not up there. She came here once, like I said. In her rage she let her ice demons rip apart my collection looking for the *Book of the Cosmics*. But that ledge is just about invisible from down here." He jerked his head upwards. "I found it the hard way when I first moved into this cave. Couldn't see straight for a week. Anyways, that book was placed up there long before even Jackass over there was born." He nodded at Spring. "And it hasn't left that ledge since."

"But how did you get it?" Lumi asked, glancing up at the invisible ledge. I looked too, wondering what other treasured possessions were hidden high above us.

"I've always had it," Vallath said through a snort. "Darling, I wrote it. And I wrote the *Book of the Cosmics*."

"You wrote it?" she gasped. He let out a growling chuckle.

"Not bad looking for a three-thousand-year-old, am I?" Vallath grinned. "Yes, I wrote it. So please, don't let my life's work out of your sight," he added with another pointed look at me.

I placed my hand over my heart, nodding, and he smiled.

"I like you three... tell you what," Vallath said. He rolled onto his side, exposing his underside and the painful-looking ice lodged in his chest.

Lumi covered her mouth and Ash stared at it. He looked down at his open hand and back at Vallath, furrowing his brow. Vallath winced as he stretched out, rubbing the scales around the awful sight. I tore my eyes away as Vallath gestured with his wing. "Why don't you stay the night? Keep me company before you gallivant off to— What are you doing? Hey!" he snapped suddenly. I jumped and looked around.

Ash had stepped forward with a determined look on his face. His clenched fists blazed to life as he darted across the cave and slammed it straight into the ice on Vallath's chest. An earsplitting crack echoed off the stone walls. Sparks flew, dazzling my eyes and fizzling out in the air.

Vallath winced before roaring furiously and rolling to his feet.

Lumi screamed, snatching up her bow and drawing back an arrow as Vallath plucked Ash off the ground. He struggled, his arms pinned to his side by Vallath's claws. Fear froze me in place as I watched my friend be raised towards the dragon's teeth.

"How dare you attack me!" Vallath screeched. Smoke began pouring from his mouth. "I'm going to rip you apart! I'm going to...to..." Vallath faltered and froze, watching the smoke curl in front of his snout. His eyes widened and he dropped Ash in disbelief. "What? How?" He drew in a breath and blew. Smoke and embers streamed from his mouth, billowing out into the room. He whipped his head to Ash, who was still lying on the ground with a sheepish expression. "What the fuck did you just do?" Vallath demanded.

"Sorry," Ash said, wincing as he sat up. "But... I figured that if I melted her ice once..." He nodded at a horrified Spring, who was clutching his heaving chest. "I mean, it was worth a shot, right? I guess I could've asked first though," he mumbled, running a hand through his hair.

The realization of what had just happened punched me in the gut and I let out an angry breath.

"Ash, I'm gonna kill you!" I shouted, clutching my face in my hands. "You're going to give me a fucking heart attack!" Lumi slid to his side and wrapped her arms tightly around his chest. Her bow clattered to the floor beside them.

"Stupid," Lumi said, pressing her face into his neck. He blushed and held her back. "Stupid, stupid, stupid, stupid."

"I'm sorry, everyone," he mumbled. "I just had an idea."

"Have your ideas out loud next time, please," I snapped.

Ash ducked his head apologetically.

I sighed again and turned to Vallath. Huge tears were flowing down his scaly face.

"I haven't taken a breath that deep in years," he whispered. He looked down at the shard of ice. Its mirrored surface was now marred by a deep gash. "I thought..." He swallowed, unable to find the words.

Ash released Lumi and stepped cautiously over to Vallath, holding up his hands.

Vallath straightened. "Please," he whispered.

Fire danced in Ash's palms, and he pressed them to the ice. Vallath dug his claws into the ground as Ash let his flame envelop the spot. He held firm, gritting his teeth for a few moments before stepping back and looking up. The ice was gone.

"Ah," Vallath let out a sigh of relief and drew in a long, deep breath. "I can breathe!" He threw back his long neck and opened his mouth wide. A blinding stream of flames burst forth, roiling up to the ceiling before it dissipated against the cold stone. Vallath laughed and blew another column of fire into the air. "Oh, that feels so good!" He spread his wings and soared into the air, flying in tight circles around the large window overhead. He swept out of view for a brief moment before returning with a bundle of cloth wrapped around one large claw, crashing to the floor in front of us, still cackling with glee. "I almost forgot what it feels like to fly!"

He looked down at Ash. "I have no idea how you did that, but... Thank you my friend. You saved my life," he said softly as he began to shrink before our very eyes.

CHAPTER TWENTY-ONE

LUMI

Scales and sharp fangs vanished before our eyes. Vallath's neck shrank into a strong column atop his shoulders. He smiled, flashing a row of straight, white teeth. His snout morphed into a round nose and a square jaw, and his wings retreated into his muscular back.

He gasped as his body stopped moving, stretching, and flexing his bulging arm muscles. His eyes had taken on a more human appearance but were still bright purple. He passed a hand across his face, a deep rumbling laugh bursting from his chest as he tossed his head back in glee.

"Oh, it feels so good to feel skin again!" His voice had lost its growling edge and become low and smooth. He ran his hands down his muscular torso, flexing his fingers against his dark skin. I blushed and looked away as I realized he was completely naked. He stretched out his legs and laughed again, glancing around. "Oh dear... Look at those blushes." He purred, grinning wickedly at us.

Rowan's face was bright red as he and I stared determinedly at each other, and Spring stared intently at the opposite wall. Ash glanced at me with a small frown. Vallath bounced on the balls of his feet, clearly enjoying our discomfort.

"Forgive my indecency," he chuckled, grabbing a bundle of brown cloth from the floor. To my relief, it turned out to be a pair of pants. He tugged them on and settled them low on his hips before pulling a leather strap from his pocket and tying his long purple hair behind his head.

"Good to know I still have that effect on people," he grinned. "Well, don't be shy." He smirked, stretching his arms out wide. "I've enjoyed both men and women. Spirits. Dragons. Only thing I won't do is take what isn't freely given or take from anyone that cannot properly consent."

Rowan coughed, his neck turning a bright red.

Vallath laughed again and ran his fingertips along the spines of his precious books with a soft smile.

"Dragon scales don't let you feel things in the same way that human skin does. In any aspect of life," he added, smirking in our direction. We fidgeted and he winked. "Sorry. But I haven't fucked anyone in a long time. I'm a little on edge."

"Anyways," Ash said loudly, frowning. Vallath glanced over at him and tilted his head to the side.

"You know something, handsome... You look really familiar. It's been bugging me ever since you strolled in here. Have we met?"

Ash shook his head.

"Are you sure?" A mischievous light danced in Vallath's eyes.

"I think I'd remember meeting a dragon," Ash replied firmly.

Vallath smirked, studying Ash with a curious expression.

"Are you absolutely sure? Because I swear I've seen your gorgeous face before."

"So, what will you do now?" Ash said, purposefully ignoring him. Vallath shot him a wicked grin, quirking his eyebrow before letting out a happy sigh.

"I can finally leave," he replied, beaming. "I can pack up and leave to be with my people!" I looked around the cavern.

"You're going to pack up all of this?" I tilted my head back and looked all the way up to the shelves closest to the top.

"I am!" Vallath rubbed his hands together excitedly. "My kind fled to the Southern Isles two hundred years ago. It gutted me to leave my precious books behind, but coming back while Lady Summer was still a herald was too dangerous to do on my own. When the seasons fell out of sync, I realized that Winter had lost her mind and came back to talk some sense into my old friend. She repaid centuries of friendship by torturing me and stranding me here. My family must think I'm dead after all this time. But now, I can bring my collection with me. It will take a long time to pack, but I don't care."

He lifted his eyes to the round window on the ceiling. "I can finally leave," he breathed.

"Will the Southern Isles be affected by Winter too?" Rowan asked, tucking the black box under his arm.

Vallath shook his head.

"No," Spring chimed in suddenly. His voice was very small. "Our powers are locked to the isle. Heralds have no influence outside of our borders."

"Jackass is right," Vallath said.

Spring winced. Rowan looked over at him sadly.

I glanced at the box tucked into his side and an idea struck me.

"Hey," I said, waving a hand at Vallath. The dragon looked over at me and raised an eyebrow. "So, Winter's power can't cross the sea at all?"

"Correct," he replied. "Why?"

"So, that means the ice demons can't cross the sea... Can *she* cross?" I asked.

"No," Vallath shook his head. "She can't leave as long as her stone is locked to the tower. Why do you ask?"

"The book!" Rowan cried suddenly, catching on.

"Just what I was thinking, Ro," I replied. Vallath cocked his head to the side.

"Care to enlighten the rest of us, gorgeous?" he snickered, crossing his arms.

"Rowan can read faster than anyone I've ever met," I said, pointing to him. "Instead of taking the book with us, could we stay here? If the *Book of the Cosmics* really was destroyed, that's all that's left. Taking it out of the cave seems... I don't know... a little stupid?" I shrugged. "Ash, Spring, and I could help you pack while Rowan reads. And then you could take the book with you to the Southern Isles."

Vallath considered me for a moment, running a hand across his jaw thoughtfully. "That makes sense... And I can't say I'd mind having someone so beautiful to look at for a while," he added with a wink.

Out of the corner of my eye, I saw Ash shift.

Vallath blew out a breath. "Fine. But gorgeous over there should probably take his shirt off," he said, shooting Ash a predatory smile. Ash's frown deepened.

"Not happening," he said tersely.

"Oh well... It was worth a shot," Vallath sighed heavily. "All right then. Let me grab the crates." He strolled away, humming to himself as Ash came to stand beside me.

"I think he might be sweet on you," he murmured, nudging me gently with his elbow.

There was a strange edge to his words that I'd never heard before. A sinking feeling filled the pit of my stomach and I had to fight to hide my disappointment.

"Maybe," I said, forcing my tone to be neutral. My treacherous heart cracked as he nudged me again.

"Oh, come on," he pressed, grinning tightly. "You didn't notice? He couldn't keep his eyes off of you."

"I think he's more interested in you, Ash," Rowan said, furrowing his brow. Ash rolled his eyes in response.

Vallath returned a moment later, balancing ten huge crates in each hand, one on top of the other, like he was hefting around a stack of pillows. He dropped them on the floor, lining them up along the shelves as he walked back towards us.

"Figured we could start with these," he said, dropping the last crate and dusting off his hands. He looked around at us gaping at him in shock and chuckled, flexing his biceps. "Dragon strength," he snickered. "Anyways…" He turned to me, smiling mischievously. "I know short and sweet is Rowan and tall, dark, and fiery is Ash. But I don't know your name, beautiful."

Ash turned away, uninterested, and my heart sank a little further.

"Lumi," I said, meeting Vallath's violet stare. His mischievous smile widened.

"Lumi," he purred, rolling my name around on his tongue. "Glad to make your acquaintance." He held out his hand. I took it and he brought my knuckles to his lips.

Ash huffed out a small breath. I glanced at him, and he smiled brightly, winking. Disappointment slapped me in the face, and I looked away sharply.

"Now, if you will follow me." Vallath motioned to us. "You can set up a place to sleep over here. Unless someone decides they want to keep me company," he added, licking his lips.

He led us through the maze of shelves and into a study area. A large oak writing desk sat against the stone wall. Bookshelves faced away from the space, lining the sides, and creating a large room.

"This is my reading area," Vallath said, spreading his muscled arms out and gesturing at the room. "The bathing area is through there, and my sleeping area is up there." He pointed up to a ledge overlooking the space. "So, make yourselves nice and comfy while I go grab more crates. We can get started after you get settled. Rowan, you can use that desk for your study." He jerked his chin at the large oak table.

Rowan thanked Vallath, who winked and strode from the space.

"See?" Ash said casually, placing his pack on the floor. "I told you." I met his eyes as he shrugged.

"I think he's just looking for some company after being alone for so long," I said, fighting to hide the disappointment in my voice.

Ash chuckled. "He didn't look at any of us like that," he replied.

"Quit teasing her," Rowan said, placing the box on the desk. "You're just jealous Vallath didn't kiss *your* hand. But I bet he would if you asked nicely."

"All right, all right. I was just curious." Ash held up his hands in defeat.

Rowan rolled his eyes before looking over at Spring. He was huddled in a corner, despair written across his ashen face.

I dropped my pack on the floor and wrapped my arms around my chest. I hadn't even had time to sort out my feelings and I already knew Ash didn't feel the same way. I tried to tell myself that it was for the best. That I could squash my feelings for him and move on.

But my heart ached anyway.

I sighed and turned back to watch Rowan and Ash chatting quietly as they set the tents up.

I just needed some time to put my head on right and let go of the fluttery feeling in the pit of my stomach. Then everything would be okay.

I steeled myself and, pushing my shoulders back, went over to help.

Ash looked up at me from where he was fixing the tent's base. His golden eyes blazed as he smiled up at me and my heart stuttered.

"You okay?" he said, cocking his head to the side. I realized suddenly that I was clutching my shirt with both hands and sucked in a breath.

"Oh," I muttered, blushing as I released the front of my tunic. "Yeah, I... uh... food." I turned away and strode back to where we'd laid our packs.

Spring barely glanced at me as I passed. His long legs were tucked in close to his chest. He was staring at the ground like he was waiting for it to open up and crush him.

I made lunch in silence while Ash and Rowan finished putting up the tents. They used their power to mold stones from loose boulders into weights to hold the ropes in place. They finished their work, wiping their brows as I handed them each some bread and dried meat.

"Spring... There's some for you," Rowan said tentatively, sitting down next to me.

Ash sat down on my other side and sank his teeth into the bread with a deep moan.

Spring didn't look up from the floor, too ashamed to meet our eyes.

Rowan glanced helplessly at me, and I shook my head, at a loss. He gave Spring a worried look before starting to nibble on his lunch.

Ash and I finished first and stood up together.

"We'd better get back to Lumi's admirer," Ash said, winking. Rowan raised an eyebrow at him but didn't say anything.

Rowan finished the last of his food and gave Spring one final glance before he plopped into the chair in front of the desk.

Ash and I bid him farewell and headed back through the shelves towards Vallath and his book crates. We walked in silence for a few moments before Ash blew out a long breath.

"So," he began, plucking a loose string off of his tunic. "No interest? At all?" I frowned at him. "Hey, I'm just curious," he said, running his fingers through his hair.

"No, Ash." I snapped to hide my sinking sense of disappointment. "I wasn't planning on fucking him. But you seem to really want me too, so maybe I will."

Ash pressed his lips together and looked away.

One thing I knew for sure was that he most definitely didn't have feelings for me. I shot him a sideways glance, watching his dark brown hair fall in front of his handsome face. He brushed it back, his full lips turned down with displeasure.

He looked at me, locking his golden eyes with mine. My heart leapt into my throat, and I looked quickly away.

"I'm sorry," he mumbled. I rolled my eyes.

"Whatever," I sighed, unable to keep the defeat from my voice. "We'd better hurry up. Vallath's probably waiting."

Ash shifted his shoulders uncomfortably and nodded, frowning.

We heard Vallath before we saw him. He was singing to himself, pulling books off the shelves near the floor and laying them with love and care into the large wooden crates.

"Ah," Vallath purred, looking up at us with a grin as we approached. "The cavalry has arrived." His smile faltered as he glanced around. "What? Jackass is too embarrassed to face me?" Ash and I exchanged a look.

"Something like that," I replied.

Vallath snorted derisively. "I should've just eaten him."

"Speaking of which," I said, jerking a thumb back towards the campsite. "We have potato bread if you want some."

"That's very kind, but I'm not all that hungry... For food," he added with a sly grin. Ash cleared his throat and looked away. Vallath winked and gestured to the shelves. "I don't care what shelf you get the books from, or which crate they go in. Re-organizing them is half the fun. Just place them nicely into the boxes so nothing is damaged."

We nodded and set ourselves to it. Despite the hollow ache in my heart, I couldn't stop myself from sneaking glances at Ash while we worked.

Why did I have to be in love with him? I wanted to kick myself for being so stupid. Especially now that I was sure he didn't love me. If he found out how I felt, it would ruin our friendship.

A trickle of fear crept up my spine at the thought. I pushed it away as I pulled a large brown book from the shelf and placed it carefully in the box that I was kneeling next to. I couldn't let that happen. But that meant I only had one choice. I had to smother my feelings, no matter how much it sucked. I needed to distract myself long enough to let the feelings die.

I glanced at Vallath and considered him for a beat. He really was stunningly handsome. And if Ash wasn't interested in me...

I shook the thought away and snatched another book from the shelf. Out of the corner of my eye, I thought I saw Ash watching me. But when I turned to look, he was stretching a hand high above his head to grab a large book. I frowned and let my eyes wander back to Vallath's muscular form for a moment.

We worked for two hours to the tune of Vallath's jovial singing and humming. As we removed books carefully from the shelves and placed them in crates, my thoughts kept wandering. First to Ash, then to Vallath.

Vallath seemed to notice my attention, because he started grinning and throwing occasional suggestive comments in my direction that made me chuckle.

Ash, on the other hand, was quiet. He kept his focus on the task at hand, sighing heavily through his nose every once in a while. He kept shooting me a strange look that he thought I didn't notice, but I couldn't place its meaning. After a few tries, I stopped guessing. My heart wanted to believe he was jealous of Vallath commanding so much of my attention, but I knew that wasn't true.

After a while, Vallath declared himself in need of a break. I stood, watching Vallath as he stretched, suddenly mesmerized by his form. His arm brushed the side of his face and he groaned, rubbing his hand across his mouth as he caressed his smooth skin.

"You have no idea how much I've missed having lips. It's been nothing but scales and sharp angles for two decades." He shot me a predatory smile. "I see you've noticed. Care to feel?" Without pausing to think about it, I stepped over, passing a thumb slowly over his lower lip.

"Very soft," I winked.

Vallath threw back his head and laughed. "Well, fuck me... I'm a sucker for a woman who's bold and knows what she wants."

I smiled and glanced up to find Ash staring at me. His expression was dark as his eyes darted between Vallath and me. He gripped the book in his hands so tightly that his knuckles were white.

I straightened, confused. "Ash?"

He sucked in a breath as Vallath came up behind me and put a lazy arm across my shoulders.

"Oh dear," he simpered. "Have I stepped on someone's toes? Are we a bit jealous, Ash?"

"Yes," Ash hissed through his teeth.

I blinked as Ash threw the book forcefully into the crate and stormed away. The fluttering feeling twisted in my gut as Vallath arched an eyebrow, grinning slyly.

"Interesting," he muttered to himself before turning to me. "It seems I've offended your... ah... What exactly is he to you?"

"He's my... friend," I replied softly, my eyes rooted to the spot where Ash had just disappeared around the corner.

"Oh, sweetness," Vallath said, smirking down at me. His violet eyes twinkled. "Surely you're not that oblivious."

I pressed my lips together and looked up into his face. "I'm not oblivious. Ash has never... He doesn't have feelings for me. He... He just..."

I was at a loss. Had I interpreted those strange looks correctly? But if I had, then that meant...

Vallath shook his head and leaned down, his lips brushing my ear as he said, "Lumi, darling. I'm afraid you are, in fact, terribly oblivious. He's been watching me flirt with you for hours and I could smell the jealous rage setting his blood on fire. All I did was touch your shoulder just now. And do you know what I felt? Heat rolled off him like a tidal wave. He had to fight not to burst into flames where he stood. Look at the book..."

I peered into the box and found the blue book Ash had been holding. Deep, round singe marks gouged the leather where his fingers had been.

"Had I not been deliberately trying to piss him off, I might be upset that he burned my book. But his fury is absolutely delicious to watch. I couldn't resist riling him up just a little bit," Vallath purred. "He really is such a gorgeous creature. I can see why you like him so much."

I opened my mouth. I had no idea what I was going to say, but he cut me off before I had the chance.

"And my dear... Would you like me to tell you where he is now?" he asked, raising his eyebrows. I nodded. He turned me slightly and pointed to where Ash had disappeared. "He thinks he's gone far enough down the cavern to not be heard," Vallath continued. "And he's probably right. I doubt *you* can hear him, but a dragon's senses are much more perceptive than a human's. I can hear a huge fire crackling and I can smell the burning air. So... perhaps... You and he should... Talk," he added with a wicked grin.

My breath caught in my throat and my traitorous heart surged. I struggled with the smile tugging at the corners of my mouth.

"Well," Vallath sighed, patting my arm. "It seems you two are going to be preoccupied for a while, so I'll check on our handsome bookish friend."

He strode away, leaving me alone with my thoughts as I stared after Ash, fidgeting indecisively with the end of my braid. A wild, dangerous kind of hope seized my heart. Vallath was right. Ash and I needed to talk.

CHAPTER TWENTY-TWO

ASH

It felt like I was on fire. I stumbled blindly down the dimly lit cavern. My whole body trembled violently as my power surged through me. I took slow, steady breaths, desperately shoving the heat crawling under my skin away until I could escape far enough into the gloom. I could feel my control slipping with every hurried step I took but I didn't care. I just had to get far enough away that she wouldn't see it.

The sound of her laughter still rang in my ears. My mind was swarming with images of Vallath's violet eyes dragging brazenly up Lumi's body. His arm draped possessively across her shoulders. His smirk when he caught me glaring at him. Her thumb pressed to his lower lip.

My blood boiled. Finally, I stopped in a dark chamber. The last of Vallath's torches sputtered on the wall, casting shadows into the tunnel beyond their light. I dropped to all fours, gasping as I relented to it at last.

Wind and swirling flames whipped around me, blowing my hair into my face. The stone beneath me shuddered and cracked under my fingertips. I gritted my teeth, breathing deeply through my nose to calm the rising fury ripping apart my heart.

Watching her touch his face had been like a knife to the chest. The moment she'd seen his human form... And her beautiful face flushed at the sight of him... A vicious, jealous beast had seized my mind. It screamed at me to stake my claim and show Vallath that she was mine.

Even if she wasn't. Not really. She deserved so much better than me.

But I couldn't help it. I had to know, so, I poked and prodded her as I tried to assuage my fears and find out what her feelings might've been for the dragon. But the only thing I'd actually succeeded in doing was upsetting her.

That, and possibly convincing her to sleep with him.

Guilt sat heavily on my shoulders, and I felt horrible. So, I'd shut my mouth and endured his endless flirting with her, grinding my teeth in frustration as my blood ran hot with each sly comment. I pressed my forehead into the floor and pounded a fist against the stone, sending deep cracks skittering towards the wall.

I felt like a monster. A gross, possessive monster. I had no right to feel this way. Lumi was her own person and she deserved to be happy. She deserved someone who could give her the world. Not a mess of a person like me.

But the thought of him wrapping his arms around her and leaning in to press a kiss to her lips made me sick to my stomach.

Suddenly, a cold gust of air swept through the cavern. It doused the flames swirling around me and silence fell.

I blinked and looked up to find Rowan staring down at me.

"Lose something?" he said. His intense green eyes burned a hole right through me as I bolted to my feet, wiping my hands on my pants.

"Oh... uh... Hi, Ro." I mumbled sheepishly, ducking my head to avoid his gaze.

"Ash," Rowan sighed. "What are you doing?"

"Nothing," I replied, running my fingers through my hair. Rowan arched an eyebrow.

"Nothing," he repeated, slowly. "Really..."

I shrugged and looked down to avoid meeting his eyes. Embarrassment and shame sliced straight through me.

Rowan exhaled sharply. "Ash, come on. What's going on?"

"Nothing, Ro. I promise. I'm fine."

"Right," Rowan snorted. He turned as footsteps approached from behind him.

Lumi peeked around the stone and peered into the chamber.

My heart fluttered.

"Oh!" she gasped in surprise. "Hi, Ro. I thought you were reading."

"I was," he said. "Vallath said I should probably come check on him."

"I'm fine," I said, forcing my tone to be light and happy.

"You didn't seem fine," Lumi replied. She tucked a loose strand of hair behind her ear as she stepped closer. "You looked upset."

Panic rocked through me, but I waved her off.

"No," I said, breezily. "Why would I be upset?"

"Well," Lumi began, shooting a quick glance at Rowan. "You looked upset when Vallath touched me." I swallowed hard. "And when Vallath asked if you were jealous, you said yes. So... I mean..." She trailed off, looking up at me with concern in her beautiful eyes.

Rowan cocked his head slightly to the side. He arched one eyebrow as his gaze slowly drifted back to me. His lips were pressed tightly together as if he were trying to suppress a smile.

I ignored him, patting Lumi on the shoulder instead.

"No," I said, shaking my head. "I uh... I misheard him. That's all. I promise I'm fine. I'll meet you back at the camp. I just have to... pee," I finished lamely. I knew they'd see right through my outright lie, but I fixed an easy smile on my face anyway.

"You have to *pee*," Rowan repeated incredulously.

I shot him a warning look, running a flustered hand roughly through my hair before looking back to her and forcing a smile to my lips.

"Yep," I said brightly.

"Ash..." Lumi furrowed her brow before snapping her mouth shut. She considered me for a long moment and sighed deeply. "Fine. See you back at camp." She turned on her heel and headed down the tunnel without looking back.

My heart sank like a stone.

"You're such an idiot," Rowan said sharply.

I rolled my eyes. "Shut up," I hissed.

He glared at me. "You are! You honestly think she didn't see right through that? Toddlers lie better than you!"

"And how do you know I lied?" I snapped, rubbing my face with my hands.

"Oh right, of course. How silly of me? I must've forgotten you *always* try to light yourself on fire before you pee," he spat sarcastically.

I didn't respond.

"Ash," Rowan sighed, exasperated. "When are you going to admit what's happening here?"

"I don't know what you're talking about," I grumbled.

"Oh, no?" He pointed behind him towards the tunnel. "So, what Lumi just said isn't true? You didn't admit to being jealous?"

"I..." I faltered, swallowing hard again. "I just don't think he's... I just—" My brain scrambled to find the right words, but nothing came. He stared at me hard before suddenly shrugging.

"You know what? It's probably for the best." I raised my eyebrows at him, and his green eyes gleamed defiantly. "It is. I'm sure Vallath could make Lumi very happy."

I gritted my teeth and still didn't respond.

He took a small step forward, watching my face. "She deserves someone, doesn't she? Someone to love her? And who knows? Maybe Vallath would be good to her."

I saw right through what he was trying to do, but that didn't stop the jealous monster from growling. I pursed my lips together and said nothing as he kept pressing.

"And you saw him." Rowan took another step closer. "Bet he's an animal in bed. He'd make her very happy there, too."

I clenched my jaw and looked away.

"Well, I for one am happy for Lumi," he said, still watching my face. "She deserves to have some fun. I'll bet he's with her right now. Maybe you and I should wait here. Make sure he has plenty of time to ravish her."

My power shot through me like lightning before I could smother it. Fire tore from my fists and licked the stone at my feet. A tendril of flames drifted towards Rowan's face. He waved a hand, and a gust of wind swept it aside. I took a desperate breath and clenched my fists shut, staring determinedly at the floor.

"That's what I thought," he said softly. He stepped in front of me, forcing me to meet his eyes. "I think it's time to be honest with yourself, Ash. And with Lumi."

My heart pounded as I stepped around him, holding up my hands. "I said I don't know what you're talking about, Ro. Come on... Let's go grab some dinner." My voice was raw as I turned away.

"Thought you had to *pee*," he hissed sarcastically. I winced and turned but he waved me down the tunnel. "Save it, Ash. I'm here to talk when you're ready. But hurry the fuck up. This is getting ridiculous." He placed a hand on the small of my back and steered me towards Vallath's cavern.

My heart beat against my ribs, but I kept my face impassive. Rowan must've guessed that my feelings for Lumi were more than just friends. He was too smart not to. Part of me wanted to turn to him and confess everything. My heart yearned to finally share the burden it carried with someone else. Even if that someone wasn't the person I wanted to tell most.

But I couldn't bring myself to say it out loud. If he told Lumi, she might hate me. I couldn't bear losing her from my life. Just thinking about it made me want to vomit. So, I trudged ahead, schooling my expression into one of carefree ease to hide the turmoil in my heart.

We rounded the corner and found Lumi and Vallath sitting together on the floor. They had apparently created a small makeshift fire pit out of loose stones and a small blaze was already crackling merrily, casting Lumi's face in a warm glow. She was speaking to him in a low voice and, as we drew closer, he wrapped a comforting arm around her.

His long fingers stroked her arm in gentle circles, and I thought I might explode. I quickly looked up at the large window. The sun had set, and stars twinkled high above us. Lumi laughed quietly and I had to grit my teeth.

"Well, my friends," Vallath began. I looked down and saw him stand, looking up to the sky. "I'll be gone for a few hours. I need help leaving and if I'm honest... There are more than a few of my kind I am eager to see." His eyes misted over, and he smiled. "I won't be gone long." He looked back down at us and smirked. "Don't let the jackass break my stuff."

Vallath crouched and jumped into the air. Wings and shining purple scales erupted from his dark skin as he flew in a tight circle above our heads. A few strong flaps and he had returned to his dragon form. He soared up to the window and shoved it open with an ear-splitting creak. He gave us a wave of his claw before sailing out the window and up into the night. His tail whipped out, slamming the window shut behind him.

"Well," Lumi said, standing up without looking at me. "I guess we should grab something to eat and get back to work."

"Okay," I mumbled, embarrassed at the mess I'd made for myself.

We prepared our food in silence. I wracked my brain for something I could say to Lumi, but she stayed clear of me. She ate quickly and set to work restringing her bow. I watched her adept hands holding the arm down as she popped the string into place and tested the tension. A deep *twang* broke the silence as she released the string and set the bow aside.

I jumped when she suddenly looked up at me.

"Are you going to tell me the truth now?" she asked.

"I..." I ran a hand through my hair as my heart started screaming at me. *I love you!*, it shouted. *Say it! Just fucking say it, you stupid idiot!*

"I'm sorry," I managed finally. "I... I was being a prick."

"Why?" she pressed, watching me carefully.

"I guess, I might be a little overprotective sometimes." Not exactly a lie. Even if saying it made my heart ache.

"I can handle myself, you know," she said sharply.

"Oh, I absolutely know you can," I replied quickly. "You're a warrior queen and I'd follow you into battle any day."

"Damn straight," she said proudly. The blush that crept up her cheeks and the small smile tugging at her lips sent a wave of unrelenting joy through my soul. I'd give anything to make her smile like that. "But seriously, I can take care of myself. You know that. Why'd you get so worked up?"

Rowan cocked an eyebrow at me, and my throat closed around the words I wanted to say.

"I just... I mean," I faltered and sighed. "If something happens to you... I can't let anything happen to you." I met their eyes. "You two are my everything."

Lumi and Rowan looked at each other.

"We love you too," Rowan said grinning.

A small cough sounded from behind me, and I turned to find Spring standing there. His hands were clasped tightly in front of him, and tears were streaming down his face.

"Hello," he whispered. "I... I owe you three an explanation." He approached the fire and sat next to Rowan, bringing his knees to his chest, and hugging them close. "I'm so sorry. I can't imagine what you must think of me." He let out a deep, shuddering sob.

"Why don't you take a breath?" Rowan said gently, laying his arm across Spring's shoulders. Spring nodded and took a few deep, calming breaths, wiping his eyes on his sleeve.

"It was nesting season," he began quietly. His vibrant, forest green eyes stared deep into the fire. He was far away in a distant, awful memory. "The elder women of a few cities made blankets for the eggs every year. Only a few of us knew the location of the nesting ground, so Calliope and I volunteered to take them up the mountains. I had no idea we were being followed."

"So, you didn't actually lead them to the nests?" Lumi asked. Spring let out a broken sound.

"Not on purpose, I swear," he gasped. "But... I was singing. They must have followed the sound of my voice. We reached the bottom of the pass, but the horses wouldn't go any further. Calliope made them nervous. They were pawing and restless. I was afraid they'd freak out and trample some of the nests. So... I left the pass open and kept the cart at the bottom. I was just going to walk the blankets up to the nests. By the time I realized my mistake, it was too late.

"Calliope was engaged to one of the dragons guarding the nests. She'd stayed with him while I went to get more blankets from the cart. Then I heard Calliope screaming for me. I ran back and..." He stopped short and shook his head. "It was horrible. I summoned stone golems and saved as many of the nests as I could, but Summer's followers had snuck in and executed so many already. Including Calliope's fiancé. He'd tried to save them while Calliope ran to find me. I was... I was careless..."

Spring paused and let out a shuddering breath. "I didn't take my sister seriously and I wasn't careful. I didn't close the path behind us like I always did. And... So many hatchlings died that day... Because of me..." He gasped and let his head fall onto his knees.

"Spring," Rowan said softly, "You were trying to do the right thing. It was a mistake."

"My mistake cost the dragons almost an entire generation," Spring wept.

Lumi sidled up to his other side. "Summer took those lives. Not you," she said, leaning into him. "If not by following you, they would've found the nests some other way."

"But I heard her say it," he said miserably. "And I let her shut me down when I tried to tell her off. The only one of us brave enough to stand their ground with my sister was Winter. And now look at her... All because I was a coward."

I watched him for a beat before sidling closer and placing a hand on his knee.

"Spring, listen to me. You can't let your past define you now or it'll ruin your whole life. Trust me," I added bleakly. "I know that better than anyone." I shoved the memories of burned buildings and long cold nights out of my mind before they had the chance to overwhelm me and straightened. "Letting your regret eat you alive does no one any good. Make what amends you can and then leave your sister and her actions in the past. You have us now. And we can't do this without you," I finished seriously. He met my eyes for a long moment before wiping the tears from his cheeks.

"All right," he said softly. "I'll try. But I don't know how I could ever make amends for this."

"Vallath would be the one to ask about that," Lumi suggested. "But for now, let's leave Rowan to his reading and get to work." She stretched and gestured towards the books lining the vast shelves. I stood and grinned.

"Lead the way, commander," I said with a wink.

Lumi rolled her eyes, turning away to hide her smirk.

Rowan rolled to his feet. "I just need a few more hours and I can join you," he said.

"Already?" I gaped at him. "That book was huge!" Rowan just shrugged.

"It's mostly diagrams and illustrations. But I've learned a lot from it. Anyways, I'd better get to it!" He sat down at the large desk as we headed off towards the crates.

Spring followed us into the maze of shelving, still wiping his eyes, and began placing books into crates as gingerly as possible. Like just his touch would cause them to disintegrate.

Lumi and I went further into the shelves and started working together. We had cleared where we could reach from most of the shelves before a strange movement caught my eye. I glanced over at Lumi. She was holding a large red book clutched to her chest, focusing on a small pebble at her feet.

It shivered and bounced once before shooting straight up into the air. It whizzed past, missing my face by inches and sailed out of sight. Lumi winced.

"Oops," she mumbled sheepishly. "I didn't mean to do that."

"It happens," I replied, waving a hand. "You'll get better with practice. It's like exercising a muscle. You just gotta... what's the word, 'hone' it? I guess?"

Lumi chuckled and I grinned.

"You know," I said, slyly. "I don't wanna say I told you so, but..."

"Yeah, yeah," she muttered, rolling her eyes. Lumi pressed her lips together to hide her smile as she placed the red book she was holding into the nearest crate. "Shut up."

"Hey," I said, nudging her gently with my shoulder. "I think I'm entitled to an I-told-you-so."

"Yeah. I guess you are," Lumi agreed, locking eyes with me.

I was utterly mesmerized. Her lips parted slightly as she stared back at me, and I stopped breathing all together. Suddenly, she sighed and looked away.

"I uh..." I stuttered, scrambling to reorder my thoughts. "I can help you. If you want... Help you get more comfortable with your powers."

"That would be amazing," she said.

"Of course," I replied. "You know I'd do anything for you."

"Yes. I know you would." She shot me a meaningful look before she blinked and glanced around. "How long have we been working?"

I looked up at the window. The moon had come into view and was shining so bright, I had to squint slightly to look at it.

“A while,” I replied, wiping the sweat from my brow. “We should probably go grab Ro and get some sleep before Vallath comes back and puts us to work again.”

“Sounds good,” she said, brushing her hands off on her tunic. “We got all these boxes filled, so it’s a start. Come on.”

I followed her back towards where Spring was working. The area looked so strange with the lower halves of the bookshelves empty.

Spring looked up as we approached. He had pushed up his sleeves and sweat had plastered some of his longer green curls to his pink skin. A streak of dust was smeared across the tip of one of his pointed ears.

“Headed for bed?” he asked, gently placing an ancient looking book inside the nearest crate.

“Yep,” I said. “We have an extra tent for you.”

“Oh, don’t worry about me,” he replied. “I’ll keep packing so we can head out as soon as possible. Winter won’t sit idle for long.”

We told him goodnight and left him filling crates. Exhaustion began to pull at me as we rounded the corner into our little camp.

Rowan was still pouring over the book. He traced one thin finger gently across the paper as he read. His other hand was pressed against his forehead, holding his curls out of his face. I cleared my throat and he jumped at the sound, staring around wildly.

“Oh!” he said, clutching his chest. “It’s just you.”

“It’s really late,” Lumi said through a wide yawn. “We need to get some sleep.”

“Is it?” Rowan said. His shoulders sagged and he rubbed his eyes vigorously. “I guess I lost track of time.” He slid a hand under the book’s front cover and closed it carefully, placing it slowly back inside the black stone box.

“How much more do you have left?” I asked.

“I finished it,” he said.

Lumi and I exchanged surprised glances.

“Already?” I asked, impressed.

“Well, yeah,” he muttered. “I told you it was mostly diagrams. I’ve spent the majority of the time studying it.”

“Do you know what we need for the ritual?” Lumi asked.

“Yeah,” Rowan said. There was a nervous edge to his voice that made me uneasy. “I have all of it.” He closed the box, eyeing it like it was about to explode and met both of our eyes fearfully. "Guys, remember what Spring said? About Winter joining the stones and killing the Two?"

Lumi and I nodded.

Rowan gulped and my uneasy feeling sharpened. I'd never seen him look so bleak. "That's... that's not what happens," he whispered.

"What do you mean?" Lumi asked.

"She wouldn't replace the Two," he said, his quiet voice shaking. "She'd undo *everything*." Fear seized my chest, making it difficult to breathe.

"What do you mean, everything?" I asked.

"I mean *everything*," Rowan shuddered. "Joining the four stones doesn't replace the Two. For that, you'd need something called the All Stone. Joining the four stones would cause a cataclysm." Rowan wrapped his slender fingers around his throat. "It would rip the very fabric of this world apart."

The ground swayed beneath my feet as I stumbled back a step.

Lumi gasped and covered her mouth with her hands. "Winter," She whispered through her fingers. "She doesn't know what would happen?"

"No," Rowan replied. "She doesn't and neither does Spring." He looked over his shoulder at the stone box behind him. "That book has to leave this isle. She can't find it. And we have to remove her stone before she manages to find the real book."

"But if she knew..." I began, "She wouldn't still go through with it, would she?"

"That's a chance we can't take," Lumi said firmly. "But now we know why Vallath hid it. You're right, Ro. We have to get that book off the isle as fast as possible."

"Looks like sleep is out of the question," I said, rolling up my sleeves.

"Let's go," Lumi nodded in agreement.

Rowan and I followed close on Lumi's heels as we raced back into the shelves.

"Hey! I thought you three were going to bed," Spring said in surprise. He looked between us, taking in our tense faces. "What is it?" he asked cautiously.

"I need to tell you something," Rowan said as he laid a hand on Spring's arm and leaned in close. Lumi and I left him to fill Spring in, rushing back into the stacks and throwing ourselves into the task. For hours, we filled crate after crate. My muscles ached from no rest, but fear fueled me throughout the night.

We finally paused when the sun came peeking over the mountains, and the giant window overhead swung open with a loud creak.

CHAPTER TWENTY-THREE

WINTER

The sun crested over the horizon, bathing the land in a soft glow. I stood on the balcony and peered through the eyes of my thrall trotting carefully through the snow. My mouth twisted in disgust. Not a single one of them had found my book. Those that weren't still out searching were marching towards Haven. In a matter of hours, fifty of my biggest demons would attempt to breach the walls. The last two human settlements had fallen with no sign of it. Haven was the last place left where it could be.

The last corner of my isle still resisting my reign.

"Still hunting that stupid book?"

I didn't turn to acknowledge Summer. Instead, I strode back towards my throne and sat with my back straight and my head held high. Summer sauntered into my line of sight. I lifted my chin to stare determinedly over her head.

The facet on the golden crown she wore was empty. But when she shifted, I could've sworn I saw the ghost of the diamond that should've been there. She smoothed a hand down the sides of her dress. It was a long, glittering gown of yellow, orange and gold. The bodice was cut low, exposing most of her large breasts and the wide skirt brushed the floor as she walked.

"Seriously, Kiora? Are you really going to ignore me? After murdering me in cold blood, the least you could do is look me in the eye," she simpered, her bottom lip jutting out in a pout.

It was a gesture I'd seen her use many times. And it was one that had never worked on me. When I didn't respond, Summer huffed in annoyance and gathered her skirt up in her hands, striding towards me until she filled my vision.

"You can't ignore me forever, *Kiora*," Summer said, drawing my name out obnoxiously. I cringed but still didn't respond.

She used to do the same thing to her brother. Whining his name until he finally gave in. Just like he always did. She did it so much that he stopped using his name all together, asking that we call him Spring. Fall and I had respected his wishes. His sister, on the other hand, had been outraged.

She'd lost her means of keeping him in line, so she'd switched to a new tactic, plucking at the guilty strings tangled around his heart until he did whatever she wanted. I never figured out why it worked, or what he felt so guilty about. But she knew and she used it to play him like an instrument. Until the massacre. After that, Spring had become a shell of who he once was. Not that she cared.

I'd asked him about his name once. He told me that he wanted to save it for someone special. He said it was the little piece of himself that he had left to give them. I didn't understand what he meant at the time, but it didn't matter anyway. He would never get that chance now.

Summer shifted, forcing me to look at her. "I'm not going anywhere."

I rolled my eyes and stood, stepping around her to stride back to the balcony.

"You're really going to ignore me. A figment of your own mind."

"Shut up," I snapped over my shoulder.

"You created me!" she laughed. "I'm only here because of you."

"In that case, go away. I banish you," I said, bracing both hands against the rails of the balcony.

Far in the distance, I could just make out Haven's huge border wall. How I would relish smashing it open wide and stamping out the plague of humanity once and for all.

"If only it were that simple," Summer sighed.

I turned and found her stretched across my throne, grinning at me.

"But you're stuck with me. Until your imminent demise and then you can come join me forever," she added with a wink. "I may even share Fall with you on occasion. We've grown so... close over these twenty years."

Rage filled me. I stalked up to her and flung my hand out, sending a spike of black ice straight through her heart. Summer blinked down at it once and threw her head back, laughing.

"By the Two, Kiora, you really have lost it, haven't you?" She smirked at me and stood, gesturing first to her unblemished chest and then to the spike embedded in the throne. "I'm not here! I'm dead! You're trying to stab a ghost!"

I growled in frustration and reached my power back out.

My thralls stood in the snow, milling about, and bumping blindly into whatever was around them. Some were still snuffling through the snow, desperate to complete their task. In my distracted rage, they had become disjointed and confused. I refocused on them, and they all resumed their searches.

I turned back to Summer. Her clothes had changed back into the nightgown. A thick collar of black ice had wrapped itself around her delicate neck and was slowly crawling up her face. She didn't seem to notice as she circled me like a hawk preparing to swoop in for the kill.

"My brother is coming," Summer hissed viciously. The black ice began to creep down her chest. "And when he gets here, he will crush you."

"Shut up," I snapped, my lip curling in a sneer. "You know nothing, you stupid bitch. You're dead."

"And you will be too. Very soon," she snickered. The ice crept across her eyes and down her nose. She began to resemble one of my thralls as she moved closer. "It's over, Kiora. End it before he does."

"Shut up!" I spat, louder. "Your brother is a useless fucking coward."

"Oh, really?" she challenged, sneering. Most of her body was covered by ice, transforming her into a terrifying beast. Her voice dropped a few octaves and she growled. "Then how did he get free? He is not alone, Kiora. And whoever they are, they are coming with him to kill you."

"Shut the fuck up!" I screamed.

Summer let out a horrible screech and began to swell, filling the room before my eyes. Deep cracks appeared in her form, spilling bright purple light.

"See you soon." Her voice thundered through me, rattling my bones before she vanished into thin air.

I screamed into the empty void left in her wake and flung my arms out in every direction. Cold sliced through my blood as I unleashed my power on everything around me. I sent my power roiling towards the ceiling and crashing across the floor in my wrath.

Everything she'd said was true, except for my death. I was going to make sure of that. I'd find Spring and tear him apart with my bare hands. Then I'd join the stones and use my new power to wipe his pathetic existence from the face of this world for good.

Finally, I stopped screaming and stood, panting. Shards of black ice were protruding from the walls and the floor, sticking out at odd angles.

My chest heaved with the exertion. Shadows began creeping in at the edge of my vision and I pushed them away, straightening my back. A new crack had formed in my shoulder and sharp points of ice were poking through my skin. My heart hammered painfully. The silence ringing in my ears was broken by a distant sound and I stilled, listening intently. A roar echoed off the mountains, followed by the beating of giant, leathery wings. It was a sound I hadn't heard in an exceptionally long time.

Dragons.

I raced out to the balcony. There, circling the peaks of the Fire Mountains, was a group of dragons, led by a large purple one. His scales shone brightly in the fresh morning light. Shock seeped through me. There was only one purple dragon I knew of, and I'd taken his ability to fly long ago.

Suddenly, all the pieces clicked into place.

Dragon's fire had proven ineffective against my power. That meant Cosmic fire must've freed Spring from my ice. I still had no idea how, but it was the only possible explanation. Which meant Cosmic fire removed the ice from Vallath's chest as well. A Cosmic had found Spring... In my purge of their kind... I definitely missed one. That was who Spring was shielding from me. And Spring had brought them to Vallath's cave. But why? Vallath didn't—

I gasped as the realization struck me in the stomach.

"You lied," I said in disbelief, watching Vallath joyously circle the mountains with his kind.

He disappeared from view and dragon after dragon followed him, diving behind the same peak. They were entering his home. "You stupid, scaly bastard... You fucking lied to me! *You* had the book! For twenty years, I've searched for it, and you've had it all this time!"

The last time I saw Vallath, he'd begged me not to destroy his precious collection. Dragons were attached to their treasure, and books had always been his horde of choice. I'd watched my thrall tear book after book to shreds while he swore up and down that he no longer had the *Book of the Cosmics*. I'd tortured him in his human form. I'd taken his ability to breathe fire, shift, and fly. And yet still he'd sworn he traded the book away. When I thought I'd seen through his cryptic confessions and went to Trithica only to find nothing there... I began to believe that he told the truth. I thought I made absolutely sure. In the face of all that, there was no way he would have lied to me. But he had. The book had been right under my nose the whole time.

Rage tore through me and I raised my hand. In unison, the hundreds of ice demons milling about stood up straight and turned to face the mountains. The fifty demons approaching Haven's great stone wall paused, turning back towards the tower. I reached into their minds and implanted a command. I showed them the way and the face of their enemy. As one, they bounded off, racing as fast as they could move.

The appearance of the other dragons could only mean one thing. Vallath was leaving the isle. I reached into their minds and urged my thrall to move faster. They had to stop him before I lost the book forever. I smiled smugly and turned, reeling back as I came face to face with Fall.

"Haedon!" I gasped, shocked. His true name felt like poison on my tongue.

"Stop," he whispered. His lovely brown eyes were full of sadness and despair. "Please."

I frowned at him and resisted my sudden urge to cup his face in my hands. I stepped back and squared my shoulders.

"You know I can't. I have to fix the mess you made," I seethed. I stepped further out of his grasp and strode around him.

"Kiora," he gasped, following me into the throne room. "Please... Don't punish everyone for my mistakes. I paid for them... Let that be that."

"And leave you dead?" I demanded, yanking the ice from my throne, and sitting down. His bare chest heaved as he fell to his knees and stared up at me with a bleak expression.

"Yes," he croaked. "Leave me in the past and rebuild the future. Please, Kiora. Don't do this."

"I have to," I replied. "I will rebuild this world for the better. No more chaos. No more greed. I will wipe that bitch from your memory and from mine and we will rule this world together. We shall be the Two."

"Kiora, please... I'm begging you." He let out a small sob and clasped his hands in front of his chest. "Don't let what I've done destroy you. You're fading as we speak," he said, desperation edging his voice. As I stared down at him, his form wavered. He looked down in shock and found his hands were vanishing.

"I will fix your mistake," I said simply. "And you will be mine again."

His body disappeared inch by inch as he watched me in despair. I looked away as fresh tears rolled down his disintegrating face.

When I was once again alone, I reached into the mind of my demons and saw them approaching the forest. They were racing through the trees like a cataclysm of teeth and claws bearing down on the world.

I smiled.

CHAPTER TWENTY-FOUR

Spring

My companions were exhausted. Dark circles had formed under their eyes and their skin had paled slightly. It had been a few hours since Rowan told me the shocking news. He and I packed up our unused campsite and dragged our things out into the main library, while Ash began teaching Lumi to create gusts of wind. Together, they knocked the books off the highest shelves, catching them before they hit the ground.

Rowan and I started working as a team in the same way. Terror edged all of our minds as we scrambled to pack as fast as possible. We were almost finished when the window overhead creaked open.

"My goodness!" Vallath exclaimed, landing in front of us with a soft thump. "You've been busy! I hardly recognize this place!"

The shelves were almost all empty and crates brimming with books lined the floor. Vallath shot me a nasty look before turning to address everyone else excitedly. "I'd like you to meet some very special guests." He pointed a wing upwards as a group of twenty dragons followed him through the opening and landed around us.

Terror squeezed my chest. I shrank back, trying to make myself as invisible as possible.

Vallath grinned at Ash, Lumi, and Rowan. "These," he beamed, "are my family and friends. They came to help me leave."

"Pleasure to meet you all," Lumi said, turning in a circle to look up into their faces. The dragons eyed her warily and Vallath nudged a small blue dragon gently.

"Easy everyone," he soothed. "She's okay. Him on the other hand..." He jerked his snout in my direction.

Thunderous growls echoed in the tense air as each dragon locked their eyes on me, baring their teeth.

Rowan reached back and wrapped a hand protectively around my wrist. The zing that shot up my arm from his touch was quickly overshadowed by the fear seizing my mind.

Vallath glanced around the group of angry dragons, grinning. "How unexpected," he snickered. "Maybe I should let them eat you."

"How about we don't," Rowan said, edging further in front of me.

My whole body trembled.

"You deserve nothing less." A silver dragon stepped forward and glared down at me. He towered over the others and seemed to fill the whole room. Even Vallath appeared small next to him.

"Ah," Vallath purred, grinning viciously. "This is Garwyn, one of the council elders. And Brynn's father."

The silver dragon snarled as understanding dawned on my face. I gently shook Rowan off and dropped to my knees.

"You know who I am?" Garwyn thundered.

"I-I knew your son," I managed to croak. "And Calliope."

"You were supposed to be there the day my son was murdered." Rage rolled off of him in palpable waves. I gulped, staring up at his vicious fangs. "You opened the pass for the humans," Garwyn seethed. "And then you left them to their brutality."

"No," I gasped, shaking my head frantically. "No, that's not what happened. I swear."

"No?" Garwyn leaned closer, baring his teeth. Terror froze me in place. "Then why did you run? Why weren't you at the nests when the attack happened?"

Movement caught my eye, and I glanced over to see Ash running his fingers through his hair. His words echoed in the depths of my mind. If I really wanted to make amends, I had to start somewhere.

"You're right. I was supposed to be there," I said, as my eyes slid back to the furious creature. My voice quaked, but I held the fierce dragon's stare. "But I was afraid the horses would hurt the hatchlings. Calliope was making them nervous, and they were restless. So, I left the cart where I should've closed the path and walked back to get the blankets. It was my fault and I... I will carry that guilt for the rest of my life. However long that will be. But I swear on everything

I hold dear, I did *not* know I was being followed. It was my carelessness that led them to the nests, but I didn't lead them there on purpose."

The dragons started murmuring amongst themselves and glancing at their leader, who had not moved.

"I know I will never ever deserve forgiveness. But if there was anything I could do—" I trailed off as Garwyn's tail flicked out, cutting me off.

"Bring them back," he growled. I blinked up at him, confused.

"I-I don't have the power to—"

"The scales," he rumbled. "Every single one of them. I want them brought back to where they belong. Do that and we will let you live with your guilt." A few dragons nodded in agreement.

"You have my word. Every last scale will be returned as soon as we right the land," I breathed, pressing a hand over my heart.

"Your word," Garwyn spat, his scaly face twisting in contempt, "is meaningless. You were trusted with the sacred location of the nesting grounds, and you were careless with it."

"If I may, Garwyn," Vallath chimed in. He bowed his head to the larger dragon, who bowed in return. "I agree with you. The jackass's words are useless. However..." He pointed to Rowan with the tip of his wing. "This Cosmic human has proven himself an ally to our kind. Perhaps he could give us *his* word?"

Garwyn examined Rowan closely. Rowan stood tall, squaring his shoulders. There wasn't a trace of fear on his kind, handsome face.

Finally, Garwyn nodded. "Human," he rumbled. "Will you give us your word? Will you promise to return the scales of our fallen to the Southern Isles?" Rowan nodded solemnly.

"You have my word," he said. "Every last scale will be returned to you. Once we retake the tower and end this winter, I will return them to you, personally," he said.

"It is a bargain then. The scales in exchange for his life," Garwyn said, swishing his tail at me.

My insides quaked with fear as Rowan pulled me to my feet, grasping my wrist.

"Deal," he replied.

The dragons murmured around us, falling silent as Vallath flared his wings.

"It's time to go," Vallath announced. His voice cracked slightly on the last word. "My Cosmic friends have done most of the work. But the lady of the tower will notice us, and the book must be brought south before she can get to it. So please, grab what you can carry and let's get out of here!" The dragons dispersed, each grabbing as many crates as they could muster and soaring out the window.

Rowan vanished for a moment, returning with the black box tucked under his arm. Garwyn and Vallath spoke to each other briefly, before Garwyn strode away to direct the dragons still loitering about.

"Judging by the shadows under your eyes and the fact that the majority of the books are all packed up, I'm going to assume you finished your reading," Vallath said, cocking his scaly head to the side.

"I did and you have to go," Rowan nodded. He held the box out to Vallath.

"I will miss you three," he said, peering down at Lumi, Ash, and Rowan as he took the box. "You will come and see me, won't you?"

"Of course," Lumi said brightly.

Vallath smiled down at her as he placed the box into a passing crate. I watched the green dragon carrying it spread his wings and leap into the air. He flapped a few times before sailing through the window and out of sight.

The book was gone.

"If there is anything I can—" Vallath began, pausing suddenly as a deafening screech echoed off the walls. The remaining dragons craned their necks, sniffing the air. Vallath took a long inhale and blanched. "Demons," he snarled loudly.

"Grab what you can and fly!" Garwyn shouted. He dug his claws into four crates and flung himself up towards the window.

The air clouded with dragons fleeing the cave. They streaked through the window until the only one remaining was Vallath. He spread his wings out over us and roared as hundreds of ice demons swarmed into his home. They crawled up the walls, clawing over each other as they poured into the cave and surrounded us.

Ash's fire burst from him, circling us, and pushing the demons back. His flames wavered and he swore. "Fuck! We didn't sleep," he shouted. Panic edged his voice as he groaned and clutched his head. "I'm gonna run out of power!"

Lumi snatched her quiver and bow from her pack and began firing rapidly. Her arrows ripped through the air and found their targets. Demon after demon exploded into dust as her lethal aim brought them down.

"Ro!" Lumi shouted over the overwhelming screeching. The ice demons were gnashing their teeth and swiping at the flames holding them at bay. "Ro! Can you help him?"

"I'm trying!" Rowan screamed. Sweat had formed on his forehead. "But I'm almost out too!"

I felt helpless. If I drew from their power, I could summon golems to protect us. But it would drain them. The golems wouldn't last long on borrowed energy and then we'd really be in trouble.

Vallath opened his jaws and blew white-hot flames down the line of circling monsters. They were quickly replaced by more as the demons crumbled and balls of light streaked through the air. He turned to me, growling. "Fucking do something!"

"I can't!" I cried helplessly, wringing my hands. "Winter took the stones, and my power is locked to mine! And if I pull their power, I'll drain them!"

Vallath gasped. His eyes went wide, and I saw the understanding of why she was so desperate for the book click in his mind.

"All of them? She has all four of them?" he shrieked. I nodded frantically.

"Shit, shit, shit." Vallath backed up a step as the screeching grew louder. Ice demons were crawling further up the walls, trying to find a way to leap over the flames.

Ash groaned and dropped to one knee, his arms shaking. Rowan blinked hard and began to sway. The circle drew closer and so did the waiting demons.

Lumi reached into her quiver and swore. "I'm out!" she screamed.

Vallath looked around the room as the fire flickered lower.

"Ah, fuck me!" he yelled, spreading his wings out wide, "Grab your packs!"

We threw our bags onto our shoulders. Rowan and I were suddenly squished together as Vallath wrapped his claws around us and reared up on his hind legs. He gave the room one last remorseful look before opening his mouth wide.

Flames billowed from him like a rolling fog, incinerating the nearest demons before they even had the chance to turn to dust. He twisted his neck, swirling the flames in a wide arc around us. Before we could blink, the whole room ignited. The giant shelves were set ablaze in a matter of seconds. A few of them crumbled and fell to the floor. Smoke filled the air, as the last of Vallath's precious books were destroyed.

Vallath roared and swept his fire across the walls. The air was filled with screams of pain. A few of the demons tried to flee from the raging fire, only to be blasted by Vallath in his fury.

Sweat poured down my face as the heat grew unbearable.

Vallath flapped his wings, rising through the smoke and carrying us out through the window. The screeches of the ice demons followed us as we sailed high over the Fire Mountains. Rowan was clutching me close, pressing his face into me.

"Are you all right?" I called over the wind whipping my hair into my face. He groaned in response and clutched me a little closer.

"I hate heights," he gasped into my chest. My pulse started racing. I wrapped my arms around him, patting him gently on the shoulder.

"You're okay," I called. "I've got you."

My heart sank into the pit of my stomach as I surveyed the land. The city of Haven looked like a fortress. A high wall surrounded it, cutting the village off from the rest of the world. Ships bobbed in the bay, and the beach was covered with tents and small wooden shelters. A few people gawked and pointed up at us as we raced past. Vallath flew faster than the wind, streaking through the clear sky like lightning through a storm cloud.

A few more abandoned settlements zipped past as we flew. I looked down in time to see the remnants of the old clock tower of Trithica square drawing closer. It was a desolate wreck. The stone wall had been charred and scoured, and the base of the clock tower was surrounded by the rubble of the once proud city.

Vallath banked towards the wreckage and landed with a soft thud before releasing us into the snow.

Rowan fell to his knees, pressing his forehead to the ground. "Fuck," he moaned. "I hate flying. I hate it. I hate it. I hate it."

Vallath sighed as he looked back towards the small column of smoke rising into the distant sky. "So many of my books," he lamented.

Lumi reached out and patted Vallath on the claw.

Rowan stood and looked up at him. "I'm so sorry," he said.

"Me too," Vallath replied. "But we're alive."

"How can we ever repay you?" Lumi asked quietly.

"Stop her. End the winter and bring my people the scales," Vallath said after a pause. He turned to face us. "This is what's left of Trithica. I brought you here to hopefully shorten your journey to the tower. I can take you a little further, but I won't go anywhere near the Crossroads Temple. I only just got my ability to fly back, and I plan to keep it."

"No." I stepped forward, shaking my head. "You've done enough for us. Go and be with your family, Vallath."

He considered me for a moment before nodding once. "Good luck." I was surprised he didn't sneer. "I hope to see you all soon. Even you, Jackass," he added with a wink. He spread his wings and shot into the sky.

We stood together and watched Vallath disappear beyond the horizon before Rowan finally broke the silence, glancing around. "So, which way do we go?"

We stood in what was once the town center of Trithica. The buildings lining the square were nothing but blackened, burnt-out husks and debris littered the snow.

"I'm not sure." Lumi turned in a circle, her bow still clutched tightly in her hands. "We should probably try to scavenge for supplies. And it wouldn't hurt to go check that clock tower and see what... Ash?" she said suddenly.

I turned and found Ash standing nearby, utterly frozen. Every inch of him shook like an earthquake and his skin was deathly pale.

Lumi and Rowan exchanged startled glances. Fear swirled around Ash like a vicious tide, sweeping him farther and farther out to sea. Dark memories flooded through his mind and began to drown him. I saw the clock tower and the square flash past his eyes, followed by a horrible scream. Unease gripped my chest and my eyes darted around. Something was desperately wrong.

"Ash?" I took a step towards him. "Ash, what happened here?" I said, slowly.

Lumi's eyes snapped to me in confusion.

"We have to go," Ash whispered desperately. He let out a shuddering gasp and swallowed, his voice trembling as badly as his hands. "Please. We have to get out of here."

Lumi grasped his hand.

"What happened?" she said, the worry clear in her expression.

He met her eyes with great effort. The darkness swirling behind his golden stare was dragging him deeper into the abyss. He shook his head, unable to force the words from his lips.

"I—" Ash gulped loudly, looking around at the burned buildings. "I can't..." He shook his head. "We have to go," he whispered. His face paled further as a small sound echoed from behind us. He whipped around, bracing for a fight only to find nothing there. I caught Lumi's eye and jerked my head.

"The main road is just a few feet that way," I said, quietly. Whatever it was that had someone as fearless as Ash so terrified was not something I wanted to meet. “We can follow it all the way to the Crossroads Temple. It’s only a few days hike once we leave the city.”

“Okay,” Rowan hissed. He grabbed Ash’s other hand and stepped gingerly towards me, tugging his distraught friend along behind him. “Let’s get the fuck out of here.”

“Seconded,” Lumi breathed. She stowed her bow away, holding onto Ash tightly as she drew her dagger from her boot. The blade gleamed menacingly in the light. She held it at the ready as we crept to the road and began making our way, slowly, out of Trithica.

I glanced around at the once shining city in despair. The Cosmic Academy lay in ruins. Walls had been reduced to piles of crushed stone and most of the remaining buildings had collapsed under the weight of years and years of snow. If we chose to search for supplies here, sifting through the rubble was going to be difficult. I opened my mouth to point this out when Ash jumped at a noise, and I snapped it shut.

A creature stumbled out of the destroyed school, howling, and snarling at nothing. We froze.

Ash turned white as a sheet, shaking violently and bracing himself to flee. The creature stumbled closer, swaying, and staggering about on two legs.

I could sense a presence in the creature’s mind. A fragment of who she once was. It called out to me in desperation, jumbled and confused. As it got closer, I realized with a jolt that she was human. Or she had been at one time.

The woman’s flesh was gray and half-rotten. Ice protruded from deep cracks in her skin. Her eyes were wide and unseeing. She sniffed the air, pausing before her rotted face swiveled in our direction.

Ash had stopped breathing all together. The creature sniffed again and opened her mouth wide to reveal blackened teeth. She sucked in a sharp breath, filling her lungs for a violent scream when Lumi’s dagger sailed through the air and embedded itself firmly in the creature’s forehead. The creature stumbled and fell without ever making a sound.

Lumi crept forward and grasped the handle of the dagger, yanking it free. She wiped the blade in the snow and stowed it back into her boot. I raised my eyebrows, marveling at the deadly accuracy.

“What is that thing?” she hissed. Her eyes darted around as another howl sounded a few yards away.

"We have to go. Now. Right the fuck now," Ash whispered frantically. Lumi took his outstretched hand. Rowan grasped my arm and, together, we crept silently towards the road.

We only made it a few feet before a bloodcurdling shriek split the air and we stumbled to a halt. Another creature staggered into the open, screaming and reaching its rotting fingers out towards us. Its screeching was soon joined by another. And another. Soon, screams and howls filled the air.

"Go!" Lumi yelled.

A debilitating fear tugged on my mind. I reached out on instinct, snatching Ash by the wrist and dragging him along behind me as we tore off in the other direction. The creatures' screams echoed all around us as more of them came stumbling into the square. We slid to a stop as a male creature swayed out from behind a building, screaming, and reaching for us.

We were surrounded.

"Quick!" Rowan shrieked, pointing. "In there!"

I kept a firm hold on Ash as we sprinted for the clock tower. Lumi rammed her shoulder into the door and held it open for the rest of us as we raced towards it. As we reached the threshold, the terror seizing Ash's mind became blinding and he dug his heels into the ground, trying to stop himself from entering the clock tower. I tightened my grip, yanking him hard through the doorway. Lumi slammed it shut behind us and pressed her back against the door.

It lurched hard as the creatures slammed into it and Rowan raced over, throwing his weight against the door to hold it closed. Nails scraped against the wood and the screaming intensified.

I released Ash and spun in a frantic circle, searching for anything to brace against the door. Several large crates were stacked against the wall. I darted over and shoved all of my weight against the closest one. It only slid a fraction of an inch across the floor.

"Ash! Ash, help me!" I cried.

He didn't answer.

I looked around and found Ash pressed against the back wall. One of his trembling hands was clamped over his mouth and the other was flat against the wall behind him. His mind was gone. Lost to a sea of terror and dark memories.

I looked helplessly over to Rowan and Lumi. Sweat trickled down their faces. The door bucked behind them, and Lumi swore.

"Lumi, go! I've got the door!" Rowan gasped, summoning what was left of his power. Two chunks of rock ripped from the floor, bracing against the bottom of the door.

Lumi rushed to my side and threw all of her strength at the crate. "What... happened... to him?" she grunted.

"I don't know!" I gasped. "But we have to do something fast!"

Lumi and I shoved and pushed until the crate finally hit the door with a resounding *thump*. We stumbled back, panting and gasping as the shrieking grew impossibly louder.

Lumi ran over to Ash and knelt in front of him. He'd slid down the wall. His knees were curled into his chest while both of his hands were pressed tightly over his mouth.

"Ash!" Lumi called out over the screaming. "Ash, look at me!" She grabbed his hands, tugging but he didn't move. His whole body shook violently, and his breaths were ragged and sharp.

Images suddenly began to flood my mind. A small, plush dragon with a crooked wing being clutched by tiny hands. Screaming and shrieking. Terrified tears shed in utter silence. The wooden door bucking against a large stone. A raging fire engulfing the walls.

I blinked the visions away as Rowan crouched down in front of Ash.

"Ash, please!" Rowan yelled. "Snap out of it!"

"Trapped," Ash gasped suddenly. His voice was raw, like he'd just been screaming. "Trapped. Can't get out."

Rowan and Lumi exchanged fearful looks as Ash pressed his hands harder into his mouth. His eyes were wide and unseeing, lost to the horrors in his mind. A single tear rolled down his cheek.

"Ash, look at me!" Lumi called.

The screeching outside intensified and the crate jolted against the door.

Lumi managed to pry Ash's fingers away from his lips and grabbed his jaw, forcing him to meet her eyes. She yanked one of his hands up, pressing it to her own heart.

"Ash, I'm right here!" she cried desperately. "Look at me. See? You're okay. We're gonna get you out of here. We're gonna—" She gasped as the crate jolted again.

"Ash! You have to snap out of it!" Rowan yelled, gripping his friend's shoulders with both hands.

I scanned the room, frantically searching for another way out. My eyes landed on a bundle of rags in the corner of the room. Sitting on top of the rags was a small toy dragon covered in soot. It had a crooked wing that looked like it had been ripped off once and sewn back on by a child's hands. My stomach dropped. The screaming from outside had surrounded us. Only then did I realize it matched the screaming in his head. I bolted back to him and dropped to my knees between Lumi and Rowan.

"Ash!" I said firmly. "Ash, look at me! How did you get out?" Lumi and Rowan exchanged bewildered looks over my head.

"Ash, focus on me!" I said, staring hard into his eyes. "How did you get out?"

"Can't," he gasped, shuddering. "Can't get out. Can't—"

"Yes, you can," I said loudly. "Listen to me! Yes, you can. You did it before. How did you do it?"

Lumi gasped softly as the realization of what I said hit her. She opened her mouth to speak but I cut her off.

"Ash, you have to tell me how! What did you do?"

His eyes focused slightly as he met my gaze. Nothing but terror and swirling darkness looked back at me.

"You can do this." I gripped his hands. "You *will* get out again, but first you have to tell me how you did it."

He gritted his teeth, taking deep drags of air. I could feel his mind fighting through his panic, struggling to focus. Finally, he managed to summon the image of a blazing inferno, directed by small, trembling hands.

"Fire," he gasped through the haze of fear.

"Fire?" I stood and looked around. Long black singe marks crawled up the stone walls.

"Opened the door," Ash gasped. "Fire. Ran."

The crate jolted again.

"You have to light the room on fire," I said to Rowan and Lumi.

"I don't know if I have anything left!" Rowan said frantically.

"But I do!" Lumi stood, shooting a quick look at Ash. He had his head leaned back against the wall and was still struggling to breathe. "We can't move him!" Lumi cried. "What do we do?"

"Leave it to me!" I called. I focused hard on Ash, reaching deep into the well of power in his chest. There wasn't much left, but I drew all of it out rapidly, pulling it into my mind. His power roared through my head like a flash of lightning, and I blinked in shock. Cosmic energy was supposed to be light and airy. Not violent, and intense like this. I didn't have time to marvel at the strange feel of it as Ash groaned. His head lolled to one side, and he slid to the floor, unconscious.

"What the fuck are you doing?" Lumi demanded.

"Trust me!" I replied. I let Ash's fiery energy flood through me and rolled my hands through the air.

The ground shuddered beneath our feet. Three hulking humanoid forms with wide torsos and long arms tore themselves from the ground. One of them lumbered over and lifted Ash carefully from the floor, cradling him close to its chest.

"Climb on!" I yelled.

Lumi, Rowan, and I climbed into the arms of the second golem, while the third lumbered over and shoved the crate out of the way. The door sprang open, and the screaming creatures began to pour into the room.

Lumi splayed her hands out wide, and fire surged from her fingertips. Rowan threw what he had left into her blaze and soon the room ignited.

The creatures shrieked in pain as they were devoured by the flames.

"Go!" I commanded.

The golems smashed through the creatures, bursting through the wall and began running across the square. The blind creatures streaked past us, all headed for the clock tower. A few creatures were stumbling about. They turned towards us as the golems stomped past before heading for the blaze we'd left in our wake, drawn to the screeches and howls.

The golems ran all the way to the edge of the city, following the road towards the Great Forest. I felt a shudder as the stone golems slipped from my control. They shattered into pieces, and we hit the ground wincing and hissing in pain.

Rowan groaned, sitting up as Lumi leapt to her feet and rushed over to where Ash had fallen.

"Ash, wake up!" she cried desperately, shaking his shoulders.

Screams echoed from the city and thick black smoke curled up into the air. I sat up quickly as the distant sound of screaming grew closer.

"Ash, please!" Lumi said, shaking him harder. "Wake up!"

Ash's eyes snapped open. He shot up, scrambling frantically away in terror. His power flared, but I'd drained every last drop he had, and nothing happened. Lumi snatched the front of his tunic to keep him from getting too far.

"Whoa! It's okay! You're okay!" she said. He yanked at her wrist, but Lumi held firm. "Look at me. You're okay," she repeated calmly.

He gasped for air as his eyes darted around fearfully. It took a few minutes for him to come back to his senses. He blinked hard and met Lumi's eyes, releasing his grip on her wrist.

"Lumi," he croaked. She nodded and hauled him upright.

"You're all right," she said.

I stood and helped Rowan to his feet. The screaming drew closer, and Lumi grasped Ash's hand tightly.

"Come on," she said. "Let's get the fuck out of here."

We raced down the road in fearful silence for a solid two hours, making our way deep into the forest before my companions finally collapsed, exhausted.

"What were those things?" Rowan panted.

Ash had not stopped trembling. He laid on his back, running his shaking hands over his face.

"I don't know what they're called," Ash said, quietly. I was relieved to hear his voice again. "But they were people once."

Lumi blanched. "That... they were human?"

"Once," Ash repeated.

"That was a horde of corrupted Cosmic humans," I said.

"I thought you said Cosmic people can't be corrupted." Lumi said.

I shook my head. "Not in the same way that spirits can. Spirits draw from the energies around us. Winter has corrupted that and the spirits with it. Cosmics draw power from an internal well of energy. However, a spirit can dip into that well and draw from it. If that spirit is corrupted, it will destroy the well and corrupt the human at the same time."

"So, she could reach into us like you do and corrupt us?" Rowan gasped, paling. "How do we stop her from doing that?"

"You can't," I replied. "But I have been."

The trio looked around at each other uneasily.

"What do you mean you have been?" Rowan asked cautiously. "She's tried already?"

"Repeatedly," I nodded. "But I have my shields out. I can protect a few people in addition to myself. It's draining every ounce of power that I get back, but I'm focusing everything I've got on it and it's holding strong. Shielding is a natural power you'll have once you're a herald."

"Wait," Rowan said slowly. His bright green eyes fixed on me, and my breath caught in my throat. "So... Is that why you keep saying you don't need to sleep?" Heat rose in my cheeks at his stare, and I nodded.

"If I fall asleep, the shield could drop and leave you all exposed," I said. "I won't let that happen."

"You've been protecting us?" Rowan gasped. "All this time?"

"Yes," I nodded again, blushing. Lumi and Rowan exchanged a long look, unsure of what to say.

"So... Those things... They were really Cosmics?" Lumi asked.

"Yes. Trithica was run by Cosmics. They ran the academy and taught young Cosmics how to use their power. Winter must've corrupted them to make sure they couldn't revolt against her when she came looking for the book." I glanced down at Ash. He was still lying on his back, hands pressed over his face.

"Ash..." Lumi knelt next to him and pried his hands away from his blanched face. "Talk to me. What happened?"

He squeezed his eyes shut. "There were so many of them," he whispered. "So many."

"Talk to us," Rowan said, kneeling on his other side.

I fidgeted, unsure of what I should do. Lumi jerked her head, indicating for me to join them. Despite the seriousness of the situation, warmth spread through my stomach. I felt like I'd been accepted. I sat next to my upset friend and placed a comforting hand on his arm.

"I'm sorry." He opened his eyes and sucked in a deep breath. "I panicked. I tried not to, but..."

"We're here, Ash. Talk to us," Rowan said soothingly.

Ash met his eyes and sat up, pulling his knees to his chest. He stared off into the distance for a moment before drawing another shaky breath.

"I was a little kid when I found out I was Cosmic," Ash began. The pain in his voice cleaved my heart in two. "My stepfather tried to... beat it out of me. And my mother... She was always so cold and distant. I could never figure out why she hated me so much. She tried lots of things to make my powers stop. And all of them were horrible. But no matter what they did I could still touch the candle. I heard them talking one night, when I was six, about how dangerous I was. So, they loaded me up and brought me to Trithica. My mother said I could stay with 'my own kind'." He flinched as the dark memories flooded his mind. "Winter had already been to the city. The other Cosmics were—"

Ash choked on his words. Lumi gently rubbed a hand across his shoulders until he regained his composure enough to keep speaking. "There were hundreds of them. I managed to barricade myself in the clock tower, but they circled it. Night and day, I heard nothing but howling and screaming. So much screaming."

He pressed his face into his knees as he continued. "There was a little food up there, but not much. I thought I was going to starve to death. And then some soldiers came... They must have been headed to the tower. I thought I was saved. I went to unblock the door and I heard—" His face turned from white to a sickening green. "Crunching. The soldiers were overrun and the Cosmics were... Eating them..." He looked like he was about to puke.

Horror filled me as flashes of Ash's memories circled my head. My stomach roiled.

"I was stuck up there for weeks. And for weeks, anyone who came too close to Trithica was eaten. I thought I was going to die. They didn't sleep so I couldn't slip away at night. I was so scared and so hungry that, one day, I just gave up... and I ran. I opened the door and blasted fire around the room. It distracted them and I just ran as fast as I could go. I didn't stop until my legs gave out, and even then I got right back up and kept going." He looked up, meeting our eyes. "I ran all the way to Haven. When I hit the wall, a guard let me in. She felt so bad for me that she didn't even test me for Cosmic powers.

"And when I got inside the city, I found some survivors from my village. Turns out my parents were followed home and were eaten along with most of the others," he said, looking up at us desperately. "I'm so sorry I panicked. But being there... I felt like I was six again. Trapped and alone."

"Don't apologize," Rowan said, wrapping his arm around his distraught friend. A single tear rolled down Lumi's cheek as she too enveloped Ash in her tight embrace.

"We're here, Ash. You're not going to be alone ever again," she whispered pressing her lips into his hair.

I reached over, taking his hand. He met my eyes and squeezed my hand gently. We sat there for a long moment, just holding each other.

They were a funny group. So different and yet so remarkably close. And now, I was starting to feel something I hadn't felt in a long time. Like I belonged somewhere. I watched as we chased the shadows from his golden eyes and the color started to return to his tanned cheeks. In that moment, we were just *there*. Together. Just me, and my newfound family.

CHAPTER TWENTY-FIVE

Ash

We walked for days to put as much distance between us and Trithica as possible, covering our tracks as we went to be sure we weren't being followed.

Despite my exhaustion, I didn't sleep a wink that first night. What little sleep I'd manage to get since was plagued with nightmares of rotting teeth and screams.

Lumi and I started practicing every chance we got. I showed her some new ways to use her power while she attempted to sharpen my pathetic hand-to-hand combat skills.

Standing with my hands curled in front of my face, I tried to dodge her next blow. She just barely missed catching me in the chest and I threw out a fist in response. She parried and struck back hard, knocking me off balance.

Lumi smirked as she dropped and swept my legs out from under me.

I hit the snow with a groan, staring up at the trees surrounding the clearing. The branches overhead swayed in the icy breeze.

"I really do suck at this," I panted.

"You're getting better," Lumi said. She smiled down at me for a moment before holding out her hand and helping me to my feet. "You just have to be more aware of your body. You give a skilled fighter an open angle and you're sunk."

"Well, I'm very aware of the ground. Does that count for something?" I said, stretching out my aching muscles.

"No," Lumi chuckled, and my heart did a somersault.

"Maybe I'm just not cut out for hand-to-hand combat," I sighed. "I should stick to what I do best."

"Throwing fireballs will only get you so far with someone trained to fight," she replied, arching a dark eyebrow.

"It's worked for me so far," I replied, shrugging.

"Fine," Lumi said with a smirk. "Let's see if you can beat me with your fire." Her grin turned wicked as she dropped into a fighting stance.

"That's not happening," I said flatly, crossing my arms.

"Scared?" she challenged. She winked, laughing as I frowned in response.

"I'm not attacking you, Lumi. I don't wanna hurt—"

Lumi shifted. Her movement was too fast to track, and, in a flash, I was flat on my back again.

"I would *love* to see you try," Lumi teased.

The wild, mischievous light dancing in her eyes and the way she smiled at me ignited a spark in my blood. I was helpless to resist. I rolled to my feet and curled my hands into fists.

"All right then," I grinned. "If you insist."

Fire sprouted from my hands, dancing along my fingers. I struck, swinging a flaming fist out towards her. She dodged it, knocking my arm to the side and spinning me around. I staggered back a bit before I surged forward and swung again. Lumi answered by stepping around my strike and blocking my blow with her forearm. I attacked repeatedly. But each time, it was as though she read my mind.

I sent a volley of fire and she smirked, dodging the attack like a dancer. With each blast of flames Lumi slipped closer and closer until she was suddenly right in front of me.

Before I could blink, she landed a harsh blow to the center of my chest. I slammed into the tree behind me and wheezed as the wind was knocked from me. She was on me in seconds. One hand was balled up in the front of my tunic. The other held her razor-sharp dagger to my throat. She locked eyes with me and I blinked, holding my hands up in surrender.

Our faces were inches apart. My heavy breaths stirred the hair that had tugged free from her bun. I released my fire, and it sputtered out. Heat that had nothing to do with my power surged through my blood as we stared into each other's eyes.

Lumi slowly lowered the blade, her gaze never leaving my face. My head spun and my heart hammered against her palm. She glanced down at her hand before slowly dragging her eyes back to my face. Her lips were so close. The desire to lean down and press my mouth to hers was almost overwhelming. The whole world stopped spinning as we stared at each other. Finally, she blinked and stepped back.

"I told you." Her voice quaked slightly. "I win."

"You win," I agreed, breathlessly.

"I think..." Her eyes were dark as she looked back at me. "I think that might be enough practice for one day. We should get back to camp."

"Yeah." I ran my fingers through my hair. "Let's go."

We trudged back through the silent forest, walking side by side. Her arm brushed mine and I almost reached for her hand.

"You... uh... you did good today," she said, nudging me gently with her shoulder. I swallowed hard.

"You too," I replied hoarsely. Our eyes locked again, and the intense heat flared in my veins. "You were amazing."

"I..." she stammered, blushing. "Thanks... I didn't hurt you back there, did I?"

"I'm fine," I chuckled.

"Good." Lumi huffed out a breath, yanking the leather strap out of her bun. Her gorgeous raven hair tumbled down around her face. "I'm sorry if I... if that was too much." She gave me a sheepish look. "Guess I needed to work out some frustrations." I tried not to stare as she pulled her hair back into a ponytail.

"Frustrations?" I cocked an eyebrow in question, but she simply shrugged. Her expression was closed off, so I decided not to push her on it. "Well, I'm glad I could help. Feel free to kick my ass anytime." My voice was slightly breathless, and my heart was still pounding as we passed through the trees into the small clearing where we'd set up our tents for the night.

Rowan and Spring were sitting side by side. A large book was open on Rowan's lap, and he was reading aloud to Spring, who had his eyes closed, leaning his head back against a tree. He peeked through his lashes as we approached. Rowan looked up, pausing mid-sentence.

"You two look like you had fun," he said, raising his eyebrows.

Lumi dropped her sword onto the ground near the fire and plopped down.

"We did," I replied, sitting down beside her. "She kicked my ass again."

"No surprise there," Rowan chuckled, closing the book. A small flash of disappointment crossed Spring's face, but Rowan didn't seem to notice as he turned from me to Lumi. "And what about your powers? Any luck?"

"A little. Though not as much as I'd like," she admitted, glumly. Her shoulders slumped and I frowned at her.

"She's being too hard on herself. She's doing great," I said.

Lumi snorted. "I can't consistently use any of them. Except for ice," she added.

"And that's okay!" I replied. "We will get there. Trust me."

"I do trust you, Ash," she said quietly. "But I need my powers to get better. Now."

"Why?" Rowan asked.

Lumi sighed. She looked down at her hands for a moment before clearing her throat nervously. "Guys... Do you feel ready for this? To face Winter? I feel like we haven't really taken the time to... I don't know... Talk about it? Plan? Anything?" She huffed out a frustrated breath and flexed her fingers. "What happens if we lose? What then? What happens to you?" She looked up at Spring, who tilted his head thoughtfully.

"I don't know," he admitted, brushing his green curls away from his face. "I guess she'd just kill me. Or worse."

"What could be worse than that?" I asked.

"She could corrupt me," he replied with a shudder. "Then she'd have my power under her command. And that would mean bad news for the humans."

"More so than Winter?" I asked.

Spring nodded solemnly, his square jaw set in a hard line. "Of the four of us, my power was undisputedly the strongest. The power of earth extends not only to the plants, but also to rock and stone. The very ground beneath our feet bends to my will. If Winter were to get into my mind or if I were to use my stone before hers was removed... Haven would fall."

"Haven has only lasted this long because of the wall. If she corrupted *you*, she could use you to bring it down," Rowan gasped.

"She could. She's too vulnerable to go that far from the tower herself. And I doubt she'd leave her stone for that long anyways. But if she corrupted me..." Spring placed a hand on his chest. "She could bring the mountains down and bury Haven."

"No pressure though, right?" Lumi groaned, rubbing her eyes.

"Hey," I said gently, "You got this. I believe in you, and I'll be charging into battle right next to you." I gave her a lopsided grin and she sat up.

"Thanks," she muttered. "At least you believe in me."

"And you should believe in yourself too!" I nudged her. "Think about it, Lumi. I've lost count of how many times you saved my life."

"You've killed about three dozen ice demons single handedly," Rowan pointed out.

I nodded enthusiastically. "See? You're a badass warrior queen." She grinned meekly.

"I guess I'd feel more prepared if I could summon something useful on command," she said. "Because I know it's going to be a fight."

"It will be," Spring chimed in, leaning closer to us. Rowan blushed as Spring's arm brushed against his.

"I just wish I could use my power to fight." Lumi scowled at her hands.

"Have you tried summoning a weapon?" Rowan suggested.

"I already have weapons." Lumi waved a hand towards the sword lying next to her.

"Yeah, but you might not always have them. And aren't you out of arrows?" Rowan replied.

"True," Lumi sighed. "I can try." She looked down at the ground with a drawn and anxious expression. "Are you guys scared? Of any of this?"

"Oh, terrified," I admitted. She looked up at me earnestly. The worry creasing her beautiful face made my chest tighten.

"Really?"

"Oh yeah," I said. "I don't know what to expect. I'm not even sure I know what to do. All I know is that I'm with you guys. So, it'll all be okay."

"Agreed," Rowan said. "I'll miss my parents. And I'm scared that I'll never see them again. But I know this is the right thing to do." His gaze dropped to the ground. "We have to try. We might very well be the only Cosmic people left who can. And besides," he added confidently with a nod towards me. "We're together."

"Yeah. You're right," she said, a small grin spreading across her face.

I cast a glance towards the setting sun. "It probably won't hurt to get a later start tomorrow. We'll take some time to try and build your powers up more. Okay?"

"Thanks." A smile tugged at her lips.

"Of course," I grinned back at her. "You know I'd do anything for you."

A strange look flashed across Lumi's face and was gone before I could tell what it meant. Rowan smirked, settling back against the tree as he opened the book.

Spring watched him, a soft smile playing across his pink lips. He tilted his head back and closed his eyes as Rowan resumed reading aloud.

Lumi and I made dinner together. She was unusually quiet while we worked, keeping her eyes focused on her task.

I nudged her gently. "You okay?"

"I'm okay," she replied softly. "I'm just still worried I guess." She laid the bread out on a cloth near the fire.

"Wanna talk about it?"

"I don't know," Lumi shrugged. "I'm just... scared. I feel like we're charging into this. Our whole lives are about to change. Forever. Doesn't that scare you?" She looked up at me. Her ice blue eyes were swimming with emotion.

I swallowed and blew out a breath.

"Guess I haven't really thought about it all that much," I admitted. "But my life has always been so unstable that I... I don't know..." I furrowed my brow, trying to find the right words. "Honestly, I don't really think about 'tomorrow' until it gets here."

"My whole life was planned out for me," she said bitterly. She looked down into the depths of the fire with a heavy sigh. "Down to the very last detail. And in one fell swoop, I threw it all out the window without even a backwards glance. Don't get me wrong, it's ...exciting. But what if I fail?" Tears started to well up in her eyes and I wrapped my arms around her shoulders.

"I know you," I said, pressing my lips into her hair. "You won't fail. The way you took down those ice demons? Winter doesn't stand a chance."

She chuckled quietly and shook her head. "Ice demons are just mindless moving targets," she said dismissively. "And Winter... she's had twenty years to build her power... but that's not what I meant."

"What did you mean?"

"I meant, what if I fail the test?" she whispered, leaning in closer.

"What test?" My brain fought to stay focused as her scent filled my nose.

"What if I perform the ritual, but the Two don't take me?" She hung her head miserably. "For the first time, my life is actually mine. I can't go back. So what do I do if I fail the test?"

"Not gonna happen," I said confidently.

"You don't know that."

"I do," I replied, holding her tight. She felt so right in my arms, I had to remind myself to breathe. "You are, without a doubt, the kindest, strongest, most amazing person I've ever known. They *will* take you. There's not a single doubt in my mind. But I'll make you a deal. You perform the ritual first. If for some crazy reason they don't take you, even though I know for a fact that they absolutely will, I won't do it at all."

"You can't be serious." She sat up, frowning.

"Oh, I'm very serious," I replied solemnly. "Rowan can decide what he wants to do, although I think maybe he might want to stick with Spring," I added with a discreet nod in their direction.

She peeked at them, snuggled close together, and smiled.

"But it'll either be the three of us, or just you and me. We can live out the rest of our days together. We can stay here and build a house, far away from Haven. Or we could catch a ship and go explore the world. Whatever you want. But no matter what, you'll be free. You never have to go back to your father's house again. I promise you," I said firmly.

"You'd do that?" she whispered. Her eyes fixed on my face, sending my heart hammering beneath my ribs. "For me?"

"Lumi, I keep telling you. I'd do anything for you," I replied with a soft chuckle.

She sucked in a sharp breath and bit her lip in thought. The urge to lean forward and press my lips against hers dominated every corner of my head. My gaze inadvertently slid down to her mouth and I suddenly found myself inching closer.

I realized what I was doing and froze, locking eyes with her to keep myself from closing that distance.

"Ash, I..." she stuttered. Her gaze dropped to my mouth, and I felt like I might burst into flames. "There's something I need to tell you."

"What is it?" I managed breathlessly. She looked up into my eyes again and the whole world stopped. I unconsciously held her a little closer and she swallowed hard. Her heart was racing against mine, sending my head swimming with desire. Her lips were so close that I couldn't think straight. My resolve cracked and I found myself leaning forward again without meaning to.

Suddenly, there was a loud pop. A log rolled in the fire, sending sparks skittering up into the air. Startled, Lumi and I jumped and leaned away, blushing furiously.

I glanced around awkwardly and found Rowan peering over the edge of his book. He smirked at us and nudged Spring gently, whispering something under his breath that sounded suspiciously like 'so close.' Spring opened his eyes, glancing at us with a knowing smile.

"You two okay over there?" Rowan called, arching an eyebrow.

Lumi coughed and grabbed the food. "Yep," she said quickly. "Dinner is nice and warm."

Spring hopped up and held out a hand, helping Rowan to his feet. They joined us around the fire, and we began talking strategy as we ate.

"So," Spring said, glancing at us. "Our best course of action is the stone. Winter will be too powerful to defeat outright. But if we pull her stone off the throne, her power will be locked from her. And since her body has been corrupted for the past twenty years, she will be extremely fragile."

"So, one of us removes the stone while the other three of us distract Winter and try not to die," I said. "Sounds simple enough."

"'Try not to die' being the key words there," Lumi said.

"And we have to find the other stones for the ritual," Spring added. "Once mine has been returned to me, I will be much more useful."

"I'd say you shielding us from being corrupted has been pretty useful so far," I remarked.

Spring smiled and tilted his head appreciatively.

"And then the ritual. After she's been removed," Rowan chimed in.

"You're sure you know it?" Lumi asked.

"Oh absolutely," Rowan said, nodding as he stuffed some food into his mouth. The sun had set fully, and the firelight cast an eerie glow on his face. He swallowed the mouthful of bread and tapped the side of his head. "It's all right here."

"Everything? The whole book?" Spring said, raising his eyebrows in surprise. Rowan nodded.

"I can generally remember most of what I read. Kind of my own special superpower," he added with a lopsided grin.

"You are a truly remarkable person," Spring said, awe filling his voice.

"Yeah well..." Rowan's cheeks flushed. "I probably know more than I should. But I read the whole book so... I have everything we need. And we will need to perform the ritual *after* we take the stone from the throne. Not before."

"Why is that?" Lumi asked.

"Because we will get flooded with corruption if we do it beforehand," Rowan said.

"Ah," I said, wrinkling my nose. "Yeah, let's *not* do that."

"Agreed," Lumi said. She stood, stretching her long limbs.

I tried not to stare. Tried and failed.

"I am absolutely beat, so, goodnight, guys." She patted me on the shoulder and turned to go.

I watched her leave, turning back to find Rowan eyeing me with amusement.

"Something on your mind, Ash?" Rowan smirked.

I glared at him for a second before rolling my eyes and standing. "You've been reading too many romance novels, Ro," I said dryly, brushing my hands over my chest in an attempt to be nonchalant.

"I didn't say anything about romance, Ash," he replied slowly. "I just asked if you had something on your mind."

I paused, blushing. My heart stuttered as I slid my gaze over to Rowan and opened my mouth to say something. When nothing came out, I snapped it shut and winced.

Rowan just laughed and stood, waving his hand. "Goodnight," he said simply, heading for his tent. I watched him go. Spring nodded to me and turned, disappearing into the tree line.

I let out a long breath and ran my hand over my face.

Shit.

As I turned to go, a rustling sound drew my attention to the tree line off to my left and I froze. Flames sprang to life in my palms, and I scanned the shadows around me.

Something massive shifted just outside the light of my flames before it bounded away from our camp, retreating rapidly into the distance. I listened intently as the sound faded away. When silence had once again fallen, I exhaled through my nose and clenched my fists, smothering the flames as I turned to head for the tents. I entered mine, laying down on my sleeping bag and closed my eyes with an uneasy feeling.

"Good morning, sleepyhead!"

The sunlight streaming through my eyelids was suddenly blocked by a shadow. I peeked through my lashes and found Lumi staring down at me.

I groaned and tugged my blanket over my head, shivering in the frigid cold that seeped into the tent.

"Time to get up!" Lumi chuckled, pulling my blanket off my face.

I blinked in the bright light and squinted at her. Her hair was loose and flowed over her shoulders.

"You're awfully chipper this morning," I grumbled, my voice still husky from sleep.

"You promised you'd help me, remember?" she replied, holding out some dried meat.

I took it, sitting up and rubbing my eyes.

"Everyone's been up for like three hours," Lumi said.

My stomach lurched. "What time is it?"

"Late," she replied. "But you fell asleep with your boots still on, so I figured you were exhausted."

"I feel like I just closed my eyes," I groaned, tearing a piece of the meat off with my teeth.

"Well, it's time to get up. Come on," she said, favoring me with a bright smile.

I stumbled to my feet, and we left the tent and headed for the fire.

Rowan had set up a fresh blaze about twenty yards from the tents and was sitting on a log beside it, reading a book.

Spring was nowhere to be seen.

"Morning, Ash," Rowan said, glancing up as we approached. "Sweet dreams last night?"

I glowered at him, and he chuckled, lowering his eyes back to his book.

Lumi turned to me as I stuffed the last of my breakfast down my throat.

"Okay," she said determinedly, wringing her hands. "I need to start practicing. I'm thinking I should start with something small. Like a dagger."

I nodded.

We stationed ourselves away from the fire and got to work. She conjured countless disjointed and fragmented shapes, but nothing that even remotely resembled a weapon. On one try, she even conjured a perfect ice sphere by accident.

Finally, she furrowed her brow and formed a long, thin shard of ice. It glinted wickedly in the sunlight. Lumi whooped gleefully and threw it as hard as she could. The ice sailed through the air and embedded itself into a nearby tree with a loud *thunk*.

"I did it!" She whirled around. Her bright eyes and dazzling smile set my nerves buzzing like lightning. "Ash, I did it!" She threw her arms around me.

I was suddenly hyper-aware of her body pressed tight against mine. I swallowed and hugged her close, silently hoping she wouldn't feel my heart thundering behind my ribs. The scent of her filled my nose and I had to fight to suppress the urge to inhale deeply.

"I had no doubt you could," I said, smiling tightly. My fingers itched to twine themselves into her hair and I had the wild urge to pull her in closer and kiss her.

I clenched my jaw as she pulled away and turned to look at Rowan.

"Ro, I did it!" Lumi trembled with excitement. She turned her vibrant blue stare back to me, positively beaming.

I wasn't entirely sure I was breathing.

"If I can make a dagger... Do you think I could maybe make an arrow?" She gestured towards the quivering shard of ice lodged in the tree trunk.

"I do."

"Okay," Lumi nodded, grinning. "I'll be right back."

I watched her dart away. The sunlight glistened in her flowing raven hair as she bounded excitedly through the trees back towards the campsite.

I let out a breath as a fierce ache gripped my chest, growing tighter the further away she went. Fuck. I needed to get a grip. I turned and froze, blushing as I found piercing green eyes pinning me to the spot. Rowan had closed his book and was smirking at me.

"So," he said casually, laying his book in his lap. "You ready to talk about it, yet?"

"Talk?" I stammered, tensing as heat filled my face.

"Ash, come on." Rowan rolled his eyes at me. "I see the way you look at her. How you've *always* looked at her. You can't tell me I'm imagining things. She walked away and you look like you're in literal pain right now."

"I don't..." I tried to say, trailing off as Rowan fixed me with a knowing stare. I clutched my chest, pressing my lips together.

"Ash," Rowan said softly. "You can talk to me, you know." I met his stare, and he raised his eyebrows. The words danced on the tip of my tongue, desperate to finally break free. I'd held them for so long.

The icy forest around us was utterly silent. He smiled and gently patted the log next to him. I strode over and sat, bracing my elbows on my knees, and running both of my trembling hands through my hair as I did. Every nerve in my body was on fire.

He placed a comforting hand on my back and waited as I gathered my courage. I took a shuddering breath and met Rowan's stare.

It was pointless to try and deny it now. He knew me too well to not have guessed how I felt. He was just waiting for me to say it.

His kind face was the picture of sympathy and patience. I desperately wanted to confide in my brother and ease the ache in my chest. My resolve cracked and the words started tumbling from my mouth, cascading through the walls I'd carefully placed around my heart before I could stop myself. Bursting forth like a river rushing over a cliffside.

"Ro... I love her," I croaked, dropping my head into my hands. "I can't sleep. I can't think straight. Every single dream... Every single thought is of her. I love her. And I... I'm terrified she'll find out. I don't think I could ever stay away from her. Just being around her is more than enough but... I don't know what to do." The words hung between us in the cold air, and I breathed a sigh of relief. It felt like a weight had dropped from my shoulders.

"Well, I'll gloat about being right later. But...Have you tried talking to her about all this?" Rowan suggested gently.

I sat up, shaking my head. "No, no, no, no," I said, frantically. "I can't do that."

"Why not? She might feel the same way."

"She doesn't. There's no way," I replied sadly. He arched an eyebrow at me, frowning.

"You say that... But I saw how she looked at you yesterday. You should talk to her," he said. I shook my head again.

"No, she's so... Lumi's got her whole life ahead of her, and I'm just—" I swallowed. The ache in my chest grew sharper with each breath. "Who could love someone like me, Ro? I'm a mess with nothing to offer her," I whispered, forlorn.

"You're being ridiculous," Rowan snapped. I glanced at him, wincing under the intensity of his fierce gaze. "And you know exactly what she'd say if she heard you talk like that right now."

"I don't deserve her," I said, pain dripping from my voice. "She deserves someone who could give her the world. That's *never* going to be me. And I've put her through so much already. I can't tell her."

"Why?" he demanded. "Why can't you tell her?"

"Because!" My heart ripped itself to pieces as I struggled to admit my worst fear out loud. Panic closed around my throat, and I took a deep breath, forcing the words out. "If I tell her and she doesn't feel the same way. And I lose her from my life because of it, I... I don't..." My breathing turned ragged. Unable to say any more, I dropped my head back into my hands.

Rowan was silent for a long moment before he squeezed my shoulder.

"Ash," he began, stopping short as Lumi's voice drifted towards us. I sat up straight and whirled frantically, grasping his arms.

"Ro, please," I breathed, staring at him in desperation. "Promise me. Please, Ro, promise me you won't tell her. Please!"

Rowan glanced towards the sound of Lumi's voice and let out a heavy sigh. "Fine. I promise. But you're going to have to tell her eventually."

"Thank you," I said. Relief flooded through me as I fixed a neutral expression on my face.

Lumi appeared at the tree line. She was looking over her shoulder, chatting. Her face lit up when she glanced my way and met my eyes. "Found it!" She held up her white bow. "C'mon Ash. Come help me." She winked as Spring sidled into view behind her.

I glanced at Rowan, whose face turned a deep red as he busied himself with his book.

"Sure," I called, smirking at him. He shot me a glowering look as I turned and followed Lumi from the clearing. Once we were out of earshot, she turned to me.

"So," she said casually, "Do you think there's something between them?"

"Oh absolutely," I replied, stopping to face her. The morning light shone brightly on her face, making her skin glow. I stopped thinking.

Lumi fell silent, watching me for a long moment before she squared her shoulders and drew a deep, steadying breath.

"Listen." She stepped up to me. Her knuckles turned white as she clutched her bow tightly, taking another nervous breath and stepping even closer. "I need to talk to you." Her intense gaze set my heart pounding as she stared up at me. She was so close. I could reach out and cup her face if I wanted to. She was so impossibly close that I forgot how to breathe.

"Yes?" I managed to say. My voice sounded very far away. She bit her full bottom lip and the earth shifted under my feet.

"I need to tell you something," she said nervously. Her lips opened slightly, and my mind went completely blank.

I desperately wanted to touch those lips with mine. To run my thumb across them and watch them part in desire. My brain was swimming in images of pressing her in close to my chest and tangling my hands in her long black hair. Heat overwhelmed my senses, and I couldn't take it any longer.

Before I realized what I was doing, I reached out with shaking hands and took her face in them. Her skin was smooth under my rough, burning touch.

Those stunning blue eyes widened in surprise as I leaned down and kissed her. Her lips were softer than I could have possibly imagined. Fire seared through my blood and my head swam with desire.

I pulled her in closer, parting her lips with mine and reaching up to tangle my fingers in her unbound hair. Her bow dropped to the snow in her surprise and suddenly, I came crashing violently back to my senses. I released her quickly and stumbled back, pressing my fingers to my lips.

"Oh!" I gasped. "L-Lumi! I—" Panic flooded my senses and overrode everything else as I took in her shocked expression.

She blushed and reached up, touching her lips gently with her fingertips.

Shame and regret seared every nerve in my body. What the fuck was I thinking? I took ragged breaths and waved my hands quickly. Oh, what did I just *do?*

"I shouldn't have... I'm so sorry!" I gasped.

"What?" Lumi's eyes snapped to mine, and her face fell. She looked crestfallen. I knew instantly that I'd crossed a line and betrayed her trust. I had to fix this.

"I'm so sorry," I said, desperately wringing my hands. Hurt flashed in her eyes and I felt like my heart was cracking in two. "I... It was a mistake." My chest heaved as Lumi stepped back and wrapped her arms around herself protectively.

"A mistake?" she asked, shrilly. The pain on her face was killing me. I nodded frantically, desperate to fix my mess before it was too late.

"It was. I'm so sorry. I shouldn't have done that. I just got carried away. But I didn't mean it. It didn't mean anything," I said breathlessly.

Tears formed in her eyes as she took another step back.

"Why would you... I thought—" Her voice broke and I wanted to die. I dropped my hand, wishing the ground would split open and crush me.

She took a shuddering breath and met my stare. Her eyes burned into my soul. "Why would you kiss me if you didn't mean it?"

"I-I don't know." I wrung my hands. "I'm so sorry. I know I shouldn't have, but I just... I'm sorry," I finished miserably.

Lumi looked away, squeezing her eyes shut before turning on her heel, and storming off. I watched her go, sinking to my knees. Tears blurred my vision as she strode through the trees and out of sight. I dropped my head into my hands as despair tore through me. My heart was shredding itself to pieces.

I'd just ruined everything.

CHAPTER TWENTY-SIX

ROWAN

Spring watched Ash and Lumi scurry off before sitting down next to a tree. He gave me a sideways glance, a small smile playing on his lips.

"Would you read to me again?" he asked.

"Of course," I said, hopping up to sit next to him, and settling in close to his side. I let the pages run through my fingers, backtracking through the plot to where he and I had stopped the night before.

Spring leaned against the tree and closed his eyes. I couldn't help but glance over at him. His handsome face was tilted towards the sky, letting the sun soak into his pink skin. Loose green curls fell over his forehead, and I had the sudden desire to wrap one around my finger. My heart did a little flip in my chest, and I dropped my eyes back to the book, trying hard to make my mind focus on the page. As I opened my mouth to begin reading, he suddenly reached out, grasping my wrist gently.

I looked up at him surprised, but his eyes were still closed.

"You really are a remarkable person," he murmured. "Just... remember that. Okay?"

"Um... T-Thank you," I mumbled, blushing.

Spring pressed his lips together before releasing my wrist. I studied his handsome face for a moment. His sharp jaw was tense, and his handsome brow was furrowed in thought. Part of me wanted to ask what was on his mind but that felt too intrusive. Instead, I turned to the book and began reading.

He sighed in contentment.

I only got through a few paragraphs when Lumi came crashing through the trees. Her fists were clenched tight, and tears were streaming down her pale face. She didn't look over at us as she shoved her way into her tent, out of sight.

Spring sat up and looked around with a bewildered expression.

"What was that?"

"Lumi," I replied, frowning. I closed the book and handed it to him. "I'll be right back." I pushed myself up and followed her into the tent. She was shoving her things into her bag, swearing under her breath.

She didn't look up at me as I entered.

"Hey. Are you all right?" I asked tentatively.

"I don't want to talk about it. It's time to get moving," she said sharply.

"Um... Okay. I'll uh... I'll go get the guys," I said, backing out of the tent slowly. I returned to Spring and found Ash standing there, tearing his trembling fingers through his hair.

"Ash," I said cautiously, taking in the anguish on his face. "What happened?"

"I—" His voice was shaking. "I kissed her." He ran a hand roughly over his panic-stricken face.

"You what?" I gasped. "What happened to 'no, no, no'?" He shrugged miserably.

"I don't know," he moaned. "I just... I couldn't... Ro, I fucked up." He buried his face in his hands and my heart ached for him.

"Take it easy. I'm sure you two can talk this out," I said soothingly.

"You didn't see her face," he whispered, his voice breaking. "What have I done? I ruined everything. I'm such a fucking screw up." I opened my mouth to respond, snapping it shut as Lumi reemerged. She stared straight through Ash determinedly and waved back at the tents.

"Help me pack this up," she demanded.

Spring and I exchanged worried looks before ambling over to her. Ash stood there for a moment, wringing his hands. His shoulders slumped and he ducked his head in shame as he walked over to join us. The air was thick with uncomfortable tension. The only sound was the wind whistling through the trees as we finished clearing the campsite and started on our way.

Spring and I walked side by side, shooting each other anxious glances every so often.

Lumi strode purposefully ahead while Ash followed miserably behind us. We trudged for hours, eating as we walked and finally stopping at a river that cut through the forest as the sun began to set.

"Let's stop here," Lumi said. "We can jump in and get cleaned up a bit." I looked at the river doubtfully.

"Lumi, it's freezing," I remarked. "How about we use the pots I brought? We can heat water over a fire instead of jumping headfirst into an icy river."

She jerked her head in a small nod. "Fine. I'll practice while you get cleaned up first."

"Do you want some help?" Ash mumbled tentatively.

Lumi didn't respond, spinning on her heel and stalking off towards the trees.

Ash watched her go helplessly before burying his face in his hands.

"I'll go um... I'll go put up the tents," Spring suggested, following after her.

"I really fucked up this time," Ash moaned.

"Easy, Ash. Come on. Let's get cleaned up." I took his elbow, steering him towards the river. We filled our pots with fresh water and Ash flicked his wrist, conjuring a small, hovering flame. We placed our pots close to it. Ash spread his fingers wide, and his fire formed a ring around the pots. Small bubbles formed along the inside.

"What do I do now?" he said, anguish wracking his deep voice. "I'm such a fucking mess. I don't think I can live with her hating me." I looked up at him sharply.

"Hey. None of that," I snapped. "Don't make me kick your ass."

Ash cringed.

"Just relax, okay? We'll figure this out," I said, averting my eyes as we both stripped and doused ourselves with the warm water. We scrubbed up quickly with my mother's special blend of soap and doused ourselves repeatedly to wash it away.

"Ah," I said, tossing Ash a cloth from my bag without looking at him. "It feels nice to be clean again." I dressed quickly before summoning my power to draw the water from my hair, leaving my tight red curls dry. I glanced over as Ash finished dressing and used his power to dry himself. His face was the picture of misery.

I sighed and patted him on the back. "How about I try to talk to her? See how she feels."

"I can tell you how she feels," he mumbled thickly. "Betrayed. Hurt. Pissed. Hates me."

"What exactly did she say?" I asked. We left the pots and the soap for Lumi and headed back towards the campsite. She stalked past without so much as a glance in our direction.

"She said she had something to tell me," he explained. Spring had just finished putting up the tents and was lounging by a tree a few yards away from them. He smiled at us as we approached.

"Tell you what?" I asked.

"I don't know," Ash admitted. "I lost my fucking head and kissed her before she got the chance to say anything."

"Well, what happened after that?" I said, plopping down next to Spring. Ash started pacing, wringing his hands anxiously.

"She... she froze, and I knew immediately that I fucked up," he said, twisting his fingers so hard his knuckles cracked."I backed off and started apologizing. Told her I got carried away and it didn't mean anything. But... it was too late." Anguish twisted his expression and his voice broke. "She got really upset and she asked me why I kissed her. But... I had no answer."

He paused, yanking his fingers through his hair. Understanding tugged on the back of my mind and I exhaled slowly through my nose in exasperation. Part of me wanted to smack him. But he looked so miserable, I just couldn't bring myself to do it.

"Ash," I began. Spring shifted closer, nudging me with his knee. "Do you think that maybe you're misreading the situation?"

"Misreading?" he asked, confused. "How?"

"I'm just asking," I said, holding up my hands. "Maybe you should—"

My words were cut off by Lumi storming back into the clearing. Ash stopped to look up at her, reaching out his hand.

"Lumi," he murmured. She marched past him without so much as a backwards glance and ducked into her tent, out of sight.

Ash turned back to me, trembling. He looked like he was going to burst into tears.

"Okay," I sighed, standing up. "I'll go talk to her now."

Ash nodded glumly and turned. "I'll just go on a walk or something, I guess..." he mumbled, kicking a rock over into a nearby snowbank. Once he was out of earshot, I turned to follow Lumi into her tent, pausing when long fingers wrapped themselves around my ankle. I looked down to find Spring watching me.

"I'd wait," he said. I shot her tent a long look before sitting back down next to him.

"Why do you say that?" I asked.

"I sense something," Spring replied, tilting his head towards her tent. "She's angry and hurt. But there's something else there." His dark green eyes met mine. "I think you're right. He's missing something. And I think she is too. But she's not ready to hear it. She needs some time to cool off first."

"Hmm." I was about to glance back at Lumi's tent when a sudden realization struck me, and I stared at him in shock. "Wait. You can feel our emotions?"

"Kind of," he nodded. A deep blush crept across my cheeks, and I looked away sharply as my stomach roiled with embarrassment. Could he feel mine? Could he sense the things simmering just under the surface that I hadn't let myself admit out loud yet?

"I can," he said, looking up into the trees as he replied to my unspoken thoughts.

I jumped, blushing deeper and he winced apologetically.

"I've been using my shield to protect you ever since Winter tried reaching for your minds. I try not to pry, but I can't ignore such strong emotions. Much as I might try to." My heart sank sharply.

"Oh," I whispered softly. Tears of humiliation burned my eyes, and I went to move a little further away. "I see."

"No, wait. You don't understand," he said quickly, reaching out to take my hand.

My stomach fluttered as I let him lace our fingers together. His hand felt so strong in mine. Solid, warm, and safe.

"I'm sorry," he said. I raised my eyebrows and he sighed. "I meant it when I said you're remarkable. You're the most remarkable person I've ever met. And you deserve more than someone like me."

"Someone like you?" I asked, confused.

"Someone... with so much blood on their hands," he replied bitterly. He withdrew his hand and passed it over his face, tucking a green curl behind his pointed ear.

"You're not a bad person," I told him firmly.

"I wish that were true," he replied sadly. A hollow look filled his eyes and my heart twisted. "But if you knew everything, you'd feel differently."

"You've made mistakes," I said, reaching out for his hand again. He stared down at my palm before taking it, rubbing small circles on the back of my hand with his thumb. Sparks skittered across my skin from his touch. His voice was small and rough when he spoke again.

"My mistakes have cost so many people their lives."The depthless pain shining behind his green eyes stole the breath from my chest. I wanted to take that pain away. I wanted to make him smile again. But I didn't know how.

"Summer and Winter took their lives. Not you," I insisted. "You didn't know the humans followed you to the nests. And you didn't know Winter would lose her mind when Fall betrayed her."

"There's more to it than that," Spring whispered, his voice cracking. "Things that... If... If you knew..." He shook his head. My heart split in two. I faced him fully, cupping his jaw in my hands.

"I think you're remarkable too, Spring," I murmured. He reached up, placing his fingers on my elbows to draw me a little closer. He studied my face for a few moments, gathering his courage.

"Eli," he whispered finally.

I tilted my head, confused. His deep green eyes flickered to my lips and back up.

"My name," he said, answering my unspoken question. "I don't let anyone use it but, I... I want you to. My name is Eli."

"Eli," I repeated, smiling. The sound of his name on my lips sent a shiver through him. Heat coiled low in my gut as he unconsciously inched closer.

My heart began to pound in my chest. And from where my fingers were pressing on his jaw, I could feel his pulse racing too.

"I don't deserve you," he said.

"Oh... Not you, too..." I sighed through my nose. "You can't think like that. You're a good person, Eli." I ran my thumb gently down his sharp jaw. His eyes grew dark with desire and his breath caught in his throat.

"You're so remarkable... and I've destroyed so much. So many lives," he breathed.

"No," I whispered firmly. "You made mistakes. That doesn't make you a monster. You're allowed to be happy."

"Am I?" he said. He sounded slightly breathless. His eyes fluttered as his gaze fixed on my mouth. I bit my bottom lip, and a small moan escaped him. "You deserve someone better than me." His voice had turned dark and gravelly, sending a delicious shiver up my spine.

"You keep trying to make this decision for me," I whispered, leaning in closer until his lips were a breath away from mine. Heat simmered in my blood. "But what about what *I* want?"

"And what do you want, Rowan?" He looked up at me through his lashes and my heart stopped. I traced my thumb across his sharp jaw again, drawing a shudder from him.

"You," I whispered, locking eyes with him.

He groaned, tangling his fingers in my hair, and pulling me in close. His soft lips pressed desperately into mine, parting them as he drank me in deeply.

He tasted like bliss. Pure, shining bliss. My arms slid around his neck, pulling him to me. I never wanted to let go. Nothing in my life had ever felt as right as kissing him or holding him in my arms. His tongue swept into my mouth, gently caressing mine.

He groaned against my lips, rolling to the side, and pulling me with him. My back hit the cold ground as he pinned me beneath him, locking his hand behind my head to steer our kiss. His other hand gripped my arm tightly. Everything else disappeared except for us. Here together in this beautiful moment.

My heart swelled as he whispered my name like a plea drifting across my lips. I whispered his and he shivered with pleasure. Through the fog of bliss and desire, a single thought drifted through my mind. He *wanted* me. I wasn't the dirty little secret, buried away under the cover of darkness. He wanted me. Here. Now. Out in the open for everyone to see.

I felt his excitement growing against my stomach and shifted so he could feel mine. He moaned and thrust his hips forward slightly, pressing himself harder into me. I gasped into his mouth in response, my fingers digging into the hard muscles in his back. He broke our kiss with a shuddering gasp, his hands sliding to my hips.

My skin felt like it was burning as his lips traced their way down my jaw. He nipped once, gently, before kissing my neck, letting his tongue follow his lips.

I gasped his name, clutching his back tighter. His hand slipped lower to grip the inside of my thigh. All I could think about was shifting that hand to where I needed it. I moaned softly, letting one hand slip up to grip his hair and arching up into him. The very fabric of my soul ached for him. And I wanted to give him everything.

Suddenly, he froze. Every one of his muscles tensed against me. He pressed his forehead into my chest, gasping and panting for air. I loosened my grip on his curls and shifted to try and see his face.

"Eli?" I whispered tentatively. Unease drifted across my heart.

He shuddered and stood abruptly, stumbling away from me as though I'd struck him with something.

Cold washed over me and I missed his heat immediately. I propped myself up on my elbows to look up at him in confusion.

He balled the front of his tunic up in his tightly clenched fists. His flashing eyes, still wild with desire, were edged with panic and guilt.

"I—" he gasped. A small sob choked off his words as he looked down at me. "I can't do this," he whispered. He pressed his lips together and turned away sharply. Like he couldn't bear to keep looking at me. My heart shattered.

"W-Wait! No! Stop!" I said in shock, struggling to get to my feet and reaching out to him. "Please." He turned back, pain wracking his face.

"I'm so sorry," he said miserably. "But I can't. I can't take that from you when I know in my heart that I am the last creature who deserves it." Tears blurred my vision.

"Eli," I said desperately but he turned away again.

He wrapped his arms around his chest and fled into the trees without looking back at me.

I watched him go, the world crashing around me as I fought to breathe. A deep, jagged ache seized my heart, squeezing the life from my chest. Kissing him had felt so right that I was sure he felt it too. But he didn't. I was the dirty little secret after all.

A twig snapped nearby, and I jumped. Lumi edged her way around her tent cautiously.

Her raven hair was pulled back in a bun and her eyes were narrowed as she searched my face. Her sword was drawn and held at the ready.

I met her eyes and let out a broken sob. She raced to my side and wrapped her arm around my waist. The tip of her sword dropped to point at the ground.

"Are you all right?" she asked. I let out a sharp breath and shook my head. Tears dripped from my cheek, staining the front of my tunic.

"No," I replied, my voice thick with emotion. "Lumi, I... I think I might be falling in love." There it was.

The moment the words crossed my lips, I knew they were true. I was in love. I had been falling for him ever since he'd made the strawberry. And the worst part was knowing he might feel the same way and wasn't willing to give me a chance.

"I know," she said. "I can see it on your face. What happened?"

"We were talking, and he said he doesn't deserve to be happy. That I deserve better," I sniffed. I could still feel his hands on me. And the trail of kisses down my neck still scorched my skin. "And I asked him 'what about what I want?' And we... well..." I gestured to my mussed hair and flushed face.

Lumi nodded.

"But he suddenly just... *freaked*. And he ran," I finished, staring at the place in the tree line where he'd disappeared. "And now I don't know what to do. I think I'm in love with him... But he doesn't want me."

Once again, I was staring after a man with tears in my eyes and a broken heart. Only this time, the ache was so sharp that I couldn't breathe.

"I'm sorry, Ro," she said, lifting the sword into my field of vision. "Want me to stab him?" She met my eyes, cocking one eyebrow and I snorted in spite of my misery.

"No. Don't stab him," I sighed, before frowning at the sword. "Why do you have that out?"

"Oh," Lumi muttered sheepishly. She released my waist and sheathed the weapon. "I uh... I came out of my tent and saw you, well, you know." I blushed and she shrugged. "So, I hid. I didn't want to interrupt you. I was going to go back to the river and sit for a while. Try to clear my head a little bit. But then I heard you tell him to stop. I thought he was trying to force himself on you. So, I was going to kill him." I smiled meekly at her and wrapped her in a one-armed hug.

"I appreciate you," I said softly while wiping my streaming eyes with my other forearm.

She planted a kiss on the side of my head and took my hand. "Come on, Ro," she said, tugging me towards the trees. "I think we both need some quiet time by the river."

A small spasm of guilt shot through me as I realized I'd forgotten all about what had just happened between her and Ash. I opened my mouth to apologize, but she shook her head, reading the worry on my face.

"It's okay," Lumi sighed. "I'm still not ready to talk about it. Not yet. Come on."

I gave the tree line one last desperate look, half hoping he would come striding back for me. When he didn't, my shoulders dropped, and I let her lead me away.

We reached the river and sat, huddled together for a long time. Neither one of us said a word about our broken hearts. We were just there. Miserable together. It was comforting. Sitting there with my best friend, listening to the river rushing past us as we leaned our heads together in companionable silence.

My mind was filled with images from the past few days. Walking side by side, laughing and discussing books with him for hours and hours on end. Spring's head tilted back as I read to him from the book he'd given me. The strawberry.

His comment about sweeping someone special off their feet. At the time, I thought that maybe he could be talking about me, and I let myself hope. But now, I knew it didn't mean anything.

Finally, when the sun had set fully and the stars were shining overhead, Lumi broke the silence with a sigh.

"We should get back," she said softly. I nodded and stood.

"Thanks, Lumi," I said, hauling her to her feet and offering her my arm. She took it and we began our stroll back. "I needed that quiet time."

"I think we both did," she replied, looking down at our feet.

I shot her a quick look, contemplating whether or not I should tell her what I knew. But the look on her face told me she still wasn't ready to talk about it yet, so I kept my mouth shut. She seemed to know what I was thinking because she looked back up at me as we stopped at the campsite and exhaled through her nose.

"We can talk more about everything tomorrow. For now, try to get some sleep, okay?" I nodded and she planted another kiss on my temple before disappearing into her tent. I looked around for Spring, but he was nowhere to be found. I didn't know if him hiding from me made me feel worse or better. But my heart ached just the same. My eyes landed on Ash, knees curled to his chest, staring mournfully into the fire.

Heartache was in the air it seemed.

I debated going and sitting with him, but I knew him too well. He'd put his own broken heart aside and go charging menacingly after Spring if I told him what happened.

Ash looked up from the fire and I gave him a meek smile before slipping into my tent and sprawling out on my sleeping bag. As I drifted off, I thought I heard someone step to the entrance of my tent before sighing and stepping away.

I wanted to sit up and peek, hoping to find Spring, but I made myself stay in bed and squeezed my eyes shut tight. I didn't want to let myself hope anymore.

The next morning passed in sullen silence. Spring had returned and was determined to avoid looking at me, which I decided made me feel ten times worse.

Lumi noticed and stuck close to my side as our group packed up and resumed our trek down the road.

Lumi and I spoke quietly about nothing in particular, walking side by side and watching Spring's back as he led us through the forest.

I tried to keep my focus on our journey, but my traitorous mind kept straying. It kept picturing his eyes darkening with desire and my fingers pressing into his back. I could almost taste his lips again. On one occasion, my mind strayed to the feel of him grinding into me and I saw him falter a step, clenching his fists tightly at his sides.

I blushed, remembering what he'd admitted to me about hearing our thoughts. My sullenness gave way to a bubbling anger, and I straightened, glaring at the back of his head. I wanted to be furious with him for refusing to consider how I felt in this situation and toying with my heart. Just like every other asshole.

But the difference this time was that he could see my heartache. He could feel it. And he was still ignoring me. Didn't I matter, too? He'd let me think there was something growing between us. Didn't my feelings matter? Apparently not. It never mattered what I thought. To any man. Well, fine. If he didn't want to think about how shitty he made me feel, then I'd give him something else to stew over for a while.

I narrowed my eyes and began to think the dirtiest, most salacious thoughts I could about him, throwing them with all of my might in his direction. I pictured sliding my hands along his bare chest and kissing my way down his stomach. Slipping my fingers along the underside of his cock. I let myself imagine what he might sound like when I stroked down his length and what it might feel like if he were to do the same to me with his tongue. I imagined his soft pink fingers wrapping around my cock, while I twisted mine into his luscious green curls and thrust into his hand, moaning his name into his ear.

The thoughts reverberated around in my skull. Vivid, loud, and viciously clear.

Spring sucked in a sharp breath.

I felt a surge of petty, vindictive satisfaction as he suddenly stopped walking. His hands shook at his sides and his breathing had turned ragged.

"Spring? What happened? What's wrong?" Lumi said, concerned. Her fingers twitched towards the hilt of her sword as she glanced around us at the bleak, snow-covered landscape.

Guilt smothered the satisfaction and filled my gut. I ducked my head, ashamed of my petulance.

Spring half turned, tilting his head back. The sun caught his handsome face, giving it the appearance that his flushed pink skin was glowing. His eyes were dark, and his luscious lips were parted as he sucked in another deep breath. He glanced over, locking his molten green eyes with mine.

I swallowed and pressed my lips together in shame. He stared hard for a few moments before he blinked and slid his eyes to Lumi.

"Sorry. Nothing," he said quickly, turning away and continuing down the road.

Lumi shot a questioning look at me and I shook my head, embarrassed.

As we continued following after him, I sent apologetic thoughts towards the back of his head. He didn't respond. His hands were shoved deep into the pockets of his coat and tension lined his shoulders. After a few minutes, I stopped trying and shrunk back in despair. I felt immensely guilty for trying to torture him. And immeasurably lonely. Nothing. That's what he said to Lumi. It was nothing. And now I felt like nothing too.

We came around a bend in the road and froze.

Ahead lay the crumbling remnants of a village. Abandoned houses lined the road, surrounded by wreckage and debris. Several of the walls had deep claw marks gouged into them and an eerie silence hung heavy in the air. Not even the wind howled.

Spring swallowed and covered his mouth with his hands. Lumi grabbed my arm, staring wide eyed around at the ruins.

"Shit," she whispered, horrified.

My insides clenched with fear. We crept forward, stepping carefully over the wreckage of a farmer's cart. Scattered amongst the debris and half-buried in the snow were several skeletons. Horror gripped me as I stepped over a particularly small one.

"Ice demons," Ash whispered from behind us. He had his hands out, fire dancing along his palms and at the ready.

Lumi went to draw her sword, but Spring shook his head.

"They are long gone," he said sadly, gazing down at two skeletons wound together in a dying embrace. Deep claw marks gouged their bones. "These skeletons aren't recent."

I stopped in front of a gray corpse rotting on the side of the road.

"Look," I said pointing. Lumi stepped to my side. Ash paled and took several steps back. "It's one of those things from Trithica. But what's it doing here?" I said, glancing at Lumi.

She drew her sword and nudged the creature gently in the chest. The tip of the blade sunk into its flesh, but it didn't move. It was long dead.

"They wander," Ash hissed fearfully. "If they can't find anything to eat... After about four days, they just die." Ash waved a flaming hand towards the creature.

I shuddered at the thought. "How have the ones in Trithica lived this long?" I wondered aloud. It was Ash's turn to shudder, his face paling further.

"I said there were hundreds, remember?"

Horror coiled in my chest, and I stepped away from the creature, following Lumi and Spring as they made their way into the town square.

Lumi was staring down in dismay at a tiny skeleton lying face down in the snow. A tear rolled down her trembling cheek.

Ash came up behind me. He pressed his lips together thoughtfully for a moment before he approached her and placed a hesitant hand on her shoulder.

She jumped and glanced up at him before shaking him off and striding away without looking back.

"Let's get the fuck out of here," she said tersely, leading the way through the ruins. Spring followed behind her and Ash and I brought up the rear.

Ash shot me a helpless look which I returned in dismay, patting him on the back.

We dodged over wreckage as we made our way out of the city and plunged back into the trees.

We walked in horrified silence for a few more hours, stopping only when everyone's stomach began to growl. Ash went to collect firewood while Lumi announced she was going to find some fresh water. I sat, digging through my bag without looking at Spring as he inched closer hesitantly.

"Rowan," he said finally.

A lump formed in my throat. I had to make myself look up at his distressed face.

He knelt next to me and took my face in his hands. "You do matter," he said softly.

My heart lurched. Tears formed in my eyes, and I tried to pull away, but he held firm.

"Wait, please." He traced his thumb over my cheek bone and kissed my forehead gently. "I'm so sorry. I didn't mean to make you feel like you don't matter to me. I just... I don't deserve someone like you."

I snorted bitterly and yanked my face out of his grasp. "Fine," I muttered, turning my streaming eyes back to my bag to hide my tears. I was so damn tired of men feeding me their bullshit excuses that I just couldn't handle his and I didn't want to hear them. "I'm sorry I sent those thoughts to you. I was being childish, and I won't do it again."

Spring tilted my chin back to look in his eyes. They'd gone dark with desire at the memories of my attempt to torment him.

"Don't apologize," he whispered.

I exhaled slowly through my nose, glancing at his parted lips. My heart wrenched painfully. He must've sensed it because he frowned, his eyes searching my face. "Rowan, I..." he began. He trailed off, snapping his mouth shut when no other words came out.

I looked away, wiping my eyes, and busying myself with my bag.

"Don't bother, Spring. It's okay," I sighed.

He winced, his face falling at the sound of his spirit name.

"Rowan, I didn't mean to—"

"Don't," I snapped finally, scrubbing a frustrated hand across my face. "I get it, okay? I'm never going to be the one someone picks for forever. I'm just the dirty little secret men fuck around with before they go back to their real partners and forget I exist. The sex toy that gets used and tossed aside. But this time I thought it was different. For once, I thought someone actually *chose* me. I've been with three men, and each time I thought I loved them. Even when I knew they didn't love me. And when they inevitably threw me away, it hurt. But it never hurt like this."

My chest felt like it was caving in. "And now... I know for sure that none of it was ever love. Because... now, I finally know what love actually feels like." I hadn't meant to say the last part out loud, but there it was. My soul unwillingly bared for him to see.

"Rowan—" Spring began, his voice breaking. He swallowed hard and suddenly, it was too much for me to handle. I stood abruptly, wiping my eyes.

"Lumi worries about me all the time. Because when I fall in love, I fall hard, and I fall way too fucking fast. I try so hard not to, but I just can't help it. But it's never felt like this before. It's never hurt this bad." I met Spring's eyes. "So... now you know," I said quietly. "Though, now that I think about it... I guess you knew already. So, it doesn't matter." I turned to walk away, and he watched me go, nothing but devastation on his handsome face.

I only managed to take a single step before he was suddenly behind me. I hadn't even heard him move. I didn't have time to react as he grasped my arm and turned me around sharply.

His lips crashed into mine, opening my mouth frantically and sinking into me. I groaned in surprise as he stepped forward, backing me a few feet into a tree and pinning me against him.

Heat flared through me. He kissed me hungrily, his tongue lashing over mine as I twined my hands around him, bunching his coat under my fingers. He broke our kiss suddenly and pressed his lips into my neck, shuddering as his hands trailed up my chest to feel my thundering heart. His touch sent lightning crackling down my nerves and my mind reeled as it scrambled to catch up.

"Rowan," he gasped desperately, kissing my neck over and over. "You matter. Please don't walk away. I'm so sorry."

My mind went blank as his mouth burned a trail down to the exposed part of my chest above my collar. My head fell back against the tree as his lips seared my skin.

"S-Sorry?" I managed, grasping the back of his neck. I was terrified he was going to run away again. He shook his head vigorously in response to my unspoken fear, pressing into me tighter with a small noise of despair.

"No," he croaked. He trailed his lips back up to murmur in my ear. "I hate myself for making you feel like this. The last thing I ever wanted to do was hurt you. I swear to you, I won't run away again." He pulled away and looked deeply into my eyes. "Please, listen to me. I do feel it."

My heart stuttered and a hopeful balloon swelled in my chest, warring with the hesitancy and doubt lodged firmly around my heart. I went to say something, but he kissed me soundly before I could speak.

"I do," he whispered against my lips. "I'm sorry I panicked yesterday. I shouldn't have... but I felt you so willing to give me everything, and all I could think was that I didn't deserve it."

"But—" I started, and he kissed me again.

His lips were urgent against mine and he kissed me harder, driving whatever I was about to say from my mind. He kept kissing me fervently until I was dizzy and gasping for air.

"Eli!" I moaned breathlessly. He shuddered at the sound of his name and pressed into me tighter. My scrambled brain was still trying to form the words to make my point. Even if I couldn't remember what that point was through the fog of desire.

"I know," he said. "How you feel matters to me, Rowan. You aren't the only one who falls too hard and too fast. But before I can have anything more than this... Have you fully and freely... I need to prove to myself that I'm worthy of your heart."

He met my eyes again and a lump formed in my throat. Part of my heart wanted to sing with joy, while the other half sank. And I was lost between the two.

His gaze roamed over my face, soaking in every detail of this moment. "The last thing I'd ever want is for the man I love to regret me."

The world screeched to a halt as his words crashed into my frantic heart. My soul tore itself in two. I desperately wanted to believe that he meant what he'd just said. But it was too good to be true. I'd heard those words before, and they were always a lie. No man had ever meant it when he said he loved me. But despite the fears clawing at my mind, I couldn't quite squash the hope soaring through me.

He looked deep into my eyes, watching the war raging there.

"You—" I whispered, too stunned to say it out loud. It didn't feel real.

He didn't answer. Instead, he pressed his lips to mine, parting them and drinking me in deeply. Suddenly, my mind was filled with vivid images of us together. His head was on my lap, and I was playing with his loose curls. He was smiling up at me as I balanced a large book on his chest and read to him. We were outside in a vast garden, greener than anything I'd ever seen, picking flowers of every color imaginable. He came up behind me and tucked one behind my ear with a sweet kiss on my cheek. We were in the dark, kissing deeply, wrapped up together in a warm blanket while thunder clapped outside, and lightning flashed across the sky.

Each image was wrapped in tightly knit emotions, swirling around them like a whirlwind. Desire, longing, affection, and love. I could feel each one like they were mine. I realized, rather than just telling me, he was letting me into his heart and showing me how he truly felt. Showing me so I would know, beyond a shadow of a doubt, that he really did love me.

The images receded and I gasped. Tears filled my eyes. He loved me.

"I do," he whispered, wiping away my tears. "I love you. Please, Rowan. Be patient with me. Let me save this world and atone for some of my mistakes. Let me do this so that I can love you the right way." He emphasized his words with another deep kiss, drawing a groan from my chest.

"Does this mean no more kisses?" I mumbled.

He chuckled lightly and reached up to caress my bottom lip with his thumb. I shuddered.

"I know I should say yes, but I don't think I could stop if I tried. Now that I've tasted your sweet kiss, I'd drive myself crazy if I denied myself it," he admitted, leaning in. "I know you're probably starving, but can we stay right here for just a little bit longer? I missed you so much today, my sweet Sunflower."

I smiled against his lips, and he kissed me again. My heart surged, racing against his as we stayed locked in a tight embrace for a long while. He loved me. He really, genuinely loved me. Out loud and in the open for the whole world to see.

And as long as I had that, I could wait for the rest.

CHAPTER TWENTY-SEVEN

LUMI

My steps were featherlight to minimize the sounds of the water as I crept back towards our campsite. I'd filled one of Rowan's pots and planned to boil the water before refilling our canteens.

A hair came loose from my bun, and I blew out a breath, shooing it away from my forehead. The water sloshed loudly, and I winced, freezing in place until the liquid calmed and fell silent again.

I didn't want to interrupt the important conversation I desperately hoped was happening. The utter devastation on Rowan's face had simultaneously broken my heart and ignited a burning fury in my chest. I was at least willing to give Spring a chance to apologize, but he was still on thin ice and knocking him senseless wasn't off the table just yet.

A soft, blissful groan reached my ears and I paused, a hopeful smile spreading across my face. I crept a little further down the tree line and spotted Rowan and Spring. They were tangled together in a deep, passionate kiss, completely oblivious to everything around them. I made a small victorious gesture and crept quickly away, leaving Spring to make his very enthusiastic amends to my broken-hearted best friend.

Relief washed over me as I trudged through the silent forest. I wanted Rowan to be happy. After everything he'd been through, he deserved it. I'd held him while he wept over assholes too many times. But despite what his exes put him through, I'd never seen him that broken-hearted before. The misery on his face had made it clear that there was something different about Spring.

My relief evaporated as I entered a clearing and almost ran headlong into Ash.

He gasped in surprise and skidded to a halt, barely avoiding a collision.

My pace stuttered for only a fraction of a second before I dodged to the side and breezed past him. I kept my eyes on the ground, staring determinedly in the opposite direction of his stupid, handsome face.

"Lumi! You scared me!" he gasped. I didn't respond, choosing instead to put the pot down next to the fire he'd started. The water splashed as I slammed the pot down harder than I meant to and sat on a log near the fire. He must've dragged it out of the woods so we could sit and eat. Part of me wanted to look at him, but I squashed the urge and picked up a stick instead, jabbing it into the fire angrily. He cleared his throat, taking a step closer. Being this close to him made my aching heart race.

"I set up the tents," he mumbled awkwardly. "I was just going to find Ro. I think he—"

"Do not," I spat, without bothering to look over my shoulder, "bother Rowan right now."

"Oh... Sorry."

I had no idea how I was ever going to be able to look at him again without wanting to cry. Because now, every time I pictured his face, all I saw was that look of horror and regret after he broke off our kiss.

I straightened my back and resumed poking violently at the fire, refusing to let myself dwell on the kiss for longer than a few seconds. Any longer than that, and my heart would break all over again. It didn't mean anything.

That's what he'd said. And what I kept trying to remind myself. He got carried away and it didn't mean anything. It was a mistake. That word was a dagger to my soul. A mistake.

What he didn't know was that I'd spent the whole morning gathering my courage and had pulled him aside to tell him the truth. I loved him. But before I got the chance, he kissed me.

In that moment, I felt like I could fly. I thought he knew what I was about to say. And that he loved me too. But the kiss had only lasted a second before he'd stumbled back in horror.

And the whole world had crashed down around my head.

Ash cleared his throat, but I didn't turn around to look at him. He watched me for a moment before he ambled away. I didn't know where he went, and I didn't care. I just needed him to leave and give me some space.

I huffed sharply and put my head in my hands, fighting back the tears threatening to overwhelm me.

How could I be so stupid? Of course he didn't feel the same way. Who would love someone whose father tried to kill them all the time?

I sat there, stewing in lonely silence for a long time before I heard footsteps crunching through the snow behind me. I straightened my back, determined to ignore him again, when I heard a blissful, giddy sigh.

I turned and found a bright-eyed Rowan staggering towards me. His face was flushed, and his lips were swollen and puffy. He looked up at me with a dazed grin.

"Hi," he said, a happy giggle bubbling around his greeting. I smiled broadly and scooted over, patting the log enthusiastically.

"Hey, Ro," I said with exaggerated slowness as he plopped down next to me. "You look... well."

"I guess you could say that," he sighed happily. I nudged him.

"So, I don't have to kill him for hurting my best friend? He can stay?"

"Oh... He can stay," Rowan said. He touched his swollen lips and smiled. "He... He loves me, Lumi." Excitement filled his bright green eyes. "He really loves me."

"He loves you?" I asked. A familiar worry began gnawing at me. "And how do you feel about that?"

"I love him," he replied, beaming. The worry sharpened and I paused, choosing my next words with care.

"That's pretty fast, isn't it? For love?" I suggested, gently. The last thing I wanted to do was pop my sugar roll's bliss-filled little bubble, but I wasn't about to allow anyone to take advantage of his hopeless romantic soul with empty promises and flowery words again.

"I know," he sighed. His smile turned dreamy, and he shook his head. "And a part of me is freaking the fuck out about it. But... I don't know, Lumi. I've had crushes before, but it's never felt like this. It feels real this time. It is really fast, but I know it's the truth." His eyes turned misty. "He let me see into his heart and showed me all these thoughts and feelings he's been having about me. And I could feel it. How he feels about me. It's real. He really does love me," he finished, his expression turning hopeful as he looked at me.

I realized he was waiting. Waiting for me to sign off as his best friend. I resolved to have a long chat with Spring when I got the chance. For now, I smiled broadly and threw my arms around my lovestruck sugar roll.

“Of course he loves you, Ro! What’s not to love?” I said firmly. “I just needed to make sure you’re okay.” He let out a small sigh of relief and squeezed me tightly.

“I know. And I swear to the cosmos above, I am this time. I promise you.”

“Good. So, you two are a thing now?”

“Yes?” Rowan tilted his head thoughtfully. “Well, sort of.”

My stomach dropped. He noticed the shift in my expression and shook his head, sitting up.

“It’s not like that, I promise. Not this time. He said he wants to atone for his mistakes before I give myself to him fully,” he said slyly, blushing.

“Ro...” I began cautiously.

“I swear,” he replied earnestly. “I know what it sounds like, but I promise it’s okay this time. He’s mine. He called me his Sunflower.” He wiggled his shoulders happily as he said it. His joy was so infectious that I put aside my own heartache for a moment and basked in his radiant glow.

“Sunflower? That’s adorable,” I said. I cocked my head to the side thoughtfully. “What even is a sunflower?”

“I have no idea. Hopefully, a good thing,” he chuckled. I was still worried for him, but I pushed the thoughts aside. There’d be time to deal with Spring later.

“So... Good kisser?” I asked, raising my eyebrows.

He tilted his head back with a groan and I laughed.

“Very much so,” he grinned. “For now, that’s all I get. But I’ll take it. He loves me,” he repeated quietly. He touched his face with his fingertips as though that fact hadn’t quite sunk all the way in yet.

“I’m happy for you, Ro,” I said, gently rubbing his back. “You deserve to be happy.”

“Thanks,” he said, straightening. “All right... Enough about me. What about you?”

My stomach lurched. I didn’t want to think about myself just yet. I wanted to stay in Rowan’s happy moment with him. But the smile had faded from his still flushed face, and I knew there was no avoiding it.

I sighed and looked into the fire, frowning at it.

“So,” he said carefully, tilting his head to get a better view of my face. Mussed red curls filled my vision. “Something happened between you and Ash?” I shot him a forlorn look.

“He told you?” I guessed.

"Well..." Rowan scrunched his nose. "Not so much told me as... Panicked frantically in my direction. He said he kissed you."

The aching part of my heart felt a surge of vindictive glee that he had panicked.

"He did," I said, tears immediately clouding my vision. I blinked them away rapidly. "And then he started apologizing. He said it didn't mean anything and that it was a mistake."

I had to blink more tears away as Rowan scooted closer, rubbing my back in small, comforting circles.

"Are you all right?"

"No," I replied, my voice breaking. "I'm not all right, Ro. He kissed me. And then he called it a mistake." Rowan furrowed his brow.

"And you're upset because he crossed the line and kissed you?"

"No, Ro, I...I *wanted* to kiss him." I let out a small sob. "I've been thinking a lot about him lately. And I realized that I'm in love with him." Rowan's hand froze and shock spasmed across his face.

"Wait..." he said, slowly. "You... wait, what?"

"I love him," I sighed, wiping my eyes. The words felt like broken glass in my mouth. "I was about to tell him. And... when he kissed me, I thought he knew. I thought he loved me too. But he made it crystal clear... He doesn't." Understanding suddenly dawned on Rowan's face and he pinched the bridge of his nose.

"So," he said. A small amount of irritation tinged his tone and I frowned. "Just to be clear...You're not mad that he kissed you?"

"No," I said, sharply. "I'm angry and hurt that he kissed me when he doesn't love me. And now I know he will never feel the same way. It sucks, Ro."

"Oh, I'm gonna smack the ever-loving fuck out of him," he said, looking up and shaking his head. The sunlight streaming through the trees cast a halo of light on his red curls as he tore his hands through them in frustration. I raised my eyebrows, utterly confused. "I'm gonna smack him right in his dense, clueless face. See! If he would've just *listened* to me—" He sighed sharply through his nose and looked back at me. "You need to talk to him. Now."

"No," I retorted. Angry tears blurred my vision. "He made it crystal clear how he feels."

"He didn't," Rowan said, shaking his head in exasperation. "I promise you, Lumi, he really, *really* didn't." I opened my mouth to protest, and he cut me off, gathering my hands in his. "Do you trust me?"

"Of course I do," I said, my confusion deepening.

"Then trust me now. Talk to him," Rowan insisted. "I can't tell you his side of things. That has to come from him. But trust me. Please." His eyes slid from mine to somewhere just over my shoulder as the sound of footsteps approached, crunching through the snow.

I tensed. Rowan frowned and jerked his head at me.

"Enough is enough," he said fiercely. He stood and pointed to the log. "Sit. You two are going to talk."

"No," I said firmly.

Rowan shot me an exasperated look.

"There's nothing more to say." I shot a cold look over my shoulder and met Ash's gaze.

He was a wreck. His hair looked like he'd been tearing his fingers through it and his chest was rising and falling sharply with each ragged breath. He met my stare, wincing at the pain filling my eyes. I glared back, letting him see it all. His face fell in devastation as I turned back to Rowan, who was shaking his head.

The tears I was desperately trying to hold back started to trickle down my cheek. I held my head a little higher in an attempt to hide them. Rowan's eyes flashed.

"The fuck there isn't! There's plenty more for you to say. Both of you," he snapped.

"There you are!" a bright voice called suddenly. Spring stepped into the clearing, clutching Rowan's bag to his chest. "I've been looking everywhere for you, Sunflower. You left your... Oh."

He froze, eyeing us before raising his eyebrows at Rowan. "Oh," he repeated, shifting uncomfortably. "I was just... I uh... I was hoping you'd help me with something?" he finished, with a pointed glance at Rowan.

Rowan let out a near silent sigh of relief and dashed to his side, lacing his arm through Spring's. Spring planted a soft kiss on his lips and Rowan beamed before turning back to us with a frown.

"Talk. Now. Or I swear to the cosmos, I will tie you both to a tree until you do." he threatened.

He turned on his heel and disappeared through the trees, leaning his head against Spring's shoulder as they went. I clenched my hands in my lap and stared down at them hard, willing my breathing to remain steady and even.

"Lumi, please," Ash whispered. I shook my head and swallowed a sob, refusing to turn around. "Can we talk ab—"

"No," I hissed.

"Lumi, please." He let out a shuddering breath. "I can't stand this anymore. Please. Tell me what I can do... And I'll do it. Anything, please." The snow crunched as he took a tentative step closer.

My heart ached. Fresh tears surged forward, and I stood, clenching my fists.

"There's nothing you can do. Just go," I whispered. I'd taken three steps when he caught my wrist.

I squeezed my eyes shut as he stepped around to face me. I couldn't bring myself to face that regret again.

"Lumi. Just look at me. Please..." His voice broke. "I can't stand the thought of you hating me." His other hand came up to cup my cheek.

"Don't." I jerked my face away from his touch. Tears of humiliation rolled down my cheeks as his fingers slipped from my wrist. I opened my eyes, staring determinedly at the trees.

"I'm so sorry, Lumi. I'm so—" His voice wavered as he let out a small sob. My heart felt as though it was going to snap in half. "I'll never forgive myself for... For kissing you and—"

"Stop!" I cried suddenly, shoving him away from me.

He stumbled back a step and nearly tripped over the log.

I wrapped my arms around my chest. His words twisted in my gut like a dagger, and I couldn't bear them any longer.

"I get it." I finally faced him, reading the anguish and shock on his handsome face. "You regret kissing me. But I—"

The words caught in my throat as a tear rolled down his cheek. Every muscle in my traitorous body screamed to reach for him, but I made myself take a step back. I held myself tighter and looked into his eyes, forcing out the words before I lost my nerve.

"I don't want to hear any more apologies. I don't want any more... Any more reminders that I feel something, and you don't."

Ash blinked. For a moment, the only sounds were our breathing and the trees creaking overhead in the icy wind.

"Wait... What?" Ash said finally, his eyes wide.

I opened my mouth to repeat what I'd finally allowed myself to admit, but the words wouldn't come back. His look of regret swam through my mind, and I let out a small sob, gritting my teeth.

"I can't do this," I said softly. My heart ripped itself apart. I took a step towards the path, but Ash reached out and grip my shoulders gently.

"No! Wait," he gasped, his eyes desperately searching my face. "Please, wait. What did you mean by that? Please, I need to know... What did you mean?"

"Don't," I said, looking into his golden eyes.

There was something flickering there, and my chest tightened. If that look of regret crossed his face again, I didn't think my heart would survive.

"Don't make me say it again. I can't... I just can't." I let out a shuddering sob and tried to step back, but he held me firmly in place. "Please, Ash. I can't face you right now. It hurts too much."

"Lumi no, I—" Ash stuttered as his fingers tightened on my shoulders. His mind was moving faster than he could form words.

"Just stop." I shook my head. "Leave me alone. Please, Ash. I don't want any more apologies because you don't feel... the same way I do." He froze, staring at me in shock.

"You feel something? For me?"

Something palpable shifted in the air between us. He watched my face for a few moments, holding my gaze as a wild hope danced through his eyes.

Finally, I made myself nod. "I love you," I whispered.

A sharp, stunned sound escaped his lips. I looked away quickly, unwilling to watch the guilt and regret return. Or worse. For a moment, we didn't move.

"You... You love me?" he said, dumbfounded.

I winced, wishing I could vanish.

"But when I kissed you, you said..." he began. Understanding crashed across his face and he sucked in a sharp breath. "Oh no! Oh, I am such a fucking idiot!"

I braced, waiting for the worst. His hands trembled as they glided up to cradle my face, forcing me to look at him again. His golden eyes blazed with life.

"Lumi..." he said, drawing me in closer to his chest. "I can't breathe without you."

I blinked. A small slice of hope fluttered through me as he let his eyes roam over my face.

"I didn't apologize because I didn't want to kiss you. You're all I ever think about." He pressed his forehead to mine and traced his thumb over my lower lip.

Heat simmered in my blood at his touch.

"I apologized because I thought I crossed a line and betrayed your trust in me. I thought there was no way someone as amazing as you could ever love someone as messed up as I am. And I didn't want to do anything to lose you. So, I panicked. But Lumi..." He swallowed hard. "I love you. I love you so much it hurts. I always have."

I splayed my palms against his broad chest. His heart thundered wildly beneath my touch. I shook my head and let out a small laugh, my heart so full of emotion I thought it might burst.

"I thought you didn't." I choked back a sob as Ash pressed his lips to my forehead.

"I do," he murmured. "With everything I am. I love you, Lumi." He leaned down and his lips met mine, softly. His kiss was slow and sweet, sending the heat simmering in my stomach roaring through me. I reached up and wrapped my arms around his neck, drawing him in close.

"I love you," I whispered against his mouth.

He tugged my hair free from my bun and spread it over his hands. He grinned against my lips as my hair ran through his fingers. "Oh, Lumi," he whispered, wrapping his strong arms around my back. "I'm sorry that I'm such a fucking idiot."

I couldn't help but laugh. "I don't think you're an idiot," I replied, burying my face into his sturdy chest. His heart pounded against my forehead. He pressed his lips into my hair, holding me as close as he could get me.

"So, what would you call kissing the woman I've always loved... Misreading her reaction because I'm so stuck in my own head... Panicking before she can tell me that she loves me too... And then claiming that it meant nothing when kissing her is the only thing I've wanted for years?"

"I..." I looked up into his golden eyes and scrunched my nose apologetically. "Yeah, I got nothing."

Ash's deep laugh rumbled through his chest. I pressed in closer to him, shivering.

This close to him, I could see the flecks of green and brown in his eyes. I laid my cheek against him, savoring his warmth as it seeped through me. He pressed a kiss to my forehead.

"Well," he sighed, "Ro has earned his inevitable I-told-you-so."

I grinned up at him and his eyes darkened.

His lips parted and he sucked in a sharp breath. "Have I ever told you how breathtaking you are when you smile?" he whispered. His voice had a rough edge to it that sent a shudder down my spine. My nerves started buzzing as I was suddenly very aware of how his body fit against me.

"I don't think you have," I replied, biting my lip. He let out a soft gasp and leaned in close.

"Remind me to tell you more often," he said. He pressed his lips into mine, kissing me hard and determined.

I opened my mouth to him, caressing his tongue with mine as his hands trailed down my back, settling on my hips. Lightning coiled down low in my gut.

His mouth grew more insistent, drinking me in desperately. I bit his lower lip gently and he gasped.

Ash pulled back suddenly. I reached up to kiss him again, but he tilted his head back, struggling to draw breath.

"Wait," he hissed. His fingers gripped my hips tightly, holding me still.

I could feel him growing hard against my stomach and I shifted. My mouth went dry, and my heart pounded at the size of him. The heat pooling in my abdomen started boiling over. I needed him. Now.

Ash groaned at my movement, gritting his teeth, and holding me impossibly tighter. "Wait...Lumi... if we don't stop now, I won't be able to control myself."

I looked up into his bright, golden eyes and parted my lips, lost in his intense gaze. I grinned wickedly and lowered my head, running my tongue slowly across the exposed part of his chest above his collar and up the length of his throat.

His head fell back, and he let out a soft moan through his clenched jaw. "Lumi," he warned roughly. He fisted the back of my coat in an effort to keep control of himself.

But I wanted him to break. I wanted to feel and kiss every inch of his body. I wanted him to lose control. His cock throbbed against my stomach, sending another surge of heat flashing through me like a spark blazing through dry tinder.

I slid my fingers across his broad chest and locked my gaze with his. Those brilliant golden eyes were glazed over with passion and his handsome face was flushed.

"Do you want me to stop?" I asked softly. He swallowed hard.

"No," he gasped, shuddering. "But... I don't want to get you pregnant." It was like he threw cold water at me. I exhaled sharply and stepped back.

"Right," I said breathlessly.

He plunged his hands frantically through his pocket, withdrawing two small vials of shining red liquid. I looked at him, arching one eyebrow. "What's that?"

"Spiceberry wine," he said, his eyes still flashing with desire. "I took it from the storeroom in the palace. Remember what Rowan said?"

I shook my head.

"It was what people used to prevent pregnancy." He held it up for me to see and I arched an eyebrow, grinning.

The red wine glimmered in the sunlight. I was reminded of a gem I'd seen once in my mother's vast jewelry collection. A ruby, or at least that's what I thought it was called.

"You just so happened to have those in your pocket?" I asked and he shrugged, blushing.

"I was curious how it tasted... But I thought trying it by myself might be a little rough and I didn't want them to break in my bag. I meant to get rid of them. Thank goodness, I didn't," he said breathlessly.

Ash's hand trembled as he held one of the vials out to me. I took the small bottle and turned it over in my hand. The liquid inside radiated heat and I winced slightly as my skin brushed the scorching glass. I palmed the vial, looking up to meet his eyes.

Vallath was right. Ash was undeniably gorgeous.

I bit my lip and just let myself look at him for a moment. The sharp cut of his jaw. The hint of his muscular build visible even under all those layers. The burning glow of his molten gold eyes. My heart stopped and my breath caught in my throat. I needed him. And now, I was going to make him mine.

I reached for the cork, but he grasped my wrist. "Hold on," he said. "Just because I had these doesn't mean I'm expecting anything from you. If this isn't what you want, I—" He trailed off with a soft gasp as I locked eyes with him and yanked the cork out of the bottle.

I downed the wine, shuddering as it burned down my throat and tossed the empty glass behind me into the snow.

He licked his lips and drained his vial quickly. White hot lava coursed through my veins. My face flashed hot and the aching need between my thighs grew unbearable. It took all of my willpower not to throw myself at him on the spot. He must have felt it too because his breathing turned ragged.

His sharp exhale was the only warning I got before he rapidly closed the distance between us and pressed me tightly against his body. I locked my fingers in his hair and kissed him hungrily. Desire roared through me so strongly, I could hardly breathe.

He hitched his hands around my thighs and lifted me, wrapping my legs around his waist as he carried me through the trees.I moaned against his kiss, desperate for more of him. His lips opened mine and his tongue invaded roughly.

He tasted like fire and delicious heat. I gripped his hair, drawing a groan from deep in his chest. He kissed me deeper and slid a strong hand farther under my body, cupping my ass. His fingers were so close to where I needed them that I arched into him.

"Please," I moaned breathlessly.

He turned and, before I could blink, we were inside his tent. He laid me gently on his sleeping bag and ravaged my lips with his. I slid my hands under his tunic and splayed my fingers wide across his bare chest.

He was so warm.

I craved that delicious heat against my skin. I shoved at his tunic, and he yanked it roughly over his head, tossing it aside. I paused, taking a minute to drink him in as I ran my hands across his muscled torso.

The spattering of dark chest hair tickled my palms. My hands trailed down his lean stomach, causing his breath to catch. He pulled off my tunic and undergarment, letting his eyes rove over my bare breasts in absolute awe as he laid down beside me, propping himself up on one elbow.

"Fuck, Lumi," he gasped. He reached up and palmed one of my breasts gently, feeling the weight of it in his hand. His touch sent sparks flying across my skin and I moaned, arching my back.

He lowered his head and took my nipple into his mouth, flicking his tongue over it and grazing it with his teeth. Heat jolted through me, and I cried out, bowing into him.

Ash groaned and sucked harder. His hand slid down my bare stomach, slipping just inside the waistband of my pants and pausing.

My heart hammered beneath my ribs. He looked up at me, his lips parted and his eyes dark with passion. Slowly, he slipped his hand between my thighs and slid two fingers straight into the center of me.

I gasped. Every part of my soul was focused on his touch. Nothing else existed. His fingers began working in a steady rhythm as he lifted his head to watch my face. My hips started moving, riding his hand.

"Oh, Lumi..." he murmured. His voice was low and dangerous, sending shivers down my spine. "You're so perfect." He flattened his hand against me as I ground myself into his palm. "That's it, love. That's it," he groaned, his fingers tracing small circles against me before dipping back into me again. Sweet, intense pressure began to build deep inside me.

I reached for the front of his pants, desperate to wrap my fingers around him. His free hand shot out from under his head and caught my wrist, pulling my arm up over his shoulder. He pressed closer, pinning my arm behind his back.

"Oh no you don't," he whispered roughly. "I've dreamed about this moment for too long, my love. I want to focus on every second of this." His golden eyes were gleaming. His fingers began to move in larger circles and the pressure filled me.

"Ash, please," I moaned. My fingers twitched against his skin, but he held firm. I raked my fingernails up his muscled back as he edged me closer and closer to release. "Ash—"

My body began to tremble in his arms, and I clung to him tighter, anchoring him to me. The pressure was quickly reaching its breaking point and I tightened around his hand. He pressed his lips into my collarbone and moved his fingers faster.

"Ash!" I cried out. I dug my nails into his shoulder. His cock was hard and insistent on my hip, and he pushed himself firmly into my side.

"Not yet," he growled, dragging his tongue up the side of my neck. "Give me what I want first. Come for me and maybe then. Come for me, Lumi," he commanded, biting the shell of my ear. My body responded immediately to his deep voice as a sharp wave of pleasure crested over me. I cried out, gasping his name. He held my writhing body close to his chest, stroking me through my release.

I slowly came back to myself, slumping and gasping for air. He planted soft kisses to my ribs, his hand still probing gently.

"Oh..." he moaned into my stomach. "That was more perfect than I could've ever imagined." I frantically tried to catch my breath, running my fingers through his hair.

"I'm glad I could... make you happy," I panted, passing a hand over my face. "Fuck... I can't even see straight right now."

"Oh, Darling... I'm just getting started," he said with a wicked grin. He sat up, shimmying my pants and undergarments off. I laid before him, naked and vulnerable, shivering with anticipation.

"Fuck," he hissed, eyes wide as he reached out and ran his hands across my stomach.

I smiled and let my hands flop to the sides. I was surprised that I didn't feel self-conscious or uncomfortable. But this moment felt right. He felt right.

"By the Two, Lumi I… fuck." He let his trembling fingers trail across my bare skin and sucked in a sharp breath. His gaze felt like a brand as he stared in awe at every last inch of me.

"You got what you wanted. Now it's my turn," I said, propping myself up on my elbows and waving a hand at his waist. "Pants off." His expression turned mischievous as he stretched out on his stomach in front of me.

"I lied," he smirked, throwing my knees over his shoulders.

"Ash," I said sharply, but my protest died on my lips as he lowered his mouth between my thighs and licked me.

I gasped and flopped onto my back as his tongue began to work in earnest. My core tightened with each kiss and caress of his mouth and my fingers tangled themselves in his hair, holding him close. Release began to build, faster and more intense than before. I gasped his name, shuddering as he drew me in closer. Every nerve in my body was on fire.

Ash groaned against me, and his tongue dipped impossibly deeper. I wasn't prepared for the orgasm that rocked through me, sending stars winking before my eyes. My body bowed off the ground at the sheer force of my release. He reached up, placing a strong hand on my stomach to hold me down as he stroked me through it with the flat of his glorious tongue. I panted, clutching his hair as the wave of pleasure slowly receded. He turned his face, peppering light kisses on the inside of my thighs while I went limp and struggled to catch my breath.

"Are you okay?" he murmured.

"I've never been so okay in my life," I gasped.

He chuckled and licked me playfully. "Good. I aim to please," he whispered. As he crawled back up to lay next to me, I threw out my hand, catching the front of his pants, and hooking my fingers into them. He hissed sharply as my fingertips grazed the tip of his swollen cock.

"Take your fucking pants off," I demanded. He locked his molten eyes with mine before sliding his pants off of his hips and shoving them away.

My breath hitched as I took in the size of him. He didn't stop me this time when I reached out, wrapping my fingers around him, and caressing his heavy cock. Ash let out a shuddering gasp as I slipped along his length, working in a slow, steady rhythm. He was enormous.

He moaned, clutching me and brought his mouth to mine again. I could feel his heart pounding in his chest. I squeezed my fingers tighter, and he growled into my kiss. An aching need began to spread low in my abdomen and I squirmed once again, rubbing my thighs together.

"I need you," I whispered against his lips. He broke our kiss and met my gaze. I could get lost in that gorgeous golden stare.

He rolled me under him and spread my legs with his knees as he lowered his body to mine, bracing his weight on his elbows. His eyes flared with need but there was something flickering behind them.

"Lumi," he moaned, his breaths turning ragged as his bare skin touched mine.

His cock brushed my entrance, and I bit my lip at the bolt of lightning that zinged through me at his touch. His eyes dropped to my mouth and his lips parted as he thrust forward slightly, drawing his tip across the most sensitive parts of me.

He paused. "Lumi, I—" he gasped. His cock was hot against me, and I tilted my hips, inviting him in to where I wanted him most. To where I desperately needed him.

A strangled sound escaped his lips, but he still didn't move. His arms shook beside my head with the effort to keep himself still. Self-doubt and passion warred in his eyes as he watched my face carefully. I furrowed my brow as I saw a flash of something that looked like fear cross his flushed face.

My heart lurched and I realized that he was holding himself back because he was afraid. Afraid I was going to regret this. I reached up, cradling his face as I planted a soft kiss on his forehead.

"I've wanted this for so long," Ash sighed. He closed his eyes as my thumb traced a line across his jaw. "But..."

"Do you want to stop?" I asked, trailing my fingers lightly down the back of his neck and onto his shoulders. He shook his head frantically.

"No! No, no. Fuck no. But... I just don't want you to feel... forced? Or feel... Shit, I don't know. I know I'm being stupid right now. I'm sorry. I just don't want to do anything to lose you or... Fuck, you're so amazing and I'm such a mess. I just..." He huffed, words failing him and pressed his forehead into mine. I had to fight not to arch into him as he brushed my entrance again. My body ached for him.

"Ash," I breathed. I caught his chin with my finger and brought his face up to meet my eyes. "I wouldn't be here if I didn't want to be. I want this. I want *you*," I said sincerely. He opened his mouth, sucking in a breath as my hips tilted up further.

"I... I love you," he groaned.

I wrapped my legs around his waist, and he thrust forward, sliding inside, and burying himself deep in me. I gasped, arching my back as he filled me completely. He paused, giving my body the chance to adjust to him.

"Fuck, I love you so much," he cried breathlessly, drawing back slightly, and sinking back into me.

I moaned, wrapping my legs tighter around him and gripping his shoulders, desperate to get as close to him as I could.

"You feel so... Oh, Lumi," he groaned. With each thrust, he drew back farther and rocked into me. His whole body trembled as he pulsed into me gently. He locked eyes with me, and I moaned his name, raking my nails sharply up his back. His golden eyes flashed dangerously.

Whatever it was that had been holding him in check vanished and he drove into me with delicious, unrelenting force. Sweat shimmered on his heaving chest as he thrust deeper and harder, pushing me slowly back towards the brink.

I cried out, squeezing my thighs around him as white-hot pressure started building. I began to move my hips, matching his steady rhythm and drawing him in as deep as I could get him. He rocked forward hard, and I shattered, tightening around him as he sent me spiraling back over the edge. He drove into me through my orgasm, sucking in long, desperate drags of air.

"That's it. Oh, fuck that's it. That's my girl. Oh, Lumi," he cried. His pace stuttered as I came down, whimpering and shivering with intense pleasure. "You feel so good, I... Oh. Fuck... Lumi!" he groaned breathlessly.

I reached up and gripped his hair. "Give me everything," I said, still panting from the intensity of my release. "Everything." He came undone and cried out, slamming himself into my hips as his cock throbbed deep inside me. He pressed his forehead into mine, clinging to me as he gasped and shuddered. We rode out his orgasm together until he collapsed in my arms.

I held him and stroked his hair while he caught his breath. I never wanted to let him go. I could stay in this moment until the end of time. Finally, he looked up and studied my face.

"Are you all right?" he panted.

"Are you kidding?" I arched an eyebrow at him, smiling dreamily. "I'm better than all right. Can't you tell?" I asked, flexing my pelvic muscles around him for emphasis. He gasped softly before withdrawing to lie next to me.

"I just had to make sure," he said quietly. "I was worried I hurt you. I got a little carried away."

"You didn't hurt me," I replied, rolling to face him. "Not at all."

He pulled me to his chest and began stroking long, lazy circles along the length of my spine. I draped an arm across his hip and sighed happily.

How could I ever think he didn't feel the same way? His kiss had ignited a fire in my soul, but it was nothing compared to the inferno I felt now. I turned my face and rested my ear on his chest to listen to his heart's steady beating. My eyes fluttered closed as his warmth enveloped me.

Wrapped up in his strong arms, I felt safer than I had in a very long while. Nothing could touch me as long as I was here. I meant to tell him that. I meant to tell him how safe he made me feel, but his heat combined with the exhausted bliss creeping through my bones pushed me down into the dark and I drifted off before I got the chance.

CHAPTER TWENTY-EIGHT

WINTER

Wind whipped my hair as I stood on the balcony, impatiently awaiting the return of my remaining thralls. Vallath had put up a tremendous fight, and I'd sensed the deaths of many of my followers.

I skipped from mind to mind, searching for the one that had what I wanted, but none of them seemed to be carrying anything. Finally, they prowled into view, stalking their way towards the tower before stopping under the balcony.

"Whichever of you bears my book, come forward!" I called. I waited with bated breath as I scanned the crowd below for movement.

My thralls turned their blank eyes towards me, waiting. None of them moved.

Panic seized my chest, and I gripped the railing tightly. "I said come forward!"

Still, none of my thralls stepped out from among the crowd.

"They don't have it."

I snapped my head around as Summer sauntered into view. Her skin was gray and cracked, with ice jutting from her broken skin. Her eyes were coal black and gleaming. Her hair had lost all its shine and was darker than the night sky. Shadows dripped off her as she came to stand at my side and looked out over the crowd gathering around the base of the tower. She pushed out her bottom lip in a pout. Her voice echoed strangely as she crooned, "The book was either destroyed in the fire, or Vallath took it with him. Now what, Kiora?"

I ignored her, flashing from mind to mind and searching through the memories of my thralls. Countless images of Vallath's billowing fire raced across my mind. I paused on one, examining it. Vallath's purple wings were spread wide over four people standing inside a ring of flames.

So, there were three of them. Spring had managed to find three of the only Cosmic people left. They must've come from Haven.

I looked closer. The two males had their hands spread wide and were gritting their teeth as they strained to hold their flames in place. The taller of the two was handsome, with brown hair that fell just past his chin and a muscled frame. The second had red hair and a kind face that reminded me of someone I'd met a long time ago. Beside them was a pale, lethal looking female with raven hair. She had a long, white bow drawn back and was frozen in the act of releasing a razor-sharp arrow.

I frowned as I found Spring. He hid behind the trio like the coward he'd always been. He looked exactly as he had the last time I'd seen him. Before I'd thrown him out the window.

"Lord Spring," I whispered, viciously. "It's been a while."

"He's coming for you," Summer whispered in a deep, hollow voice.

"He's a coward," I replied bitterly, snapping out of the creature's mind, and moving on to the next one. Suddenly, a familiar voice echoed to me. I slowed my search, lingering in the mind of a thrall just joining the crowd.

I flashed into a dimly lit memory. The creature stood outside of a campsite. Spring was talking and telling the three Cosmics about the stones. My face twisted in wrath as my suspicions were confirmed. Spring was leading them here. The fact that he had not one, but *three* Cosmics with him could only mean one thing. He intended to replace his sister, my lost love, and myself. The creature had crept closer as Spring turned with a surprised expression to the curly haired Cosmic, who tapped the side of his head.

"I can generally remember most of what I read. Kind of my own special superpower." The creature shifted closer and froze again as the male said. "Yeah well... I probably know more than I should. But I read the whole book so... I have everything we need. And we will need to perform the ritual after we take the stone from the throne. Not before."

It took a moment for the realization to hit. The book he was talking about had to be the *Book of the Cosmics*. And he said he remembers what he reads. He had what I needed.

I shoved my way out of the creature's consciousness and rounded triumphantly on Summer.

"Well, Mirela," I sneered. "It looks like I don't have to lift a finger. Your idiot twin brother is bringing the book straight to me." Summer's face was blank.

"He wouldn't do that," she hissed sharply, her coal black eyes widening in uncertainty. "He would've left the book with Vallath."

"That he did," I conceded. My smirk widened as I turned back to my thrall. "But Vallath let one of the Cosmics read the book. He knows the ritual I need to join the stones."

She blanched and took a step back.

I snickered. "After centuries of your incessant whining, you're finally speechless? Look at that. Miracles do happen." I turned away as she vanished, and I was once again blissfully alone. I stood tall and raised my hand to command the attention of my horde.

"Find Lord Spring." My voice bellowing across the valley. "He travels with a Cosmic male that has red hair. You will bring him to me. Alive and unharmed. I care not for the rest. Go!"

My thralls turned in unison and bounded off in different directions. I watched them race off into the distance before turning back to my throne. Part of me expected to see Fall waiting for me. I scanned the shadows and frowned slightly when I didn't find brown eyes staring back at me.

I shook myself mentally and strode across the room before sitting proudly on my throne.

My ultimate goal was finally within reach.

I threw out my power and collided with that damned rose-scented shield. I grinned as I stroked a mental finger threateningly across its surface.

He was closer this time.

You can't save him from me, Spring, I whispered. The shield flexed and reinforced its walls in response. I felt a ripple of panic and desperation squirming under the shield and laughed.

Something else drifted underneath the sense and I paused, focusing on the strange feeling.

There was something there, behind the shield and under the panicked urgency. A strong emotion that flooded through him like a tidal wave crashing to shore. I tried harder to sense what he was feeling but Spring was working very hard to conceal it from me. Whatever it was, he desperately didn't want me to find out. I hammered on the shield for a few moments with my power before I smirked and withdrew.

It didn't matter. He'd heard my threat. I was sure of it. The panic had been swift and strong, assuring me that Spring was still the whimpering coward he'd been twenty years ago.

It was a shame and yet another of the many failings of the Two that they had wasted so much power on that sniveling fool.

My gaze drifted to the horizon. Off in the distance, Haven's wall was still marring my view. If only the Two had made *me* Spring. Then that wall wouldn't be such an obstacle. A sudden, delicious thought struck me, and I sat up, my spine as straight as an arrow. That hideous wall had kept the human filth from falling to me for two decades. My demons couldn't get over it without being destroyed, and the humans had somehow managed to stay warm despite my frigid cold. I could cross the wall myself, but leaving my stone for that long was much too dangerous.

However... if I could command Lord Spring's power, I could shatter the wall. I could bring down the mountains and flatten the village. With his unbridled power at my command, I could open the very ground beneath their feet and swallow the village whole.

I grinned wickedly as I reached out with my power and stroked it across the shield. If only there was a way to get inside... I could flood his mind and completely take over his senses.

The answer presented itself and my grin widened. His emerald sat in the treasure room below me. All I needed to do was corner him. I'd give him no other choice but to use the stone and reclaim his power. Then... He was mine.

And I knew exactly how to do it. He had to be headed to the Crossroads Temple. From there, he could follow the road straight to the World's Tower. Or he would have, had I not destroyed the path two decades ago.

I reached into the minds of my thralls as they scattered across the land and watched them search, sniffing out their prey. I sent them a new command and they responded immediately. The mountains dissolved into trees as I flitted from mind to mind.

It was only a matter of time now.

I swept from my throne, striding through the room and out into the dimly lit stairwell that spiraled down the length of the tower. I descended quickly, gathering my skirt in my hands as I reached a large stretch of blank wall and placed a hand on the stone. It split under my touch.

I smirked and stepped into the treasure room. Sitting in the center, on a large stone plinth, were three large gems. A diamond, an amethyst, and an emerald. Each one glowed with an intense light. They sat clustered together like fearful children hiding from a monster.

I crossed the room and scooped them up, running my fingers along their smooth surfaces. They felt cold in my hands. Cold and wrong. Stabs of discomfort shot up my hand, but I ignored them.

"Come, lovelies," I crooned. The gems seemed to shudder under my touch. "It's almost time." I stowed them in my pocket and retreated back up the stairwell, striding to the balcony.

Excitement set my heart racing as the gems bounced against my thigh. I looked up at the sky and grinned viciously.

"Your time is up!" I screeched to the cosmos. "I'm coming for you! I will right your wretched mistakes and put an end to your worthless existence!"

The cosmos stayed silent, and I laughed, letting my power swell from me and blanket the skies in thick gray storm clouds. I splayed my hand and let them roll across my land.

My victory was inevitable. Once my former best friend was under my command, the world would finally be mine.

CHAPTER TWENTY-NINE

ASH

I'd give anything to stay in this moment forever.

Lumi was fast asleep in my arms, her deep breaths tickling my chest. I pulled my sleeping bag around us and closed my eyes, stroking her back in long, languid circles. We must have been there for at least an hour. Maybe two. As far as I was concerned, we could lay there, wrapped up in each other until the end of time. I was in no hurry to let this moment end. I was terrified that if I did, it would all evaporate. Just like everything else good in my life.

I placed a soft kiss on her forehead, and she shifted closer, sighing happily in her sleep.

I desperately wanted to stay there, locked in her embrace forever. But my body had other plans.

My stomach grumbled and I realized that I'd been so upset, I'd not only skipped breakfast but lunch as well. It was loud enough that it made Lumi stir. With a regretful sigh, I gently slid my arm out from under her head, pulling away slowly.

She groaned and caught me around the waist, yanking me back into her and pressing her face into my chest.

"No... Where are you going?" she groaned. Before I could respond, my stomach growled again, and she let out a breathy chuckle. "Oh. Okay, fine. But don't be gone long," she said through a yawn. She planted a kiss in the center of my chest and rolled onto her back, settling into the warm blanket.

My stomach grumbled again, and I frowned, finally reaching for my clothes, and tugging them on against my will.

I stepped out of the tent, shivering in the cold and glancing around. Rowan and Spring were still off somewhere together, and the fire had died out. I grabbed my pack from where I'd left it and dug out some potato bread, tearing off a chunk as I flicked my wrist absentmindedly to summon a fire. Stifling heat flashed through my body. A giant inferno exploded to life from my fingertips, engulfing a tree nearby.

"Fuck!" I shouted, staggering back in panic. I splayed my hands wide, and the blaze died out swiftly. Thick black smoke curled into the air from the remains of the smoldering tree. A soft chuckle sounded behind me and I whipped around to see Rowan strolling through the trees, arm-in-arm with Spring.

"You drank spiceberry wine, didn't you?" Spring mused with a sly grin.

"I uh..." I swallowed and ran a hand through my hair, blushing. "I might have. Why?"

Rowan's smirk widened and Spring tilted his head towards the tree.

"Spiceberry wine has a lot of uses," he explained, suppressing a knowing smile. "But in a Cosmic, it also intensifies their fire for a while."

"Oh." Heat filled my face. "I... I didn't know that."

"Where'd you find spiceberry wine?" Spring asked.

"Oh," Rowan said suddenly. "That's what you took from the storeroom! I saw you stick something in your pocket, but I wasn't sure what it was."

"I was curious what it tastes like," I mumbled, shifting my weight from foot to foot. Rowan raised his eyebrows.

"I see," he grinned. "And... Where's Lumi?"

"She's uh... She's in there," I mumbled, gesturing at my tent.

A wicked smile spread across Rowan's lips. "Is she now? And what on earth would she be doing in there?"

I rolled my eyes, fighting a smile. I could still taste her kiss on my lips. Among other things.

Spring pressed his lips to Rowan's hand and stepped away, grinning.

"So," Rowan said, arching an eyebrow at me. "Can I say it yet?"

"Do you have to?" I grumbled and he chuckled.

"Oh, absolutely," he replied gleefully. "And, all things considered, I'd say I earned it."

"Fine," I sighed, unable to hide my smile any longer.

"I—" Rowan threw his head back to shout at the cosmos. "Told you the *fuck* so! I told you so. I told you so. I fucking *told. You. So!* Damn, I love it when I'm right." He met my eyes again and smiled brightly. "I mean, it's about fucking time! Shit!"

"What do you mean 'it's about time'?" I said, arching my eyebrow at him.

"I mean..." he replied slowly, "You two have been dancing around each other forever. And it's about damn time you did something about it! If that tension got any worse, I was going to tie you both to a tree until you either talked it out or fucked. Oh wait, she's not waiting for you, is she?" He said, glancing over at my tent.

"No. She's sleeping," I said around the mouthful. Rowan shot me a mischievous grin.

"Well damn, Ash," he chuckled, nudging me in the ribs. I swallowed my bite and rolled my eyes.

"Knock it off," I replied, grinning. "And yes, Ro. You were absolutely right. I misread everything." A sudden wave of suffocating anxiety hit me. "Hopefully, I'm not misreading now..." I trailed off meeting his eyes nervously.

"Don't be silly, Ash. You know her too well for that," he said, waving a dismissive hand. "What, you think she slept with you just because you asked her nicely? She wouldn't if she didn't want to."

"I know that," I frowned. "I just... I can't shake this awful feeling." I pressed a hand to my chest. Anxiety tightened around my racing heart. "That I don't deserve this. And I'm going to lose everything all over again."

"How?" Rowan demanded, crossing his arms. Irritation flashed across his face, and I winced under his intense gaze.

"I don't know, Ro. It's just... nothing ever goes right in my life. Why would it start now?"

"I have no idea," he replied. "All I know is that she loves you and you love her."

"I do love her," I said, letting my eyes drift back to the tent.

"Then don't screw this up for yourself by worrying you're gonna screw it up!" Rowan said forcefully, pinching the bridge of his nose in frustration.

"I'm sorry! I know I'm being stupid. I... I just... Ro, I'm terrified that—" I said, running my trembling hands through my hair. He cut me off, stepping in front of me with an exasperated sigh and grasping both of my shoulders.

"Look," he said firmly, "I get it. You've had this fear sitting on your shoulders for years that she was going to find out how you feel and run away screaming. But Ash..." He gestured to the tent. "You told her and look what happened. She certainly didn't bolt, did she?"

I opened my mouth, but he pressed his hand over my lips and shook his head before I could reply.

"Shut the fuck up and just listen to me. I know that fear won't go away overnight. But, you trust me, right?"

I nodded in response.

"Then trust me now, Ash. I promise you, she's not going anywhere. And I swear I will beat your ass if you don't stop freaking yourself out, okay?" he added, his mouth pressed into a hard line.

I wanted to scowl at him, but he had a valid point.

Lumi hadn't run away screaming. In all my years of silently loving her, I'd never let myself consider that she might love me back. But she did. She loved me. And I was going to have to tell myself that every second of every day until it finally sunk in.

I forced my thoughts back to her breathtaking face, flushed with pleasure as she cried out my name. I replayed it in my mind, reminding myself that it wasn't a dream. My shoulders sagged and I nodded, pulling my face away from his hand.

"You're right," I mumbled, sighing. "I'm being an idiot and I'm sorry."

"Thank you," he said, winking. "Life goes a whole lot smoother when you just accept that I'm right."

I snorted and raised my hand to summon a fire. Rowan made a startled noise and snatched my wrist.

"Maybe, you should let me do it?" he suggested, nodding towards the blackened tree.

"Ah... right... yeah." I blushed and nodded. He splayed his fingers wide, and a small blaze flickered to life.

I was just sitting down when Lumi stepped out of my tent, stretching, and adjusting her coat. My heart fluttered as she met my eyes and beamed.

"Hey you two," she said. "Is lunch ready?"

"Not quite," Rowan smirked. "How was your nap?"

"Marvelous," she sighed happily, coming over and plopping down in my lap. My heart skipped a beat as she wrapped my arms around her waist.

I pressed my forehead into her hair and closed my eyes with a deep sigh of relief. *See? It's gonna be okay,* I told the anxious shadows lingering in the corners of my mind. I was discovering very quickly that everything felt better when Lumi was in my arms. She caught the small loaf of bread Rowan tossed her and stuffed some into her mouth.

"So," she said thickly. "Where are we?"

"We are about a half a day's walk from the Crossroads," Spring said reappearing and lacing his fingers into Rowan's outstretched hand. "I just had a look around and we're really close. From there, the tower is only about two days away."

"What exactly is the Crossroads?" Lumi asked, tracing small circles on the back of my hand absentmindedly. I felt ridiculous for worrying.

"It's a temple," Spring said, sitting as Rowan dropped cross-legged in the snow beside him. "It's the only jumping point to the World's Tower. It was actually where I—" Spring suddenly flinched hard, clutching his forehead.

Lumi sat up a little straighter, glancing at Rowan in confusion. Rowan was watching Spring's face fearfully. Lumi's fingers clutched my wrists as Spring's pink skin paled and he gagged as though he were about to be sick. He bowed his head, wincing.

"What happened?" Rowan said nervously, cupping Spring's face in his hands. Terror flashed through Spring's eyes as he met Rowan's stare and gulped.

"I'm sorry," he said breathlessly. "I'm all right. But we need to get moving." He stood quickly and pulled Rowan to his feet at the same time.

"What is it?" Lumi said, standing as I hopped to my feet.

Spring shook his head, wincing again as though something were hammering on the inside of his skull.

"It's nothing," he said, waving a hand. Rowan caught his wrist and sharply turned Spring to face him.

"Don't lie to me," he snapped, his bright green eyes flashing. Spring blew out a long breath, dropping his gaze to the snow.

"It's Winter," he admitted. "She tried to break through the shield again. And this time, she was very... persistent."

We exchanged nervous glances.

"All right," Lumi said. "Let's get going."

We scattered and packed up the campsite with lightning speed before throwing our packs onto our backs.

"This way," Spring called.

We'd taken three steps towards him when a long screech split the silence around us.

Lumi drew her sword, looking around carefully.

I splayed my hands wide and summoned my power. My palms blazed brightly.

Another screech sounded from behind us, and we turned, scanning the trees as we backed away.

"Ice demons," Lumi hissed.

Screeches began to echo all around us. The sounds drew closer, and the shadows of the forest began to writhe.

"They're surrounding us," Rowan gasped. "What do we do?"

Gleaming teeth and razor-sharp claws appeared between the trees, glinting in the late afternoon sun.

"Ash," Spring said, gripping my elbow. "How much wine did you drink?"

"What?" I hissed, eyeing the ugly heads leering at us as they stalked closer.

"The spiceberry wine!" he said frantically. "How much?"

"I... I have no idea! It was a small vial! About the size of my hand! Why?" Panic and confusion laced my voice.

"Light the trees," Spring commanded. "Put everything you have into it."

"I drank some, too," Lumi said. She sheathed her blade and stood shoulder-to-shoulder with me.

"Both of you!" Spring said, taking Rowan's hand as we continued to back away. "Put everything into it and light the trees. Then we make a run for the river."

"I've never used fire like this," Lumi said nervously.

The screeching grew louder as the demons called out for more forces. I looked into her ice blue eyes.

"You can do this. Just breathe and focus. Let the heat flow through you," I said.

She swallowed hard and nodded.

I squared my shoulders and spread my fingers wide. She turned towards the tree line, mimicking my movements. I summoned up every drop of my power. Intense heat unlike anything I'd ever felt before scorched through me. Flames exploded from my palms and set fire to the trees around us instantly.

Lumi growled in frustration. For a moment, nothing happened. Then suddenly, she staggered back a step as a roaring blast of flames shot from her, adding to my fires. She whooped gleefully and together, we let our powers swell, turning the forest into a blazing inferno.

Screams of agony echoed around us as we focused every ounce of energy we had into the flames. It swirled around us, blinding us and sending unbearable heat searing across our skin. Pain sliced through my skull and my muscles grew heavy as the exertion began to drag on my body.

Unable to hold it any longer, I released my power, panting and gasping. Spring grabbed the back of our coats and yanked us towards him.

"Run!" he screamed over the roaring blaze.

We took off, sprinting through the forest as the fire devoured tree after tree in our wake. More screams sounded as the mindless demons tried to follow us zigzagging through the burning forest.

"This way!" Spring called, leading us off to the left. We burst through the tree line and skidded to a halt at the edge of the river. "Quick!" he said, grabbing Rowan. "We need ice!"

Rowan nodded frantically and cast a hand towards the water. A chunk of ice appeared on the surface, and we leapt onto it as it began to drift down the river, carried away by the strong current. Rowan gritted his teeth. Sweat glistened on his brow as he held the ice above the water with his power. I looked back at the bank as flames engulfed most of the trees in sight.

"Shit," Lumi whispered. She clutched her heaving chest as she stared wide-eyed back at the raging fire. "That was from the wine?" She looked at me for a moment before bursting into laughter.

I smiled and huffed out a chuckle. "Now, I'm really glad I saved it," I gasped.

"I hope you have more," she joked, turning to Rowan and Spring. They were both staring ahead in horror.

Lumi furrowed her brow. "Ro? What's—" She trailed off with a soft gasp.

I heard it at the exact moment she did. The unmistakable sound of water rushing over a steep cliff. I turned and swore as we rounded a bend and found ourselves staring down a waterfall.

"Fuck," I shouted, reaching deep down into my well of power. I threw my hands out and summoned a gust of wind, but my power was weak, and it wasn't enough. "Lumi! Ro!" I thundered.

Rowan jumped and threw his free hand out. The gust strengthened, but it still wasn't enough. Lumi stared down at her palms in anguish.

"Come on, dammit! Come on!" she roared, throwing her hands out. Nothing happened. She swore and tried again, but still nothing happened.

The ice raft bobbed along at a steady pace and the roaring of the waterfall grew closer as I locked eyes with her.

"You can do this," I said.

Lumi blinked and nodded determinedly, focusing with all her might. The gust grew stronger, shoving the ice to the side of the river. We leapt onto the riverbank and looked back just in time to see the ice careen over the edge of the waterfall and out of sight.

"Yeah!" Lumi yelled. She threw her arms around my neck, planting a triumphant kiss on my lips.

I kissed her back as my limbs began to shake.

She withdrew, beaming. "I did it! I actually did it!"

"I had no doubt you could," I said breathlessly. Exhaustion seeped through me, and my knees buckled. I staggered and sat down hard on the riverbank. Lumi knelt beside me.

"Are you okay?" she asked, concerned. I winked, gasping for air, and flopped onto my side.

"I'm fine," I said through ragged breaths. "Just... running on empty.

Lumi sat down next to me and brushed a soothing hand across my chest.

"Ah," I groaned, closing my eyes. "That helps. Ro, are you okay?"

"Fine," he replied weakly. "Just drained."

Lumi looked over at him and frowned. "Why am I not out of it like you two?" she asked.

I grinned slyly up at her. "Because you took a nap."

"Oh." Lumi grinned at me, sending my heart racing in my chest.

"We should keep moving," Spring said anxiously. I lifted my head and found him sitting near my feet, cradling a deathly pale Rowan in his arms.

"I don't know if I can," I panted.

"Same," Rowan agreed. "I'm so tired I can't see straight."

Spring stood, looking around the area.

"Well, we can't stay out in the open," he said. "We're getting closer, and Winter knows it. There's going to be more of them... There!" He pointed off to the left at the opening of a small cave situated near the riverbank. "Come on." He threw his arm around Rowan's waist and helped him stagger towards the cave.

Lumi hauled me to my feet. My knees sagged and she threw her arms around me, helping me stay upright as we hobbled after them.

"Are you sure you're all right?"

"I'm fine." I blew out an exhausted breath and leaned my head against hers. She met my eyes, her expression filled with worry, so I put my hand over my heart and said, "I promise. I'd never lie to my fierce warrior queen."

"Oh no?" she cocked an eyebrow at me, smirking. "Never? Because I remember being told a lie not even a few hours ago."

My blood simmered as the memory of her heels digging into my shoulder blades flashed through my mind.

"Fair enough," I said roughly.

She laughed, her eyes gleaming as we crossed the threshold into the dark cavern. Rowan turned, gritting his teeth, and splaying his hand wide.

A large boulder slid across the stone floor and landed with a loud crack in front of the cave's entrance, plunging us into pitch blackness.

I raised my hand to summon a spark. Instead, a roaring fire blazed to life in my palm and scattered the shadows around us. I chuckled.

"Guess the wine hasn't worn off yet," I remarked absently.

"Good," Lumi replied, so quietly that only I could hear.

I swallowed hard and looked down into her intense blue stare. Her eyes were dark, and her cheeks flushed.

Heat that had nothing to do with the flames burning in my hand coursed through me as we examined our surroundings. Spring had propped Rowan against a wall and was already throwing up a tent, leaning it against the cold stone.

"I think you two need some sleep," he said quietly.

Rowan had his head back against the wall, eyes already closed. A small, faint fire danced in his palms.

Spring looked around and pointed off to the left. "I think there's another chamber right through there if you two want to set up somewhere with a little more... privacy," Spring said, suppressing a smile.

I blushed and went to shake my head, but Lumi hitched her arm around my waist and began walking me purposefully in the opposite direction. We stumbled through the tunnel and out of earshot.

"Are we a little eager?" I whispered. The brazenness of her actions surprised me.

She shot me a smoldering look that sent heat rushing straight to my groin.

"I'll take that as a yes," I said. We rounded the corner, and she released me. I let my pack fall with a groan and shirked off my coat, wiping the sweat from my brow. I sat against the wall and flicked a hand, sending a hovering ball of fire sliding across the stone floor as she put up the tent. It crackled, throwing a flickering light across the walls, and filling the chamber with a soothing warmth.

Lumi summoned stones to hold the tent's ropes down and tossed her pack down against the wall, placing her coat on top of it. When she was finished and had ensured the tent's stability, she turned and crooked her finger at me.

"Come here, my love," she whispered.

My heart jumped at the sound of her sultry voice, and I obeyed immediately, staggering to her side.

She gripped the front of my tunic and shoved me roughly into the tent. I stumbled backwards and fell onto the sleeping bags she had laid out for us, landing flat on my back. She followed, straddling my waist, and stretching my arms above my head.

"Lumi, I—" I began, but she silenced me with a deep, passionate kiss. I tried to reach for her, but she pushed my arms back up, running her fingers up to my wrists.

She kissed me, letting her tongue explore mine until my head spun and I couldn't form a coherent thought. The front of my pants became unbearably tight as my cock hardened against her. I didn't even realize my hands were tied above my head until she sat back and ran her hands down my chest possessively. She flicked her fingers and a rock tumbled across the floor at her command. It landed on the end of the rope, locking my arms in place.

I glanced up. The knot was sturdy, and the rope was wound tightly around my wrists. I looked back at her and shivered at the hungry look in her eyes.

"What's this for?" I asked, wiggling my bound hands. My words came out low and rough with desire.

"You promised," she said, her voice silky. She lifted her hips and reached down to stroke the front of my pants. I jerked and moaned softly at her touch. "You said if I came for you, then it would be my turn to touch you. And then you said, 'I lied.' Remember?"

"I remember," I gasped, rubbing myself into her hand. "And I remember saying 'maybe'."

Her expression hardened. She glared at me, drawing a breathless laugh from my chest.

"There's no 'maybe' about it," she said firmly, shifting to the side. "You got yours. Now I want mine."

"Is that so?" I said, arching an eyebrow at her. My challenge died on my lips when she pressed her hand harder against my groin.

"If you don't want this, I can always untie you and let you get some sleep," she said, reaching slowly for the rope.

I shook my head vigorously.

"That's what I thought," Lumi smirked. "Now hush and let me have my fun."

"You didn't have fun earlier?" I gasped as she pulled my pants down over my knees and wrapped her soft fingers around my cock. It hardened almost painfully in her palm.

"I didn't say that," she whispered. "But you got your chance to claim me. Now it's my turn to claim you. You are *mine*."

Hers.

My heart pounded at her words. I was hers. I always had been. But now I knew that she felt it too.

The lingering doubts I had were chased further back into the shadows as those words seared themselves into my mind, loosening the death grip my anxiety had on me.

She sat back on my thighs, working her fingers up and down in a torturously slow rhythm. Lightning flashed down my nerves and I had to fight the urge to thrust into her hand. I bit my lip and gasped for air, my chest heaving with the effort of holding still. She squeezed gently, sending a shiver down my spine.

My hips shifted involuntarily, and she smiled, tightening her grip. The heat burning through me felt like it was searing every inch of my soul. I fought to focus on her face as her hand sped up just a fraction and she leaned closer. I clenched my fists, straining lightly against the rope with a deep groan.

"Say it," she demanded, suddenly. I blinked, raising my eyebrows.

She leaned even closer. Those icy blue eyes were absolutely paralyzing.

"Say it, my love," she said roughly. "I heard you and Rowan talking. I was awake and I heard what you said. What you're afraid of. I want to hear you say it so I know you will never doubt it again. Say it, Ash. What are you?" she hissed, sliding her hand faster along my cock. My name sounded dangerous on her lips, and I shuddered, arching into her palm.

"I—" I gasped, trying desperately to form a coherent thought through the fog of desire. I opened my mouth to say it, but she adjusted her grip and my head spun. "I'm... Oh fuck... Lumi!" I moaned, tilting my head back. Sparks flew across my skin.

She shook her head and sped her pace.

Aching need surged through me, stealing the breath from my chest.

"No," she said, her eyes were dark with passion. "Say it, Ash. I need to hear you say it. I need to hear the words come out of your mouth, so I know you understand them. What are you?"

My mind reeled, drunk with pleasure. I sucked in a deep breath and blinked hard, fighting to focus my thoughts. But my head was spinning so fast, all I could think about was her hand and what it was doing to my body.

"I... Oh, Lumi... I'm yours," I managed to groan finally.

"Say it again," she breathed, keeping her eyes locked on mine.

"I'm... yours," I gasped, thrusting my hips as she worked her hand in a steady rhythm. Everything in me was tightening as she drove me towards the edge of a cliff.

"And what am I?" she asked.

"Mine," I whispered, breathlessly.

"Say it again. What am I, Ash?" she demanded. Her hand tightened deliciously around me, and I almost lost control, bucking my hips, and thrusting hard into her palm.

"Mine," I cried out, closing my eyes. Heat surged through me. I was caught in the eye of the storm, fighting tooth and nail to hold on. "Fuck... Oh, fuck, Lumi... Mine... You're mine!"

"That's right," she purred, slowing her strokes.

My whole body trembled with intense pleasure, and I throbbed in her hand. My release had come dangerously close, but she hadn't had hers yet and I couldn't allow that. Even if I *was* entirely at her mercy.

"And don't you ever doubt that again. Not for one second," she said.

"I won't," I panted, struggling to open my eyes and meet her gaze. "Oh fuck... I won't. I'm sorry, Lumi. I was... Oh... I was... being..." She silenced me by placing a finger on my lips.

"I'm not looking for an apology," she said softly. Her eyes sparkled with emotion. "But you broke my heart today. I don't ever want you to worry you'll lose me just like that. It's killing me to know you're this terrified and I need you to understand. I really do love you, Ash. I'm yours and I'm not going anywhere."

"I love you too," I gasped as my heart swelled.

She leaned forward, gently pressing her lips to my brow before she stood. Her eyes gleamed and her lips stretched in a mischievous smirk as she reached up and removed her clothes. She slid them off inch by inch, giving me a breathtaking view as she did so.

A soft moan escaped my lips. I started throbbing with need. Staring up at her glorious form, stark naked and shining in the light filtering into the tent was almost too much for me to bear. I let my gaze rove over her, drinking in the swell of her breasts and the soft curve of her waist. I met her blazing eyes swallowing hard as she turned to face me fully.

"Fuck, Lumi," I gasped.

"Now," She grinned and dropped down to her knees as she straddled me again. "It's my turn to claim you."

I shivered as she grasped my cock and gently guided it to her entrance. I bit my lip, utterly transfixed as she lowered herself down onto me, sinking until our bodies were flush and I filled her. She squirmed, pressing me even deeper with a soft moan. She was wrapped so tightly around me that I couldn't breathe. Couldn't think past where our bodies were connected.

She reached forward, shoving my tunic up to my neck and raking her nails down my stomach. Fire erupted along every nerve ending in my body.

"Mmm," she purred, shifting her hips in a small circle. "Oh, my love. Feel how deep you are."

She felt so good that my head swam. Stars winked in front of my eyes, and I clenched my fists tighter, my nails digging into my palms. My back bowed, lifting her up with my hips as I thrust impossibly deeper. A brilliant red flush crept across her face and her eyes were bright with desire. I relaxed my body and she shifted, bracing her hands on my chest. She groaned, rocking her hips back and forth in a steady, swaying rhythm.

"Oh, Lumi, you feel so—" I trailed off, gasping as she rocked her hips hard, driving me even deeper. I moved in sync with her thrusts and pressed tightly into the most sensitive parts of her. A strangled sound escaped me as she rode me as hard as she could. Her nails dug into my skin as she ground her body roughly into mine. Her body squeezed around my cock, and I shuddered.

Every muscle in my body grew taut with each long drag of her hips. She ground herself into me harder and harder, moaning and scraping her nails across my chest.

Suddenly she tightened around me, and she cried out, throwing her head back as her orgasm barreled through her, hard and fast. Watching her beautiful face filled with intense pleasure and the sound of my name ringing through the air was too much and I lost control.

Heat coursed through the very fabric of my soul. I rocked into her desperately as my release tore through me, thrusting as deep as I could get until my cock finally stopped throbbing. My whole body slumped, and I gasped, dizzy and dazed. Sweat trickled down my neck. She sighed and leaned forward to press her lips to my damp forehead.

"Mine," she whispered into my skin.

I smiled and bobbed my head in agreement. She reached up, tugging at the rope and freeing my trembling hands. Exhaustion pulled at me as she slid off of my body and curled up in my arms.

"I love you," I said sleepily.

"I love you too, Ash," she whispered, running her fingers through my hair.

I sighed deeply and closed my eyes. Her gentle caresses sent me drifting into the warm shadows of sleep.

She slipped my pants back up over my hips and straightened my tunic as I found myself struggling to stay awake. A blanket was thrown over me and, after some rustling of fabric she sidled in close.

I rolled to the side and wrapped my arms around her. She pressed her face into my chest and sighed, content. As sleep took me, her words echoed over and over again in my mind.

Mine. You are mine.

And I would do my best to never doubt it again.

CHAPTER THIRTY

SPRING

The ominous threat was still ringing in my ears hours later. I sat in the flickering shadows as Rowan slept soundly in my arms. To ease the fears tying my stomach into anxious knots, I stroked my fingers across his thick curls as gently as I could, so I didn't disturb him.

Could she sense my feelings for him through the shield wrapped around my mind? Or had she discovered my sweet Sunflower read the book? I couldn't decide which one would be worse. But Winter had made one thing abundantly clear. Rowan was in danger. There was no other explanation for the threat hissed against my shields.

I let my head fall back and closed my eyes. I had no idea what I was going to do. Logically, I knew we needed to make it to the tower and remove Winter's stone from the throne. But even as I considered it, my heart screamed at me to scoop Rowan up and whisk him away across the sea. He'd be safe. But… this land and the people would be left to suffer.

I exhaled slowly through my nose and covered my face with my hands.

"You're very tense," Rowan murmured. I jumped and looked down to find him peeking through his lashes at me.

"Did I wake you up?" I whispered. He yawned and sat up, stretching.

"No, but your rock-hard thigh muscles did," he replied, eyeing me cautiously.

I smiled meekly at him, trying, and failing to portray confidence.

Rowan's kind face was illuminated by the dancing firelight which, now that he was awake, burned even brighter. "Talk to me," he said softly, lacing his fingers through mine.

"I'm sorry," I mumbled. "I wasn't completely honest with you."

"Yeah, I figured as much," he replied, frowning and I winced guiltily. "Come on, Eli. I saw the look on your face. Tell me what happened." I exhaled slowly and attempted to gather my nerves.

"Winter knows about you. When she tried to get into my shields, she said, 'you can't save him from me forever.' And she could only be talking about you," I said, fighting the panic closing around my throat. He blinked.

"Oh. I see. How does she know?" he replied. His voice had remained steady and even, but his face paled.

"I don't know. And I don't know if she knows about us," I said, gesturing between us with a slightly frantic hand. "Or if she knows you read the book."

"Either way, it's not great," Rowan said with a grimace. "But she had to know you were coming for the stone, right? And she was bound to find out about us eventually. It's gonna be okay, Eli."

I pressed my lips together. Despite the anxious fears flitting about in my brain, my heart pounded when he said my name. Kissing him was amazing but hearing my true name on his lips felt more intimate than any act of passion. Whether it was in the heat of the moment or a casual conversation. It didn't matter. When he said my name, everything felt right with the world.

Terror gripped me again as the thought of losing him slashed across my mind.

"And what if it's not?" I said, unable to stop the anxious words from tumbling out of my mouth. His grip tightened on my hand. He looked up at me and I just wanted to lose myself in those gorgeous green eyes and forget about everything else.

"You can't think like that. Besides, she doesn't scare me," he said, beaming. "I have my Lord of Spring to protect me." He trailed off and tilted his head to the side in thought. "What do I call you?"

"Um... Eli?" I replied, confused.

He laughed and it was like the sun coming out after a long storm. Even the darkest shadows in my mind fled from his light.

"No," he chuckled. "I mean, what are you to me right now? We aren't lovers... yet," he added with a sly grin and my heart skipped. "But we're more than just friends now, right?"

"I'd like to think so." I couldn't help but smile. I lifted his hand and placed a gentle kiss on each one of his knuckles. "I don't really know what to call us, but we are definitely more than friends," I said finally. "And once I have a free conscience, I intend on fully making you mine, Sunflower."

He frowned slightly at our joined hands and my heart stopped.

"What's wrong?" I croaked as worry gripped my chest tightly. "Is that not—"

"What?" He blinked at me in surprise. "Oh. No, Eli, don't be silly," he said, waving his hand dismissively and cutting me off. "No. Look... I know what you said, and I respect your wishes. But if I'm being completely honest with you, I already consider you mine." The tension eased from my shoulders, and I relaxed visibly. My heart did a joyous flip in my chest.

"I like the sound of that. But... Is something wrong?"

"Nothing's wrong. It's just... I don't want to sound stupid," he mumbled, his cheeks turning red. I took his face in my hands and ran my thumb across his jaw.

"Nothing you say ever sounds stupid, Sunflower. What's wrong?" I urged him gently.

"It's just..." He met my eyes and frowned, embarrassed. "You keep calling me that... Sunflower," he said, fidgeting.

"You don't like it?"

"I do. But..." he huffed, lacing his fingers in his lap.

I stroked the pad of my thumb down his jaw again, encouraging him.

"But..." Rowan met my eyes again. Heat filled his face. "Eli, what's a sunflower?" The stark innocence in his question almost drew a startled laugh from me. I clamped down on the urge, beaming at him instead.

"It's a flower I used to grow in my garden," I explained. He huffed and shot me a look.

"Well I figured that much. I meant what kind of flower is it? I don't know what they look like," he replied.

"Ah I see," I said lightly. "Here... I only need a little." I held out my hand.

He took it and shifted, leaning into me to brace himself for the inevitable wave of nausea.

I reached a thin tendril of my power into him as gently as I could, sifting carefully past his pure heart to the well of power deep within his chest. I fished out just enough and withdrew quickly as he groaned. "I'm sorry," I said quickly, kissing him on the brow.

Rowan's energy felt light and airy. It soared around my heart like a bird on a summer breeze. I held my hand in front of his eyes and focused.

Sunny yellow petals sprang from my palm and grew, until my whole hand was covered in the large face of a beautiful sunflower.

"Oh!" he gasped, reaching out to touch a petal gently. "Oh, Eli! It's beautiful! I didn't know a flower could get that big!"

I smiled at his wonder and wrapped my arms around him, placing the bloom in his hands. He brought it to his nose, inhaling deeply.

"They're my favorites," I said, leaning my head against his. "It's impossible not to smile when you see them. Just being near them fills my heart with joy. And that's why I call you my Sunflower."

He looked up at me. Emotion swam in his lovely green eyes. "I love you," he said, planting a swift, firm kiss on my lips.

"I love you, Sunflower," I replied pressing a longer kiss to his. He pulled away. As he lifted the sunflower back to his nose, I felt a horrible crack in my head. I gasped, clutching him tightly as my mental shield was struck again. It wavered but held firm.

"Eli?" Rowan said nervously. He sat up and faced me as I winced at another sharp blow. "She's trying again, isn't she?" he whispered, horrified.

I managed a nod as another blow sent bright spots flashing before my eyes.

Rowan stowed the sunflower in the pocket of his coat and gripped my hands. "Can I help? Can you take from me?"

I shuddered. "No," I croaked, pressing my forehead into his hands as another strike rattled my skull. "But she's getting more desperate. I don't know how long I can hold out."

Winter unleashed a devastating blow, and I cried out, clinging to him. The pain in my head was blinding.

I felt her power slide along my shield. She leaned closer and whispered, *I know you're hiding him from me.* Her voice was a hollow echo of the rich, melodious tone she'd once had. *My thralls are coming. And when they find him, even you won't be able to keep him from me. I will torture him slowly and make him tell me everything.*

She withdrew and resumed hammering on the outside of the shield. Bile rose in my throat, and I squeezed my eyes shut. The shield caved slightly, nearly shattering as Winter unleashed an agonizing blow.

Suddenly, I felt a strange pressure building on the inside of my head. The pain eased tremendously, and my shield thickened and held strong.

I sat up in a panic and found Rowan staring intently at me, sweat dripping from his bright red face.

"Rowan," I breathed, shocked. I could sense him, shoving his power upwards into my shield and reinforcing it against the onslaught.

"Did I do it?" he grunted, gritting his teeth. "Did I... help?"

Interesting, Winter hissed. Her voice sounded much farther away.

Rowan's eyes went wide.

You taught your little Cosmic pet a trick. How like you to use another to fight the battles you don't have the stomach to face. But it doesn't matter. I will see you very soon, human. You have something of mine. She withdrew and the pressure vanished from inside my head.

"Shit," Rowan groaned and slumped into my chest. His whole body trembled violently. "Your shield weighs a ton."

"Are you all right?" I gripped his shoulders gently, searching his face anxiously as he smiled meekly in response.

"I'm fine. But how do you keep that thing up all the time? It's so heavy." His grin widened. "I did it! I'm not even sure what I did... I just tried it, and I found an opening to your mind and pushed through." His face fell and his eyes sharpened anxiously. "I'm sorry. I probably shouldn't have done that. Are you mad? Did I cross a line?"

"No," I whispered, pressing my forehead into his. "No, I'm not mad. I'm just worried about you. That's all. My heart is yours, Sunflower. So my mind will always be open for you."

Rowan grinned sheepishly and sighed before his face fell again. "Was that..." he trailed off fearfully and I nodded.

"That was Winter," I said quietly.

"I thought she couldn't get into your head," he whispered.

I took his hand, threading my fingers through his. "She can't. But I don't have my power, so my shield isn't as strong as it's supposed to be. Normally, I wouldn't be able to hear her through it." I looked down at our interlocked hands, studying them. "When you three become heralds, you will naturally have shields around your mind. For Lumi and Ash to step into your head, you would have to give them permission and open your shield first. The connection between you and I is much deeper than that. There is no opening in my mind, Sunflower. My shield doesn't exist for you." I looked up and met his eyes.

"If you decided you wanted to, you could search through my head for anything you wanted. You could look through my eyes. You could even reach in and yank the power from my chest if you felt the need to. And there would be nothing I could do to stop you." I kissed his knuckles again. "It's what made Fall's betrayal so much worse for Winter. For a very long time, she thought she held his heart like you hold mine. But she didn't." I shook my head sadly. Rowan was quiet for a long moment before sucking in a sharp breath.

"You love me that much?" he gasped. "That you'd trust me to—" He stopped short. His bright green eyes were brimming with tears.

"Of course, Sunflower," I said with a confused frown. "Why would you—" I paused, my frown deepening at the look on his face.

I felt it then. The lingering heartbreak. The loneliness. The acrid sting of rejection.

I pressed my lips into a hard line and gathered him up in my arms. I held him tightly to my chest. "Of course I do," I whispered into his red curls.

"No one ever has," he mumbled. I sat him up to look him in the eyes.

"Well I do. And once we put a stop to Winter and right the world, you'll see." I ran my thumb across his jaw, and he shuddered.

"Well... She definitely knows I read the book," he said. "But I don't think she knows about this." He placed a hand on my chest.

"I agree. But that's still not a good thing," I said, pulling him close again. He settled against me and clutched the front of my robes tightly.

"What do you think she would do to me?" Rowan whispered. I drew him impossibly closer, bracing his back against my knees and leaning against the stone wall.

"Nothing as long as I can help it," I said firmly. He smiled and tilted his head back onto my shoulder.

"See? Told you. I have my Eli to keep me safe."

I smiled, tucking my arms around him as he settled into me and fell silent. I held him like that for a long while. At one point, he drifted back off to sleep.

I did my best not to think about Winter and her threats. Instead, I let myself envision the future. I thought about my sweet Rowan and the life we would have. Seeing his face when he'd taken his first bite of that strawberry had been one of the most magical experiences of my long life. I wanted to watch him experience a world set right.

I'd had a few relationships early on in my heraldship, but each one ended as quickly as it began. Including an extremely brief, ill-advised encounter with a foreign herald. After that, lovers were never something I had ever been overly concerned with and had taken a very rare few of them. But Rowan... He was so much more than that already. With one crooked grin, he'd stolen my heart and I never wanted it back.

I sat there cradling him against my chest all the way through the night and into the morning. He slept soundly with his ear to my heart while I dreamed of a future worth fighting for.

Lumi was the first one to stir. She rounded the corner into the cavern and paused just inside the chamber.

"Hello," I called softly. She stepped over and peeked her head into the tent. Her raven hair was messy, falling wildly around her face.

"Hi," she said, arching an eyebrow at the sight of Rowan sleeping in my arms. "Did you sit there like that all night?" I smiled down at him.

"I don't want to be anywhere else," I whispered. She cocked her head and sat in front of us, crossing her legs underneath her.

"About that," she said, fixing me with a piercing stare. "You and I need to talk."

"Oh?" Unease slithered through my stomach.

"Yeah. You know he loves you," she said bluntly. "Right?"

"And I love him," I said. She frowned, examining my face for any sign of a lie.

"He's my best friend." There was a vicious edge to her voice, and I swallowed. "He has a sweet soul and a trusting heart. When he falls for someone, he falls really hard. Every time he's given his heart to someone, he's gotten it back in pieces. I won't let anyone hurt him like that again."

"That's the last thing I'd ever want to do," I promised.

"Yeah, well..." She met my eyes fiercely. "That's what Trent said, too. Swore it right to my face. He told me he was in love, and they were going to be together forever. But he neglected to mention the fact that he was already *married,* and Ro found out the hard way.

"Or Rodger. He treated Ro like shit the entire time they were dating. You could see it on his face. He didn't smile or laugh. He was really withdrawn. But no matter how hard we tried, Ro wouldn't talk to us about it. He kept insisting he was happy, so we let it go. Until we found Ro sobbing in his bedroom. With a black eye." She ground her teeth in anger. "Rodger broke up with him the next day. Rowan never knew why. But Ash and I paid Rodger a visit that night and we made sure he'd *never* go near Ro again.

"He's had enough heartbreak to last him a lifetime," she spat. "He's had guys promise him everything, only to use him and forget he exists. And I still haven't forgiven *you* for hurting him. You may already have him wrapped around your finger, but I will not let you hurt him like they did. He really believes you love him. He even told me it feels different this time. He's already so in love, his heart will never recover if you're lying to him."

I stared at her in horror, slowly reaching up to cradle the back of Rowan's head. He sighed in his sleep and a small smile tugged at his lips. My heart dropped into the pit of my stomach and shattered.

My poor Sunflower. That's what he'd meant when he said no one chose him.

"No," I croaked. My voice was stricken and tight. "I... I would never—" She held up a hand cutting me off.

"The only thing Rowan has ever wanted was for someone to love him. The kind of love he reads about in his books. And he's convinced that could be you. If you are? Wonderful. I'll give you my whole-hearted blessing and I know Ash will too. If not? You need to end this now. Because if you aren't and you string him along... If you break his hopeless romantic heart and hurt him..." She let her words trail off threateningly.

"Lumi, I swear I'm not," I whispered, clutching Rowan a little tighter. "I love him. I would never do that to him." I clenched my teeth, fighting the feral urge to slip into his mind and find the faces to go with those names.

"Well, you can understand why I might be... skeptical." Her eyes were like chipped ice as she stared me down.

"I do understand." I swallowed my rage and horror. "And I hate myself for that. I let my guilt get the better of me and I didn't consider how I was making him feel. It was wrong. And I am so sorry," I replied, holding out my hand. "But I can show you my feelings for him are real," I explained. "May I?"

She nodded, exhaling, and took my hand tentatively.

I let my thoughts flow to her mind, showing her everything. I let her see a memory of how my heart sang when Rowan smiled at me for the first time. And how it felt like the whole world tilted when our hands had first touched. I let her see the memories of our conversations about books and how happy they made me. I showed her how my feelings grew stronger with each passing moment I spent in his presence and how he'd started to dominate every single thought. I showed her the devastating pain that had consumed me when he'd been so heartbroken because of me. I showed her the hopeful future I desperately wanted. I let her see everything. Every deep, dark corner in my mind that screamed I would never be worthy of him. The sharp ache I felt every time his hand slipped from mine. The way my heart raced when he locked eyes with me. And the deep, fathomless love that consumed my very soul.

She released my hand and sat back, studying me for a long moment. Finally, she blew out a breath, glancing at her friend as I slipped my arm back around him carefully.

He stirred slightly and drifted back off.

"Fair enough," she said, meeting my eyes with a grin. "In that case, I'm glad he found someone who wants to make him happy. But that doesn't change anything. Hurt him and you will answer to *me*," she added, arching a dark eyebrow. I smiled and nodded.

"If I ever hurt him, I'll turn myself over to you willingly. If Ash didn't kill me first," I added with a wink. She snorted and relaxed.

"Yeah. Nothing personal. Ash will probably give you the same speech," she said.

"He already has," I replied.

"Doesn't surprise me." Her eyes sparkled as her thoughts turned to Ash. I could feel the love gleaming from her mind and I smiled.

"I'm happy you two found your way to each other."

"Me too," she sighed. "Took us long enough." She absently twirled a lock of hair around her finger. "We weren't on the same page there for a while. But I'm happy we finally worked things out. And I think I can safely say that he is too."

"Definitely," a deep voice replied. Ash sidled into the tent, smiling at us through his curtain of mussed brown hair. His golden eyes landed on Rowan, and he looked up at me with a hard expression. The smile vanished from his handsome face and a muscle jumped in his jaw.

My smile faltered.

Ash's expression darkened and, for a tense moment, he looked utterly terrifying. A low, vicious sound rumbled through his chest.

"Easy, my love," Lumi chuckled. She hooked her fingers into his collar and pulled him down for a soft kiss. She held him there for a beat before pulling back to wink at him. "I already threatened him for the both of us."

"Oh. Okay then," he said. He blinked once and his dark expression vanished, leaving that bright, warm smile behind. "In that case, welcome officially to our little family." He sat next to Lumi and threw an arm across her shoulders. A lump formed in my throat and my heart stuttered.

"That means more to me than you know," I said softly.

Rowan rolled in my arms, yawning, and glanced around the tent.

"Oh... Why are you all in here staring at me?" he groaned, his voice still gravelly from sleep.

"We had to make sure he didn't take advantage of you while you were sleeping," Lumi joked.

"If that's his plan then get out and let him," Rowan replied, grinning.

Lumi and Ash laughed, and I smiled, kissing Rowan on the head. He sat up, stretching.

"I guess we have to get moving, huh?" he said, shooting me a knowing glance. I nodded.

"We need to move quickly," I said, looking towards the others. "Winter is getting desperate, and we have to get to the Crossroads. From there, we can follow the road to the World's Tower. It's about a two-day hike."

"Yikes," Lumi shuddered. "You guys had to hike that far after using your power for months?"

"Oh, no," I said quickly. "We used the bridge."

"There's a bridge?" Ash said, sitting up. "Well, fuck walking! Let's just use that!"

"It's not a structure," I clarified. "We'd use the last dregs of our power to summon a strip of pure cosmic energy. The bridge acts like a slingshot, catapulting you rapidly to your destination. Usually, we had just enough left in us to make it to the Crossroads. Then the other heralds would meet us there and bring us back home. I tried to make it home on my own and ended up face down in the dirt."

"Won't Winter be expecting you to head for the Crossroads?" Lumi said.

"She might be," I admitted. "But other than the Cosmic Bridge, that path is the only way to get to the tower. We have to take our chances."

"Can you open the bridge?" Rowan asked.

"No," I sighed heavily. "I mean yes, technically I could. But there would be nothing stopping Winter from closing it again. And it would be quite a drop."

"Ah, yeah... No thanks," Ash said, wrinkling his nose. "Two-day hike it is. All right then. Let's do this."

We stood and exited the tent. I packed up our campsite while they scarfed some food down around Rowan's small fire. Once they were done, they joined me in finishing up the packing. Ash rolled the rock away, leaving us blinking in the vicious sunlight.

"Fuck that's bright," Lumi said, squinting.

As soon as the words crossed her lips, a shadow fell across the land.

"Ah that's better... Oh... Fuck," she gasped, looking up.

Horror clenched my stomach as dark, heavy storm clouds rolled overhead.

There you are, Winter whispered to me.

I blanched and grabbed Rowan's elbow. "Run!" I yelled as a blood curdling shriek pierced the air.

Cracks and snaps echoed as something came thundering through the trees. We took off, flying through the forest as more screams sounded behind us.

"Look!" Ash shouted, pointing ahead to a group of boulders in our path. "I have an idea!" He ran up to it and leapt onto a long, pointed one. "Which way?" he demanded.

I pointed off in the distance and he nodded, bracing his feet on the stone.

"Let's go sledding!" Ash grinned wickedly. He reached out his hands and yanked each of us up onto the boulder with him. Snow began to fall in a thick curtain around us.

"Ash, that's genius!" Rowan called, bracing his feet next to Ash, who rolled his eyes.

"Don't act so surprised! Ready?" He glanced at them.

Lumi nodded and splayed her fingers wide.

The screeching was growing closer.

The three of them focused on the boulder under our feet. It jolted slightly but stayed half-buried in the earth. They tried again but still, it wouldn't budge.

"It's too heavy!" Lumi cried, sweat breaking out on her forehead from the strain.

The crashing sounds grew louder as the monsters came barreling through the forest.

Ash growled in frustration, throwing more of his power at the boulder, but it refused to yield.

"Come on, dammit!" he hissed through a clenched jaw.

Rowan looked up at me suddenly. His face was set with determination and his green eyes gleamed wildly.

My eyes went wide. I shook my head vigorously as I watched the idea forming in his mind.

"No! No, don't!" I cried out. Pressure built rapidly inside my head, and I was suddenly filled with his light, sunny energy as he poured everything he had into me. He dropped to his hands and knees, groaning.

Lumi stooped to hold him up. I clutched my spinning head, gasping.

"Rowan, stop! Please!" I yelled, pressing my hands into my temples. He shoved every ounce of power he had through his mind and into mine. I swayed, dizzy from the rapid buildup.

Ash grabbed my shoulders and held me steady.

I felt Rowan's consciousness flicker and dim. "Sunflower, please! You're hurting yourself!" I cried desperately. He shuddered and clung to Lumi, looking up at me with difficulty.

"Eli... You... You have to... Get us out of here," he moaned, before his head lolled back and he passed out.

"Rowan!" I cried, reaching for him. Blinding panic ripped through me. I took a step towards his limp form, but Ash grabbed my elbow, swearing.

"Go!" he shouted. He stooped and wrapped his arms around Lumi and Rowan, bracing himself against the stone. His power zinged, locking his feet to the boulder.

I looked down at Rowan helplessly before letting his bright energy flood through me.

The boulders shuddered at my command and lifted themselves out of the earth. I turned and glared at the ice demons as they leered at us, circling the boulders. I sent a large round one spiraling around us.

The boulder bounced and crashed against the ground, shattering the monsters attempting to surround us. The other three boulders followed as I commanded ours to move. It slid across the snow, turning towards the Crossroads and took off, picking up speed as we tore through the forest.

Wind whistled past my ears as we shot through the trees like a speeding arrow fired from a bow.

Ash huddled further around Lumi and an unconscious Rowan. I threw my arms out and released my hold on the other three boulders, sending them careening into the demons trying in vain to gallop after us.

The borrowed energy began to ebb. I gritted my teeth, throwing every ounce of Rowan's power into the rock beneath my feet. It zigzagged through the forest like a flash of lightning until the energy was spent and it finally shuddered to a stop.

I wheeled around and gasped in panic, dropping to my knees.

"Oh... Sunflower," I moaned frantically, taking his unconscious form from Lumi. I pressed a shaking hand into his chest and blew out a sharp sigh of relief as I felt his heart beat against my palm. Ash sat back hard, panting.

"How did he do that?" he said through deep, trembling breaths.

I shook my head to clear the swirling panic and fear wrapping around me. The small bit of Rowan's borrowed energy that remained flitted through me like a bird on a soft breeze. I took it and let it wrap around my heart.

The connection between us was quiet.

I reached across with what little power I had left and was met by nothing but darkness. Beneath the darkness, I could feel his energy already starting to return.

"I gave him my heart." My voice cracked as I watched his pale face. "He can step in and out of my mind whenever he wants to."

They glanced at each other.

"So he can just... Whoa," Lumi trailed off, standing up. I turned and found myself face-to-face with a huge marble structure.

Or what was left of it.

"Oh no..." I said, my heart dropping. Despair pooled in my gut as I looked up at the temple. Despair, disbelief, and fear.

Most of the temple lay in ruins. Walls had been blown out, and the rubble was scattered in a wide circle around the base of the building.

The Crossroads Temple had been destroyed.

CHAPTER THIRTY-ONE

WINTER

One by one, the minds of my thralls rapidly went dark. Balls of light streaked into the sky as Spring wrought a path of destruction through my forces. I glared down at the forest as several trees were leveled by his power, chewing on the inside of my cheek.

When Summer's minions followed him to the nesting grounds, his grief sent several towering mountains crumbling into the Black Sea. This display of Spring's abilities was not nearly as powerful as his full potential. But this was still more than he should have been able to manage.

I reached into my pocket and withdrew Spring's emerald. It felt wrong between my fingers, but I held it tightly, reassuring myself that I still possessed it. I looked back towards the sky and threw my consciousness into the storm clouds.

Far below me, I saw Spring maneuvering through the trees on a boulder. One of his three Cosmics was slumped against the other two, unconscious.

"Hmm," I said to myself. "And here I was thinking you *liked* your Cosmic pets." I looked closer at the Cosmic's pale face and broke out into a vicious, cackling laugh. Even from a distance, his vibrant red hair was unmistakable. "Oh, you're such an *idiot!*" I grinned triumphantly. "You drained the one I need. This is almost too easy."

"Too easy," a scratchy voice echoed.

I turned, lifting an eyebrow at the black shadow undulating before me. It had glowing, purple eyes that sliced jaggedly across its skull, and a gaping maw that spilled violet light each time it opened. Deep cracks in its form flashed purple as it moved. The shadow had no distinct limbs or form. It was just a dark stain on the surrounding air.

"Ooh," I wrinkled my nose in disgust. "You don't look so good, Summer."

The shadow's head lolled to the side.

"Brother," she screeched.

"Your brother," I purred, sweeping my arm in a wide arc towards the forest below, "is bringing me exactly what I need."

The shadow screamed and swiped at me, missing by inches. I didn't flinch away, setting my face into an expression of pity and glee.

"Oh, come now, Mirela." I drew out her name tauntingly. "Surely you could try to muster *some* decorum," I cackled, pointing. "See? He's arriving at the Crossroads now. And you will be pleased to know, I won't be killing him after all." The shadow tilted her head and I smiled broadly. "No. I'm going to claim his heart. Then I'll use that tremendous power of his to crush the last remnants of humanity. Once and for all." I let a hand drift lazily to the side and a large frozen spike formed in my palm. "So," I purred, "If you'll excuse me. I have to go and meet him. He and I have so *much* to catch up on."

She started screaming again. I flung my hand out, sending the ice spiraling into the shadow's open maw. The scream cut off immediately, and she exploded into a cloud of billowing smoke and dust.

Blissful silence fell.

Finally, I was rid of her.

I strode through the clearing smoke and up to the throne. Sitting on the platform at the top was my garnet, glowing like the eye of a vicious monster. I placed a hand on the throne and thick ice crept up the back, encasing the platform and locking the stone in place. Satisfied, I strode out to the balcony and spread my hands wide.

"Time to go collect my newest follower," I chuckled. A thin strip of shimmering purple light appeared at my feet and curved off towards the forest. I stepped up onto the Cosmic Bridge and called out to my remaining thralls.

They turned as one and bolted in the direction of the Crossroads Temple.

I stepped forward, waving a hand through the air. Immediately I felt the pull of the bridge and vanished from the balcony with a thunderous crack. I tore across the sky like a banshee in the wind. The land seemed to shudder at my presence as I screamed by.

I arrived at the temple in a matter of seconds, landing on what was left of the roof. A section of wall crumbled on the outside of the temple and crashed to the ground, covering the sound of the Cosmic Bridges arrival.

The marble building lay in ruins, just as I had left it twenty years ago. Most of the ceiling was gone, exposing the interior to the frigid elements. Thick columns and pillars had been demolished and lay in large pieces around the base of the structure.

I stepped off the bridge just in time to hear voices below me. I crept across the roof and paused, staring down like a cat cornering its prey.

Spring stepped out of the shadows, staring around at the destroyed interior, crestfallen. For a moment, I considered skewering him where he stood out of sheer anger.

But then Spring turned, revealing the unconscious form cradled in his arms. A thrill shot through me as I beheld the Cosmic human Spring carefully placed on the ground.

Spring had brought him straight to me, subdued and ready for the taking. The only thing he was missing was a bow on his head and a tag addressed to me.

Spring stepped away and turned in a slow circle. He pressed his feeble fingers to his lips as he examined the walls in dismay.

There used to be huge murals of the four of us. On my journey to take the tower, I'd destroyed three of them. The only mural I'd left intact was mine.

I was depicted with a book in one hand and water swirling around the other. Snowflakes danced around my upturned, placid face and my robes billowed in a soft breeze. The other three murals were now nothing more than marble fragments scattered about the floor.

"The road's gone," Spring said, his soft lilt echoing in the empty space. The raven-haired female glanced his way, frowning.

"What do you mean?" she said, her eyes nervously shooting towards the dark-haired male standing in the corner.

Flames danced in his palm, scattering the shadows across the marble floor.

I examined them carefully. Power rolled off the dark-haired male in waves. For the briefest of seconds, I could've sworn that I knew him. A name flashed through my mind, but I dismissed the thought quickly. The man whose name danced on the tip of my tongue had been murdered many, many years ago.

The female carried herself with confidence. She was armed to the teeth, on top of the power she possessed. They were going to be a problem.

"The road leading to the tower," Spring whispered. I could hear the panic rising in his voice. "It's gone."

I smiled wickedly as I stepped over a jagged stone and into view. The sun was behind me, casting my shadow across Spring's face. He looked up and froze in horror.

"You didn't really think I would leave it for you, did you?" I purred.

The dark-haired male's flames blazed ferociously, and the female drew a long white bow from her back. She summoned an arrow made of ice, drawing it back and aiming at my face.

I snorted and flicked a finger at her, shattering the ice.

Undeterred, she tossed the bow aside and unsheathed her gleaming sword.

I leapt and landed soundlessly in the center of the room.

"It's been a very long time, Lord Spring. You're supposed to be dead," I sneered, meeting his dark green eyes. They shined with fear and pity.

"Kiora," he breathed, clutching his chest. Despair wracked his sharp features. "What have you done? Look at you." He gestured to my body.

Prolonged exposure to the tower had robbed me of much of the plumpness I once had. My skin was stretched thin over my bones, and the cracks in my flesh had worsened in recent days. I glared at him.

"A minor setback," I said, touching my face gently. I fought the urge to look over at the mural and the face I no longer had. The one that Fall had loved once.

Or so I had thought.

I straightened my spine and flashed a malicious grin. "One I will remedy quickly enough. As soon as you hand that one over."

The two Cosmic humans shot fearful looks at each other.

The female swung her sword in a wide arc, drifting off to my left while her fiery companion took a step to my right.

How adorable. They were going to try and attack me.

Spring put himself squarely between me and the unconscious Cosmic, baring his teeth.

"Not a chance," he snarled.

"What have we here?" I raised my eyebrows in surprise. "Given the easy way out and you don't take it? Have you finally grown a spine?" I crooned, watching the circling Cosmics out of the corner of my eye. "I will only offer you one chance, my old friend. Stand aside," I growled.

He squared his shoulders, a gesture I'd never seen in all my time of knowing him. If I'd had a spare moment, I might've contemplated the source of his newfound boldness.

"You'll have to go through me," he said ferociously.

"Gladly," I grinned.

Several towering columns of ice erupted from the ground, smashing holes in what remained of the walls. Sunlight poured through for a fraction of a second before my swarm crawled their way through them, descending on the four like a cataclysm.

The dark-haired male unleashed his devastating fire. It sizzled through the air, blasting some of my creatures from the wall. His blazing power roiled out in every direction and incinerated several of my forces that got too close. He rolled up his sleeves and began shooting fireballs driving my forces back.

The raven-haired female fought viciously. Her gleaming blade whistled through the air, cutting down any demon that came too close.

One demon attempted to snag her unconscious friend's foot from behind her and lost its head as a result.

She reached into her boot and retrieved a dagger that she wielded in her other hand. Spring crouched down and shielded the unconscious male from the heated battle raging on either side of him. The fighters took a few steps back, forming a tight circle around Spring and their companion.

I sent my power out and commanded my thralls to attack all at once. The fire-wielding male's power began to falter as sweat gleamed on his neck. The female swung her sword wide, but one of my monsters was waiting. It slashed upwards with its long claws and sent her lethal blade sailing through the air.

Without hesitation, she summoned her power and commanded the stones at her feet, sending them flying in every direction.

I watched as their powers flickered and waited. Spring's power might be gone, but he had two wells on hand. All he had to do was take it.

Suddenly, the two humans paled. The female's back slammed into the marble wall, and she slid to the floor, dazed and weak. The male hit the ground on his hands and knees before he collapsed, unconscious.

Spring stood, glaring at me. His dark green eyes glowed like light streaming through the forest canopy. His power rumbled through the walls, fracturing the stone, and bringing the remnants of the temple crashing down upon our heads. I summoned a shield of black ice and held it over me. Marble rained down, cracking the ice floating above my skull.

My thralls screamed as they were crushed under the tumbling debris.

Then silence fell.

I tossed my shield aside with a smirk.

Chunks of marble floated around him, and he flung his arms wide, sending them careening towards me.

I dodged them, dancing across the floor as he sent chunks of the walls streaking through the air. Borrowed power was nothing. It barely scratched the surface of his potential. I grinned, watching the desperation growing on his face.

Spring's control over the marble began to falter. The stolen energy was deserting him like water slipping through his fingers. He gasped as the glow faded from his eyes and the marble clattered to the floor, no longer bound to his will.

"Nicely done," I smirked. "You drained your companions and didn't so much as ruffle my hair."

He took a staggering step backwards, delicious terror on his face. I flicked my hand, sending a large chunk of ice colliding with his chest, knocking the wind from him. He staggered back and I sent three more.

They hammered into him, blasting him off his feet and into the far wall. He hit the floor hard, gasping for air. I flicked a finger and ice sprang from the ground, locking around his wrists. The raven-haired female staggered, reaching out for him and fell to her hands and knees at my feet.

"Pathetic," I sneered.

Suddenly, she surged to her feet and lashed out with her dagger, lunging for my heart. I sidestepped her weak strike and wrapped my fingers around her delicate neck.

Her pulse beat wildly under my grip. She struggled against me and slashed upward. I jerked back, but not quickly enough. My cheek stung and black blood trickled down to my chin from the deep gash left by her dagger. I struck her hard and she slumped. I tossed her to the floor, pressing a hand to my cheek as the wound closed itself slowly.

"You found quite the spirited group," I chuckled. I raised my hand and summoned three snow golems. They were vaguely human shaped with wide torsos and long arms. "This one." I gestured towards the red-haired Cosmic.

A golem mindlessly lumbered forward and scooped the unconscious male up off the floor. Spring gasped in fear, trying desperately to wrench his hands free. He yanked at his arms, raising himself to his knees.

"You've been such a huge help," I crooned. I took a long look at the other two before I turned back, grinning at him.

"Wouldn't want you getting any crazy ideas now, would we? I'd better take all of them."

I pointed at the humans and my last two golems lifted their unconscious forms from the ground.

Spring looked up at me helplessly as I turned away and reached out with my power, instructing my remaining thralls to flood the area. My final trap was set. All Spring had to do now was step right into it.

I turned to him and feigned a look of pity. "Thank you again for your help, old friend. I didn't think you had it in you. But you've never minded having blood on your hands, right?"

Spring's face twisted in agony as I swept away from him and raised an arm to open the Cosmic Bridge.

He let out a panicked cry. I waved a hand at the golems, and they obeyed, stepping onto the shimmering purple light. I shot one last look of triumph over my shoulder.

"No," he gasped, his chest heaving. "No!"

"So long," I sneered.

Right on cue, my thralls came bounding through the trees.

"Kill him," I pretended to instruct them. I paused, stretching my hand out as if to activate the bridge, watching the agonizing decision play across his face.

For a moment, I doubted he had the nerve and wondered if I should just kill him instead.

But then my demons froze in their tracks.

A shudder rolled through them like an earthquake, and they crumbled into dust. Spring broke free and clutched his head, letting out a long, anguished scream. His pink skin paled and his eyes darkened to a dull gray as he stripped the energy from the beasts around him.

I smiled wickedly and waved a hand, activating the bridge and rushing away.

We flew faster than lightning across the sky. The forest below was a blur as my tower came into view. The red-haired male groaned and stirred feebly as wind whipped his hair. We'd almost reached the balcony when I felt a tug on the bridge. We were being followed.

I stepped off of it, instructing my golems to bring my guests into the throne room and relieve them of their bags. They obeyed, ambling off as the red-haired male opened his eyes and let out a startled squeak.

I turned toward the bridge and saw Spring streaking towards the tower like a comet across the sky. I reached out my power, startled as it collided with Spring's mental shield. His mind was somehow still his.

But it didn't matter. He clearly just needed more time to *think*.

I grinned and placed a foot on the shimmering purple light, shoving downwards with all my strength. The light shattered and vanished.

Spring's screech echoed across the land as he dropped through the air and crashed into the trees below. I knew he'd survive and head straight here, but the longer I delayed him, the more time my will had to take hold of his mind. I was surprised that it hadn't taken him already, but I didn't pause to dwell on it. I had work to do.

I swept away from the balcony and strode into the throne room. The red-haired male gave a shout and began thrashing against the golem holding him.

"Let go of me!" he yelled. I sauntered over to the golem holding one of his companions.

"I'd be more cooperative if I were you," I hissed.

The red-haired male's green eyes went wide as I grabbed a fistful of his friend's brown hair and wrenched his head back.

I summoned an ice shard and pressed it to the unconscious male's throat. A small trickle of blood sprung from where the tip grazed his skin.

The red-haired male seethed but fell silent, watching me hatefully.

"Better," I said. I released my grip, waving a hand at the golems. "Secure them in the treasure room in case I need them later. And tie that one to the throne. There's some rope in his bag. He and I have some business to discuss."

The red-haired male watched his unconscious friends be carried from the room helplessly. The golem holding him complied with my command, dragging him over and binding him to the throne. I flicked my hand and the golem vanished.

"So," I hissed, stepping closer to the glaring Cosmic. "You have something for me."

"I don't have shit for you," he spat. I raised an eyebrow at him, smirking.

"Such fire," I crooned, running a finger down his soft cheek. He jerked away from my frigid touch. "But I'm sure Spring told you what I want."

"I don't know what you're talking about," he said firmly.

"Oh I think you know *exactly* what I'm talking about. And you're gonna tell me," I said.

The male pressed his lips together stubbornly and I sighed. "I am not a patient being, stubborn one. If you don't start telling me what I want to know, I'll have to start ripping you and your friends apart. Perhaps I'll start with your fierce little raven-haired friend? Gouge out those pretty blue eyes of hers?" I tilted my head. His green eyes flashed, and he spat at my feet.

"Eli will crush you," he snarled.

I began to laugh. Until his words clanged through me and I froze, trailing off to look at him incredulously.

"What did you just say?" I hissed. I must've misheard him. There was no way he could've known. Unless...

He drew up his shoulders, straining against the ropes binding him to the throne. "I said Eli will crush you. You'll be nothing more than dust under his heel when he's through," he sneered proudly. A pulse of surprise raced through me.

"That's what I thought you said," I mused. "And you just called him... Eli." Horror twisted his face as a slow smile spread across mine. "How do you know his name?"

"I—" he stuttered, his face turning white. "I-I just..."

"I find it very interesting that you know his name when he hasn't answered to it in centuries. And you used it so casually. It's almost like... He *told* you to," I crooned circling the throne slowly. My footsteps echoed off the icy walls as my prey shivered in fear.

I stopped in front of him again and he gulped.

"See," I said, leaning forward to bring my face level with his. "I've known him for a very, *very* long time. So, I know that, after he took the heraldship, he stopped using his true name and only answered to Spring. Not even his own twin sister was allowed to call him by his name. He told me once that he felt giving someone permission to use it was an act of... *intimacy*." I raised an eyebrow as the male clenched his jaw. His eyes widened with fear. All of the pieces finally clicked into place, and I smirked.

"So. That's how you did it." I stood, towering over him. "That's how you got into his mind. It all makes so much sense now! His sudden courage. His insistence on shielding you from me. His desperation. How easily he fell into my trap. Oh! How utterly delectable! He loves you!" I cried, clapping my hands together as I met the male's terrified eyes.

He shrank back against the bindings.

"Well, then my stubborn little friend. Let me assure you that your Spring is in fact coming for you. But he won't be the man you know when he gets here."

A flash of confusion and apprehension crossed his face.

"You see... He was so angry that I took you. But he'd already drained your friends of every last drop of their power and still couldn't stop me. So, he drained the only other creatures near him," I finished, grinning wickedly. Horrible understanding dawned on his face and tears clouded his green eyes.

"No," he whispered.

"Oh yes," I nodded, feigning pity. "He was so desperate to save you. Still is. In fact, why don't we reach out to him? Hm? What do you say?"

I drew a large circle in the air with my hand and created a small, crackling storm cloud before me.

"Normally I don't share the sight with anyone," I said, winking at him as I threw my power out into the skies and summoned a massive storm system. I brushed my hands out and the clouds began to drift away from the tower. "But he was so helpful in subduing you all that I can make an exception. Just this once."

He watched, horrified as the small storm cloud flickered and swirled. Trees slipped past as my larger clouds trailed over the forest. A small figure appeared.

Spring raced at breakneck speed through the dense forest. He was moving so fast, he was nothing more than a blur.

I grinned. The more power he used, the faster he'd fall to my will. All I had to do now was wait.

"Oh, Spring!" I called into the cloud.

The figure slammed to a halt, whipping his head around for the source of my voice. I let my power drift closer as he turned to face us.

The red-haired male let out a sob as he took in Spring's gray skin and his dark eyes. A small crack had appeared on his cheek and something black and thorny peeked through it.

"Spring," I crooned again. "I've been having such a lovely chat with your little pet here. And do you know what he just said? He told me that you love him! How unexpectedly perfect is that?"

"Don't you touch him!" Spring screamed into the sky. His soft lilt had turned scratchy and had a strange, empty echo to it. The red-haired male stared in disbelief, tears rolling down his round cheeks.

"Eli," he croaked.

Spring's face went from being filled with hate to panicked as he turned in a circle and scanned his surroundings. "Sunflower!" he cried out desperately. "Oh, Sunflower… I'm so—" He gasped and clutched his head briefly. He froze for a moment and a tiny, relieved smile tugged on his lips. "Sunflower," he said, his voice shaking. "I'm coming for you. Hang on, all right? Hang on."

His sunflower let out a soft sob and opened his mouth to respond. Before any words could escape his lips, I conjured a small ice shard and jammed it deftly into the male's knee. He screamed in pain, writhing against the ropes as the blade sank deep into his flesh. His warm blood spilled across my fingers. Spring's face twisted in fury.

"Kiora! Don't you dare—"

"That was just his knee," I snarled, cutting him off. "It might be his ribcage next. Your precious little pet is running out of time, *Eli*."

Spring's chest heaved with rage as his sunflower whimpered in pain behind me. I reached out to him with my power. I could feel the anger, guilt and terror swirling through his mind. Darkness had gathered at the edge of his consciousness and was slithering over the wavering mental shields encasing the last shreds of his sanity.

I removed the ice shard and stabbed it into another spot on the same knee. The sunflower's screams of pain rattled the icicles hanging from the ceiling.

I ran my hand through the cloud, dissipating it and severing the connection. Panic, anguish, and unbridled wrath flitted through Spring's mind. I chuckled softly as I withdrew my power and turned to face my prisoner.

He was panting. Sweat coated his face and he'd squeezed his eyes shut against the pain. I patted him lightly on the cheek, wiping the shard off on his coat.

"Nicely done, Sunflower," I sneered. "But while we wait for your hero to come and meet his inevitable fate... You and I have some things to discuss."

He glared up at me, his eyes glazed with agony and pressed his lips together stubbornly.

I looked up at the ceiling with a shake of my head and twirled the shard, stabbing it roughly into his shoulder. His screams were so loud that I was sure Spring could hear them as he approached the tower. I wrenched the shard free, and he slumped.

"The *Book of the Cosmics*," I said quietly, holding the shard over his thigh. "It described a ritual for joining the stones and replacing the Two. What did it say?"

The male shook his head vigorously, gasping for air through a clenched jaw.

I sighed and drove the shard into his thigh, relishing his screams. In the distance, the earth rumbled.

"What did it say?" I repeated, flexing my blood-soaked fingers.

"It said that you should go fuck yourself," he panted.

I exhaled through my nose and chose another spot on his arm, ramming the blade so hard through his flesh, it glanced off bone.

His throat was raw from screaming by the time I ripped the dagger free.

"I'm already getting tired of this game, Sunflower. Or should I go get your friends? Would you be willing to let them endure this?" I stabbed his other arm and he thrashed, screaming in agony. I twisted the dagger before yanking it free.

The sunflower jerked and cried out, slumping against the bindings. I huffed impatiently and reached into him with my power. Only to recoil as I hit that damned rose-scented wall. Somehow, it was still up.

"Your precious Spring won't be able to protect your mind for much longer," I snarled. "He's fading quickly." The sunflower blinked and shook his head.

"Eli will... crush you," he gasped, letting his head fall back against the throne with a thump.

"He's slipping to my will," I snorted. "Soon that shield will crumble and he—" I froze, my body going rigid.

The sunflower locked his gaze on me. His green eyes were burning, bright and defiant.

Understanding suddenly tore through me and I whipped around, taking in the sweat trickling down his temples. "It's you," I gasped. "You're still holding his shields up. Or you're funneling your power to what's left of him."

He bared his clenched teeth, his chest still heaving with the pain and the exertion on his power.

I threw my head back and laughed. "Oh, how adorable! You're trying to save him!" I grinned maliciously as I reached into my pocket and withdrew the emerald, holding it up for him to see. Fear flashed across his pain-stricken face.

"You're wasting your power," I purred. "Because once he gets here? I'll make sure he gets this back. And in his desperation to save you... He will lose his heart. To *me*. My power will flood his mind and soul, and he will cease to exist. So go on and waste away your only means of saving yourself to protect his heart. I will make you watch as your beloved Eli smashes your friends to a pulp. That is, unless you are ready to tell me what I want to know."

He pressed his lips into a hard line and frustration seared through me.

I lashed out, jamming the dagger into his limbs over and over, drenching my fingers in his blood.

His screams filled the room. And this time, when the ground trembled in anger, it was much closer.

CHAPTER THIRTY-TWO

LUMI

I opened my eyes, squinting in the flickering torchlight. My cheek throbbed painfully, and my head felt like it weighed a ton. I blinked, trying to clear the fog away.

Memories of Winter's sneering face followed by a burst of pain filled my mind. I took a deep breath to fight back the panic and tried to brush a hand over my eyes, realizing with a jolt that my hands were bound behind my back. Something solid and warm was pressed against my spine. I flexed my fingers and found another hand. I was tied back-to-back with someone.

Ropes were wound firmly around my torso, binding my arms in place. As I shifted again, attempting to loosen the ropes, a deep, familiar groan sounded behind my head, and I sighed in relief. I was tied to Ash.

I lifted my head to examine our surroundings. We were bound in the center of a round chamber. The pale stone walls were covered in thick black ice and icicles hung ominously over our heads. Our packs had been taken from us and laid against the far wall. I wriggled and jerked against the binding, causing Ash to cough and sputter behind me.

I shifted, locking my fingers with his.

"Oh... What happened?" he groaned, laying his head back on my shoulder.

"Last I remember, Winter punched me in the face," I said, leaning against his forehead. "I think she took us."

"We're in the World's Tower?" he gasped, sitting up quickly. The motion yanked the ropes hard and caused me to wince.

"I think so," I said with a grimace. "Do you see Ro or Spring?" I felt him shake his head and my stomach dropped. "So... If we're alone in here, then—" I trailed off fearfully.

"She has Ro," he finished, horrified. As though in answer, a long, guttural scream sounded from somewhere above our heads.

Ash began to struggle against the ropes, compressing my lungs. "We have to help him!" he cried, desperately.

"H-Hold on! Wait!" I gasped. He stilled and I drew a deep, calming breath. I released his hand and tried to summon my power, but it sputtered and failed. "Dammit," I hissed. "I can't get it to work." I focused again and called upon my power. It responded, conjuring a small ice spike that grew from the ground and surged upwards, slicing the ropes.

"Nicely done!" Ash said, shaking the ropes from us and standing up. He hauled me to my feet as another scream of pain shattered the silence. We looked up fearfully before glancing around in desperation.

"Where's the door?" Ash said, frantically. I turned in a circle, searching the walls for any sign of the exit. But there was nothing. Just unblemished stone.

"She got us in here somehow," I said, striding over and pressing my palms into the nearest wall, searching for a seam. A hinge. Anything.

"Fuck it," Ash said. He brushed his hair away from his face and spread his hands wide. "We'll just make one." He threw his arms out and the wall next to him exploded outwards. Pale, ice-coated bricks careened into the valley far below as a frigid wind whipped through the opening. He stepped to the edge and peered out of the hole, looking down. "Shit," he said, stepping back. "Not that way."

He threw out his arms again and blasted another hole into the side of the tower. I could see the Fire Mountains in the distance. Ash swore and tried again, smashing yet another hole that led to the dizzying drop outside.

"Dammit! Where's the fucking door?" Ash shouted as Rowan screamed again. He raised his arms, preparing to blast another hole in the wall. I caught movement out of the corner of my eye and looked over as a dark figure clambered through one of the holes.

I yelped and threw my hands out, sending a chunk of stone flying at it in a panic. The figure shoved it away and straightened up, clutching its stomach with shaking arms.

"Lumi... Ash..." the figure whispered as it stumbled into the room. It looked up, meeting my eyes with dark gray ones. My heart stopped.

"Spring?" I gasped, rushing to his side, and catching him before he fell. He winced and straightened as much as he could.

"Thank the Two you're all right," he said. His voice was gravelly and echoed like he was calling to us from deep inside of a cave. His skin had turned a pale gray and had fractured in several places. Poking through the cracks were black, prickly vines. Even his hair had dulled to a shineless black.

"What the fuck happened to you?" Ash breathed, gripping Spring's arm to hold him upright.

"She took you," he croaked. "I ran out of energy."

"Yeah, thanks for that," I said.

"I'm sorry," he gasped, clutching his forehead. "But I was desperate. And when she took you, I had no choice. I drained her demons."

"Shit... You're corrupted," Ash breathed.

"I don't have much time," Spring nodded weakly. "And neither does Rowan. He's been funneling his power to me so I can hold back the corruption with a shield around my heart. But he's slipping. And if his shield fails then..." He trailed off, swallowing hard. "We have to remove her stone. Then I can reclaim my power and use it to purge the corruption before it's too late." He staggered over and fished around in the bags. "Thank the Two we took these," he said, drawing out the rose crown and placing it on his head.

Another scream echoed from above us and Spring's eyes darted up at the ceiling. Fury twisted his face and he straightened, striding towards a spot in between two of Ash's holes in the wall.

He placed a hand on the stone, and it split beneath his fingers. The wall parted, opening to a dimly lit stairwell spiraling up the tower.

"Seriously!" Ash threw his hands up in frustration. "I was that close and didn't find it?"

Spring poked his head out and scanned the shadows for movement before motioning for us to follow him.

"The throne room is at the top," he whispered. Another long scream echoed through the tower and Spring blanched, clutching his chest. "He's fading," he said, frantically. "He's not gonna last much longer! Come on!"

We'd only managed three steps when something big blocked our path. It looked like a large, misshapen human made entirely of snow. The creature grunted and swiped at us with a long arm that ended in thin, icy talons.

I dodged back as Spring drew his hands together quickly. The floor underneath the creature shot upwards, smashing it into the ceiling. It shrieked and exploded in a cloud of white powder.

"What the—" Ash began, trailing off as another creature lumbered around the corner. He sent a blast of fire roiling through the creature's chest. It dropped and disintegrated.

"Quick!" Spring said, motioning towards the open door behind us. "Those are golems. They will regenerate in a few minutes. Move them in here."

I summoned my power and splayed my hands wide. The snow jumped at my command and skittered across the stone steps, flowing like a river into the open treasure room.

Spring placed his hand on the wall and the doors slid closed. "Hurry," he exclaimed. "That won't hold them for long."

We raced up the stairs, pausing at a large black door at the top. Spring pressed his hand to it, listening carefully. Deep, shuddering gasps filled the cold air.

"You're running out of spots, little Sunflower. Soon this is going to get lethal," Winter crooned.

Spring bristled. His eyes darkened, turning the irises almost black.

"Fuck you," Rowan croaked. His voice shook with pain. Winter sighed. There was a sickening crunch and Rowan screamed again.

Spring bared his teeth and shoved the door open wide. He dug his hand into the floor like he was plunging it into a pool of water, gouging out a ball of stone that he sent barreling across the floor.

Winter barely had time to register his presence before she dodged away from the boulder, grinning.

"Spring," she purred. "Right on time."

He growled and sent another volley of stones at her head, forcing her to back away from the throne.

I'd never seen a more dreadful place. The black stone walls and dark ice hanging from the ceiling gave the impression that we were standing in a dark, forgotten cavern. A large obsidian throne sat in the center of the circular room, facing a massive archway leading out to a balcony overlooking the valley below. Ropes were wrapped around the throne, and I heard a small whimper coming from it.

Ash gripped my arm. "Get Ro," he hissed, stepping around me.

I crept around the edge of the room, watching as Ash squared his shoulders. His fire lashed out, striking an unsuspecting Winter square in the face.

She sputtered, stumbling back as another fireball hit her in the chest.

"How did you... No matter," Winter hissed, eyeing Ash as he let his fire crawl up his arms. She threw a hand out in his direction and paused, frowning. "Still shielding them, Spring?" she hissed, dodging another volley of rocks.

"I'd think you'd be expending a little more power shielding yourself. But I can see from your eyes that it won't be a problem much longer." She cast a hand out and spikes of black ice shot up from the floor.

Ash and Spring rolled away, the ice missing them by inches. Ash stood and began rapidly throwing fireballs while Spring sent a stone table flying from the edge of the room.

I crept around the throne and froze, gasping.

Rowan was deathly pale. He had several wounds in his legs, arms, and chest. An ice shard was lodged in his left knee and his clothes were drenched with a terrifying amount of blood. He cracked his eyes open, crying out in relief when he saw it was me.

"Lumi!" he whimpered.

"I'm here, Ro. Hang on," I said, summoning a long ice blade. I sliced through the ropes binding him. "Come on! We gotta get you out of here."

"Eli!" he gasped, shoving himself to his feet. He peered around the throne at the battle raging behind us and let out a terrified sob. "Oh no!" he cried. "He doesn't have much time! Lumi, quick! You go help them! I'll get the stone!" He pointed a shaking hand towards the top of the throne.

There, encased in a block of thick ice, was a large, glowing garnet.

Rowan clambered up to stand on the seat, wincing in pain as he dug his fingers into the ice and started trying to use his power to peel it back. "She's still got her power focused on it. And if I drop my power from the shield around Eli's heart, we'll lose him! I need you to buy me as much time as you can! Distract her so I can get through this. Go!" he shouted.

I turned sharply and summoned my power. A cool breeze kissed my skin as I sent a powerful gust of wind tearing through the room. It slammed into Winter, knocking her into the wall and down to the floor. She scrambled back to her feet just as Ash sent a blast of flames down where she had fallen, missing her by inches. She sneered and sent a column of ice smashing into him, sending him sprawling across the room.

He landed next to the throne, groaning.

She turned as I sent a chunk of the floor flying up from between her feet. It caught her in the chin, snapping her head back as she stumbled a few steps.

"I'm getting tired of you," she growled at me viciously, sending a spike flying straight at my chest.

I dodged, wincing at the crunch as it embedded itself in the wall behind me and sent a small blaze sailing through the air. She leapt to the side to avoid it, pausing as she caught sight of Spring and grinned wickedly. "Almost there, Spring. Almost mine," she purred.

I followed her gaze and found Spring on his knees, clutching his head. His eyes had turned black, and his skin was completely gray. His chest heaved from the effort of staying awake and his whole body was trembling.

I threw my hand out behind me and summoned the ice bolt. It shot from the wall and zinged back towards Winter.

She was distracted and barely avoided being impaled, catching the spike with one hand. The tip caught her dress, tearing open the pocket. Three large, shiny objects dropped out of it, rolling away in different directions across the floor.

She turned to me and raised the bolt. I braced myself to dodge the spike. Suddenly, pain sliced through me as a thick column of ice slammed into my gut, sending me crashing into the wall behind me. The air whooshed out of my lungs, and I gasped for breath, swaying as I scrambled to get back on my feet. She leveled the spike at me again and froze. A shudder ran through her sickly frame.

"Come on, dammit!" Rowan shouted. I looked over as Rowan pressed harder on the ice, trying to force the surface to open.

"No!" Winter screeched, raising her hand. The ice opened, swallowing his fist, and locking both him and the stone in place.

"Shit!" he cried, yanking at his hand. "Shit! No!"

Winter lifted the spike, preparing to launch it at Rowan when a fireball collided with her stomach, knocking her off balance. Ash leapt onto his feet and stepped between Winter and Rowan. His golden eyes flashed.

I threw a gust of air at her, throwing her further off balance. Ash took the opportunity to rush at her, sending a wall of flames that forced her back.

Winter summoned another column of ice below Ash, and he just barely managed to dodge it as I sent a rock flying towards her. It caught the edge of the spike, nearly knocking it out of her hand.

Another blast of ice shot towards me, and I leapt out of the way as Ash sent another fireball smashing into Winter's nose.

Together, Ash and I backed her against a wall, sending everything we could muster at her.

She threw an ice shield up, which Ash shattered with a well-placed fireball. She screamed in frustration and sent waves of black ice crashing towards him. Ash stumbled back and blocked the ice with his fire.

Winter strode towards him, dodging my ball of fire. She stomped her foot hard on the ground, sending ice shooting up from the floor. Ash gasped and sidestepped the attack.

I sent a tidal wave of rock and debris crashing across the floor. She dodged my power as she rushed at Ash and swiped a hand through the air, sending a row of spikes shooting up from the ground. Unaware of her movement, he stepped to the side, dodging Winter's ice blast as she reached him. He didn't even have time to register what was happening as her hand closed around his throat.

Horror froze the blood in my veins. I threw my hands out, willing my power to stop her. To do something. Anything.

But I was too late.

Ash screamed as the spike found its mark deep in his abdomen. She released him and he fell to his knees, clutching his stomach. Dark blood stained the front of his tunic and flowed freely between his fingers.

Rage blinded me. I gathered my power and threw everything I had at Winter.

She cackled with glee, dodging my attack. She sent a spike hurtling in my direction, missing my shoulder by inches as I drove her backwards, stepping between her and Ash. I attacked with unrelenting force. Winter's sneer vanished and she gritted her teeth in frustration as I struck her with a storm of ice shards. Fire slammed into her, knocking her off balance before a gust of wind smashed her backwards into the wall.

She hurt my family. I was going to tear her apart. I sent a chunk of the wall straight at her face and she gasped, wobbling before falling to the ground in a heap. Seeing my opportunity, I rushed forward, yelling in surprise when I jerked to a sudden stop beside the throne. Winter had trapped me by locking my feet to the floor with a mass of black ice. I blasted the ice creeping up my legs with a ball of fire. But it was no use. The ice started crawling up my legs, burning my skin.

Ash sputtered and coughed, clutching his bleeding stomach, and dragging himself towards me with his other hand.

I glared at Winter and launched a volley of strikes at her. I threw everything I could at her sneering face.

She dodged it all, grinning at me as my power sputtered. I'd expended so much of it that my muscles ached, and a sharp pain had started behind my eyes. Winter smoothed her skirts, cackling wickedly.

"Oh, this has been fun," she sighed, summoning a spike. "You fought so fiercely. It's such a shame really. If only I could corrupt you without it destroying you. Oh well. It's time we ended this."

My heart stopped as she lifted the spear and aimed it at my face. I braced myself, staring her down hatefully.

"Kiora, no!" an eerie voice cried.

Winter froze, turning around in surprise.

Spring had crawled to the center of the room. In one hand, he held his golden crown of roses. In the other, he grasped a large, glowing emerald.

Winter's eyes went wide with glee as Spring fit the stone into the empty facet on his crown.

"Eli, no!" Rowan screamed, desperately. "No! That's what she wants you to do! Don't do it! Please!"

Spring met his eyes before placing the crown carefully on his head.

For the span of a heartbeat, time screeched to a halt.

Then, Rowan cried out in pain, clutching his forehead with his free hand. He slumped against the throne, held up by the hand still locked in place.

Spring let out a shuddering gasp. He leaned forward, holding his head and began to scream like he was being torn apart. Huge cracks ripped into his skin and thorny black vines sprang out, wrapping themselves tightly around his arms and torso. They trailed up his neck and tangled into his hair, locking the crown to his head. Shadows consumed his eyes, snuffing out any trace of light. His screams echoed through the air and rattled the walls until, suddenly, he fell silent.

He lowered his hands and looked up slowly. His face was blank and terrifying. Any trace of who he once was had vanished, leaving nothing behind but a monster.

"No," Rowan sobbed, clutching his head. He flinched hard, tears streaming down his face. "No, no, no."

Winter threw her head back and laughed triumphantly.

"Yes! He's mine! The unbridled power of spring and earth are mine to command!" Winter called to the cosmos gleefully. She turned back towards us, grinning. Terror froze my heart. "He will be the downfall of your pathetic kind. I will make him destroy everything and everyone." She glanced at the spike in her hand before she tossed it aside. "And how poetic that he gets to start with you." She turned towards the dark figure kneeling obediently on the marble floor. "Kill her."

Spring stood at her command, stepping past her, and stopping directly in front of me.

I summoned what was left of my power and sent a fireball colliding with his face in desperation.

Spring didn't flinch as the flames broke on his cheek and died swiftly.

He raised his hand behind him and the ground beneath the tower shook. The huge balcony split itself in two. He raised his hand higher, and the massive stone chunk came to hover directly over my head, taking the ceiling off the tower as it glided into place.

I looked up at it helplessly. I couldn't move. Couldn't think around the terror gripping my heart. I was locked to the floor, unable to escape the ice slowly devouring me.

This was it. Ash's hand slipped into mine and I looked down to meet his golden eyes.

"I love you," he whispered.

"I love you too," I whispered back to him, squeezing his hand.

"Eli!" Rowan sobbed. "Eli, please." His free hand dove into his coat pocket and he withdrew a large bloodstained and battered-looking yellow flower. He held it out for Spring to see. Sweat poured down his pale face and his expression was twisted in agony.

Spring's face remained empty and emotionless.

"Please, Eli," he begged. The flower shook in his trembling hand. "I won't drop the shield. I know you're still in there and I'm not letting you go. Come back to me. Eli, please! I love you!"

Winter laughed as she sauntered over and ripped the flower from Rowan's hand. She threw it on the floor and crushed it under her heel before striding away from him.

"You stupid creature," Winter sneered. "His heart belongs to me now. So, you can drop your pathetic shield. The only way to spare your friends from a horrible death now is to tell me what I want to know."

I squared my shoulders to muster my courage, looking back at Spring in time to see something spread slowly across his face. He was *smiling*. I froze and Ash's hand tightened on mine.

My eyes widened in shock as Spring looked up at Rowan. They locked eyes and Spring mouthed a single word.

Sunflower.

Rowan let out a startled cry and pressed his hand to his mouth in shock.

Spring mouthed it again. *Sunflower.*

He gazed up at Rowan, who let out a sob of utter relief.

Rowan's green eyes hardened as they slid back to Winter, who was still laughing and hadn't noticed anything.

"You're wrong," he said quietly.

Her laughter died away and she tilted her head, confused. "Excuse me?" she hissed.

"You heard me," he spat, defiantly. "You're wrong."

Spring's smile widened.

"Wrong?" Winter snorted. "You think you can save his heart *now*? Look at him. He's mine."

"No," Rowan said, his voice surging with savage triumph. "No, you're wrong! He's never been yours, and he never will be! His heart is *mine*!"

As the last word crossed his lips, Spring turned, rounding on Winter. The ground shook violently and the section of the balcony slammed into the ground right where Winter stood.

She blasted herself backwards, barely avoiding being crushed.

The stone on Spring's head gleamed as he bared his teeth with a vicious snarl.

"That's not possible!" Winter screeched. She stumbled backwards as her face contorted with fear. "I can feel my power flooding you! It completely consumed your mind! That's not possible!" She sent a shard of ice streaking through the air. He flicked a hand out, redirecting the ice away from his chest with his palm. It sailed over his shoulder and shattered against the wall.

He spread his hands wide, and the tower trembled as it began tearing itself apart around us.

Winter screamed. She was sent flying as stone after stone smashed into her. Spring attacked relentlessly, tossing her around like a rag doll.

His power enveloped the room and the very earth trembled under the might of his rage. Every attack Winter managed to send his way sailed harmlessly by him as he raised his hands and sent the rest of the balcony hurtling towards her. She rolled out of the way, only to be tossed into the air by a column of stone. She hit the floor hard with a shuddering wheeze.

She looked up just as a tree sprung from the ground under her, growing faster than I could blink and slamming her into what was left of the ceiling high above us. The tree vanished and she crashed to the floor.

Ash's fingers slipped from mine. I looked down and saw him raising a blood-soaked hand, aiming his palm carefully at the ice.

"Ro!" he managed. Rowan blinked before squeezing his eyes shut, leaning away from the throne. Ash summoned his fire and sent a blast of roiling flames at the block of ice. A loud crack split the air as the ice fractured and exploded.

Rowan threw himself backwards, stumbling off the throne and landing hard on his back. He sat up and held the garnet over his head. Its glow dulled instantly.

"No!" Winter screamed. Her black eyes went wide with terror. Desperately, she threw her hand out, but her power failed her. "No! That's impossible!" She took a shuddering breath. Large flakes of skin broke and fell away from her body like shards of glass falling from a shattered mirror. Black smoke curled from the cracks, dissipating in the air. She swung her head wildly around, locking her furious eyes on Rowan.

"I'll kill you!" she screeched, wrenching a spike of ice from the floor nearby and lifting it. Spring brought his hands crashing together. Two large patches of the tower's walls tore themselves from the structure and collided with a thunderous crack, crushing Winter where she stood. He tossed the pieces away, revealing a tattered white dress bunched around a pile of black dust on the floor.

A blast of freezing wind tore through the room, shattering the ice creeping up my thighs and knocking me off of my feet. I blinked and looked up. A dull ball of gray light hovered in the air before it winked once and dissipated.

Spring dropped his power and hit the ground on all fours, gasping.

"Eli!" Rowan cried, hobbling to Spring's side.

Spring retched and thick black smoke spewed from his mouth. It curled around his face and pooled on the floor before vanishing. He heaved again and his skin lightened significantly.

"I'm... fine," he panted. "Help him." He wrenched his crown from his head and forced it into Rowan's hands, spewing more black smoke as he did.

My heart stopped. I turned around frantically and found Ash leaning against the throne.

His face was deathly pale, and an alarmingly large pool of blood was still spreading around him.

"Ash!" I gasped, rushing to him.

He grinned weakly at me and winced, sucking in a sharp breath. "Lumi," he croaked. "See? I told you that you were a fierce warrior queen." I gathered him up in my arms as tears stung my eyes. My heart hammered in my chest.

"Hang on, Ash," I said, pressing a firm hand to his stomach. He hissed, flinching hard.

My stomach lurched at the feel of his blood soaking my skin and panic swirled through my mind.

Rowan let out a terrified squeak and scrambled across the room.

"You have to hang on for me. Okay?" I told Ash firmly, locking eyes with him as his breaths grew more labored. Dizzying terror surged through me, and I gritted my teeth. I tried not to look down at the spreading pool of Ash's blood. There was so much. I shifted my hand, but I couldn't seem to stem the flow.

"You promised. Remember? You promised me that you wouldn't die on me."

He swallowed hard as Rowan raced over, clutching the four stones.

"Lay him flat! Quick!" Rowan said frantically. "We have to do this now!"

I laid Ash on the ground as Rowan fumbled with the stones. He knelt beside Ash's head and placed the garnet and the emerald side-by-side on Ash's chest. Then he laid the diamond and the amethyst next to each other on Ash's sternum. Rowan touched a finger to Ash's bloody hand and placed a small drop of blood on the surface of each stone.

"Repeat after me," he said, panic lacing his frantic voice. "Every word, okay?" Ash gasped and nodded. Rowan locked eyes with him. "Okay... You have to say, 'I pledge my body and spirit to the Ethereal Two. I ask them to grant me a heraldship in their service.' That's it. That's all you have to say. Just like that," he finished, quickly. Ash swallowed again.

"I pledge my body and spirit... to the Ethereal Two," he said between labored breaths. He locked eyes with me as a single terrified tear rolled down my cheek. "I ask them to... grant me a heraldship... in their service."

Time stood still. We waited, hardly daring to breathe. But nothing happened.

I looked up at Rowan desperately, my heart racing in terror as I saw tears start rolling down his cheeks.

"It should've worked," Rowan said in disbelief, clutching his heaving chest. "I... I don't understand. Those were the words. The stones... The stones are right... It should've worked." Understanding dawned on Ash's face.

"They won't take me," he whispered.

He sucked in a sharp breath, wincing at the pain and gripped my hand weakly. A few tears filled his golden eyes. He struggled to focus on Rowan, who started shaking his head vigorously.

"Ro," he croaked. "You know... You're my brother. And I love you."

"No... Please, Ash." Rowan sobbed, crouching next to me. "No goodbyes. We'll think of something. We could... We can... Water!"

Rowan spun in a rapid circle, scanning the room, and wringing his hands. "We need water! And a tub! I... Mother does it! I could try! I... There's no... No..." He let out a hopeless sob and wiped his streaming eyes, pressing his trembling lips together. Ash smiled meekly at him.

"It's okay, Ro," he said softly.

"I love you, brother," Rowan whispered. I felt lost. This wasn't happening. It couldn't be.

"Spring," Ash said. "Take care of them. Please."

Spring swallowed hard, stepping into Ash's line of sight. "You have my word," he replied thickly.

Ash nodded and let his eyes slide to me.

"I love you, Lumi. I'm so sorry," he whispered, reaching up to wipe a tear away from my cheek. "I didn't... keep my promise."

"No," I sobbed as tears blurred my vision.

This was not happening. I refused to accept it. Even as my heart was ripping itself in half.

"No, Ash. Please. Stay with me. We... We were supposed to do this together. Remember?" Tears streamed down my face. "Ash, I can't do this without you." He smiled weakly.

"Yes, you can. My fierce warrior queen... can do anything." He lost focus and closed those beautiful golden eyes.

I pressed my trembling lips to his forehead.

"I love you," I sobbed.

He took a sharp, shuddering breath and fell silent. His hand went limp in mine.

"Ash, no!" I cried out, cupping his cold face in my hands. I shook him slightly, but those gorgeous eyes stayed closed. "No, no, no! Ash, stay with me! Please!"

I reached out in a blind panic and pressed my hand into his chest. I felt nothing. Not the steady beat of his heart or the shift of his body as his lungs filled with air. I shook my head, unwilling to accept it and pressed my hand down harder, searching for his heart beat. It had to be there. It just had to. But there was still nothing. Just a horrible silence that seemed to spiral on forever. He was gone.

Ash was dead.

CHAPTER THIRTY-THREE

LUMI

Every part of me went numb. I couldn't breathe. I couldn't move. My soul was shredding itself to pieces and I started screaming.

I clung to him, unwilling to let go as I pressed my forehead against his. My throat started to sting from sobbing and screaming, but I couldn't stop.

Rowan's arms wrapped around my shaking shoulders as he wept into my back. Spring came to crouch next to us, holding us both tightly as we cried.

My chest felt like it was cracking open. My heart desperately tried to deny it. To convince me that he'd clutch my hand again and kiss me. Any second now, he'd chuckle at me for being so worried. Those breathtaking golden eyes would open, and that beautiful, deep voice would rumble through his chest.

Because it couldn't be true. The love of my life couldn't be dead. But no matter how hard I tried, I couldn't escape it.

He was gone. Ash was gone.

"I'm so sorry," Spring whispered, his voice thick with emotion. "He was—" He trailed off suddenly with a loud gasp. Blinding light flooded through the back of my eyelids.

I opened them, startled, and found the diamond on Ash's sternum glowing like a star. Ash's forehead flashed lava hot against my skin and I reeled back in shock.

"He's burning up!" I gasped. Spring sucked in a panicked breath.

"Oh shit!" he shouted. He snatched the other three stones off of Ash's body and grabbed the backs of our coats, tossing us away.

Rowan and I hit the ground and clutched each other tightly.

"Stay back!" Spring cried, rolling away.

Ash's body started to glow like molten metal. His skin ignited, and he was suddenly consumed by a blazing inferno. The flames stretched all the way to the ceiling and swirled around him, billowing out before vanishing as quickly as they had come.

Rowan and I sat up, clinging to each other. The whole world seemed to be holding its breath. A loud, startled inhale broke the silence and Ash suddenly sat up, panting, and clutching his chest.

"What the fuck just happened?" he demanded, looking around frantically. I let out a broken sob and ran, sliding on my knees and colliding with him.

"Ash!" I cried, wrapping my arms and legs around him and burying my face in his neck. His skin was warm against my cheek. Relief pulsed through me as Ash's chest rose and fell in my arms. His heart pounded behind his ribs and his gasping breaths tickled the hair on my neck.

Ash was alive.

His arms circled around me, and he held me tightly as a fresh wave of tears overtook me.

"I thought I lost you," I sobbed into his skin. My tears rolled down his collar as he clung to me.

"I thought you did too," he whispered.

I sat back on his thighs and took his face in my hand. Ash's skin had turned a bright, sunny shade of yellow and his hair shined in the light like spun gold. His golden eyes had lost every last trace of their brown and green hues. They looked like flecks of metal and glowed with power as they searched my face.

Rowan let out a sob and dropped down next to us. We wrapped our arms around him in a tight hug. I held out my other arm, beckoning Spring and pulling him into the group.

"You scared us for a moment there, Ash," he said. "Or rather, Lord Summer."

Ash chuckled as we detangled ourselves and stood up. He ran his hands across his sunny skin and brushed his fingers through his hair, revealing pointed ears. He lifted his shirt, running a finger across a thin, dark yellow scar on his stomach.

"Guess I'll never have to worry about being cold again," Ash grinned. His smile held all the force and the radiance of the sun.

I wound my arms around his neck and kissed him, my heart overflowing with too many emotions to count. He tasted like citrus and fire. He broke our kiss and held up the glowing diamond.

"Ready, my love?" Ash said. I stepped back and glanced nervously at Rowan. His face was deathly pale, and blood was still dripping onto the floor under his feet. Fear clenched my stomach.

"You go first, Ro. You look like you're about to pass out," I said. He nodded and wiped his hands on the only clean spot on his pants excitedly.

"I'm ready, Lord Summer," he grinned. He took the diamond from Ash who rolled his eyes and smiled. Spring handed Rowan the other three gems, planting a firm kiss on his lips, and drawing us away to a safe distance. Rowan arranged the stones carefully and dabbed one of his wounds.

"I pledge my body and spirit to the Ethereal Two. I ask them to grant me a heraldship in their service." Rowan's voice was clear and confident as he placed a drop of blood on each one.

Spring tensed, watching him carefully with bated breath. Immediately, the amethyst began to shine brightly. Spring stretched his hands out and threw up a stone wall as Rowan was consumed by a vicious, swirling wind. We clung to each other, pressing our backs to the wall as the howling wind threatened to knock us off our feet. Suddenly, the wind died away and Spring dropped his wall.

Rowan's skin had become a patchwork of orange, red, and yellow. The colors shifted back and forth like they were swaying in a soft breeze. His red hair had turned a vibrant orange, and his eyes were a deep, rich brown. Spring grinned and strode purposefully up to him, kissing him soundly.

"Hello, Lord Fall," he breathed, beaming.

Rowan smiled and kissed him again before turning to me and holding out the stones. Anxiety crept up my spine.

"Your turn, Lady Winter," Rowan winked. I reached for the stones, hesitating. I shot Ash a fearful look and he wrapped an arm around my shoulders, kissing my temple. His reassuring warmth seeped into my bones.

"I promise you," he whispered into my hair. "Do it."

My heart hammered wildly. I took a calming breath and summoned a small ice shard. I shot Ash another glance and sliced my finger, pressing it to each of the stones. My hands shook as I arranged them in my arms. They backed away slowly.

"I pledge my body and spirit to the Ethereal Two. I ask them to grant me a heraldship in their service." My voice wavered and I squeezed my eyes shut tight.

For a moment, nothing happened. The only sound was the blood pounding in my ears. Anxiety hit me like a tidal wave, and I held my breath, silently begging and pleading for something to happen. But it wasn't working. The Two didn't want me. I opened my eyes, and my heart broke in dismay.

Suddenly, a blistering cold tore through my very soul. The garnet began to glow like a hot coal pulled from a blazing fire and my body was encased in a large block of ice.

I couldn't move.

Then the inside of the block melted, and I found myself spinning rapidly through water, spiraling like a ship caught in a cyclone. I squeezed my eyes shut and fought the rising nausea. My feet slammed into solid ground, and I stopped spinning with a gasp.

Silence pressed in around me. Tentatively, I opened my eyes.

The whole world had disappeared, and I found myself standing before two massive thrones. Light flickered in the darkness all around me as I collapsed to my knees, looking up into the beaming faces of the figures seated before me. They stared down at me as I gaped, speechless.

One was a shining purple being, and the other was a swirling dark blue. My brain took a second to comprehend what I was seeing. I was looking up at the smiling faces of the Ethereal Two.

"Hello Lumi," the purple being chimed brightly. They patted their partner on the elbow. "She's perfect. Just like he said she would be." The purple being's voice echoed like thousands of voices blended together as one.

"He was right," the blue being agreed. Their voice reminded me of crackling storm clouds, the roiling sea, and the rumbling earth all rolled into one. They looked at me, their glowing blue eyes crinkling in a smile. "Our brand-new Lord Summer was quite insistent we choose you. Which we would've done anyways."

"Absolutely," the purple being agreed with a nod of their round head. They straightened excitedly and leaned closer. "So," they said, winking. "Do you have any questions for us before we begin?" I closed my mouth and got shakily to my feet.

"I'm honored to meet you," I croaked softly.

The Ethereal Two exchanged knowing smiles.

"No, dear," the blue being said. "We are eternally grateful to the four of you. These past twenty years have been horrible." They shuddered. "We're already trapped up here, unable to walk among our creations. But because of Kiora, we had to cut ourselves off further to prevent becoming corrupted."

"We thought when Kiora, Haedon, Mirela and Eli took the heraldships, our land would be properly taken care of. The Forsaken Isle had been neglected severely by the heralds before them," the purple being lamented. "Alas, we chose those heralds poorly as well. All except for Eli, that is," they added with a wide grin to their partner. "The poor thing has certainly had his moments, hasn't he?"

The blue being nodded in agreement.

"He told us about the dragons," I said quietly. The Two exchanged a quick glance.

"Just the dragons?" the blue being asked. "Nothing about what happened when he was human?"

I shook my head.

"Ah well," the purple being said. "That isn't our story to tell. But he's proven his heart. Which... By the way, my dear..." The purple being waved their hand and conjured a shimmering purple light.

"That is a message for our Lord Spring," the blue being said. "Will you make sure he gets it?"

I nodded. It floated towards me and landed in my outstretched hands. I clutched the ball of light to my chest. Even though I could see it, it felt like nothing. Like my hand was clenched around the air. I glanced back up at the immense beings before me and cleared my throat.

"Ash... is he... And... And Rowan..." I began.

Emotion clogged the words I tried to force out. The blue being understood and nodded.

"They are good as new. Don't worry."

"What about Spring?" I asked, wringing my hands. They nodded in unison.

"He will be just fine," the blue being replied. "The corruption didn't do any permanent damage and he got it all out of his system."

I blew out a breath, my shoulders sagging in relief. Tears stung my eyes, and I blinked them away as the purple being smiled kindly at me.

"Our new Lord Summer loves you very much. Though you probably already knew that," they said. "Your poor darling has been through so much already in his short life. It's a wonder that his heart has stayed as pure as it has."

"It's a good thing he *has* such a pure heart with that fire of his," the blue being remarked, giving their partner a knowing look. "That's a mistake we can't make again."

"What's wrong with his fire?" I asked, confused.

"Nothing's wrong," the purple being replied. "If he were a different person then there might've been a problem. But he has a good soul. His fire is just... formidable. That's all."

"Considering who his parents are, I'm not surprised," the blue being said. "And on top of that, we gave him dominion over fire too."

"Indeed. I pity the wayward soul that chooses to cross him," the purple being replied.

"What's that supposed to mean?" I said fiercely. "He doesn't have a malicious bone in his body!"

The purple being nodded. "Our point exactly, dear. We meant nothing by it. But your vehement defense of him is sweet," they grinned. I ducked my head apologetically.

"Sorry. Old habits, I guess," I mumbled, embarrassed. I paused and looked up at them, hesitating. "So... You know who his parents are? Were?"

"We know a lot about him. Some of which I don't think *he* knows," the blue being replied. "But again. That isn't our story to tell. All we can tell you is that his heart is a good one."

"So, if there's darkness in someone's heart, they can't be a herald?" I asked. The purple being tilted their head to the side.

"Well..." they explained, "Everyone has a bit of darkness. That's human nature. Your darling has so much good in his heart that the darkness is balanced out. But there are some that let the darkness consume them. Such as Kiora did. And giving the heraldship to a Cosmic consumed by too much darkness, like your father for example, would be extremely dangerous." I blinked.

"What?" I said, stunned.

The Two glanced at each other.

"You didn't know?" the blue being asked. I opened my mouth, but no words came out. The floor dropped out from under me.

"Oh dear," the purple being said, sympathetically. "We are so sorry to drop that on you. We thought you knew. Cosmic ability is genetic."

"No," I said. Shock and confusion swirled through my mind as I shook my head in disbelief. "My father can't be Cosmic. He *hates* Cosmics. My father is a farmer. He farms thermal crops like potatoes and... and..."

"A thermal crop?" The blue being repeated, confused. "Darling, there's never been such a thing."

"No... Yes, there are," I asserted with a shake of my head. A small part of me piped up, reminding me who I was talking to. Who I was arguing with. But the stubborn part of my brain had a hold of my mouth. "They grow really fast. And they use the thermal energy from the volcanoes, so they don't need sunlight. I've seen them." I looked up at them and they both shook their heads at me.

"No, dear," the purple being said softly. "All plants need sunlight to grow. Unless they are made to grow somewhere without it." My mind reeled with questions.

"But... but he—" I stammered. "He can't be..."

All of the pieces started rapidly falling into place and a vicious anger bubbled through me. Those crops were the only thing that sustained Haven during the long winter. They were the back bone of my father's whole empire. If he were challenged, it could've toppled everything he was trying to maintain.

I sucked in a sharp breath. The hatred for Cosmics... The desperation to murder my best friend... So many things suddenly started making sense. I wanted to rage and scream. But I pushed the thoughts aside, looking up at the Two instead. First things first.

"Sorry," I huffed. "I guess he and I have some things to discuss. But I'm ready." I squared my shoulders.

"Are you sure you're okay?" the purple being asked cautiously.

"Yes," I said firmly, nodding once.

"Okay. Well, before we offer you the heraldship, there's a few things you need to know," the blue being said. "The heraldship grants you awesome power. So, we have placed some restrictions on it. Your power will be cut off when you leave your Isle. Or if your stone is removed from the throne. You will have a few days to put it back before we take any action. But if you're neglecting your post, we will intervene.

"If you try to remove another herald's stone from the throne, it will flood you with corruption. So be mindful when visiting. And you cannot stay with another herald at the tower for longer than six days at a time. Otherwise, your powers will tangle, and you will both suffer the consequences."

"You will have a shield around your mind to protect your power from other heralds," the purple being added, patting their partner on the elbow. "And now, thanks to the actions of the previous Lady Winter, we have decided it's for the best that we further restrict your movements during your cycle."

"Further?" I tilted my head.

"Yes," the purple being sighed. "It used to be that you could leave the tower for two days at a time every week. But Kiora took advantage of that to spill so much innocent blood. So, from now on, a herald cannot leave their stone while it sits on the throne."

"Okay," I said, nodding.

"There's one last thing you should know," the blue being said. "If you accept our heraldship, you will not age. And you will not be able to have a child." I paused, staring up at them.

"Ever?" I asked.

"Ever," the purple being replied grimly. "Your body's reproductive cycles will cease. You can try all you like," they added with a small smile. "But you cannot produce a child. No herald can."

"There is a way to produce a spirit between two heralds," the blue being said. "But it is forbidden."

"Why?" Unease settled in my chest as they exchanged a dark look.

"The spirit created would be a force of chaos and destruction," the purple being said with a small shudder.

"Oh," I said, pressing my lips together. "Then we won't do that. Um..." I fidgeted slightly, my cheeks heating in embarrassment. "Do they... I mean. Does..."

"No," the blue being chuckled. "The spirit is a product of your power. Not your body. Sex will not create one."

"They come from our powers? Like the golems?" I asked. The blue being shook their heads.

"No. Golems are just an extension of your power. The moment you stop thinking about them, they will disappear. The creatures we're talking about take pieces of your power from you and become a new entity altogether. They can use herald abilities and have been the cause of a lot of strife in the past. So, they are forbidden."

"Oh. I see," I said, hesitating. "Does... Does Ash know? That he and I can't..." I trailed off.

"He was adamant that it did not matter to him in the slightest. As long as you were okay with it," the blue being said.

I couldn't help but smile. Of course, that was his answer.

"Having a child always felt like something I'd be forced into," I admitted. "If things were different, then I would've liked to share that with Ash. But... I'm okay with it. As long as I have him."

"Are you sure?" the blue being asked.

I nodded.

The Two exchanged another glance before the purple being patted their lap excitedly.

"Once you accept and the Forsaken Isle has four heralds, we can start rebuilding. So, without further ado," they said gleefully and cleared their throat, sitting up straighter.

"You have been brought before the Ethereal Two," the purple being thundered. The very air around me shook. "We have judged you pure in heart and worthy of our heraldship."

"We offer you dominion over the powers of water, ice and snow," the blue being's voice rumbled like thunder through my soul. "Will you forsake your Cosmic power and accept the heraldship of winter?" My heart raced with fear and excitement.

"I accept your heraldship," I said. The purple being beamed and gave me a small thumbs up.

"Then let it be so," the blue being pronounced.

The Two held out their hands in unison. Purple and blue light swirled around me.

Suddenly, I felt like I was falling.

"Good luck!" The purple being called gleefully as I plunged down into the water. The ice around me shattered and vanished. I found myself back in the throne room, dry, and blinking in the light.

CHAPTER THIRTY-FOUR

ROWAN

The ice vanished, leaving a dazed Lumi standing in the center of the room, blinking rapidly in the light. Her hair had turned snow white, and her light purple skin sparkled like early morning frost on the window.

She reached up, sucking in a breath as her fingers probed the tip of her pointed ear. Her deep, ocean blue eyes glowed with power as she glanced around the room.

"Lumi!" Ash cried, rushing forward, and sweeping her into his arms. "Are you all right?"

"I think so," she said, stretching her hand out to examine her purple skin. She turned to Eli and smiled broadly. "I have something for you."

He raised his eyebrows as she opened her fist and released a small ball of violet light. It flashed, and the purple being's voice echoed through the throne room.

"Lord Spring," they said, "It's time for color to return to our land. And for you to forgive the ghosts in your past."

I smiled, my mind flashing back to standing at their feet.

"*He is good,*" the purple being had said to me. "*Despite what he may think of himself sometimes. And his love for you is true. Be good to each other.*"

Eli's deep green eyes filled with tears, and he wiped them away quickly. "I could not agree more," he said, scooping me up into his arms and kissing me deeply. My stomach fluttered. He pulled away and faced Lumi, who placed the emerald gently in his outstretched palm.

It started to glow under his touch. He stepped up onto the seat and placed his stone on the small platform at the top.

There was an immediate shift in the air. Purple and blue light flooded from the throne and flashed around the room. The ice and the black sludge marring the walls faded away.

Eli rolled out his shoulders and closed his eyes, letting his power sweep across the land. The air suddenly smelled sweeter, and the frigid edge vanished, replaced with a soft, warm breeze. He opened his eyes and they glowed brighter than the sun.

The tower was slowly repairing itself around us. The black throne had vanished and was replaced by pristine white marble. More purple and blue light swirled about in small circles, leaving behind plush reading chairs and a large, soft bed with an armoire and nightstand that were sectioned from the rest of the room by partitions.

Eli hopped off the throne and stretched a hand out to me. I took it and let him lead me out onto the freshly mended balcony. Ash and Lumi followed, arm in arm. Eli stood behind me and wrapped his arms around my waist.

Together, the four of us stood and watched the snow begin to melt for the first time in twenty years. Icicles began to drip. Shoots of green appeared on the tree branches.

Eli kissed my temple and swept his hand in a wide arc. The snow vanished from the grounds around the tower, and the area was suddenly covered in a sea of huge, yellow blooms, their faces upturned to the brilliant blue sky.

Sunflowers. It was the most beautiful thing I'd ever seen. My heart swelled and I choked back a small sob.

"I love you too," I said quietly, and he kissed my head again, pulling me away from the railing.

I looked up at him, tracing a finger along his wrist. I didn't want to ask the question that formed in my mind. But I knew I had too. "How long can I stay with you?" I murmured. He sighed, frowning.

"At most, only six days at a time. And never with your stone," he said, kissing the tip of my nose. "But you only have to spend three nights away before you can come back."

"Didn't the Two tell you about the limits on our powers?" Lumi asked. I shook my head.

"They didn't tell me either," Ash said.

"I'll fill you in later," she replied before turning to Eli. "But they told me there's a new one. We can't leave the stones anymore." Eli sighed and nodded solemnly.

"I had a feeling something like that was going to happen," he said sadly.

Lumi handed the diamond to Ash and held out the amethyst for me to take. As soon as my fingers brushed the surface, it glowed brightly.

It was as if it were happy.

Eli kissed my cheek and sighed. "They can't stay here. You have to take them back to the altar in the palace," he said, glancing at Ash and Lumi. "Having them here with mine on the throne is dangerous."

"We don't have to walk back, do we?" Ash frowned. Eli chuckled and shook his head.

"No, no. You're all at full power, so you can take the Cosmic Bridge. One of you can open it from here to the Crossroads Temple, and then you can open it from there to Nature's Palace. You just have to hold hands to use it together," he said, kissing mine for emphasis.

My chest tightened at the thought of leaving him.

Lumi shot me a sly, knowing smile before her gaze drifted innocently to Eli.

"Do we all have to leave now? Or can, say, two of us take the stones back?" she asked casually.

Eli grinned wickedly and my heart started racing.

Sometimes, I could swear Lumi was a mind reader.

"You don't all have to go," he replied, his arms tightening around me. "Because the stones were here, you all do have to go for the reset. But it doesn't have to be right this second. There are markers on the altar to show you which stone goes where, and I have a feeling the Two have already made some repairs there as well."

"Well then," Ash said, catching on and slipping Lumi's hand into the crook of his elbow. "Why don't we bring the stones back? Ro can stay here and make sure you get settled in all right. He can meet up with us in a few hours or so." Eli's grin widened and he nodded vigorously.

"A few more hours won't hurt him. And I wouldn't mind some company while I get... *settled*," he replied. His eyes locked with mine and stole the breath from my chest.

"Terrific. We'll catch you later, Ro," Lumi chimed in, taking the stone from my hand. I nodded, swallowing hard.

Ash winked at me as he and Lumi turned towards the railing, hand in hand.

"Okay now, let me see." Lumi furrowed her brow. She raised her hands and a strip of shimmering purple light appeared in the air, streaking off towards the forest. She raised her eyebrows at Eli.

"That's the bridge," he said, his fingers clutching the hem of my tunic. I felt his muscles twitch as though he were restraining himself from yanking it over my head. "A lot of things will come to you much easier now."

"Good," Lumi said. She grinned at us before stepping onto the Cosmic Bridge with Ash. "We'll come and visit you soon, Spring," she said, leaning her head against Ash's shoulder.

"I look forward to it, Lady Winter. Lord Summer," he smiled.

Lumi flicked her hand. There was a deafening crack, and they were gone, leaving us standing on the balcony alone. Heat simmered in my blood.

Eli pressed his lips against my neck and let his fingers slip under my tunic to caress my bare skin. I grinned, leaning into him.

"What now?" I asked. My heart pounded as his fingers drifted higher to trail lightly across my chest.

"Now I'm going to make you mine, Sunflower," he whispered into my neck.

"Hmm," I said, closing my eyes, "Can't."

"I can't?"

I felt a smile against my skin and shuddered. He kissed up my neck, letting his tongue follow his lips, scorching my skin.

"Nope."

"Why not?" He pressed his lips against my ear.

"Cause it's too late. I'm already yours," I breathed, reaching back to rake my fingers through his hair.

"I see," he chuckled, letting his other hand settle low on my stomach. Every nerve in my body buzzed at his touch. "In that case, allow me to properly worship my Lord Fall. If he would like me to." His fingertips dipped lower on my stomach, toying with the waistband of my pants and fire seared through my blood.

"Very much so," I said breathless with want, tilting my spinning head back onto his shoulder.

"Gladly," Eli whispered, letting his hand trail back up to my tunic. He slipped it over my head, planting gentle kisses across my back that sent a hard shiver rolling through me. He stroked his fingertips across my bare skin, pausing suddenly as he brushed over a rough spot on my shoulder.

"What is it?" I said, turning to meet his eyes.

He looked crestfallen and my heart lurched. He let out a soft, anguished sound, tracing over four small scars on my shoulder.

"This is where..." he whispered, his voice breaking. He took a small step away from me as tears filled his eyes, pressing a hand to his mouth.

I frowned and looked down. Small scars spattered my arms from my wrists up to my shoulders. I counted twelve in all. There were two more on my chest and three on my stomach.

"Look what she did to you." His lilted voice was filled with despair. I closed the distance between us and reached up to cradle his jaw.

"And you saved me. Just like I knew you would. And I'm not the only one she hurt. She did a number on you, too," I said, taking in his pink skin and the loose green curls falling over his forehead. He nodded and pressed his lips to mine.

I opened my mouth to him, desperate to chase away the shadows gathering in his eyes.

Eli shuddered, sinking into our kiss with a sigh. One hand pressed into the center of my back and the other locked into my hair.

He deepened our kiss, letting his tongue gently explore mine. His kisses were measured at first. Soft, sweet, and slow. I flicked my tongue across his bottom lip, and he groaned, pressing his lips harder against mine. His tongue plundered my mouth as our kiss turned urgent and gloriously messy.

I locked my fingers into the front of his torn shirt, desperate to hold him closer as he hooked his thumbs into the waistband of my pants and shoved them lightly off my hips along with my undergarment. They pooled at my feet, and I kicked them and my boots away.

Eli's moan was almost feral as his hands slid across my naked body. Heat coursed through me, and I clutched his robes tighter.

"Hey," I gasped, breaking our kiss to arch an eyebrow at him. "That's not fair. You have all those clothes on."

Eli chuckled, kissing down the side of my neck. His hands slid down to grip my hips.

"Never fear, my love," he murmured against my collarbone. He stepped forward, walking me backwards until my back found a wall. "You will feel properly and thoroughly worshiped when I'm through with you. I promise."

"I believe you," I said.

His lips burned a trail down my chest as he slowly sank to his knees before me.

My heart started racing. "Oh! Eli, wait! I've never... No one's ever..." I stammered, eyes wide with desire as his knees hit the floor and he looked up at me. His fiery gaze branded my very soul.

I gasped, pressing my palms flat against the wall behind me for stability. I tried again but the words wouldn't come out. Somehow, Eli understood anyway.

He tilted his head slightly and reached up, letting his fingers caress my swollen cock almost absentmindedly.

I sucked in a sharp breath as his touch sent lightning coursing through my veins.

"Never?" he said, his eyebrows knitting together. "Never ever?"

"N-No," I mumbled, blushing. His fingers were making it difficult to think straight as they stroked up and down slowly.

"Oh, absolutely not," he said seriously, shaking his head. "I'll have to fix that immediately. Unless—" His hand stilled. "Unless you don't want me too?" I blinked, trying desperately to focus.

"No, I do. I really, *really* do. I just, I mean, what if I..." My head reeled as his fingers began moving again. "I don't want you to... think... Oh... Fuck."

His chuckle was low and dangerous. "Don't want me to think what, Sunflower?" I sucked in a steadying breath that did absolutely nothing for my spinning head.

"I just don't want you to... I don't know... Hate it? I mean, what if I don't... taste... good." My voice got smaller and smaller with each word, and I cringed at myself. Eli's wicked grin was blinding.

"Would you like me to find out?" He arched a thin eyebrow at me, and his glowing eyes flared.

I nodded, biting my lower lip anxiously.

Eli kept that intense gaze locked on my face as he leaned forward and dragged his tongue down the underside of my cock.

My entire existence narrowed to the feel of his mouth as he ran his tongue back up and sat back on his heels. "Ah," he grinned, sighing deeply. "See that, Sunflower? Nothing to worry about. Sweeter than a strawberry."

Words failed me. I suddenly realized I wasn't breathing and sucked in a deep, jagged breath.

Eli chuckled.

"Eli..." I managed to croak finally. "I... Oh..." My head fell back against the wall with a muffled thump. "You do that and this... This will be over way, way, *way* too soon," I rasped breathlessly. His eyes blazed a little brighter.

"Oh, my sweet Sunflower. I have so much to show you." His handsome, upturned face caught the light and he looked positively ethereal. "When I told Lumi that things are much easier now, I didn't just mean your powers. Your body will be much more... *receptive*. When it wants to be.“ He smiled mischievously.

"Receptive?" I repeated slowly. "So, no... um..." I trailed off, flexing my fingers for emphasis. He shook his head.

"Nope. We don't have to. But I will if you want me to."

My heart leapt into my throat. A shadow from the past tried to force its way into my mind and I tensed, pushing it away. I refused to let anything from my previous life ruin this moment for me.

"No," I mumbled, shaking my head slightly. "I... I don't want to."

"Then we don't have to," he said gently. I stifled a sigh of relief that he didn't press the issue. "It's not necessary. And you will recover from fatigue much faster."

"How much faster?" I asked. His grin stretched wider.

"Why don't I show you?" He arched an eyebrow at me again and I nodded.

Before I could draw another breath, Eli slipped his mouth around me and began working his tongue in a strong, steady rhythm. My soul left my body. My breathing turned ragged and shallow as I tangled my fingers through those luscious green curls. My heart raced and my muscles all began to tighten rapidly. I'd never felt anything so deliciously magical. Eli's tongue rolled across my skin and sent jolts of fire tearing through me.

I let out a small, strangled noise.

Eli's groan reverberated around my cock, sending me sliding towards the brink. Stars wheeled before my eyes.

"Eli... Oh fuck, Eli, I'm—“ I managed to gasp.

But then he looked up at me through his lashes. Locking those glowing green eyes on my face.

I came undone. Never before had I ever felt something so intense and so earth shaking. The force of my release overwhelmed my senses and sent my head spinning. His fingers dug into my hips. That glorious tongue never slowed its devastating pace until I finally came down, gasping and shaking. Eli sat back on his heels again, eyebrows raised as he watched my face carefully. I tried to focus on him, but my knees suddenly wobbled. I tipped sideways and slid down the wall, landing in front of him in a panting, speechless heap.

"Sunflower?" he grinned, tilting his head.

My answer was a long, shuddering moan.

He chuckled. "Was that okay?"

I moaned again.

"Good." He took my hand, gently kissing my knuckles while I slowly regained the ability to function.

"Eli, I… I have no words…" I blinked at him. "Do… Do you want me to…" He cut me off with a shake of his head.

"Yes, but later." He smirked, dragging me to my feet and pressing me back into the wall. "I'm not done with you yet."

Heat coiled once again in my stomach. He ran his fingers up my sides and raised my arms over my head before pinning my wrists with one hand. I could feel his excitement pressed into me and I throbbed in response, growing painfully hard against him. I looked down, surprised I was ready so quickly. He winked.

"Now," he grinned, pressing his body tighter against mine. "A certain fantasy was used to torture me a few days ago. Do you remember it?" I shuddered as his voice dropped low. His eyes were dark with promise.

"Who would do such a thing to you?" I said, feigning surprise. He let his fingers circle my collarbone before drifting down my stomach.

"I wonder," he whispered, brushing his fingertips against my cock. I gasped and arched towards him unconsciously. He ducked his head, lightly biting the shell of my pointed ear which, I discovered with a thrill, was very sensitive. "Do you remember?" he hissed, wrapping his fingers around my cock.

I groaned and rolled my hips, sliding further into his hand.

He smiled. "That's the one." He shifted, rubbing his excitement against my leg as he did so. My head spun. "I've been thinking about it for days now," he moaned against my skin. I bit my lip.

"Oh?" I gasped, tilting my head to give him better access to my neck. Eli's tongue flicked across my racing pulse.

"Please, Sunflower," he whispered.

I shuddered and slowly rocked my hips forward again.

He smiled and loosened his grip ever so slightly so that I could slide across his palm easier. I moved my hips in a slow, gentle motion while he nipped and kissed my neck, letting his tongue trail over my skin. His hand began working in a delicious rhythm with my hips, stroking down the length of me while I thrust into his fingers.

Fire scorched through me as my muscles began to tighten and ache. I sped up my pace, groaning as release began to build alarmingly fast. He let go of my wrists, letting his hand trail down to cup my ass. I tangled my fingers in his green curls as his teeth grazed my neck.

"Eli," I moaned, pressing my lips into his hair. "Oh... Eli!" Release barreled through me, hard and fast. I cried out, clinging to him as I throbbed in his hand, gasping his name. My body calmed and I stopped shuddering with a soft moan lacing my hands behind his head.

He groaned against my neck and wrenched me away from the wall, dragging me over to the bed and shoving me onto it. My back hit the soft sheets as he tore the shredded tunic from his body, tossing what was left to the floor before kicking away his pants. My breath hitched.

Eli was a glorious sight to behold. All hard lines and lean muscle that I was itching to dig my fingers into. I drank him in, pausing just below his waist with a shiver. He was a rather impressive size. I could feel the power thrumming through him as he stretched over me, claiming my mouth with his.

I wrapped my legs around his waist, and he groaned as he rubbed his swollen cock against me. He drew back with a shudder, and we locked eyes. The intensity of his gaze made me temporarily forget how to breathe. He held himself over me on his elbows, his face inches from mine.

"I love you," he said. The sudden sincerity in his voice made my heart flutter.

"I love you too," I replied, reaching up to stroke his face.

"I just need you to know," he began, pressing his forehead to mine. "I've never felt this way about anyone. I've never wanted to give away my heart. But you?" He kissed the tip of my nose. "I want to give you everything. I'd pull the moon from the sky for you." His fingers stroked lovingly through my hair.

I blinked away the tears swelling in my eyes, my heart too full for words.

Eli kissed my brow before locking eyes with me again, grinning. "Before we go through with this, I need you to understand. You aren't my first choice. You're my *only* choice. There is no one else for me, Sunflower. I just want you."

I wasn't breathing. My heart could barely handle the emotions raging through me. How long had I waited? How long had I hoped for someone to say those words to me? For the first time, I was someone's one and only. It was a beautiful, overwhelming feeling.

"Eli..." I managed to say, choking back a sob. "Eli, I love you so much... You have no idea what that—" I shook my head and took a shuddering breath. I needed to tell him. Needed him to understand what his words meant to me. But my voice was stuck. Eli smiled.

"I love you too, Sunflower." He leaned in, kissing me softly. His hand trailed over my thigh, wincing as he found more small scars. He sat back to peer at my legs, running his hands across my skin.

"Oh no," he whispered. "Oh, my poor sweet Sunflower, I'm so—" His face fell, and I sat up, catching his wrists.

"No," I said firmly. "Please, Eli. Don't do that to yourself." I reached out to cradle his sharp jaw. "I'm fine, my love. I promise you I am." He frowned, his eyes still on the scars marring my skin.

"There's so many."

I drew him closer and lifted his chin so that he'd meet my eyes. "Eli, I'm all right. See?" I took his hand, pressing it over my racing heart. "Feel that? I'm okay. You saved me."

"No." He shook his head. "You saved *me*." He laced his fingers with mine and brought them to his own chest. His heart was thundering. "You never let go," he breathed. "She almost had me. It must've hurt so much. But you never let go."

"Of course not. I finally found my storybook prince and I wasn't going to let her take him from me," I smiled. I cupped his face, pulling him to me as I laid back. My lips parted his and I held him closer, determined to wipe the painful memories from his mind. I kissed him deeply, until his breath came in rough gasps, and he drew back, gripping me tightly. Forgetting all about the scars. His lips were parted slightly, and his eyes were wild with need.

I bit my lip and his eyes flared. "Eli, please," I whispered.

He reached down between us, guiding himself and filling me with a long, slow thrust.

I cried out, smiling as he froze to savor the sensation of our bodies connecting.

"Rowan..." he gasped.

I shuddered against him. He started to move, slow and hard, ravaging my mouth with his as my muscles tightened. I gasped, throbbing against his stomach as he pressed into me. I tilted further and he moaned my name in response, locking his arms around me as he drove into me as deep as he could go. Lightning flashed through me.

"Eli," I moaned as another release built hard and fast. "Eli, I'm... oh, fuck!" I gasped desperately, locking my fingers into his hair.

He groaned through a clenched jaw as he pressed his forehead to my shoulder and pulled me tighter to him. He rolled his hips forward hard, and my soul fractured.

Nothing else mattered except for the feel of his body and the sweet pressure building in the very fabric of my existence. He watched my face hungrily as I bowed into him, overwhelmed by the bliss, and needing to get him impossibly closer all at the same time. I started throbbing hard against his stomach. The pleasure coursing through me sharpened unbearably and I cried out.

My entire body shook with the force of my orgasm as it stole the breath from me, spilling onto the both of us. He rode it out, gasping. His pace stuttered and became more urgent. I moaned his name over and over as my mind shattered from the intensity of my release.

"Oh, Sunflower, I love it when you say my name like that. Fuck, it drives me so crazy." he groaned, locking eyes with me.

I tried to speak, but a soft, blissful moan escaped my lips instead. My knees trembled against his hips as he sucked in a shuddering breath and dropped his head to kiss me hungrily. I felt him throb as his pace became rough and frantic.

"I love you," he moaned against my lips. Over and over, he kept repeating those three beautiful words. Each time he said it, he was a little louder and sounded a little more out of breath. "I love you. I love you. I love you."

"I love you too, Eli," I groaned.

He shuddered hard and slammed himself deep into me. Our lips crashed together, and I opened his mouth with mine, letting my tongue explore his as he went spiraling over the edge.

He locked his hands into mine, crying out against my kiss as his orgasm raced through his shivering body.

I held him through it until he finally stilled.

Eli pressed his forehead into my neck, panting. I reached up and stroked his hair away from his eyes.

"You were right," I murmured, tucking a green curl behind his pointed ear. "I feel very properly worshiped."

He laughed breathlessly, withdrawing before he hopped off the bed and disappeared from sight.

I missed his touch immediately.

He returned moments later with a warm cloth and began to lovingly clean me up. I grinned shyly, stretching out as he got to work. Watching him made my heart flutter and a lump of emotion form in my throat. Sex with him was phenomenal, but this was a whole new level of intimacy that I'd never experienced before. And I loved it so much. I felt like I was cared for. Like I was cherished. Every other sexual encounter had ended in one of two ways. With a cold indifference or with me being shoved from the room and hidden away.

Eli moved quickly, cleaning off my skin before turning to his own. My stomach jolted as the cloth moved and I caught sight of my body. The orange, red, and yellow patches were still swaying gently back and forth across my skin.

I frowned.

"What's wrong, Sunflower?"

I glanced up as he drew the cloth across his stomach, watching me carefully.

"I'm gonna have to get used to this." I trailed my fingers across a large orange patch on my stomach. "Will they ever stay still?"

"The colors? Not that I know of," he replied. "But the colors are like the fall leaves dancing in the breeze. Just wait, Sunflower. Your cycle is truly remarkable. Just like you." He kissed me softly and laid down, curling his body around me, and pressing his chest into my back.

I sighed and stroked the arm he draped around my waist.

I wanted to stay wrapped up in his arms forever. Even if I knew I couldn't. The thought of leaving made my heart ache. So, I pushed it away and focused instead on the lovely murmurings that had set my heart racing. Something in particular stuck out in my mind and I paused mid-stroke.

"Can you actually do that?" I asked, suddenly.

"Can I do what, Sunflower?"

"The moon." I shifted closer to him. "Can you actually pull the moon out of the sky?" I felt his smile stretch across the back of my neck.

"Are you asking for it?"

"No, no," I said quickly. "I'm just... curious, I guess."

"If you wanted the moon then yes, my love. I could pull it from the sky for you. Especially now when my stone is on the throne and I'm at my strongest. But our power is locked to the isle, so it would need to be directly above us." I gaped, gripping his arm.

"Have you ever actually tried?" I breathed and he sighed sadly.

"Once. But it was an accident. I wasn't actually trying."

"Wow," I said, resuming my idle circles across his arm. "That's incredible, Eli! I knew you were powerful. But—"

He chuckled and pulled me a little closer.

"I'm not the only one who has awesome power," he said, kissing my shoulder. "Yours can level cities. We'll have time to practice with it but trust me, Sunflower. You are truly remarkable."

"You keep saying that," I smiled, and he chuckled again.

"Because it's true. And now I have forever to prove it to you."

"I really like the sound of that," I sighed happily.

"Me too," he replied, snuggling me in close. "You're all mine. Forever." His words made me pause.

"I've never been someone's forever," I admitted, tracing idle circles on his wrist. Emotion clogged my throat, and I took a shaky breath to muster my courage. "I've never been anything to anyone. Just a toy that gets thrown away after a few fucks."

His arms went rigid around me, and his sharp, angry exhale sent a tiny shiver down my spine.

"I fucking hate that so much," he hissed softly. "It disgusts me. I swear to the Ethereal above that if I ever meet those assholes I'll..." He paused and took a steadying breath. "Sunflower, I swear on my life. You will never *ever* feel like that again." He pressed his lips to my neck. "You'll see."

"Eli, I don't doubt that you love me," I began but he shook his head.

"It's more than that, Sunflower. I want to know everything there is to know about you. I want to know your favorite book. Your favorite color. Your favorite food. I want to know what your favorite flower is so I can grow them for you all the time. I want to know what makes your heart race and those gorgeous lips of yours part with desire." He reached up and trailed his thumb over my bottom lip for emphasis.

I couldn't breathe. Silent tears rolled down my face and I wiped them away quickly.

"Eli, I—" Words failed me, and I shook my head, unable to say anything more. I was so overcome by emotion that my lips trembled against his thumb. He planted soft kisses along the back of my neck.

"You're not a toy to me," he whispered. "And no one's going to treat you like one ever again." I pressed my hands over my eyes, fighting back the tears spilling down my face. Eli tightened his hold on me. "I'm sorry," he murmured. "I didn't mean to make you cry."

"No," I replied thickly. "No, I'm just—" I huffed out a sharp breath. "I've never felt like this before."

"Me either," he replied, peppering my shoulder with kisses. "I've never wanted someone so much. But I think you stole my heart the second I met you."

"Well, you can't have it back. I'm keeping it," I said, smiling meekly.

"Good. It's all yours." He grinned against my skin. We laid there for a few more minutes, holding each other like we were never letting go. Finally, I let out a soft sigh.

"So..." I wiped my eyes again, sniffing. "Before I forget..." I held up a hand, counting off on my fingers. "My favorite book is called *Phantom in the Dark.* My favorite color is blue. I don't really have a favorite food yet, but I have a feeling that will change. My favorite flower... I really wanna say a sunflower, but definitely a rose. For obvious reasons. And as for the rest..." I trailed off nervously. "No one's ever cared enough to stick around so I could find out. So... I honestly don't know. I know what I like in books but when it comes to the real thing..." I shrugged.

"Well, I'll fix that," he replied confidently. "We'll find out together."

My heart swelled at the thought. But my bliss was short lived as I remembered I still had to leave soon. Already a small, uncomfortable pressure was building behind my eyes.

"I don't want to leave you here alone," I said, frowning.

"I know, Sunflower," he whispered, pressing a kiss to the back of my neck. "I don't want you to go either."

"What would happen if I stay?" I pouted, linking my fingers with his.

"Your power will start to flare," he replied grimly. "It will tangle with mine, and then the cycles will be all messed up for the world."

"Even without my stone here?"

"It will take a few days longer, but... yes," he said, kissing my neck again. "Then we'd have to stay away from each other for a whole year until our powers untangle themselves."

I blanched and shook my head. "That's so long! Why?"

Eli sighed again. "Because my power is locked to the tower. So, tangling it with yours would be much more intense. If we tangled our power outside of here, it would only have to be a few days."

"Does that happen a lot?" I raised my eyebrow.

"No," he replied, shaking his head. "Outside of here, we would have to force it. But from what I understand, it hurts like crazy."

"Oh," I said. "Yeah, no. None of that. I don't wanna do that."

"I agree," he laughed, brushing his lips against my skin.

"Fine," I huffed grumpily, rolling to face him. "I guess I can handle a few days if you can."

"Sunflower, I waited for six hundred years to find you," he said. "And if I had to, I'd wait thousands more."

The sincerity in his voice made my breath catch in my throat as his eyes roved over my face. A sharp pain rose behind my eyes, and I winced.

"Let's just stick with three nights," I said as the pain receded. "Besides, it'll give me a chance to raid the palace library for books to read to you."

"Mmm, that sounds wonderful."

I have no idea how long we laid there curled together, caressing and kissing. But it wasn't until another sharp pain sliced through my skull that I sat up with a deep, unhappy sigh.

"I'm going to miss you," I said. The pain receded slower this time, leaving behind a dull ache.

"I'll miss you too," he replied, kissing me on the shoulder.

"I'm gonna hate not being able to talk to you," I grumbled, scrubbing a frustrated hand over my face. The ache in my head was growing sharper.

"Oh..." Eli said. "Well, I gave you my heart. And you gave me yours." His smile spread across his face, and I heard his voice clear as a bell in my mind. *You can talk to me whenever you want to.*

I grinned in relief for a brief moment before wincing at another sharp stab of pain. "I guess I should go," I grumbled. He frowned and kissed me softly.

"I'm sorry. But it's only for three nights." He brushed my messy curls back from my forehead. "Unless you don't want to come back," he added with a sly smirk. I scoffed and bit his bare shoulder playfully.

"Shut up," I grinned, rolling off the bed and ambling reluctantly over to the wall for my clothes. He slipped his pants on and lifted the tatters of his shirt.

"Ah... Right... I guess I was a little eager... When you come back, would you mind?" he asked, tossing the scraps aside. I pulled my pants over my hips, grimacing at the dried blood and nodded.

"Of course," I said, yanking my tunic over my head. He wrapped me up in his arms. We kissed for a long while, drawing out my goodbye as we inched our way to the balcony.

"Fine," I grumbled, waving a hand to summon the Cosmic Bridge. "I'm going..."

He laughed and planted one last kiss on my lips before I made myself step onto the shimmering light.

"I love you, Eli," I said. His smile lit up his handsome face.

"I love you, Rowan," he replied.

I sighed. My heart lurched and I activated the bridge, racing away before I could change my mind. The trees below zipped past at lightning speed, and I suddenly found myself standing in an opulent temple.

The ache in the back of my head vanished instantly. I took a deep breath and paused to look around at the room. The marble walls were carved with depictions of the four of us.

Eli was smiling, surrounded by all manner of blooms. Rocks floated over his head and clutched close to his heart was a large, radiant sunflower. Ash held fire in both hands, crowned by the shimmering rays of the sun. A thick chain was wrapped around his neck and, hanging from it, was a small snowflake. My own face smiled back at me. Leaves danced around my head and a rose was tucked behind my ear. On the last wall was Lumi, her face gleeful as snow fell around her and water circled both of her hands. A sun pendant hung from a thin chain around her neck.

It was poetic. Here in the Crossroads, each one of us got to stare at the person we loved. We never had to be separated.

My heart started to ache. I missed my Eli.

Has it been three days yet? His voice rang out in my mind clear as crystal.

I smiled and closed my eyes.

I miss you so much already.

I miss you too, he said. *I promise I'll make it up to you.* Images of sweet and salacious things filled my mind.

Tease, I hissed, and he laughed.

I sighed and opened the bridge again, stepping carefully onto it and racing away swiftly. The mountains rushed up to meet me and I found myself standing at the front gate of Nature's Palace a moment later.

Only, it looked much different than the last time I saw it. I gasped and pressed my fingers to my lips. The palace had been remarkably transformed. It stood, sparkling and opulent in the sunlight. Pristine white stone and marble towers scraped the sky with windows scattered across them that glistened like diamonds.

Eli, I called out, *Can you see the palace?* I felt something gently shift in my head.

It looks beautiful, he breathed.

I can't wait to see that garden of yours.

Eli chuckled. *No wait necessary, my sweet Sunflower.*

I got the overwhelming sense that he was near and blinked. The air was filled with a sweet fragrance, and I suddenly found myself surrounded by flowers of every size and color imaginable.

Oh, Eli! I exclaimed, clutching my heart. *It's amazing.* I felt him smiling as I strolled through the garden, stopping to smell just about every flower that lined the path. I was so absorbed in the blooms that I didn't immediately notice someone was standing by the large oak doors until they shifted.

"Oh!" I looked up in surprise. In the back of my mind, I felt Eli's prickly barb of fear. Three men were standing by the door, waiting.

Large crates stood open behind them. The one in the center smirked and stepped forward with a deep bow. I smiled in recognition.

"Vallath," I said, smiling. "Nice to see you again."

"You as well, Lord Fall," he said, winking as he straightened. "My cousins and I are hoping to make good on your word. This is Cadmus and Finnigan." He gestured to the two young men behind him.

They inclined their heads politely.

"Of course," I said, gesturing towards the doors. "Please. You came quickly."

"First time anyone has ever accused me of that," Vallath grinned. His violet eyes flashed mischievously. "But yes. The council is impatient, so we've been waiting. Even the South felt when the shift happened. We knew the long winter was finally over and so we made our way here."

They stepped aside and let me throw the doors open wide. The entrance hall was glowing in all its dazzling splendor. Gilded walls adorned in gold and silver stretched to the high vaulted ceiling. I stifled a gasp as I strode across the floor, leading the dragons to the grand staircase.

I paused, placing a hand on the banister, and wracking my brain as I glanced around, half expecting to find directions posted on one of the walls.

Eli, I called nervously. *Help.*

Up the stairs and go left, he whispered into my mind.

I smiled and strode confidently up the stairs.

"I must say, my curious friend," Vallath purred from behind me. "You were stunning before, but the heraldship looks absolutely delicious on you."

I felt a far-off stab of jealousy as I turned, suppressing a laugh.

"Well, thank you," I smiled. "But my heart belongs to someone else."

"Ah... Such is my luck I guess," Vallath sighed heavily.

I felt Eli's puff of triumph and snickered to myself.

Eli, you're adorable, I told him softly.

Adorable?

Yes, I grinned. *All the things we did to each other not even two hours ago and you're jealous?*

Well yeah, but... He sighed heavily. *I'm sorry, Sunflower. I'm being ridiculous.*

"You're being awfully quiet, curious one," Vallath said with a sly smile. We reached the second floor and turned left, heading down the corridor. "Reconsidering my offer already? I'd be happy to oblige if the one who has your heart isn't satisfying you properly." He winked and Eli grumbled darkly in my head.

"No. Thank you though, Vallath," I chuckled as Eli continued to grumble.

"Well..." Vallath sighed. "If you ever change your mind, you know where to find me. I have a considerable amount of skills I'd be more than willing to demonstrate for you."

Before I could respond, the air around me rippled. A huge yellow sunflower formed in my hands. I snorted, smiling down at it, and shaking my head.

See? I teased. *You're adorable.*

Eli started to mumble an apology, but I cut him off.

Don't apologize. I've never had anyone feel jealous over me. I'm not about to pretend that I don't love it just a little bit.

I looked up from the bloom and met the dragon's eyes.Vallath raised an eyebrow.

"Oh, I see," he grinned. "Though I probably should have guessed as much when you willingly stepped between him and a horde of angry dragons. In that case, tell Jackass I said hello." I frowned at him, and he laughed.

"He's not a jackass," I said as I pushed the door open to the treasure room.

"Well, all things considered... I think I deserve a few barbs," the dragon said. His face fell as he stepped inside. I felt the apprehension give way to guilt in the back of my mind as Vallath turned in a slow circle. Anguish filled his violet eyes as he took in the rows upon rows of colorful scales. After a long moment of silence, he met my gaze.

"I'd forgotten how many she stole," Vallath whispered. He beckoned the two smaller dragons to get started.

"There's a ritual to honor the fallen," Vallath explained, withdrawing a large bundle of cloth from inside one of the crates. "They need to be wrapped carefully before they get placed in the crates. And there's a special recitation we say. Would you like to help us?"

"Can I?" I asked.

"Of course," Vallath nodded.

"It won't be seen as disrespectful?"

"Oh, not at all," Vallath replied, shaking his head. "In fact, it will go a long way to repairing relations between the heralds and the dragon council."

"Then absolutely I will. What do I need to do?"

He taught me the words to say and the proper way to wrap the scales as we set to work.

We carefully wrapped each scale in a special, soft cloth before placing them gently into the large crates. I murmured softly over each one, taking extra care to be sure I said the words exactly right. It took an hour. Finally, I placed the last tiny scale in the crate. Vallath flipped the lids closed and secured them with lengths of sturdy rope. Each dragon hoisted a crate onto their shoulder like it weighed nothing and carried them out into Eli's garden.

"Well," Vallath said solemnly, "We'd better be off. As much as I would love to stay and visit, the council is very eager for our return. Tell Jackass..." He trailed off as I frowned at him and sighed. "Ah. I guess I have to stop calling him that, huh?"

"Please," I said, and he raised his hands in surrender.

"Fine," he lamented. "I'll stop calling him that... If the handsome Lord of Fall will give me a kiss." He raised an eyebrow flirtatiously. Before I could respond, the ground beneath our feet shook, rattling the palace windows.

Vallath threw his head back and cackled with laughter. "Tell him it was a joke," he said, grinning.

The ground stilled but the grumpy feeling in the back of my head remained.

"He was not amused by that," I chuckled.

"All right, all right. Tell Lord Spring that he and the dragons are square. We won't eat him." He bowed deeply to me and transformed before my eyes into his full size. Violet scales glinted in the sunlight. The other smaller dragons followed suit. One was a deep blue and the other was a bright emerald green.

They each grabbed a crate and took off. A few beats of their huge, leathery wings carried them over the Fire Mountains and off into the distance.

I watched them go before ambling back inside of my new home and closing the door.

Thank you, Eli said softly. I smiled, closing my eyes.

Of course. I really don't want them to eat you considering that I love you and whatnot.

He laughed. *I love you and whatnot too,* he said. I opened my eyes and took a step further into the entrance hall to search for my friends.

CHAPTER THIRTY-FIVE

ASH

The second our feet hit the ground, we came together like a cataclysm. Her hands raked through my hair, dragging my mouth to hers desperately. I lifted her up into my arms and wrapped her legs around my waist as I carried her blindly down the drive of Nature's Palace. The heat flashing through me was so intense, I thought I might explode. Her tongue tangled with mine, drawing a deep groan from my chest.

We reached the door and I paused, fumbling blindly for the latch before finally throwing it open. I hitched her up higher and steered us into the nearest room, slamming the door behind us and laying her on the floor. She ripped her clothes away as I removed mine and slid over her.

"Ash," she moaned, her eyes glazed with desire. "I was so scared... I-I thought—" The words stuck in her throat, and she gulped.

"I'm so sorry, my love," I whispered, trailing a soft line of kisses down her stomach. "I'm sorry."

"I thought you were..." Lumi trailed off, gripping my hands fearfully as though I might suddenly disappear. I planted light kisses on the inside of her thigh.

"I know," I breathed against her skin, sending a delicious shiver up her spine. "I thought so too. But it's all right. See?"

I dipped my head, dragging my tongue across her seam. She tasted like pure bliss. She shuddered and buried her fingers in my hair.

"See?" I whispered against her, and she arched, moaning. "I'm right here, my love."

I gripped her hips and set my tongue to work in a torturously slow rhythm. I took my time, letting my mouth draw soft shivers and moans from her. Her whole body shook but I kept my pace soft and slow. Her heels dug into my back, and she arched again, unable to escape the feeling overwhelming her.

I kissed and licked, tasting her deeply until she tugged hard on my hair and cried out. I held her hips, stroking her through her climax with the flat of my tongue until she came down, panting and whimpering. I feathered some more kisses on the inside of her thighs before covering her body with mine.

She wound her arms around my neck and pulled me down roughly to her chest, wrapping her legs tightly around my waist.

The feel of her bare skin against my stomach sent heat rushing through me and I hardened against her.

Lumi let her hand drop to my chest and pressed it firmly into my skin. My heart raced under her touch. She let out a small, broken sound and leaned her head against my neck. My cock brushed her entrance, but I fought to hold still, giving her the minute she very clearly needed.

"My love," I whispered. "I'm so sorry."

She pressed her lips together and closed her eyes, letting my heart beat against her palm for a long moment.

I brushed across her again and clenched my teeth to fight back the moan rising in my throat. She slid her hand back up to cup my jaw and tilted her hips, drawing me closer.

"I need you," she said, breathlessly. "Please."

I groaned and thrust forward, pushing deep into her. She felt so perfect that my head started spinning and I nearly lost control.

She dragged her nails up my back and locked her hands into my hair. I pulled back and thrust slowly into her again, relishing the way her body clung to mine. Her fingers tightened in my hair and lightning sizzled through me.

A dark, fiery part of my soul demanded that I take her hard and rough. But she was still upset, and I couldn't bring myself to do it. So, I fought my baser urges and rode her as gently as I could.

"Oh... Lumi," I groaned, dropping my head onto her shoulder. She lifted her hips and drew me in deeper with each thrust, gasping my name softly into my ear.

My willpower started faltering and that fiery piece of me was getting too loud to ignore.

I bit my lip and focused on keeping my movements slow and measured. Trying desperately to give her exactly what she needed from me.

Suddenly, she raised her hips and jerked her thighs towards her chest, slamming me deep inside her.

My breath caught in my throat, and I grit my teeth. She locked her legs tighter around my waist and pulled my hips back before ramming me into her again.

A deep, feral growl rumbled through my chest and my willpower failed.

She cried out my name and arched into me. Every inch of her trembled under me as I pushed her rapidly towards the brink. Everything in me started to tighten and ache with need, but I didn't slow down. I wanted her to break for me, and from the way she was moving, I could tell she was getting close.

I rode her hard until she gasped, yanking my head back roughly as I sent her over the edge.

I didn't stop. I drove through her orgasm until her knees shook on my hips. She squeezed around my cock so tightly that my head swam and release tore through me. I shuddered and throbbed violently, clinging to her as fiercely as she clung to me. I came down and slumped against her, panting, and shivering as she drew her nails lightly across my back.

"Are you okay? I didn't hurt you, did I?" I gasped. She shook her head.

"No. I needed that."

Concern washed through me. I braced my hands against the floor and was about to roll onto my back, but she grabbed my arms.

"No!" Her voice was thick with emotion. "Please. I just... I need you," she pleaded. "Please, can we stay here? Just for a few more minutes. Please?"

I nodded. My heart ached fiercely. I laid my head on her breasts and listened to her heart pounding.

"I'm sorry," she whispered. "I know I'm being stupid."

"You're not," I groaned as her nails scratched lightly across my scalp. She sounded like she was on the verge of tears, so I cast my mind around for something to lighten her mood. "Are you going to miss the brown hair?" I joked. She took a shuddering breath.

"I don't care what color it is. Or if you have no hair at all," she breathed, her voice breaking. "As long as you're still here."

My heart stopped.

Lumi let out a jagged sound. I planted a kiss on her sternum before looking up at her. Her face was twisted in anguish and her hands were pressed over her eyes. Tears were flowing between her fingers. They froze on her pale purple cheeks before they clattered to the floor.

"Hey." I scrambled to sit up, pulling her into my lap and cradling her close to my chest. "Please don't cry, my love," I whispered, pressing my lips to her hair. "Please, don't cry."

"You were dead," she wept. "I felt you die. Felt your... last breath. Your blood was everywhere. There was so much of it."

"I'm so sorry, Lumi," I said quietly.

"I lost you," she cried, wrapping her arms around me. I didn't know what to say, so I fell silent, holding her tightly. "She killed you and I couldn't save you."

Sharp stabs of ice peppered my skin as she wept into my chest.

After a few moments she sat up, wiping her eyes.

"I'm sorry," she murmured, her deep blue eyes meeting mine. I gave her a cautious grin that she returned meekly. "I'm okay," she sighed, leaning back into my chest.

"What do you need?" I asked, stroking her back.

"This," she replied, pressing her face into my skin. "Just hold me."

"I've got you."

I glanced around. We were in a small receiving room that was completely empty except for the plush red carpet we'd just made love on. I scooted us over and braced my back against the marble wall, leaning her against my chest.

We sat in silence for a long while, caressing each other gently. Finally, I tilted her chin up and kissed her.

"Are you sure there's nothing else I can do? Anything?" I said.

"You could make the world move again," Lumi suggested with a sly, mischievous grin.

"Mmm," I growled, desire flaring through me. "I can do that." As I dipped my head towards her, the ground beneath us started to shake violently. The windows rattled and the chandelier above our heads danced and swayed. Her eyes went wide, and she drew back to gape at me.

"How the fuck did you do that?" she demanded, astonished. I shook my head, glancing around in confusion.

"That's not me!" I insisted.

"Are you sure?"

"I..." I ran my fingers through my hair. "I don't think it was me."

A soft voice called out to us from the entrance hall. We froze before scrambling back into our clothes in a panic.

I yanked my pants up and was about to pull my tunic on when I spotted the huge blood stain. I grimaced and tossed it aside before Lumi could see it. My pants were stained as well, but I had to wear something.

Lumi had just pulled her tunic down when the door creaked open.

"Lumi? Ash?" Rowan called, poking his head around the door. He grinned at the sight of us, flushed and disheveled. "What have you two been up to?"

"Making the ground shake apparently," Lumi replied, eyeing me. I shrugged.

"Making the... Oh..." Understanding dawned on Rowan's face and he laughed. "No! Oh, no guys! That was Eli."

"He's here?" I tilted my head in surprise. "I thought he had to stay at the tower." I glanced behind Rowan, and he chuckled.

"No, he does. But you guys just missed Vallath and his cousins. Vallath got flirty and Eli wasn't happy about it." He patted a large yellow flower poking out from his pocket. I raised my eyebrows.

"If he's not here then how did he know?" I asked. Rowan's grin widened.

"Oh... you two don't know yet," Rowan said gleefully. "So, you're linked now." He tapped the side of his head. "Watch. I'm gonna ask Eli to shake the ground again." Rowan fell silent, his eyes straying towards the window. The earth rumbled beneath our feet, and he beamed. "See? You can talk to the one you gave your heart to whenever you want. Try it." Lumi and I looked at each other and she raised her eyebrows.

Ash? I heard Lumi's voice in my head as though she'd spoken out loud.

"Whoa!" I exclaimed. "That's insane!" I reached out with my power, slipping it into her mind.

I love you, I said.

"I love you too!" she said, grinning.

Rowan chuckled and shook his head.

"Eli thinks you two are adorable," he said.

"Can he see us too?" I asked incredulously. Rowan smiled and tapped his temple again. I turned back to Lumi as something soft brushed the inside of my mind.

"Whoa," she breathed. "I look so different now. You try." I reached out again and blinked. Suddenly, I was staring up at my own face. A lock of shining hair fell over my forehead and my eyes were solid gold. My skin had turned bright yellow and gleamed like sunlight was filling my face. I blinked again and found myself looking at Lumi.

"That's crazy!" I let out a low whistle.

"We can try that out again later," Lumi said, stepping back. "For now, let's go get changed. We need to go to Haven and let the villagers know the long winter is finally over. But before we go, I have to tell you something. The Two told me..." She trailed off. Anger glimmered in her deep blue eyes.

Rowan and I exchanged a glance.

"My father is Cosmic," she spat roughly. "He's been using his power to grow crops underground. That's how he managed to get control of the village's food supply. Thermal crops aren't a real thing. It was all a lie."

For a split second, I swore I must've heard her wrong. I stared at her for a beat before a wild laughter burst from me. Lumi arched her eyebrow at me as I held my stomach, throwing my head back.

"Ah, that's too much," I gasped.

"I'm serious, Ash," she huffed.

"Oh, no I know," I managed, wiping my streaming eyes. "But as many times as he tried to kill me because he thought I *might* be Cosmic? And he's... Oh, I just can't!" I took a deep, shuddering breath as my amusement finally subsided. "All right, I'm sorry." Lumi frowned and I held my hands up in surrender. "I'm done. I promise, I'm done." Rowan tipped his head to the side, his eyes straying towards the window.

"Oh, that's right!" he gasped. "Eli just said that could've been where that block he kept sensing came from. The one that held your powers back."

"He can do that?" Lumi gaped at him.

Rowan tilted his head again.

"Well..." He held up a finger, still listening intently. "Yes, and no. He could when you were human. But Eli says that he can't do anything now that you're a herald. Only the one you gave your heart to could do something like that. So, Ash. Though... Eli says that he's not sure how your father did it. He knows Cosmics can do it, but it's not something he was ever taught how to do."

"So... he reached into my head? And blocked my powers?" she said. Anger flashed in her eyes.

"That must be why your powers popped up when we left Haven," Rowan pointed out. "You were too far away, and he lost his hold."

"He's such a fucking asshole!" Lumi spat. "Why would he do that to me?"

"If he could block power, then why'd he never try to block mine?" I said, crossing my arms over my chest. "He could've killed me just by cutting off my fire."

"I'm guessing because you never got close enough for him to try," Lumi said.

Rowan nodded. "That's probably why he kept trying to kill you. You were a threat to his little empire. Especially if you and Lumi actually did team up. You two could've toppled his reign."

"And why he kept trying to marry you off to his lackeys," I put in, glancing at Lumi. "He had to keep you under his thumb. Where you weren't a threat."

"And why he tried so hard to isolate me and my family," Rowan added. "The three of us together would've ended his dictatorship. Throw in Mother and Father, he wouldn't stand a chance."

"Well, his little empire is finished," Lumi said fiercely. She straightened her back and met our eyes. Like a commander rallying her troops.

"What's the plan?" I said, rubbing my hands together excitedly.

"We're going to tell everyone what he really is. He can't hide behind his lies anymore," she replied. "I'll go put the stones on the altar. You guys go get changed and meet me back here."

Thirty minutes later, we met in the entrance hall clean, dressed, and ready. Lumi wore a flowing purple and blue dress with shimmering silver snowflakes. Rowan wore red and orange robes with golden leaves stitched all over the fabric and brown pants. I had donned a shining golden robe with a yellow sun stretched across my back and black pants. The Two must've adjusted the wardrobes, which was lucky for me. The former Summer's clothes would *not* have fit me, and I'd been dreading checking the closet.

We stepped out of the palace and into the sunlight. A deliciously sweet scent hung low in the air. Lumi gasped and grabbed my hand in shock.

The grounds were covered with flowers of every size and color. Rowan chuckled.

"Eli's garden," he said proudly.

We strolled to the end of the drive, taking our time to admire the vibrant colors all around us. Lumi splayed her hand wide. The bridge dropped in front of us, and we stepped onto it, hand-in-hand. A loud crack split the air and a second later, we found ourselves staring up at the massive stone wall surrounding Haven.

Guards were sent into high alert at our sudden appearance and were scrambling and shouting to each other frantically. Bows were being notched and arrowheads were flashing along the structure.

"We better hurry before they shoot us," I remarked.

Lumi nodded and conjured a sheet of ice under our shoes, lifting us up into the air and over the wall. Arrows pinged off the ice and embedded themselves below our feet.

"I know it's a little late for this," Rowan said slowly as he looked down. "But the thought just occurred to me that ice may not have been the best way to go about this."

"Yeah," Lumi said, wincing as she glanced at the horrified, screaming villagers below us. "The thought just occurred to me too. They're going to be terrified of us."

"Welcome to my life," I snorted. "They've always been afraid of me."

Lumi set the sheet of ice down in the middle of the town square. We were instantly surrounded by terrified people, swords, and arrows.

"Winter has come for us!" One of the villagers shouted over the screams filling the air.

"Quick! Pierce her black heart!"

"Open fire!"

A volley of razor-sharp arrows screamed across the square.

Rowan raised his hands and a blast of air tore through the sky, knocking the arrows off course and dropping them harmlessly to the ground. I blew out a breath and sent a protective ring of fire dancing around us.

The villagers screamed and cowered.

"People of Haven," Lumi cried to the terrified crowd. She raised her hands innocently. "I am not the Winter you fear! My name was Lumi. I was Jasper and Celeste's daughter. Look at me! You know me!"

My eyes darted through the petrified crowd as a soft murmur echoed around us.

Lumi gestured towards Rowan and then to me. Now that she had their attention, I dropped my power and the flames vanished.

"You know them," she said. Her voice softened as the terror around us slowly gave way to curiosity and disbelief. "They were Rowan and Ash. My friends. We came to tell you that Lord Spring has returned. We rescued him and took him to the World's Tower. He destroyed the former Winter! Feel the warm air. Smell the sweet flowers blooming!"

The villagers huddled together and glanced around nervously at the ice and snow that still lingered.

Lumi tipped her head towards Rowan. "I could use a little help," she hissed.

Rowan looked off into the distance, a smile lifting his lips. A soft, warm breeze swept over the square and giant yellow flowers sprouted from the ground. They chased away the snow and towered over us, swaying happily in the wind.

Someone in the crowd let out a startled gasp.

"Sunflowers!" A man said as he stumbled forward. Rowan let out a long breath of relief.

"Father!" he cried. My heart leapt as we rushed in, pulling Kaelin into a massive group hug. He laughed and kissed each one of us on the head in turn.

"Look at you!" He stood back, beaming down at us as we wiped our eyes. Another familiar voice called out and Lucia came barreling through the crowd towards us.

"Mother!" Rowan called. He wrapped his arms around her as she crashed into him. She pulled back to cup his face in both hands, her expression positively shining with pride.

"Look at my handsome boy!" Lucia tucked one of Rowan's curls behind his ear. "Did I ever tell you that fall is my favorite season?"

Rowan let out a small sob and hugged her tight.

"You saved us!" she cried. She released him and grabbed Lumi, pulling her into a bone crushing hug. "Look at you! You look so lovely, my sweet Lady Winter."

Tears clouded Lumi's eyes. Lucia turned to me, and I threw my arms out wide, ready, and grinning broadly as she yanked me into a hug.

"Oh! My handsome Lord Summer! Look at you! I never have to worry about you being cold again! You saved us!" She released me and stood back, dropping to her knees. "You saved us all," she said again, clasping her hands over her heart. Villagers around us began to cry, dropping to their knees. Many started approaching us slowly. I shifted, unsure of what to do as they grasped our hands, sobbing and kissing our knuckles.

This is new, I whispered into Lumi's mind, swallowing hard.

She winked at me. News traveled extremely quickly and soon, we found ourselves surrounded by a huge crowd. Villagers poured into the square, cheering, and sobbing with joy. Someone had started a fire and villagers were tossing their old, worn-out winter coats into the flames.

So many familiar faces appeared before us, teary eyed and grateful. The old woman who spit at me and her son. A few of the farmers who hissed at me.

Even Tom. They all passed before us to thank us profusely. It was the strangest experience I'd ever had.

A tall, lean figure pushed through the crowd to the front and grabbed Rowan's hand roughly.

Rowan took an automatic step back as the man pressed his lips to his knuckles. He tried to gently pull his hand away, but the man clung to him. The man brushed a stray blonde hair from his face as he stood back up, smirking. The moment he stood up, I recognized his face and a white-hot anger sparked in my chest.

"Rodger," Rowan faltered, glancing over at me nervously. I raised my eyebrows in question, taking a step closer. Waiting for Rowan to give me the go ahead. Lumi stood next to me, tense and ready.

"Rowan, my love. How wonderful to—" He was cut off as the ground trembled under his feet.

I smirked. Lord Spring was still watching. And he was pissed.

The surprise startled Rodger enough that Rowan managed to yank his hand away.

"My name is Lord Fall," Rowan said firmly. "And my heart belongs to another." Rodger frowned, taking a step closer.

"Oh, come on," he simpered. "I know we've had our differences. But I'm willing to give you another chance if you—" The ground shook again.

Rowan chuckled, looking off into the distance and the ground stilled.

"Look, Rodger," Rowan said flatly. "Maybe I wasn't clear. I'm dating Lord Spring and right now, he's begging me to let him smash you with a boulder. So, I suggest you take a step back."

Rodger's face contorted in anger, and he grabbed Rowan's arm roughly.

"And just who the fuck do you think you are to talk to me like..." Rodger faltered suddenly, releasing Rowan's arm, and taking a step back as a vicious wind whipped around their feet.

"I am Lord Fall," Rowan snarled. "I am a herald of the Ethereal Two and the only thing standing between you and the anger of my fellow heralds. Who would all gladly crush you if I asked them to."

Rodger glanced over. Lumi and I glared back at him. Fire danced in my palm, and I let it grow menacingly.

He gulped and took another step away from our best friend. He looked back at Rowan and dropped to his knees.

"Forgive me, Lord Fall," he whispered, his voice shaking. Rowan stared down at him and waved a hand dismissively.

"Get out of my sight or they won't have to squash you. I'll do it myself," he said, releasing his power.

As I watched, beaming with pride at Rowan's courage, roses began blooming on his head. They sprang open wide, circling his head like a crown. The stems were threading their way through his vibrant curls, holding the roses in place.

Rodger scrambled to his feet and raced away for dear life. Rowan released a breath and pressed a hand to his chest before turning to us.

"Nicely done," I grinned, clapping him on the shoulder.

"Thanks," he said. "It's a whole lot easier to face him with Eli in my head."

"The roses were a nice touch," Lumi chuckled. "We're proud of you, Ro."

Rowan smiled shyly as Lumi thread her arms through our elbows and turned to survey the crowd. We stood arm in arm, being thanked repeatedly until a horrified screech cut through the noise.

Lumi's mother shoved her way through the crowd, tears pouring down her furious face.

"What happened to you?" she demanded.

Lumi swallowed and drew herself up proudly as her father stormed to his wife's side.

Silence fell around us.

Jasper's eyes locked on me, and his face twisted in vengeful fury. "You did this!" he screamed. He yanked a dagger from his belt and charged. "You took her from me!"

Before I could react, he drove the dagger straight at my heart. The blade bounced off me, crumpling like he'd just stabbed a stone wall.

I pressed my hand into my chest in surprise as Lumi summoned her power and blasted her father off his feet. Celeste screamed in horror and rounded on Lumi.

"Look at what he did to you!" she cried.

"What *he* did to me?" Lumi spat incredulously. "What about what you two did? To all of us!" She pointed at her father who staggered back to his feet. "Go on!" she snarled, stepping closer. I stepped to her left and Rowan to her right. Knights flanking our queen.

"Tell them all!" Lumi spat. "Tell them what you really are! What you've done to keep all of them under your control!"

"Lumi," Jasper breathed, his expression turning murderous. "You don't—" She cut him off.

"Don't what? Know what I'm talking about? Because as a matter of fact, the Ethereal Two told me everything. How there's no such thing as a thermal crop. And crops can only grow in the dark if Cosmic power makes them."

A confused murmur ran through the watchful crowd.

"She's lying!" Jasper bellowed, and the crowd fell silent again. "Thermal crops have kept us fed for years! Don't listen to the filth that creature filled her head with." He jerked his chin at me, and I had to fight to keep my face impassive.

"And what about what *you* put in my head?" she spat. "You reached into my head and blocked my power!" She turned to the crowd. "How many of you had family? Or friends? People you loved that were Cosmic? Only to have him murder them for the so-called 'safety' of the village! And he was a Cosmic this whole time!"

You could've heard a pin drop. Expressions all around us shifted from confused, to horrified, and enraged.

Celeste took a sharp step back, looking up at Jasper in shock.

"Cosmic people are not evil!" Lumi cried beseechingly. "He lied to you! He lied to all of us! Thermal crops only grow because he makes them. Look around you! Lord Spring made sunflowers grow out of the cobblestones!"

"You're a liar!" Jasper bellowed. He turned to the onlookers. "Who do you believe? The one who's kept you alive for two decades? Or this worthless bastard poisoning her mind? Well, I won't stand for it!" He rounded on me and took two steps when I had a bold, crazy idea.

I let my power swell and flash out, reaching into the vast well of power in his chest. I could sense the rotted feel of it as I drew his power out swiftly and let it flow up my arm. I held my hand up and released the funneled energy out into the air. It curled like smoke from my fingers and dissipated.

"A liar, huh?" I said with a smirk as Jasper's eyes widened. "Then how is it that I can draw out your power? For everyone to see?" He staggered and dropped to his knees, gasping.

"You see?" Lumi shouted, turning to the crowd pressing in around us. I released my power and he slumped. "He lied to you! He killed and maimed Cosmics just so that no one would challenge him! But the long winter is over and now you all know the truth! We will help you rebuild, and no one will answer to him ever again!"

"Lumi!" Celeste squeaked, eyeing her daughter with a fearful expression. "You have to stop this now and......" She trailed off looking around. It was then that she noticed the faces of villagers around us. She took a step back, vanishing as they began jeering and pressing closer.

Jasper regained his footing and stared me down.

"You mark my words. I'll take my daughter back from you," he snarled. I opened my mouth to respond but Lumi stepped in front of me.

"Your daughter," she spat, "is gone. Lumi is gone. I am Lady Winter. Threaten Lord Summer again and you will answer to me. Now leave my isle. And don't *ever* come back." She turned, grabbing my face in both hands, and planted a long, passionate kiss on my lips.

I groaned in surprise and swayed into her. Jasper's face twisted in revulsion as he stormed away, turning his back on us, and striding away through the crowd. Lumi broke our kiss and met my eyes as the crowd cheered and carried on celebrating.

"That felt amazing," she said.

I smiled and kissed her again. She pulled away and threw her arms around mine and Rowan's waists. "We'll help these people rebuild their villages," she said. "And my father won't control anyone's life ever again."

"I love it," I said, watching the crowd grow as more villagers learned the news and more familiar faces came to see us.

Anni and Lumi hugged tightly before Lumi declared her the official blacksmith to the heralds and commissioned four new crowns for us. Rowan said that Eli was excited for something new after so many years of just roses. Killian's mother came forward and clung to Lumi for a long while, begging forgiveness. It was then that we learned Killian's father had tried to fight Jasper on sending his son after us. But Jasper was hellbent on having Lumi returned to him. So, he'd sent Killian after us anyway and killed Killian's father for daring to challenge him.

Lumi held onto the widow tightly as Rowan and I took over the greetings. The distraught woman didn't look in my direction. Not even once. But I couldn't honestly blame her. She finally sniffed and sidled off, freeing Lumi to join us.

"Look!" someone screamed. A hush fell over the crowd and a strange high-pitched sound floated through the air. The smallest creature I'd ever seen darted swiftly through the breeze. It flapped its tiny wings and landed on a tree, staring down at us with its beady black eyes. Another one came swooping past and landed next to the other. They chirped and chattered as the hushed crowd looked on in awe.

"Birds!" a villager sobbed, wiping her eyes on her apron. "The birds are returning!" As we watched, a flash of purple light dazzled our eyes and the sky darkened. Birds of every shape and size came swooping down over the land. Villagers clapped and cheered. We stayed for four hours, dancing, laughing, and celebrating with our people. Rowan told his parents the whole story while Lumi and I twirled and sang with the joyous villagers.

Finally, we managed to peel ourselves away, stopping to hug Rowan's parents as we left Haven behind. I opened the cosmic bridge, and we raced back to the palace together. The air was quiet and peaceful as we walked arm-in-arm up the drive of our new home.

"That," Rowan said, turning to us with a wide grin, "was one crazy fucking adventure."

I chuckled and threw my arm around Lumi.

"It was, Ro," she laughed. "When you said you wanted an adventure, you really weren't kidding." We laughed and he looked off into the distance with a happy sigh.

"If you two will excuse me, I'm going to poke around my new library. Eli and I have to pick out a new book." He hugged us tightly and strode off, stopping every few feet to take in the scents of his love's flowers along the way. I turned to Lumi and wrapped my arms around her.

"I love you," I said, leaning my forehead against hers.

"And I love you," she whispered as she wound her arms around my neck with a sigh. "We still have a lot of work to do. But I think today was a good start."

"We got this," I replied, grinning. "Or more accurately, you got this. Last time I tried to lead I fell down a hole. So, I'll stick to following yours."

She rolled her eyes, grinning and pressed her lips to mine. As we stood, kissing deeply under the clear night sky, I couldn't help but think of the future and all the bright promises it held. For the people of the Forsaken Isle rebuilding their long-lost lives. For the flirtatious dragon who finally got to go home. For Ro and his storybook prince...

And for me and my fierce warrior queen.

Acknowledgements

It's been my dream for as long as I can remember to write a book. I never would have gotten here without the amazing people I have around me. Thank you to my husband, Blake, who has been unfailingly supportive throughout my entire journey. Thank you to Hannah (I big love you!), Tracey, Breanna, Nikky and Azea for never getting tired of listening to me go on and on and on about my story, and for helping me make my characters come alive. Thank you to Jeff and his gorgeous cover design, and to Jamie who helped me polish my manuscript and make it something I can be really proud of. And thank you to my kiddos, Iris and Harper. I hope I make you as proud as you make me!

ABOUT THE AUTHOR

I'm a boring person really, so I won't be offended if you skip this page. If you decide not to though, here's a little bit about me! I live in Florida with my two amazing kiddos and my awesome husband. He was my high school sweetheart, so the poor guy has been stuck with my special brand of crazy for a very long time. I try my best to be a productive member of society, but all bets are off when hockey season starts! I love to read (when my brain quiets down enough to let me) and I like to pretend on occasion that I can paint. I can't... but it's fun to try. I've wanted to write a book since I was twelve years old. This book is a long-awaited fulfillment of my life long dream. Hopefully, there's someone out there that has as much fun reading it as I did writing it.

Made in the USA
Columbia, SC
31 July 2024

9c978570-6dc7-4cb2-aff6-b5eb5822ae9fR01